IMMORTALS:
THE RECKONING

JENNIFER ASHLEY
JOY NASH
ROBIN T. POPP

LOVE SPELL®

March 2009

Published by

Dorchester Publishing Co., Inc.
200 Madison Avenue
New York, NY 10016

Wolf Hunt copyright © 2009 by Jennifer Ashley
Blood Debt copyright © 2009 by Joy Nash
Beyond the Mist copyright © 2009 by Robin T. Popp

ISBN 10: 0-505-52768-5
ISBN 13: 978-0-505-52768-4
E-ISBN: 1-4285-0615-2

The name "Love Spell" and its logo are trademarks of Dorchester Publishing Co., Inc.

Printed in the United States of America.

10 9 8 7 6 5 4 3 2 1

Visit us on the web at www.dorchesterpub.com.

Contents

Immortals: The Reckoning

JENNIFER ASHLEY

WOLF HUNT

*To my fellow Immortals authors, Joy and Robin,
for making the Immortals process so much fun.*

CHAPTER ONE

Logan got the call while he was making an arrest.

The vampire he cuffed in a West Hollywood club had been running a slavery ring of "blood donors," people who fed a vampire a little at a time without being drained.

"Septimus will hear about this," the vampire hissed.

Logan locked magically charged cuffs around the vamp's wrists. "Septimus gave me his blessing. You're embarrassing him."

The vampire paled as much as a vampire could pale, and Logan's cell phone chirped. Logan passed the vamp to his partner, Tony Nez, and snapped open the phone.

"Yeah?"

"Logan." A female voice went breathless with relief.

"Nadia?" Everything stopped.

He'd seen the demon woman Nadia twice since he'd interviewed her six months ago in her hospital bed. She'd been through so much, and still her smile was sensual, her dark eyes defiant. Each time he saw her, he wanted to spend more time with her. Dangerously so.

Her pleading tone nearly broke the self-control he'd been battling for the last six months. "What's wrong?"

"I don't know where I am. There's lots of woods, and they're coming."

"Slow down, slow down. Who's coming?"

"Hell." She broke off, the one word filled with terror. "Logan, please." The phone clicked off.

"Nadia?"

Logan glared at the unfamiliar phone number that slid neatly to the top of his recent calls list.

"Shit." His wolf was growling and snarling, his hand gripping the phone so hard the plastic began to crack.

"Trouble?" Tony asked, giving the vampire over to uniformed cops who marched him outside. It was nearly dawn, and the vampire screamed at them to hurry and put him in the van.

"I don't know." Logan slid into their unmarked car and punched up the new computer system that had been installed in all the paranormal detectives' vehicles. In theory they used it to quickly find priors and other information on suspects, but it came in handy for other things as well. All searches for the phone number Nadia had called from turned up blank.

Seething, Logan called a uniformed sergeant at the station to trace the number. Experienced sergeants trumped computer searches every time. Just as he'd finished, his cell rang again, same number.

"Nadia?" he bellowed into it.

"She ran away," a male voice said. He sounded wrong, keyed up, filled with adrenaline and excitement. "More fun that way." *Click.*

Tony got in the driver's seat and started the car. "Where to, boss?"

"Station," Logan said, staring at his phone.

"Bad news?"

"What?" He snapped his attention to Tony. Logan's new partner hated to butt into Logan's personal business, though Tony never minded talking about his large and boisterous extended family back home in the Navajo Nation.

"The phone calls," Tony said in a patient voice. "You look like I did the first time I saw a ghost."

"A woman I know." Logan tucked the phone into his pocket, his heart drumming. He quickly told Tony what had happened, and his partner blenched.

"Best we find out where she is, then." Tony put his foot

down, turned on the siren, and zipped through LA freeways toward the paranormal division headquarters.

What Logan didn't tell Tony was that the second caller had been a werewolf. The man's voice had grated with excitement, which meant he was keyed up enough to lose control of the change.

And worse, Logan knew who it was—the man who had cost him everything, and forced Logan to lonely exile on the streets of Los Angeles.

CHAPTER TWO

By the time Logan and Tony strode into the paranormal division headquarters at the Parker Center in downtown LA, Logan's uniformed sergeant had traced the phone number.

"It's a pay phone at a gas station in a place called Brookside. That's a wide spot in the road on the California-Oregon border, according to the gas station owner. He said he never noticed anyone using the phone."

A demon, even one pursued through the woods at the crack of dawn, was stealthy enough to use a pay phone without anyone seeing.

Logan nodded tersely, thanked the man for his help, and went to his lieutenant, McKay, a small, black half-Sidhe woman, to ask for a leave of absence.

Tony wanted to go with him.

"It's way out of our jurisdiction," Logan said, grabbing a duffel bag out of his locker.

"So why are you going?"

"Nadia's a friend. I'm making this personal."

"All the more reason you need someone at your back."

Logan strode out to the garage and slung bottles of water and extra ammunition into the duffel bag. He thought of the triumph in the man's voice on the phone and knew he would be dealing with whatever this was as a werewolf, not a cop.

"You have a family to support. I don't want them pissed off at me for getting you hurt . . ."

"You worried because it's a werewolf thing? I'm a shaman.

I grew up dealing with Four Corners werewolves, and don't think that wasn't a picnic."

"If it were a Navajo thing, I'm not sure you'd welcome *my* help," Logan said.

Tony grinned. "Hey, next time I have to face my grandmother, I'd love to have you as backup. Tell you what—you run into trouble up there, you call me. I can get there fast. Deal?"

"Deal." Logan finished strapping down his duffel, slid on his helmet, and straddled the Harley.

He thought of other help he could ask for, the most formidable being Tain, his ex-partner's Immortal boyfriend. But he wanted to figure things out before he called for backup.

The bad blood between Logan and this werewolf ran deep, and anyone who got involved could die. Logan had thought that when he left the pack in Minnesota, everything was finished. He realized now that the problem had only festered. It was time to end it—no matter what it took.

Ten hours later, Logan pulled into the gas station in the tiny town of Brookside, a stop on the way up to Klamath Falls. The morning attendant at the convenience store had gone, but his replacement knew that the police had called asking about someone using their phone.

"If I'd been here, I'd have seen her," the kid said. He had greasy hair, an acne-scarred face, and a rawboned body. "I see everyone and everything around here."

"Maybe she's come in here before," Logan said. He had no photo of Nadia, but he described her as he remembered her—five foot six, short curly dark hair, coffee-brown eyes, slim athletic body.

The kid shook his head. "Nope. But if I do see her, I'll let you know. You got somewhere I can reach you?"

Logan left his cell phone number without much hope. She'd been out of breath, scared, running for her life. She wouldn't come back here.

He thanked the kid and left the convenience store after

purchasing a packet of instant coffee and some disposable razors. He stashed the purchases in his saddlebag and approached the two lighted pay phones on the left side of the building.

In this day and age, pay phones were relics, usually graffiti-laden and forlorn under their plastic half domes. But there were still dead zones where cell phone signals didn't reach, and land lines had their uses.

Logan knew which phone Nadia had used before he reached it, because her scent was all over it. He closed his eyes and took in the brimstone smell of demon coupled with a flowery fragrance that was Nadia's own. That scent was overridden with Nadia's fear and the heavy musk of werewolf.

He'd been here. Logan couldn't tell if he had Nadia or whether she'd gotten away, but he knew one thing—the Challenge had been made, and Logan would meet it. And this time, he'd win.

Nadia kept running. Her feet ached, her naked body was coated with sweat and dirt, and her breath grated like sand in her lungs.

She'd been running for two days and two nights, sometimes in her demon form, sometimes in her human form. But she knew her trackers wouldn't let her drop dead of exhaustion, because that wouldn't be as much fun. If she lay down and died, they couldn't do anything to her.

She heard them coming, the werewolves running on all fours, followed by a human on an off-road motorcycle, its headlight slicing through the woods. They'd enjoyed that she'd laid false trails and doubled back, enjoyed locating her scent again with howls of triumph. Now they simply wanted to catch her, no more games.

Being able to call Logan had been an incredible piece of luck. Nadia had dashed out of the trees and found the convenience store in the middle of a crumbling parking lot, two lit phones turned toward her like friends.

She'd crept to the edge of the trees, then morphed into

her human form before cautiously approaching. She was naked, of course, and could only hope that no one would come around the building and spot her. But the parking lot remained deserted, the only sign of life the hum of the ice machines next to the building.

Her fingers shook as she keyed in her phone card number, then the number of Logan's cell. She'd had to try three times—so many numbers, and she kept missing one and having to start all over again.

She'd never told Logan she'd memorized his phone number. The few times they'd met since he'd interviewed her in the hospital they'd kept the conversation neutral on topics of mutual interest: motorcycles, movies, music, TV shows. No reason they should remember each other's numbers, but she thought of calling him often. Every day, in fact. She'd never been able to quite forget the werewolf whose tawny eyes had burned with compassion for an injured demon.

When Logan's deep tones had floated into her ear, far too much relief had flooded her.

They were coming. Dragging in deep breaths, Nadia scrambled up another hill and turned to run just below the ridgeline. She stumbled more than once, and she knew that soon she'd fall and be too tired to rise. And then they'd have her.

She drew in the last of her strength and shot forward, just as she heard the howling wolves crest the ridge and come for her.

CHAPTER THREE

Not far from the convenience store, Logan found a motel, a single-story, rundown lodge with a few pickups in front of the blue-painted doors. A tired woman at the reception desk told him the rates and handed him a key.

Logan parked his bike in front of room Five and dumped his backpack and plastic grocery bags on the sagging bed. He locked the door and closed all the blinds, pressing a chair against the door's blind to close the gap between it and the wall.

Out of habit he checked the room for spying devices, both magical and mechanical. Satisfied that there were none, he opened his backpack, took off his jacket, and went through the weaponry he'd brought with him.

He laid his police-issue 9mm on the bed, and stacked the magazines of ammo he'd brought beside it. He'd picked up a heavy, fleece-lined jacket at a Target on the way out of LA, knowing he'd have to start his hunt in the mountains. Even in March, he could run into snowstorms up here.

Next to the gun he laid a sheathed knife his partner Samantha had given him after she quit the police force. She worried about Logan, she said, and the blade, spelled by an air witch named Leda, would help him against demons and others resistant to conventional weapons. Samantha was a sweetheart, even though she was now queen of her demon clan.

Matriarch, she'd correct him. *Only pretentious demons from the deeper hells make themselves out to be royalty.*

Logan had brought one more weapon, a Colt .45 revolver he'd never told the LAPD about. He'd never used it beyond target shooting at a range to keep in practice, and he always stored it unloaded.

He loaded it now. He had to wear leather gloves to slide the bullets into the chambers, because the bullets were pure silver.

When he'd been Packmaster up in the wilds of Minnesota, he never had to put down a werewolf. They'd obeyed his every command because if they didn't, they'd have to face the Pack Leader. And if they were afraid of Logan, they were downright terrified of Matt Lewis.

Logan's job had been to enforce Matt's decrees and werewolf law. He'd worn a sword with a silver blade, which he'd kept safely in its leather sheath—the quiet threat of the executioner.

He'd never had to use either the sword or the silver bullets. No wolf except Matt had ever Challenged Logan.

But Logan kept the gun. Werewolves, no matter that they were life-magic creatures and perceived by the public at large as "good guys," were still dangerous.

Logan slid the collection of weapons into various holsters strapped to his body. They'd be useless when he turned wolf, but he believed in being prepared for all situations.

He pulled on the fleece-lined jacket, tucked the sheathed knife into his boot, locked his room, and started his bike.

He rode back to the convenience store, then took a side road that led up into the foothills, away from the highway. He rode this as far as he could and turned down another dirt road, going slowly, his headlight picking up rocks and branches in gathering darkness.

When he decided he was far enough from civilization, he stopped the motorcycle and killed the engine. He found a clump of brush in which to conceal it, then he took a trowel from his saddlebag and dug a hole to hide his weapons, carefully wrapped in the plastic grocery bags.

Last he removed his coat, shivering in the sharp March

cold. He'd gotten spoiled in Los Angeles. March there was merely cool, while up here the mountains still clung to winter.

He stripped, folding his clothes into another plastic bag and burying it among leaves and branches. Before the shivering got too bad, he stood, stilled his mind, and willed the wolf to come.

Legends said that werewolves changed at the full moon whether they liked it or not but were perfectly normal humans the rest of the time. Those were fairy tales.

Wolves did have to change at least once during the full moon or they risked going insane. At full moon, the wolf wanted to take over, and it was best to let it.

But werewolves had evolved over the centuries just like any other species. The ones who could change at will, whatever the phase of the moon, ultimately survived, while those who only changed when their wolves compelled them to slowly died out.

Logan felt his body growing more powerful, brute strength and instinct overtaking cautious intelligence. It was more than just the sensation of sprouting fur and claws—he felt his entire being subsumed into the beast, whose senses of smell and hearing and ability to read body language far outstripped those of the human Logan. Human thoughts and knowledge weren't lost, but Logan tucked them away to be accessed later.

He landed on all fours, the world taking a strange convex perspective, scents and sounds becoming far more important than sight.

He made his way back down to the convenience store and picked up Nadia's scent a little way above it. Her trail blazed like a white-hot streak, her unique scent vivid to him.

Logan picked up other smells as he went along, the nose-curling but familiar smells of exhaust and oil, the burned odor of rubber. Tracks of a motorcycle wound up the hill under the trees a little way from the wolf tracks.

The wolves had left their own unmistakable smell. He didn't personally know these particular wolves, but the scent of Logan's pack and their leader had been imprinted on them. Logan growled low in his throat as he ran on.

Nadia had run so long she must be close to dropping. Logan loped up the hill, the Packmaster's instinct to find and protect spurring him on.

He spotted the glare of firelight in plenty of time to crouch down and come in low. He found four men around a campfire drinking coffee, one with an uncocked shotgun slung over his arm. Typical hunters, except three of them were werewolves.

Logan didn't recognize the wolves or the human, but he could smell that they'd been around Matt. Where *was* Matt?

The human, the man with the gun, stood among them with the air of a leader—or more accurately, a tour guide. Logan could smell the nervousness on him, though.

Crawling on his belly, Logan edged closer. A motorcycle was parked just outside the circle of light.

"Damn cold out here," one werewolf said. The crackling fire nearly drowned out their low voices, but Logan's hearing was sharp.

The human chuckled. "You can always change back to your fur coat."

The werewolves only looked at him, and the guide fell into nervous silence.

One of the wolves paced restlessly. "What's to say the bitch won't get away while we're warming our asses?"

"No one escapes one of my nets," the human said. "It's woven with spells I got from a white witch. It will hold her until we're ready."

The werewolf grabbed his crotch. "I'm ready now."

Another laughed. "Let her get her strength back. It's more fun when they fight."

A growl welled in Logan's throat, and he fought the urge to attack. His wolf wanted to taste their blood on his fangs.

He was stronger than each of the wolves individually;

Packmasters were bred for bulk and strength. But he'd have to fight them all together, and one might get around him to Nadia.

With difficulty he swallowed his fury and circled the camp. He crept behind the motorcycle and suppressed the wolf long enough to morph to his human form.

He couldn't move as quietly as a human, but he crawled on hands and knees to the vehicle, using it to shield him from the four at the fire. They were standing close to the flames, night-blinding themselves like fools.

Logan knew which wires to yank out and carry away to keep the motorcycle from starting. Cutting their fuel lines was tempting, but the bike was too close to the fire, and the whole woods could go up, Nadia with it.

Logan crept back into the woods with the wires and scattered them into the underbrush. Then he morphed back to the wolf, put his nose to the ground, and tracked Nadia.

He found her a little way up the ridge. She was in her human form, wrapped in a net that stank of magic. Her dark hair and big dark eyes were meant to entice, but now she just looked scared and tired. Her previously too-thin body had filled out to nice curves in the last six months, blatantly revealed in her nakedness. The net clung to those curves like a bizarre designer gown.

His wolf didn't want to release control again to Logan the human. He was very, very angry, wanting to savage and kill, and he didn't want to let go of the feeling. But Logan forced his limbs to become smooth flesh, his face to flatten into its human form. It was painful, and his wolf fought him all the way.

He looked down at her, a man once more. "Logan," Nadia whispered. "Thank all the gods."

CHAPTER FOUR

Logan reached for the net to pull it from her and snatched his hand back in pain. The human must have woven silver into it—to keep the werewolves from tearing Nadia apart too soon?

"Are you all right?" he asked as he tried to spot a loose cord.

"Exhausted, starving, scared." She gave him a defiant look. "Otherwise, fine."

Logan dropped a cord as it singed his flesh, anger he hadn't felt in a long time boiling up inside him. The paranormal police at the LAPD had until recently thought of Logan as a calm cop, good at his job, not taking shit from anyone but not taking out his aggressions on anyone, either. They'd never known Logan the Packmaster, whose rage was deadly, who kept the pack under control with a discipline that Matt had only wished he had.

Logan dragged in a breath of cold, damp air. He'd need the bespelled knife and other equipment to free her. But would he have time to get it before the werewolves grew impatient and came for her?

The last thing Logan wanted to do was leave Nadia alone on the side of the hill, but Logan the human could help her better than Logan the wolf.

"I have to go get some things," he said. "I won't be long."

She nodded, but it was clear she didn't believe him.

Logan carefully reached through the mesh of the net and

touched her cheek, finding it soft and warm. Instinct of a different kind punched him now.

"I won't leave you, Nadia, I promise. Sit tight and try to rest. I'll be half an hour."

Nadia nodded again without changing expression.

Logan let the wolf and its rage take over again, and slid off into the woods.

He'd found her. Nadia wanted to lie back, close her eyes, and relax all her defenses. Logan had found her. It would be all right.

The sane part of her knew nothing was all right. Even if Logan did rescue her from the hunters, this wasn't over. There was still the issue of the werewolf leader and the question of how far she could trust Logan.

She'd known Logan was a powerful werewolf the first time she'd met him. She'd been alone in a hospital bed grieving the death of her sister when a tall, hard-faced man with tawny hair and tawny eyes had stalked in to interview her. He'd reeked of werewolf and life magic, but she'd seen anger in his eyes for her ordeal.

She'd thought about the strange encounter for months— a werewolf who cared about what happened to a demon. A chance encounter at a Harley shop several months later had led them to drinks at a nearby bar, which would have been harmless if they'd both been human.

Beneath their mundane conversation, she'd sensed his restlessness, the power of his wolf. The demon in her wanted to fight him; the woman in her wanted to sleep with him. She wanted all-night, sweat-soaked, hard-pounding sex. She wanted to wake up tangled with him and screw some more.

She wondered what she desired most: the danger, or his hot golden gaze on her, his big hands on her body. She'd sworn off sex since her sister died. Maybe that had been a mistake, because being with Logan did all kinds of weird things to her hormones.

Now Logan had rushed up here from LA to find her. But

why? Until she knew exactly what his motives were, she wasn't sure how far she could trust him.

Down the hill, the argument between the werewolves escalated. Her human hearing wasn't as good as her demon's, but she could tell that one wanted to go at Nadia right away, while the others wanted to wait a little longer.

Come on, Logan.

It seemed like an eternity before she heard him making his way back. The other wolves were still arguing. In the meantime, the woods had grown black with night, and there was a cold bite in the moist air.

Logan crept across the damp leaves without a sound, fully dressed and carrying a duffel bag. His naked human body had looked good, all tight muscle and broad shoulders, but he looked equally fine in black T-shirt, jeans, and fleece-lined coat.

Logan crouched next to her and brought a long-bladed knife out of a sheath in his boot. She scented life magic on it, a witch-spelled blade.

The cords fell away, and Nadia exhaled in relief. The pain of the spelled net receded a bit, though her skin was crisscrossed with sensitive red welts.

She shook with cold. Her demon tried to flow through her and take over, wanting to keep her warm, wanting to keep her strong, but she was too tired to change.

Logan put his hand on her shoulder, and she gasped out loud. His life essence was strong, sparking through him like white fire. The demon in her wanted to reach out and pull that life essence into her.

She wanted it so bad she cringed from his touch. She was hungry, needing life essence. She could suck him dry in an instant. Or, more likely, die trying.

Logan took off his coat and draped it around her. The fleece inside retained his warmth and a tiny bit of his life essence, enough to make her want more. She shivered and pulled the coat close, tamping down her need. Get safe first, worry about life essence later.

She calmed herself enough to let Logan help her stand. Twigs and pebbles on the ground cut her already raw feet, and she bit back a moan.

Without a word, Logan lifted her in his arms and moved silently and swiftly back under the trees. After a while, they came to the end of a dirt track, where he'd left a motorcycle. It was a black Harley, sleek and lovely.

"Hold tight to me and keep your head down," Logan said in her ear.

He stowed his gear in the saddle bags and helped Nadia mount the bike. His coat was so long on her that she could pull it under her butt so she wouldn't have to sit bare-assed on the seat. Logan got on in front of her, and she bit her lip as she wrapped her arms around his middle. The jolt of his life essence behind the thin barrier of his clothes was making her crazy.

"Ready?"

She nodded tersely. Logan pushed the bike forward with his feet and let it coast silently a little way down the hill before he kicked on the engine.

Instantly he plummeted forward, the roar of the engine drowning out the shouts that sounded behind them. Nadia grinned in spite of her hunger and tightened her grip around his flat abdomen. Logan knew how to ride.

She and Logan shot out from under the trees to a jeep trail that ran down the side of the hill. Freezing air flowed over Nadia's legs, but where she pressed against Logan she was fiery warm.

He took them down the mountain to a paved road that dipped and rolled with the terrain. Nadia held on, waves of exhaustion swamping her. She fought to stay awake, lifting her head a little so that the cold air would stream over her face.

It was late enough that they were the only vehicle on the road. When they pulled into a parking lot of a one-story motel, nothing stirred. Flakes of snow began to fall as Logan stopped the bike and killed the motor in front of one of the doors. He swung off and unlocked the door, tossing his bag inside.

Nadia didn't have enough strength left to swing her leg over the seat. Without a word, Logan returned to carry her into the motel room.

He deposited her on the bed, but before she could release a breath of relief, he climbed on top of her, straddling her on all fours.

His grim face hovered above hers, his body pinning her to the bed, his life essence nearly swamping her. Anger swirled in his amber-colored eyes, a werewolf ready to dissolve in fury.

"You want to tell me what the *hell* you're doing here, and why you're being chased by my old pack?"

CHAPTER FIVE

Nadia's combined scents of fear and relief roused the beast Logan tried to keep buried. His own worry added to the mix, making him hot and pounding hard.

Nadia glared at him with coffee-brown eyes that glinted with a hint of red. "I didn't ask the wolves to chase me, and it's none of your business what I'm doing here."

"Screw that." He pinned her shoulders to the bed. "You called *me*."

"I called you because yours was the first phone number I could remember."

Not a lie, but not the truth either. Logan resisted the urge to shake the story out of her, and at the same time he had to resist smoothing the short curls that lay against her face. They'd be silky soft and so would her skin.

"Why did you need my help?" he demanded. "Why didn't you just morph to demon form and kill them all?"

"A question like that shows you know damn-all about demons. Even if you're cozy with a demon matriarch." Her voice grated, but she smelled of sharp fear.

"What did you do to make werewolves chase you? Those werewolves in particular?"

She regarded him in stubborn silence.

He had to make her tell him. He wasn't supposed to be so protective of a *demon*, but something about Nadia roused all his Packmaster instincts.

When Samantha had been his LAPD partner last year,

she'd unknowingly siphoned off a little of his life essence every day. That act had calmed the magical ferociousness of the Packmaster inside him, which had been fine with Logan. He'd been having difficulty staying under control away from his home and pack, and Samantha had unwittingly helped him.

When Samantha realized what she'd been doing, she'd stopped, but Logan had grown used to the calming effects of Samantha's siphoning. Once it was gone, his Packmaster instincts flared doubly strong, and it was all he could do to keep them suppressed. He'd been a little more vicious than he needed to be with the paranormals it was his job to arrest, more protective of his new partner, Nez. Nez never said anything, but Logan sometimes sensed the man's uneasiness. McKay had given him leave without question, which meant his control was slipping. When he was with Nadia especially, his control cracked like thin ice.

"Are you all right?" he asked gruffly. "Did they hurt you?"

He watched a swallow move down Nadia's throat. "I'm just tired. I ran for such a long time."

She closed her eyes, her face too pale in the harsh yellow glare of the bedside lamp. Logan couldn't stop himself brushing her hair back from her forehead. Her curls, soft and damp, tickled his fingers.

He softened his tone. "Do you need life essence?"

Her eyes popped open. He saw the hunger swimming in her dark demon gaze.

"What do you know about that?"

"I know demons need it or they can't survive. I learned a lot about demons from Samantha, believe me." Logan touched her cheek. "Take some from me."

She twisted her face away. "No."

"You need it. Take a little."

"You have a death wish or something?"

"I'm strong, Nadia. I'm a damn powerful werewolf and can take a little essence sucking. Do it."

With those words, he pressed his hand to her face again.

She tried to resist, but then something dark tugged at his hand. He felt Nadia start siphoning his life essence as though she couldn't get enough. It snaked from his fingertips into her body, igniting his already simmering desire.

It had never felt like this with Samantha. Logan's arousal pushed at the seam of his jeans, his body knowing Nadia was naked under the coat. He wanted to rip open the jacket and pound himself into her, stab his tongue into her mouth until he was groaning. He wanted it, needed it. Now.

She grabbed his wrist and forced his hand from her. Logan gasped like she'd slapped him. He dragged in a breath of cold air, his heart pounding.

"Shit."

"That's enough." Nadia sounded stronger, the red glint in her eyes replaced with tiny white sparks. "Get off me, Detective."

He rolled away from her and came to his feet, breathing hard. He knew that a demon taking life essence could give the donor an orgasmic high. If the person let a demon drain him too often, he started to crave the experience like a jones for a drug. This was why people went to the demon clubs— for the pleasure of letting someone like Nadia feed from them.

She smiled a little, her eyes half closed, so sensual he had to take two steps back. His hard-on rubbed the inside of his pants until he gritted his teeth.

"Get under the covers and sleep," he ground out. "I'll find you some clothes and food for both of us."

"Fine," she said. She was angry, but to his demon-craving senses her voice came out low and sultry.

Logan knew logically that he reacted to her demon glamour, the beauty that sucked in the unwary. At the same time the Packmaster in him wanted to touch her, to reassure her that she was protected.

The conflicting desires ripped at him. Logan the man and Logan the wolf weren't often at odds, but his wolf's mind was snarling and snapping at what Logan's human body needed.

He had to get out of there.

"Double-lock the door behind me," he said with effort. "Make damn sure it's me before you open it again."

The cold embraced him as he stepped outside. Nadia lifted herself on her elbow, a delectable picture of lovely woman with long legs wearing nothing but his coat.

He deliberately slammed the door, and plunged into the cold night.

Nadia heaved a sigh of release and frustration as Logan's motorcycle rumbled off into the distance. She swung out of bed and locked and chained the door as he'd instructed, then stood with her back against it.

Her body was hot and aroused, Logan's life essence like nothing she'd ever tasted. She knew it was dangerous to take from a life-magic creature, but oh gods, was his essence sweet. It surged through her body like a white-hot flame, and the temptation to lace her fingers around his neck, open her mouth, and suck it all into her had been incredibly hard to resist. He tasted like fine wine laced with hot peppers, and felt like . . .

She closed her eyes and pressed her hands to her mouth. She was lucky she'd been able to stop and push him away. He'd been aroused too, she'd seen his hard-on against the inside of his jeans. What would it be like to drink his essence and have him inside her at the same time?

Nadia groaned. She had no business thinking things like that. At the end of this, Logan wouldn't want to come anywhere near her.

But she could still feel his essence inside her, a connection to him. Damn. The heady afterglow of it gave her a strong impulse to relax, sleep, and recover, but Nadia had things to do.

She limped to the duffel bag Logan had dumped on a rickety chair, pried it open, and began to sift through it. Something heavy rattled inside a small box, and she opened it to find revolver bullets. She lifted one and examined it. Silver.

So Logan had come prepared to shoot and kill the were-wolves of his own pack. That made her feel even worse.

Nadia dropped the bullet back into the box. *I'm a demon. I'm not supposed to give a damn about the feelings of a lone were-wolf.* She shoved the box back inside, frustrated.

Logan's bag also held a couple of sweatshirts and a pair of jeans, all with the price tags still on them. Nadia slid off his fleece coat and pulled on a sweatshirt. Even brand new, the shirt already carried a trace of Logan's life essence.

The unopened package of briefs did likewise. Nadia pulled the package apart and shook out the generic white cotton. Very practical, no racy thongs for Detective Logan Wright.

Nadia couldn't help imagining Logan's butt filling out the briefs. He had the sweetest ass.

He'd fill out the front side well too. She'd felt as much when he lay on top of her on the bed. Nadia slid the under-wear on, trying to forget the heady joy of tasting his life essence.

She was pleased that her hips were slim enough for the un-derwear, though the briefs felt weird. The spare pair of jeans felt odd too, too tight in the wrong places, too loose in others.

She straightened up and caught sight of herself in the mirror, her eyes dark in a white face. Here she was, all dressed up and nowhere to go. She couldn't simply call Samantha and ask for a ride back to LA. That wasn't an option. She had to finish her part in this, or risk everything she cared about.

Nadia knew she'd be a fool to trust herself around Logan or broadcast her troubles to him. She had to play this out, for everyone's sake, even if it meant Logan might die.

She didn't want Logan to die.

She could not get any more involved with him. There were things she needed to do, a hole in her heart.

Another search of the duffel bag rendered a money clip with ten twenties in it. Interesting. Was it a spare stash he'd forgotten about, or had he left it to trap Nadia?

Damn werewolves. Just because they were life-magic creatures, people got the idea that they were on the side of good. But werewolves were for themselves when it all came down to it.

Nadia turned to the phone. She didn't really want to use the hotel's telephone for such calls, but she didn't have much choice.

The first was to a house in suburban Los Angeles. "Is everything all right?" she asked the woman who answered. "Is Joel home from school?"

"Yes, he's fine. Why wouldn't he be?"

Nadia exhaled in relief, said a few more expected and reassuring things, and hung up. She dialed another number but had to leave a message when voice mail picked up.

The sound of a bike made her jump, and she slammed down the phone. She knew it was Logan—she recognized the purr of his Harley. She tossed the money back into the bag and peeked out the tiny window to see Logan's bulk under the yellow porch light before she opened the door.

Logan swirled in on a wave of wind and snow, his hands full of bags. She closed and bolted the door behind her, then turned to find his golden gaze taking in his clothes on her body.

"I told you I'd get you something to wear." His eyes darkened. "Although you look pretty good in those."

"I was cold."

He turned away, his expression guarded. "You can always take a shower, if this dump has any hot water."

Nadia imagined herself in a steam-filled bathroom with glorious water beating down on her. Even better if Logan came through the steam to her, sliding his hands through her hair to lean down and kiss her lips.

Stop it.

"I'm more interested in the food right now," she said, trying to keep her voice steady.

"I didn't have to go far to find it." Logan held up a white bag from a fast food chain. "How many cheeseburgers do you want?"

Nadia's stomach rumbled. How long since she'd eaten? Forty-eight hours?

"Just give me one."

Logan smiled and tossed her a paper-wrapped burger. Nadia sank down at the scarred table and ripped open the paper, barely getting the wrapping out of the way before she bit.

Meat, juicy and hot, melted cheese oozing over everything. Junk food had never tasted so good.

"Demons like burgers?" Logan asked.

Nadia swallowed and wiped her mouth with a thin paper napkin. "You thought we craved the taste of human flesh? Or yummy life-magic creatures?"

"Very funny. Don't eat so fast. You'll just bring it up again."

Nadia didn't care. She could eat everything on this table and be hungry for more.

"Thank you," she said, her mouth full.

Logan shrugged, unwrapping a burger for himself. "They weren't busy. It was easy to persuade them to give me everything they'd already made."

With Logan, that probably meant looking at them with his golden wolf's eyes before they fell all over themselves to do whatever he wanted.

"Are you ready to tell me what happened?" he asked, putting his burger down after only a few bites.

Nadia sighed. "Logan, don't ask me. I appreciate your help, but please just take me somewhere safe and then forget all about me."

"I can't do that. I told you I'd protect you, and I take my oaths seriously."

"Yes, but who protects me from you?"

He met her gaze, and Nadia felt the power of a dominant werewolf touch her. The demon in her didn't like it at the same time she was fascinated by it.

"I'd never hurt you, Nadia," he said.

She gave him an ironic smile. "Unless I was sucking down too much life essence or doing something equally demonic? Especially if I did it in your jurisdiction."

"Is that what you think?"

"You're a paranormal cop—it's what you do. You're a were-wolf, the enemy of death-magic creatures. Neither of us is safe from the other, although I admit I couldn't kick your ass if I tried right now."

The hint of a smile touched his mouth. "Why would you want to kick my ass? I just rescued you."

He shouldn't smile like that. Was he trying to melt *all* her resistance? "And now I'm in your power. Samantha told me you were a Packmaster, which I guess means the head cop of your pack."

The smile died. "Used to be."

He pushed the burger aside and rested his elbows on the table. His forearms were covered with gold hair and criss-crossed with tiny scars.

"One of the wolves hunting you was my old Pack Leader, Matt Lewis."

Was it her imagination, or was he waiting to see if she recognized the name? "Oh, yeah? Does he hunt demons a lot?"

"He shouldn't be hunting them at all. I think this is about me, not you. He's using you to draw me out."

Nadia looked down at the remains of her burger. "Why would he do that? You barely know me."

Logan looked uncomfortable. "I know you well enough."

They'd met twice more after their first encounter to have beer or coffee and talk about Harleys. They'd never asked each other personal questions or gone out on a real date or gone home with each other. It didn't matter what sexual fantasies she'd spun about him, they'd never happened. Probably never would.

"I'm sure Matt has a spy in Los Angeles keeping tabs on me," he said.

Nadia sensed there was more to it than that, but she kept silent.

"Did Matt or his wolves nab you in Los Angeles?" Logan asked.

Were half-truths better than none? "Not exactly. I came up here on my own."

Logan frowned. "Why?"

Nadia carefully picked cheese from the wrapper. "I wanted a change. I thought I could look for a job up here."

He looked at her the same way he'd study a suspect across a table in an interrogation room. "There aren't a lot of supernatural beings around here. No werewolf packs, no vamps. What made you think someone would hire a demon? Or are there demon clubs even in this remote area?"

"It's not what you think," Nadia said in a hard voice. "I thought I could work at a mountain resort as a concierge or something. Planning outings for wealthy skiers. I only did the clubs in LA because I desperately needed the money." Pandering to clients who wanted the high of a demon taking their life essence, putting up with their sexual advances had made her sick, but she hadn't had much choice.

"You left the clubs, though, you and your sister," Logan said.

"Because the asshole who ran the club in Santa Monica kept after Bev to become his mistress. She was afraid of him. So I told him what to do with himself, and we walked."

"The club owner wasn't your clan, was he? You're Lamiah clan, he was Obsejan."

"Good work, Detective. Checking up on me?"

"I was curious why two girls from a Lamiah family would end up working for a rival clan's club. And why you didn't go back to a Lamiah club, like Merrick's, when you quit."

She gave him an ironic smile. "It's not as easy to get into the clubs as you think. The bosses tend to think they own everyone who works for them. Merrick was cool and left us alone for the most part, but he wasn't about to help us without something in return. I'll give you three guesses what he wanted."

Though Logan didn't move, Nadia sensed rage stir inside him. "I never liked Merrick."

"He can be a sleazebag."

"I'm glad you stopped," Logan said quietly.

"After what happened to Bev . . ."

She broke off, the emptiness inside her swelling. She and her sister had been abducted and beaten because they were demons, rendered helpless by spells so they couldn't fight back. Bev had lost her life at the hands of a fanatic, and Nadia had vowed never to put herself or anyone she loved in that kind of danger again.

She'd even found herself talking to demon girls in clubs and on the streets about what kind of dangers they faced. A crusader, that's what she'd become.

The club owners started to not allow her to come around, because demon clubs made money off the idiots who wanted the demon experience. Fortunately, some of the girls had listened to her and had already given up the life.

"What did you need the money for?" Logan asked.

Nadia jumped. "What?"

Logan pinned her with another critical gaze. "You said you worked the clubs because you needed the money. Since you came up here looking for a job, I assume you still do."

"Now that is none of your business."

"It's my business now. You aren't safely home with your Lamiah clan, and my Pack Leader is pursuing you through the woods."

Nadia folded her arms, feeling slightly queasy. Her cheeseburger wrapper still held a bit of melted cheese, but her appetite had disappeared. She probably shouldn't have eaten so fast.

"My clan disowned me and my sister. You knew that."

"Samantha is your clan leader now, and she's made it clear you're welcome back."

"Leave it alone, wolf-man."

"I can't, hell-spawn." Logan's expression was humorless. "You called me for help, and I consider you a friend. Doesn't matter that you're not werewolf. I'm the Packmaster, the protector. And now I protect you."

Nadia stood, every fear flaring. "You're not my protector. I'm grateful to you for helping me, but once we're out of here, that's it. We're done."

"And yet, when you were in trouble, you called me."

"Because I couldn't think of anyone else," she nearly shouted. "I had to risk it—I didn't know what else to do."

He met her toe-to-toe, towering over her. "Tell me why you really wanted to come up here."

Gods, was he not going to leave it alone? She backed a step, her worry returning. "I told you. To get a job, start a career. You know, have a life."

"On your own."

"Yes, on my own."

"You wouldn't be alone." Logan's voice was harsh. "You'd be unprotected, prey to every shark looking for a victim. Look what's happened already."

He came for her, and she backed up until she was against the wall. He caught her shoulders with strong hands and leaned over her, as intimidating as ever.

He had the best eyes, tawny like a lion's, a stare that stabbed through her like he knew all her secrets.

All but one.

"It wasn't exactly my fault," she said with heat. "I didn't run up to the werewolves and say, 'Hi there, I'm helpless and alone, why don't you chase me?'"

"You didn't have to."

"You don't know a damn thing about me," she flashed. "I'm surprised you bothered to help me when I called."

Logan leaned closer, touching his own temple. "How could I not? You've been burned in my brain since the day I met you."

"Why? Because the mighty werewolf cop likes to keep track of the demon element in his city?"

"No. Because of this."

He cupped his hands around her head and covered her mouth with a bruising kiss.

CHAPTER SIX

Gods, she tasted good.

Logan felt her fingers lace around the back of his neck, her lips open to his. He slid his tongue inside and let it play there, tasting her fear and anger, her desperation.

Forget about her? Never.

Logan had wanted her the minute he'd seen her, with her dark brown eyes in a softly curved face and the set of her shoulders that said she'd not break down. Logan's interest in her had grown as he'd kept tabs on her these last six months. He'd felt more than interest, more than desire. He'd felt the bonding magic a werewolf high in the pack felt for his mate, and he'd resisted. He should resist now.

Logan deepened the kiss and leaned Nadia against the wall. Her body was slim and small but so strong. Even the weakest demon was stronger than any human could be.

Her tongue swirled around his, finding the depths of his mouth. She wasn't afraid. She welcomed this.

Logan furrowed her hair as he eased the kiss to a close. Her face was dirty from her run through the woods, scratched and cut from sharp branches.

He traced his fingers over the cuts, wishing for the healing powers of Tain, who could have closed up Nadia's wounds in two seconds flat.

The urge to heal her, to hold her, to take care of her was strong. He wanted to put her over his shoulder and carry her home, to have her stay there until he made the world safe for her.

He should feel that for a pack mate, not a demon woman, no matter how beautiful she was. If Logan were still connected with his pack, Matt could have sensed Logan starting a mate bond. Packmasters were deeply connected to every nuance of every wolf in the pack, and Logan was willing to bet that simply walking away hadn't broken the connection. Matt was exploiting it, like he exploited everything else.

"You should shower," he said softly. "And sleep. You need the rest."

The spark of desire in Nadia's eyes made his heart hammer. The bed was right next to them, a rickety thing covered with a threadbare blue plaid bedspread.

He saw Nadia glance at it and then back at him.

Heat flared. She wanted it.

No.

He pushed away from her. "Go take a shower. We'll talk about what to do with you later."

She flushed. "What to do with me? Is it too much to get your brain around that you don't have to *do* anything with me?"

Without waiting for answer she slid out from between him and the wall, strode into the bathroom, and slammed the door. The thin-walled room shook with the impact.

Logan stared at the bathroom door, hearing the shower snap on, pipes groaning as hot water was dragged through them.

He thought of her peeling off her clothes—his clothes—and letting them fall one by one to the cold bathroom floor. Naked, she'd pull back the plastic shower curtain and step under the steaming water.

Logan took a step toward the bathroom and stopped, his gut clenching.

He'd come to protect her, not claim her. He wouldn't be as bad as Matt.

He turned away from the bathroom, his body tight. He ached for her, and his arousal hated him for not pulling her down onto the bed. Logan wanted to have her, to show her how much he'd really thought of her all this time.

He wanted her for a more basic reason—the need for her warm female body under his. He wanted to look into her eyes when she came, feel her writhing with climax, her sheath squeezing him tight.

Stop.

He took his cell phone from the table and flipped it open. He stared at it for a long time, then slowly punched in a number that he'd wanted to forget and hadn't been able to.

A woman picked up on the other end with a breathless "Hello?"

"Kayla," Logan said.

He didn't have to tell her who it was. She sucked in a sharp breath.

"Logan."

"Where's Matt?" he asked.

"You're not supposed to call, Logan. You're not pack. You're outcast . . ."

"Where the hell is Matt?" Logan growled. The Packmaster in him was strong enough to cut off her words but not allow her to hang up the phone. "Do you even know?"

"I know."

"He's after me, isn't he? Why?"

"Matt can travel where he wants to," Kayla snapped. "He's Pack Leader, asshole."

To think, Logan used to be in love with her.

No, not love. She'd been promised to him, and he'd been loyal to her and protective. His reward for taking care of her all those years was her running to Matt and sparking the Challenge.

"Matt has come here to kill me," Logan said in a hard voice. "Why is he bothering? I left the pack, like you said. I walked away so you two could live happily ever after."

"Because it's not over," Kayla said.

"Yes, it is." Logan was over and done with it—he'd turned his back on his old life and that was that.

"You never fought him." Kayla's words tumbled out, frantic. "You didn't take up the Challenge. You ruined him. Half the pack thinks you're the stronger wolf, that you would have won if you'd fought. The rebellion started small, but it's escalated until they won't listen to Matt anymore. They say you should be Pack Leader, and him driving you out was against pack law. Karl, the new Packmaster, can't keep order. Not like you could."

"So Matt came out here to Challenge me again?" Logan asked when she finally slowed down.

There were tears in her voice. "Yes. Please don't kill him, Logan."

So Kayla also believed that Logan was the stronger wolf. Interesting.

"Why didn't he just confront me? He kidnapped one of my friends and tormented her to get me up here. Why didn't he come to me instead?"

"I don't know. I don't know anything about that."

Matt had done it to lure Logan alone into the wild, of course, far from any help he might have from his LA friends. Stealing Nadia served two purposes: First, the beginnings of the bond would ensure Logan would come after her. Second, the other wolves would hear about how much Logan cared about a demon. What kind of werewolf did that make Logan?

"Are you going to kill him?" Kayla asked in a small voice.

"That all depends on Matt," Logan said.

Kayla started to bleat something else, but Logan hung up on her.

He wanted to throw the phone across the room, to punch the wall, anything to release the rage inside him.

Logan heard the water go off, the shower curtain slide back, and then Nadia came out of the bathroom, wrapped in a towel.

His breath caught in his throat, his rage giving way to roaring desire. Damn it, was she sexy like that on purpose?

Of course she was. Nadia was a demon.

The motel's one thin towel barely came together around her torso. Her limbs were shapely but strong, muscles playing as she walked across the room toward the plastic bags Logan had brought in.

"Oh, good, you bought toothbrushes." She rummaged in the bags, pulling out sweatshirts and jeans made for women. "How did you know what size clothes to get?"

"I remembered."

She turned around, her short hair slicked to her head. "Remembered from what?"

"The matriarch's records."

"You looked at my file?" Nadia said, outraged. "Samantha let you?"

"She didn't exactly let me." Logan's detective instincts, much like his wolf instincts, died hard.

Nadia glared at him, the towel baring the cleavage between lovely round breasts. "Do you mean you snooped? We should have kept the policy that non-demons are barred from the matriarch's mansion."

"It would put a damper on Samantha's marriage," Logan said dryly.

"What were you doing? Making sure I hadn't broken any of your paranormal laws? What were you going to do if I had? Shed on me?"

"I was making sure you were all right."

"You couldn't just ask me?"

"Someone hurt you, Nadia. Bad. I was making sure that hadn't happened to you again. I won't let it happen again."

She started to answer, then broke off. Logan wished she weren't so damned delectable, that he didn't want to ease her to the bed and pull the towel off her.

"Who were you talking to on the phone?" she asked abruptly. "I have good hearing. You sounded pissed."

Logan's mouth hardened. "Kayla. Matt's mate."

"The woman you were supposed to marry?"

"How did you know about that?"

She gave him a little smile. "You check up on me, I check up on you. Why didn't you marry her?"

Logan turned his back, surprised at how angry it still made him. "We were pledged to be mates since childhood. My father, who was Packmaster before me, and her father arranged it. When it came time to take Kayla as my mate in truth, Matt stepped in and said he wanted her. I either had to answer his Challenge or go. I decided to go."

"Werewolves arrange their marriages? I've never heard that."

"Most don't, not anymore. But werewolves at the top of the pack marry for the good of the pack. Kayla's family is high-ranking, and she was a good match for Packmaster. Matt decided she was better for Pack Leader."

"So why didn't you fight him?"

Logan heard the plastic bags rattle, the thump of the towel as it hit the floor. He kept his back firmly turned.

"Because Kayla wanted one of us to die. If I won, I'd become Pack Leader. If Matt won—I'd just be dead. Kayla wanted to be Pack Leader's mate, and she'd have it over Matt's dead body or mine. I didn't want to give her the satisfaction of getting one of us killed. So I walked."

"I bet that was hard." A note of sympathy entered her voice.

"The hardest thing I ever did. The wolf inside me wanted to kill Matt and hang his body out for the vultures. But I wasn't dying for Kayla, or killing for her, either."

"She sounds like a real bitch," Nadia said. "Pun intended. You can turn around now."

She was settling a sweatshirt over her new jeans as Logan turned. His blood pounded as he saw a sliver of her belly, the shadow of her naval before the shirt came down.

He wanted to push her back on the bed and lick across that belly until he was satisfied. Which he wouldn't be. He'd have to unbutton and unzip her jeans and tug them down, dipping his tongue below her panties to taste the heat of her.

Logan dragged a chair from the table and straddled it wrong way around, hoping that hid his pounding erection.

"So tell me what happened," he said, forcing himself into the role of investigating officer. "Why did you come up to this particular area to hunt for a job? Did you have a specific place in mind?"

His voice sounded so natural, so normal. Nadia sat cross-legged on the bed, resting her elbows on her knees, her expression still wary. Logan stayed in the chair, hanging onto the back of it for dear life.

"I got an e-mail," she said. "A job offer."

"What kind of job offer?"

Nadia studied her fingernails, now clean, and he had the feeling she was choosing her words carefully. "To come up to a lodge here in the mountains and work as a concierge. I saw it as a chance to start over. So I left LA and hitchhiked north."

Logan clutched the chair until the wood dented. Imagining her out on a dark rural highway, all sexy in her tight jeans, sticking out her thumb for any lust-starved lunatic to pick up—it made his blood boil.

"What lodge?"

"A resort near Crater Lake that's always looking for people. Apparently it's so remote people don't like to stay long, but that sounded perfect to me."

"How did they get your e-mail? Or was it bulk mail?"

"It was addressed to me personally. They named a woman I'd met when I worked in Santa Monica. It seemed like a good offer."

"But you never made it."

"I almost did. I hitchhiked to Sacramento, then got a bus up to the mountains. It took forever, but it was so beautiful." She sounded wistful.

"And you met the guy who sent you the e-mail? What was his name?"

"Dan Martin, but I never met him. When I got off the bus, a van with the resort logo on it was there to pick me up.

There was a man in the back, and as soon as we got down a road out of sight of other traffic, he shot me with a tranquilizer dart."

Logan's growl came from deep inside himself. "Go on."

"When I woke up, I was in deep woods. I was naked, and the man who'd picked me up from the bus station had a gun pointed at me. He explained that he'd brought men out to hunt me, and I had to give them a good chase or he'd shoot me. If I survived the hunt, he'd give me two thousand dollars and a ride to anywhere. I didn't have much choice. I ran like hell. They chased me, three werewolves and the first guy, who was human. I did everything I could to lose them, but I couldn't. Damn wolves could track me anywhere."

Logan's growls wouldn't stop. They rumbled up in his throat and rippled through his body. He felt his skin flash hot, like it did just before he changed.

"What was this resort called?" he managed to ask.

"The Lodge of the Pines."

Logan got up from the chair and paced the small room, trying to keep the beast inside from breaking free.

"Do you know where it was?"

"Not exactly. The e-mail said a van regularly took guests up from the bus station, so I didn't worry about directions. I thought I'd figure it out once I got there."

"Bus station."

"That's what I just said. What do you plan to do, go to the station and wait for another van to show up?"

Logan turned around, feeling his skin rippling as he fought the change. "Yes," he said.

CHAPTER SEVEN

Nadia leapt to her feet and planted herself in front of him on his next restless stride across the room. His eyes had gone strange, yellow flecked with red.

"What makes you think they won't shoot *you* with a tranquilizer?" she demanded. "If one of these wolves is your Pack Leader, don't you think he'll be waiting for you?"

"I hope he is."

Her heart beat swiftly with fear. "Don't, Logan."

Logan faced her, his body vibrating with rage. She'd never seen him like this. The couple of times she'd met him, he'd been hard-faced but quiet, calm but not overly friendly, seeming alone even when he was with other people.

She could imagine his wolf sitting unmoving on a hilltop, the wind gently ruffling his fur, while the other members of his pack avoided coming too close. Wolves were beautiful— she wasn't immune to that—and the wolf Logan became was a magnificent creature.

She wondered how lonely he'd been.

"Don't?" he asked incredulously. "Why not?"

"Because he might kill you, that's why not. You're alone, and this guy brought friends."

"They hunted you. It's my job to show Matt what happens when he messes with one of mine."

He looked down at her with an expression that must have scared the bejesus out of whatever wolves he'd punished as Packmaster.

"Gods, you're an arrogant bastard. What's this 'one of mine' crap?"

Logan's golden-eyed stare burned her. "I made a connection with you that must have vibrated through the pack. I didn't mean to, but I did it. So you're under my protection, now. It doesn't matter that you're not werewolf. I'm still bonded by laws that go way beyond what Matt understands."

He closed his eyes briefly, and when he opened them, a little more of Logan the man looked out. "And I want to get the bastards that did this to you."

Nadia put her hands on her hips, her breath hurting her. A connection? If she was honest, she'd admit that she'd felt something sliding into place when she and Logan had talked over beers. She could talk to him so easily. At least, she could when nothing had been at stake.

Matt had already gone back on his bargain with her, but the hold he had over Nadia terrified her. She had to make sure Logan stayed alive long enough, or nothing could help her.

"If you go charging in there with nothing but your arrogant attitude, you'll get the shit kicked out of you," she said. "We need a plan."

"Who's 'we'?"

"I want to get them too, Logan."

Logan closed his mouth. His lips turned down and his eyes went quiet, making him look like the LA cop who'd stayed distant even when he talked to her across a restaurant table.

Except now she'd kissed that mouth, felt his lips respond to hers, tasted his life essence. The magic of him had singed her primal core, tightening her body and making her crave more.

"I can call for some backup," he said. "I have a new partner, a Navajo shaman who's good at misdirection magic. I don't really want to bring him into it, but he'd be good if I need help." Logan picked up his gun and holster from the table. "In the meantime, I'm going to find this resort. You stay here, lock the door, and get some sleep."

"Don't be stupid. I'm going with you."

"Like hell you are."

"You aren't *my* Packmaster, Logan, and we aren't in LA. You have no authority over me."

Logan's glare held both anger and surprise, and she suddenly realized that he'd never been disobeyed before. She suspected every wolf in his pack had fallen all over themselves to do whatever he said. The perps in LA certainly never gave him any trouble.

"Can I point out that it's common sense?" Logan growled. "You're exhausted, and I can look around more easily if I don't have to worry about you every step of the way."

"You don't have to worry about me at all. We'll be two people going to a mountain lodge. If the only thing they did up there was hunt demons, I'd think every matriarch in the country would know by now, and be up here raising hell—literally. It's likely it's a secret sideline, or else the hunters are using a van with their logo as a blind."

"Or the resort doesn't exist at all."

"Another possibility. One way to find out."

She opened the drawer of the bedside table and pulled out a tattered phone book.

Logan leaned over her shoulder, his breath hot on her neck as she flipped through the yellow pages to hotels and resorts. Not many were listed and she easily found a small ad for Lodge of the Pines.

"That's it." She rested her finger on the logo that had adorned the side of the van. "Oh look, they've even printed a helpful map."

Logan gave her a withering glance, then sat next to her and reached for the phone. The sagging bed rolled his thigh to hers, and her breath stopped.

She glanced up at him to find him looking down at her with glittering eyes, the warmth of his leg shooting heat up and down her body. Nadia's gaze went to his lips, remembering his kiss, the spark of his life essence.

Logan looked away and grabbed his cell, frowned at it,

then tossed it onto the bed and picked up the black phone on nightstand. He punched a number and waited.

"Nez," he said in a low voice. "Can you do something for me?"

"Sure thing, wolf boy." A smooth voice come out of the phone plenty loud enough for Nadia to hear. "You got a mountain lion I need to tame for you?"

"No, a suspicious resort. Find out anything you can about a place called Lodge of the Pines in . . . Point Grace, Oregon. Not far from Crater Lake."

"Got it. Want me to call you back at this number?"

"Try my cell first, then here."

"Right, partner. Your friend all right?"

"I think so. I found her in time."

"Good. You need backup?"

"Not yet. I'm going up to the resort to check them out."

"Be careful, my friend."

Logan glanced at Nadia. "I'll report in if I find out anything."

"Me too. Good luck."

The phone clicked on the other end, and Logan hung up, but not before Nadia heard a second click.

"Someone was listening," she said, alarmed.

"I know, I heard them breathing." Logan stood.

He moved to the table, and Nadia couldn't stop herself admiring the view of his rear in tight jeans.

He turned around with the .45 in his hands, clicked open the cylinder, checked the bullets, then shoved it into his shoulder holster.

"Do you know how to shoot?"

Nadia nodded. "I know how to fire a nine millimeter. Samantha taught me. She likes to keep her hand in."

Logan's brows lifted, but he didn't comment. "Take the Glock then," he said, handing it over. "And don't shoot me."

Nadia checked the safety, then buckled on the holster as Logan replaced the witch-spelled blade in his boot.

"Nice knife," Nadia commented. "What made you bring it? I thought only silver bullets worked on werewolves."

The look Logan shot her made her stop. She expected the cold eyes of the Packmaster, but she saw sadness, fear, and relief.

"It was for you," he said. "In case it was all I could do for you."

He turned around, shutting her out. He swung on the fleece-lined jacket that he'd let her wear and banged out of the room.

CHAPTER EIGHT

Logan was very aware of Nadia on the motorcycle behind him, her slim body hard against his back.

The jacket he'd bought her fit her snugly, and the jeans nicely cupped her ass. He wanted to turn the bike around and ride straight back to his apartment in LA, peel the jacket and jeans from her, and kiss every inch of her flesh.

Nadia leaned against his back, her helmet hard on his shoulder as she tried to hide from the wind. It was tempting to make sure she rode behind him the rest of his life.

The map to the lodge was easy to follow—Logan remembered passing the turnoff to the narrow numbered road. A small sign beyond the intersection proclaimed that Lodge of the Pines was five miles away.

It all looked legit. Logan's bike hummed under the trees in the early morning light. The woods here were so thick the snow hadn't gathered on the road yet.

Around a few bends, the road widened a little and ended in a parking area in front of a cluster of buildings. A wooden sign with burned-in, stylized lettering proclaimed LODGE OF THE PINES.

Logan parked the bike next to a line of SUVs. He waited for Nadia to hop off, then swung his leg over the seat and settled the bike on its stand.

"It looks nice," Nadia said, taking off the helmet and ruffling her hair. "Like a place humans would have a honeymoon, if they were into hiking and snowshoes and skiing."

Or cuddling in front of a fire, Logan thought. He imagined lounging on a sofa with Nadia curled up next to him, her head on his shoulder. Her warm curls would tickle his cheek, and he'd have his arms around her waist.

His imagination shifted to them being naked on the sofa under a blanket. Her bare body would be flushed with warmth, her soft bottom rubbing his hip. He banished the picture before his swift physical reaction could embarrass him.

Inside they found a huge lobby with split-log walls and a fire warming one end of the room. A huge elk's head peered down from above the fireplace, and other unlucky deer decorated the walls. Chairs and tables were scattered across the wooden floor, with people in sweaters and jeans reading or talking or admiring the sunrise over the mountains.

The clerk looked up as Logan approached the check-in desk in the corner, then he did a double take. Logan realized he must look like hell, pale and dirt-stained from his long trip and then the hunt through the woods for Nadia. He put up his hand and felt a day and a night's beard growth on his face.

Nadia looked better for her shower and clean clothes, but dark shadows of exhaustion marred the delicate skin beneath her eyes. Logan half expected the clerk to call security and throw them out.

Logan jerked his badge and ID out of his pocket. "LAPD, paranormal division," he said, laying the ID down so the clerk could see it clearly. "I need to speak to Dan Martin."

"Dan?" The clerk looked at Nadia, then Logan, obviously not recognizing Nadia. "I'll see if he's free."

He disappeared through a door into the back, and Nadia looked around. "On second thought, I don't like this place."

"I know. It smells wrong."

"No werewolves, though."

Logan shook his head as he looked around the room. Everyone here was human. Ordinary average, everyday humans. No witches, no demons, no vamps, no werewolves. So why did his hackles rise?

The clerk came back with an apologetic smile and told them Dan would be out in a moment. He turned to a newly arriving customer, banishing Nadia and Logan from his sphere of attention.

Logan moved to the window and looked out, feeling Nadia stop beside him. It would be the most natural thing in the world to slide his arm around her.

"It's beautiful out there," she murmured. "From in here, that is. Trying to survive being hunted through a beautiful landscape changes your perspective of it."

Logan imagined her alone, frightened, hurt, running for her life. When he found Matt, he'd punish him slowly.

A man in a dark suit and navy tie approached them. "Can I help you? My clerk said you were with the police?"

His tone and look, though polite, requested they prove it. Logan flashed his ID again, and the man didn't change expression.

"You Dan Martin?" Logan asked. "Manager?"

"Yes." He motioned them over to an isolated corner. "Why?"

Logan believed in the direct approach. "Do you know why one of your resort's vans was used to kidnap my friend and take her out into the woods to be hunted?"

Dan Martin's face paled. *"What?"*

"It wasn't a mistake," Nadia said in a hard voice. "It was a Lodge of the Pines van. And they were werewolves. One human."

"Couldn't have been. Not werewolves."

"Why not?" Logan asked.

Dan had trouble meeting Logan's gaze, but that might not be because he was lying. Logan was ready to take the place apart, and he could feel his wolf's rage glowing out from him. Not all humans could stare down a wolf.

"Paranormals aren't allowed here. Humans only." Dan lifted a brochure from the rack next to them and showed them a tiny symbol at the bottom, a horned head with an X through it. "That means this is a haven from vampires, demons, werewolves, and the like." He gave Logan a disparaging look.

"I wasn't planning to check in," Logan said. "I'm looking for someone to arrest for kidnapping, assault, attempted murder, and maybe conspiracy to assist in all these crimes."

Dan went whiter. "Well, I can't help you. All our vans are accounted for, and no werewolves are guests at our lodge."

"I can check that, you know, with a warrant."

"Go ahead." The man's lip curled. "You won't find anything."

"Then you won't mind if I talk to the drivers?" Logan asked. "If you have a van driver conspiring with paranormals to commit crimes in your pristine community, wouldn't you like us to find him?"

Dan hesitated a moment, then nodded. "Fine. The garage is in the back. Tell them I said you could speak to them."

"You don't want to come with us?"

"No. I'm busy. It wasn't one of my drivers. Anyone can copy a logo and paint it on a van. The sooner you figure that out and leave, the better."

Logan felt Nadia looking sideways at him, but he shrugged as though he didn't care one way or the other what Dan did. He thanked the man, gave him a half smile, put his hand on Nadia's shoulder, and turned away.

"He sounds sure," Nadia said as they descended the steps outside. "But it still smells wrong." She glanced at the stone balustrade of the wide porch, at the steep mountains rising through the trees to the cloud-ragged sky. "Guess I won't be staying here for my honeymoon."

"You planning on getting married anytime soon?"

She shrugged, her slim shoulders moving under the thick coat. "Who knows? I might meet someone."

A basic, primal instinct made Logan want to turn around, gather her against him, and tell her like hell he'd let her meet "someone," let alone marry the bastard.

They walked around the lodge to the garage. The garage

had four bays, all open with a van parked inside each one. An office lay on the left.

Nadia looked at the identical vans, her expression puzzled. "I can't be sure, but I don't think any of these were the one that picked me up. It was smaller. My memory is fuzzy—I was tranquilized, and I'm working on no sleep."

"Let's see if you recognize a driver."

But she didn't. Logan introduced himself in the office, which was warmed by a space heater, said he was making a routine inquiry about their vans. He didn't mention werewolves.

Martin had apparently called them, because the head driver readily showed Logan the log of when each van had been used in the last few days. None had gone to the bus station at the time Nadia had arrived.

When they left, Nadia shook her head. "I didn't see the guy who picked me up."

Which left them back where they'd started. "All right." Logan took up his helmet. "We tried this the polite, legitimate way. Now let's do it the werewolf way."

"What's that? Glare at everyone until they confess?"

"Very funny. Where did you get such an adorable sense of humor?"

"I've always had it, Logan. You just didn't notice."

Logan seized her shoulder and turned her face up to him. "Believe me, I notice everything about you."

He bent down and gave her a swift, intense kiss.

CHAPTER NINE

Logan's mouth on hers was hot and bruising, and she almost whimpered when he took it away.

Gods, if he kept kissing her like that, she would follow him around and do whatever he said. The urge was strong, the need to taste his incredible life essence again even stronger.

Maybe he knew that. *Damn him.*

Logan's eyes gleamed through half-closed lids as he curled his fingers through her hair before releasing her. He mounted the bike, adjusted his weight as she climbed on behind him, and started it up.

Nadia slid her arms around his waist as he guided the Harley onto the road. It scared her how safe she felt hanging on to him.

Logan took them where she'd feared he would, to the campsite where she'd been held captive. The fire had long since been buried, but the motorcycle still lay there, useless.

Logan crouched by the remains of the fire. "They didn't bother to cover scents. I can easily track them from here."

Nadia felt a cold prickle of fear, not for herself. "They're werewolves out to get you."

He looked up at her with a feral smile. "So I'll hunt the hunters."

"And then what? Attack four men on your own? What kind of a plan is that?"

"I'm not going to attack them."

He could have fooled her. Logan's eyes sparked with raw intent, the need to kill pouring off him in waves. He might claim to have gone civilized in Los Angeles, be an integral part of the paranormal police, but right now Logan the Packmaster was ready to rip the wolves of his pack apart. By himself.

"So you'll morph into a naked human and have a serious talk with them instead?" she demanded.

"I'll locate them and then decide what to do."

He'd attack. She knew that an angry werewolf, especially an überdominant one with a score to settle, wouldn't let anything like bad odds slow him down.

"This isn't your fight," Nadia said.

"Yes, it is."

"You don't have to take vengeance for me. I'm not a little wolfie in your pack."

"They need to be stopped."

"Of course they do. So round up the paranormal police and help them stop it."

His glare would have sent a weaker woman scrambling for cover, but Nadia lifted her chin and met it.

He said, "Don't keep telling me this isn't personal. It's damn personal. It always will be with you."

The intensity with which he looked at her made her skin tingle. "I just want you to be careful."

He looked at her a moment longer before finally turning away. He hid the bike in a stand of scrub and shed his coat and sweatshirt.

He had the hard chest and abs of an athlete, a man who regularly ran and fought. A dusting of golden hair swirled across his chest and pointed downward to his waistband.

Nadia didn't realize she was intently watching his hand on his fly, waiting for him to unzip, until he turned away and finished undressing behind a tree. The tree wasn't wide enough to hide his nice ass when he slid out of his jeans and bent over to bundle his clothes and boots. She started to grow fond of that tree.

Nadia could help him hunt the werewolves, but only if she too changed her form. She hesitated.

Most humans and life-magic creatures were repulsed by true demon forms. People could handle demons in everyday life as long as they retained their glamour as beautiful humans. Physical beauty tended to disarm even the angriest person. Scales and horns made them bring out the weapons. But not all demons had scales and horns.

Nadia stripped off quickly and willed the glam that kept her in human form fall away. She felt herself growing taller, her limbs smoothing, at the same time they became stronger, more muscular.

A wolf trotted out from behind the tree, a huge gray animal with tawny eyes and a flat, heavy-muzzled wolf's face. He looked up at her, the fur on his neck rising. Then he sat down and gazed at her in silence.

Nadia's body took on its white sheen, a glow she could escalate or dampen at will. Her hair fell black and long to her waist, her face took on its triangular shape, and her eyes enlarged, her vision strengthening. She could see shapes that shadows would hide from the ordinary person, and a spectrum of colors humans didn't have names for.

Black feathery wings emerged from her shoulder blades and cascaded to her heels, and she felt herself float a few inches above the forest floor.

Logan regarded her intently, his wolf's gaze never dropping. After a moment of them watching each other in silence, Logan rose and moved toward her.

She held her breath, knowing that as strong as she was, a werewolf, especially one with Logan's power, could still take her down. Logan kept his tawny gaze fixed on hers as he came straight at her. At the last minute, he swerved and brushed by her, his hard body sliding against her legs.

She reached down and ran her slender-fingered hands across his back. His fur was rough and wiry but tickled at the same time.

He circled her again, and Nadia crouched down to meet

him, her body shimmering as her fears flowed away. Logan looked straight into her eyes, then he rubbed his muzzle under her chin.

"Mmmm." Nadia wrapped both arms around his strong wolf's body, burying her hands in warm fur. "Nice doggie."

Logan snarled gently, lips peeling back from ferocious-looking canines. He pushed with his whole body, and Nadia toppled lightly onto her back, two hundred pounds of wolf on top of her.

Her wings cushioned her fall, and Logan shifted his weight to not crush her. His paws rested on her shoulders, pinning her, his breath hot on her face.

"Wolf breath, yum. Just what I've always wanted."

Logan growled again. His entire body rumbled with it, like a cat purring but ten times as powerful. Nadia brought up one wing to touch his back.

His life essence was so heady she feared she'd pass out. She wanted to wrap her body around his, put her face against his muzzle and draw the essence into herself. She'd drink him so greedily she might not stop. She'd only ever taken the life essence of humans who were permanently half drained by their addiction to demons. They'd had nothing like the wild, powerful life essence of this wolf.

"My," she said. "What big teeth you have."

Logan very gently touched those teeth to her throat. A dominant gesture, the wolf equivalent of saying, *I outrank you.*

While Nadia wasn't about to let him think she'd be submissive, she made a noise of pleasure. His hot breath did things to her insides, made her wish he'd morph back to his human self and kiss her until she begged for more.

Logan took his teeth from her neck and licked it instead.

She made another low noise. "My, what a big tongue you have."

Logan growled, licked her cheek, and got off her.

Nadia stretched, letting her wings flow out against the ground, in no hurry to leap up and chase the hunters. In spite of the danger and her ongoing worry, she felt relief.

Logan didn't hate her in this form. If he'd hated her, he'd have let his wolf take over and do what werewolves instinctively did—killed demons. She suddenly wanted to celebrate.

Logan watched her with his yellow gaze as she climbed reluctantly to her feet. "I suppose we have werewolves to track," she said.

Logan gave her an admonishing look, rumbling low in his throat. Nadia realized she was glowing, a beacon in the dark woods. With effort, she dampened the fires within and followed Logan under the trees.

Logan sniffed around a few moments, then raised his head and loped off. Nadia followed, his life essence leading her like a glowing trail.

Her heart fluttered as she remembered the terror of her flight through the woods, of her desperate fight when the hunters finally caught her, the burning pain when they'd thrown the net over her.

Logan thought he'd already solved the problem—he'd use these wolves to track down his Pack Leader, put Matt Lewis in his place, and take Nadia back to LA. But Nadia's predicament wasn't over yet.

Matt had her over a barrel, and the man knew it. His instructions had been clear—Matt got Logan and Joel would be safe. Matt hadn't mentioned he would have his wolves hunt Nadia until she dropped. She assumed that had been to make sure her fear was real, so she'd sound truly desperate when she called Logan.

Her heart felt like ice. She couldn't get away from Logan until Matt gave her further instructions. She'd called like he'd told her to, but he hadn't answered, and she didn't know what to do now.

Damn all werewolves. She'd just been putting her life back together when they'd decided to tangle her in their problems. Nadia hadn't had much, but she had Joel, and he made her existence worth it.

And then Matt had threatened to destroy her happiness forever. She wanted him to pay for that.

Ahead of her, Logan slowed and came to a silent halt. Nadia crept to stand just behind his shoulder while he watched the air with intensity.

Logan walked forward slowly, then he crouched, slinking like a cat to the top of a rise. Nadia folded her wings close to her body and sidled beside him.

They looked down at a ring of tents around a camp stove and three werewolves lounging in canvas chairs. They were drinking coffee—espresso, she put a name to the smell. Damn arrogance.

Logan was flat to the ground, his nose working, his ears pricked. Nadia watched with him, saw the human guide come out of his tent, didn't miss the way the werewolves glanced at the guide with contempt.

"You know," one of the werewolves drawled, "if we can't find the cute demon, we can always hunt a human."

The human stopped, his stance wary.

"Not as good," another werewolf agreed, "but fun in its own way. You let that little sweetie get away before she got filled up with werewolf cock."

Nadia made a noise of disgust, then cut it off. Logan was utterly silent, but the look in his yellow eyes was murderous.

Logan watched another few seconds, then backed carefully away. He sped noiselessly the way they'd come until they reached the spot where they'd left their clothes and the bike. Nadia relaxed the glowing magic inside her, taking on her human features again.

Logan circled her, pressing her legs hard with his wolf's body. Nadia gave a half laugh as she stumbled and caught herself.

She got down on her knees and wrapped her arms around him, smiling as he let her rub her face against his. He'd never do anything so affectionate human to human, but he was still thinking like a wolf.

His body began to change, his essence flowing into the limbs of a human male, his face flattening, his hair becoming the mussed mane she'd liked the first time she'd seen him.

Logan's arms remained around her, and the tongue-swipe he'd begun ended with their mouths meeting.

She expected him to push away, but he tightened his hold on her. Her breasts pressed into his chest, his body warmth covering her.

He cradled her head in one hand, and his other hand went to the base of her spine. He drew her up to him, his kiss hard and hot.

Nadia parted her lips for him, loving his taste. She slid her hand down his back, finding the taut muscles of his backside, daringly caressing him. It was still cold out here, but with Logan against her, she no longer felt it.

Her heart beat double-time. She was falling in love with this man—a dangerous thing to do. When she'd opened her eyes and seen him through the tangled hunter's net, she was thrilled that he came for her so quickly. He'd come himself. He'd cared.

She pulled him closer. He smelled like the woods and the musky odor of wolf and the salt tang of man. Logan, the Packmaster, the strongest of them all, gentling his touch for her.

Not too gentle, though. Logan bit her cheek before he kissed her lips again. His weight pushed her to the forest floor, never mind the mud and dead leaves everywhere.

He lifted his head, his breathing hard. But instead of leaping off her, he smoothed her hair, his touch as gentle as it had been rough. "This isn't the time or place."

"No kidding." *But maybe the only chance I'll ever have.*

Logan kissed her softly, then took away his lovely heat. He got to his feet and helped her to hers. He pinched her chin between his thumb and forefinger, caressing her lips once more.

"Now it's time to get some justice."

CHAPTER TEN

Nadia tasted disappointment, but he was right, of course. They couldn't make love here in the woods with Matt's werewolves just over the rise.

Logan pulled on his jeans, covering his enticing body, while Nadia watched disconsolately.

"What are you going to do?" she asked.

"Find Matt."

Nadia's eyes widened in alarm. "Now?"

"After I take you someplace safe."

Nadia shivered as she slipped back into her clothes. "What are you going to do? Attack the werewolves? Force them to lead you to Matt?"

"No, I'll just keep an eye on them. They'll meet up with him sooner or later."

"What if they see you?"

Logan stood, shrugging on his coat. "I'm armed and dangerous."

Dangerous was right. Logan was still angry. He wanted vengeance, which was different from seeking justice for wrongdoing.

"How about we watch them together?"

Logan's eyes glowed yellow. "I want you out of here. You'll do as you're told."

"Screw that, mighty Packmaster." Nadia met his gaze squarely. "What guarantee do I have that as soon as you have me 'safe,' you won't go back and all-out attack them?"

He would, she saw it in his eyes, and she'd seen it in his wolf's eyes. He was telling her what she wanted to hear, not the truth. He wanted her stashed away so she couldn't stop him.

"I'll go only if you give me your word you won't go after them while I'm gone," she said quickly. "Give me your pledge."

Rage rose in Logan's eyes. Werewolves didn't lightly pledge anything, not like demons, who had many different levels of oaths. For demons, there were the offhand promises that had no binding, handclasping oaths that were only binding if both parties had decided beforehand that they planned to keep their word. Then there were the serious oaths, done in secret, in dark places with blood symbols drawn and ancient incantations recited. Those oaths were the ones that bound you until death.

"I can't," Logan said.

"Then I'm not leaving, not without you."

"Damn it, Nadia, we don't have time for this."

"Make it quick and easy, then. Swear on your blood that you'll get backup before you confront them, and I'll let you take me out of here."

Her words were calm, but her breath came fast. She was too afraid to not have his promise. If Logan died, there was no guarantee the rest of her life would be worth living.

"I'm not going to lose you too," she said.

The fury in his eyes sparked. "What do you mean, swear on my blood? Is this some demon thing?"

"It's a level-nine oath. A pledge binding you until the circumstances change. Werewolves keep their word, I've heard."

"I've heard that too," Logan said dryly. "What do I do?"

Nadia told him. His movements stiff, Logan pulled a pocketknife from his coat and nicked his palm. As blood trickled across his skin, he came to her and clasped her hand.

"I pledge on my blood that I won't attack the camp or go after Matt until I can get help. All right?"

His hand burned hers, his powerful latent magic tingling

through her fingers. A part of his life essence seeped into her, so heady she gasped. The little he'd given her before had lit up her whole body. What would it be like to take even more?

Nadia stepped back with difficulty and looked into his eyes. She saw the honor in him. He wouldn't break his word, no matter how angry he was.

She raised on tiptoe and kissed his lips. "Thank you."

Logan's eyes darkened. "Unless they attack me first. I reserve the right to fight back."

"I'm not that unreasonable." She kissed him again, withdrew her hand, and turned to the bike. "Can I drive? This is one awesome machine."

Logan rode back to the hotel room with his arms firmly around Nadia's lithe body. While the position drove him into a frenzy of lust, he also admired the way she handled the bike. She was good at it, leaning into the turns just right, compensating for his weight as well as hers, playing the throttle like a musician played a fine instrument.

He'd love to ride behind her out on the open road, letting mile after mile of the world go by. They could head out everywhere and nowhere, sleep curled up together by the side of the road if they wanted.

Werewolves liked the night, and Logan fought the instinct to drowse in the growing light. His body reminded him he hadn't slept for a day and a night, and he'd eaten only one small cheeseburger during that time.

His instincts were telling him to hunt, kill, eat, then drop into sleep. Whenever he punished his human body, his wolf liked to take over. His overwhelming protectiveness reared its head as well, screaming at him to keep Nadia safe.

I am keeping her safe, he told himself irritably. *I'm taking her in the opposite direction of the danger.*

He knew this logically. Logan still wanted to lock Nadia in a guarded room while he hunted down and murdered those who dared hurt her.

Her demon form had surprised him. Demons were more varied in looks than any other species, ranging from small batlike creatures to tall horned beings with cloven hooves. But Nadia was like nothing he'd ever seen before.

Her demon was tall, like a Sidhe, her body lush and beautiful and glowing white. He wasn't certain which part of her had been light and which flesh. Her face was delicate-boned, her black eyes almond-shaped, wide and beautiful.

And the wings. Her long, black, feathery and warm wings had caressed his body. Logan had wanted to morph back into human form and wrap himself in those wings. He'd wanted to rub himself all over them and have her hold him while he did it.

He wondered if his longing was part of her glamour, the demon's call to life-magic creatures. Nadia was full demon, and although Logan was strong, she could drain him. And he'd smile all the way down.

He thought of how Nadia had wrapped her arms around him and rubbed her face against his. The wolf in him had reacted strongly.

She'd been behaving like a mate.

His heart throbbed. *Yes.* That felt so right. The bond he'd begun twined more tightly around them.

She's a demon, his common sense snapped at him.

She knows what it's like to be separate, apart. I no longer belong to my pack. Her family and clan disowned her, let her drift until she ran into tragedy.

He never wanted her to know tragedy again. He'd protect her as his mate, he'd kill for her.

Logan's palm tingled, and he looked at the dried cut on his hand. He'd blood-pledged not to kill any of them until he had backup. She'd made him promise.

Damn her cute little ass and big brown eyes.

They arrived at the hotel room without meeting any other traffic. Nadia parked the bike and dismounted after he did. She leaned against the bike and ruffled her hair, yawning.

"I need a nap."

She stretched like a cat, and Logan's libido soared.

He snaked his arm around her waist and yanked her against him. Nadia looked surprised, then smiled and snuggled in under his chin like she belonged there. They were silent a moment, sharing warmth, sharing the touch.

He could stand like this with her indefinitely, but danger was too near.

Logan pressed a kiss to her hair. "Let's get inside."

Once he shut and locked the door behind them, he unfolded a map and pinpointed where they'd seen the camp. He called Nez again, and Nadia slumped tiredly in a chair and watched until he hung up.

"Nez said he'll try to put together an investigation team," he told her, "but he's not getting much cooperation. The locals here deny that anything bad is going on with Lodge of the Pines. Nez can smell a lie like I can smell blood, and he thinks the local authorities might have been in on your abduction. Or at least aware of it and decided to take no action. I'm guessing Matt paid them off, paid the lodge to use one of their out-of-service vans."

Nadia chewed her lip. "Makes sense. And anyway, people who have 'no paranormals' lodges wouldn't care much about the abduction of a demon. They all think demons are evil."

"I'm just glad you got lucky enough to call me. How did you know my number, by the way?"

To his surprise, Nadia blushed. "I remembered it. You gave me your card once."

"That was months ago."

She shrugged, looking away.

"Thank all the gods you did," he said.

The embarrassment left her face, and she looked gray and exhausted. Tears started in the corners of her eyes, but she blinked them back.

Her bravery twisted his heart. Nadia had gone through hell last year when demons had been hunted on the streets of Los Angeles, and now she'd gotten mixed up in Logan's stupid life.

He had no business bonding with her, but he'd been interested in her the first time he saw her. He'd liked how her brown eyes had gazed at him in fury from her hospital bed, liked how she'd agreed to testify, liked her determination to get the bastards who'd hurt her and killed her sister.

He'd learned from Samantha that she liked motorcycles, and managed to run into her at a popular Harley spot. He'd enjoyed their conversations about bikes, telling himself that was all it would be, friends who shared an interest. His wolf had had other ideas, and started bonding with her before his human self could stop it.

His wolf's interest in her had nearly got her killed.

Logan went down on his knees beside Nadia's chair and pressed his face to her thighs. He felt her hand on his hair, a tender caress.

He was supposed to fear and hate her kind; she was supposed to hate him. Death and life canceling each other out? Or yin and yang, two opposites that made a whole?

She stroked his hair, and he remained still, loving her touch.

"Thank you, Logan," Nadia whispered.

She couldn't believe Logan knelt beside her with his head so tenderly on her lap. She loved the feel of his hair, rough but silken, so thick and warm.

He raised his head but remained on his knees, bringing his face to her eye level. Rough stubble covered his jaw and chin, and his skin was creased with red scratches. From his smudged face, his eyes blazed yellow-gold, the wolf awakened.

Nadia leaned forward and kissed his mouth, letting her need surge. He touched his palms to her face, his thumbs opening her lips.

Nadia furrowed his hair, pulling him closer. No matter what happened next, she could have him now. After this was over, he'd never want to see her again, but she could be with him now.

To her acute disappointment, Logan gently eased her hands away.

"I need to shower. You get some sleep."

Nadia laced her fingers through his, still holding on. "We're both a long way from home, and there aren't any rules out here. It's just you and me."

"I know." Logan stood, letting his hands go slack so hers slid from them. "That's why I'll be in the other room."

He turned and walked into the bathroom, closing the door with a firm snap. The sound hurt Nadia's heart, but it couldn't erase the heady vision of his fine backside as he walked away from her.

CHAPTER ELEVEN

Logan's hand shook as he adjusted the temperamental faucets. Fatigue, anger, and fear didn't cause this reaction—holding himself back from Nadia did.

He shed his clothes and stepped under the water, liking the bite of heat on his cold and weary body. She was right that they were far from home and had no rules to keep them from each other. It had been hard to reject what she'd been offering.

His skin might be cold, but his body was hot and hard, his heart still jumping from his decision to walk away from her. He wanted her, but too many things bothered him.

For instance, where was Matt? If he'd wanted Logan out here so bad, why hadn't the Pack Leader followed him or attacked? Why had the werewolves stayed in camp with their human guide instead of spreading out to look for Nadia?

Logan had no illusion that Nadia was safe in this motel room. The door had a lock, and they had weapons, but he remembered the click of the second phone when he'd talked to Nez. The motel clerk could just be nosy, or she could be in Matt's pay.

So why hadn't Matt shown himself? Why had he let Nadia get away?

Nadia had been very lucky to find a phone, lucky to remember Logan's number. And if she'd made it to the phone, why hadn't she called 911 or run inside the convenience store for help?

The questions nagged his fatigued brain, but wouldn't resolve.

The bathroom door opened. The draft sent the thin white shower curtain against him and the plastic stuck to his skin. Before Logan could peel it away, the shower curtain moved back, and Nadia stepped over the tub rim.

She was naked. Steam curled her hair into ringlets, and moisture beaded on her skin.

As he stared, Nadia stepped close and twined her arms around his neck. Her eyes had widened and darkened, like her demon eyes.

A low growl sounded in Logan's throat and rapidly filled the room. She growled back playfully and kissed his chin.

Logan's resolve vanished in the face of his need. He pushed her against the tiled wall and nuzzled her, inhaling the scents of outdoors, sweat, and her own musk. She smiled under his lips, her eyelids heavy.

He cupped her waist with his hands, liking how it curved beneath the swell of her breasts. He'd seen her naked in the woods as they'd shifted back and forth, but when he was so close to his wolf he paid little attention to nudity. Not until he'd settled back into human form a while did clothes and modesty seem to matter.

Now his human body throbbed at the beauty of her. Nadia smiled against his lips, then licked them.

The feeling of her small tongue made his already stiff erection rise. She rubbed against his hardness, sliding her body against his so that his tip poked at her naval. She laughed.

"Stop that," he hissed.

"Stop what?" Her eyes held challenge.

"Being so damn adorable."

"Adorable?" Nadia's eyes widened. "Adorable is for kittens. I'm a demon, sweetheart."

And her demon was seducing the hell out of this werewolf. Logan skimmed his hands to her breasts, holding the weight of them, brushing his thumbs over her hard nipples.

He'd wanted her for months, had been resisting her for too damn long.

Logan lifted her and slid her up against the tiles. He felt his own eyes burn golden, and her answering smile made everything go dark.

The cold tiles pressed Nadia's back so hard she thought they'd leave an imprint. Logan hadn't shaved yet, and his jaw was shadowed with stubble. Nadia gave in to the urge to lick his throat, to feel the sandpaper roughness on her tongue.

Logan grunted and seized her face between his hands, tilting her head up so he could slant his lips across her mouth. He tasted so good, the hint of toothpaste he'd used before he got into the shower blending with his own spice.

Her nipples burned where they brushed his chest. Nadia reached between them until she found his hard arousal wedged against his abdomen. He was hot and huge.

By all the dark gods, why was Logan so sexy? And why did she want a *werewolf*? She must have gone completely insane.

She moved her hand to his wide knob, liking the heat of it against her palm. When she closed her fingers around it, he groaned into her mouth.

How fate let her stand in this shower and hold this beautiful man in her hands, Nadia didn't know. She'd always wanted his body, his strength, his touch. And now she had all of him.

Logan's eyes were fierce and hot when she pulled out of the kiss. Nadia licked her way down his throat again, tasting sweat in the hollow at his collarbone. She went on licking as she slowly sank to her knees.

"Damn it, Nadia, don't kill me."

"I don't want to kill you." Nadia smiled. "I just want to suck you."

He put a heavy hand on her shoulder. "You need to stop."

Nadia shrugged, pretending nonchalance. "If you want me to."

"No." He balled his fist and pressed it into the tiled wall beside her. "I *don't* want you to."

"Good." Nadia opened her mouth—wide—and teased his rampant cock with her tongue. Swiping it once made it dance, and then she caught it in her mouth.

Logan groaned. He tasted smooth and hot, the hard cock stretching her mouth wide.

"Why are you doing this to me?" he whispered hoarsely.

Her mouth was too full of him to answer. She suckled him gently, then rubbed the underside of his flange with her tongue. She withdrew a little, but only to nibble on the tip.

Logan threaded his fingers through her hair, his other hand remaining fisted on the wall. He rocked back on his heels, begging for her with his body.

She glided her hand to his hard balls, liking the warm firmness of them. She squeezed one.

"Shit," Logan moaned.

He rocked faster, driving his cock into her mouth. Nadia licked and suckled, squeezing his balls once more.

Strong hands landed on her shoulders and dragged her firmly away from his gorgeous penis. Nadia looked up in surprise, and Logan yanked her to her feet.

"Not yet."

His eyes blazed gold, a hint of fang poked from his curled lips.

"Why not?" she asked. Her body throbbed for him, her cleft burning.

For answer he lifted her slippery body in his arms. He got them out of the tub and ran with her, both dripping wet, to the bedroom.

"Aren't you going to turn off the water?" Nadia asked as she landed on her back on the rickety bed.

"Screw that."

The water continued to patter merrily in the bathroom as Logan landed on the bed over her. His cock pointed firmly toward her as he positioned himself on hands and knees.

The bedroom was cold after the roiling heat of the bathroom, but Nadia's flesh was plenty hot. Hotter still when Logan lowered himself to her.

"What do you mean, not yet?" she asked him with a smile. "Didn't you like what I was doing?"

Logan put his face to hers. "When I come, I want it to be inside you."

"Fine by me."

Logan pressed her thighs apart. She spread for him, wanting to show him how ready she was. She snaked her fingers down and parted her folds, revealing moisture that wasn't from the shower.

"Damn you," Logan growled.

"What?"

"Why are you making me hurt for it?"

"I'm not," she said, startled.

His hair tickled her skin, his legs rigid inside the V of hers. Every muscle on him was hard, from his strong neck down his back, his thighs, his calves, his backside.

When he finally eased inside her, it was all she could do not to scream. He was huge and hard, and she was tight with need.

"Logan." She bit her lip, her eyes welling with tears.

He stilled. "Are you all right?"

"Yes. Why are you stopping?"

His breath was ragged. "I don't want to hurt you."

"You can't."

"I could. Believe me, I could. But I won't."

Nadia's heart beat faster. She slid her hands to his hips. "Come on."

Without answering, he slid in all the way with one swift stroke. She dragged in a breath as he filled her. He was so damn big, but it didn't hurt. It felt *good*.

"Logan. Please."

He was beyond questions, beyond talking. He kissed her, his lips bruising, then began to move his hips.

Their lovemaking was silent and intense. The bed creaked

and rocked, both of them holding each other with bruising hands while Logan drove in and in.

Nothing slow, nothing sweet about this lovemaking. It was pounding hard, need held back for too long. Nadia thrust her hips up to meet his, and their bodies came together again and again.

They were both strong enough to take it. Nadia skimmed her nails down Logan's back, and he nipped her throat, his fangs scratching her. He held himself back and didn't bite, and Nadia's body writhed as she wondered wildly what would happen if he let go.

She was demon; she could take what he gave and give it right back to him. She'd never been with anyone as strong as Logan, someone who made her feel petite and delicate. She laughed at the thought of it.

He stared down at her, his wolf's gaze intent. "What?" he growled.

"I like how strong you are."

He growled again and nuzzled her, very wolflike. "I like how strong *you* are, Nadia. And how beautiful. I want to make you feel good."

He kissed her, his body opening hers in a way it had never happened before. She hadn't made love like this since she'd been eighteen, and that encounter paled next to this one with Logan. Then she'd been little more than a child and madly in love; now she was an adult and better understood adult needs.

She felt the tingle of his life essence, and the demon in her couldn't resist reaching for it. It sparkled across her hands as she brushed her fingers across his face.

She made herself pull back, not wanting to steal it like she would from an addict at a club. She didn't want that with Logan.

"Take it," he whispered, his eyelids heavy.

"I don't want to hurt you."

"I'm a big, bad werewolf, sweetheart. Your matriarch fed off me for a year and it never touched me."

Nadia's heart squeezed in jealousy. "She did?"

"She didn't mean to. Take it. You're dying for it, and I have it to spare."

The demon in her was snarling, starving for what she'd tasted before. She held his face between her hands, letting the darkness in her reach out to the light.

CHAPTER TWELVE

Nadia screamed at the sensation. Logan's life essence poured out of him and swamped her with light. She rocked her body, hips arching to take him all the way inside.

She grabbed his face and forced his mouth to hers. His beautiful life essence sparkled over her tongue, and she drank like a woman dying of thirst.

Her body moved with his, he thrust hard into her again and again. She shouted his name, and he groaned hers. Sweat slicked their bodies despite the cold, Nadia hotter than she'd ever been.

His life essence coupled with the climax was the best thing she'd ever felt. She had all of him, drew all of him into her body. *Gods, Logan, I love you.*

Logan gasped out loud and shot his seed deep inside her, his eyes flicking to lupine and back to human again.

"I love you," he whispered hoarsely. "I love you, Nadia."

He collapsed onto her, breathing hard, kissing her with hot, swollen lips. Nadia wrapped her arms around his body, making the demon in her ease back from his life essence.

It was over. Logan's life essence tingled through her fingers a moment longer, then it was gone. She closed her eyes so he wouldn't see her tears.

Logan lay heavily next to Nadia while she slept. Her chest rose and fell with her even breathing, her nipples dark against pale skin.

Taking his life essence seemed to make her rest peacefully. He was glad of that, because the exhaustion that had been etched on her face had finally smoothed away.

Logan was tired too, but he didn't feel drained. This mating between himself and Nadia had sealed the bond between them. For the first time in his life he felt fulfilled rather than empty.

She'd looked stunned when he'd said he loved her, her eyes betraying her deep shock. Logan smiled a little. He'd have to get her used to the fact that a life-magic creature loved every bit of her. He'd also have to explain that he wanted her as his mate. His wolf had already decided that, but Nadia needed to choose.

Restless, he rose from the bed and quietly pulled on his jeans. Nadia continued to sleep, her lashes black crescents on her white face. He gently tucked the cover around her and went to the table to pack for the journey back to LA.

It was more important to get Nadia home to safety than to find Matt right now. Logan knew that Samantha would let Nadia stay in the matriarch's mansion in Beverly Hills, a place with security so tight Matt would never be able to penetrate it. Samantha and Tain could make damn sure Nadia stayed safe.

After that Logan would hook up with Tony Nez and return to flush out the werewolves and find Matt. He was tired of Matt's games and ready for a final confrontation. If it had to be a fight to the death, then so be it.

In the bathroom, Logan turned off the water, which had gone ice cold. He pocketed the hotel room key and stepped out into the snow. He'd pay the bill so he could wake Nadia and they could go.

In the office, the tired woman fished out his bill and took his credit card. In the room behind her, two children yelled at each other over the blaring television.

"What's this charge?" Logan asked, pointing to a number.

The woman glanced at it. "Phone calls."

Logan had only made one, to Nez. "Can you break it down for me?"

She gave him a blank stare, sighed, and pushed keys on the computer keyboard. Another sheet printed and she shoved it at him. She turned away to the back room, obviously finished with him.

Logan looked at the list. One call to Nez. One call to a 805 area code—a Los Angeles vicinity—and two calls to a number that made Logan's blood freeze.

He stared at the white sheet with the sharp black numbers on it, stark and damning, but they didn't change.

Someone in room Five had called Matt Lewis.

Logan slammed out of the office and strode back to the room, never noticing the chill. His fury mounted at every step, as did the bile in his throat.

Why the hell would Nadia call Matt? Matt had kidnapped her, brought her up here, let his wolves hunt her so Logan would run to her rescue.

Against the odds Nadia had found a pay phone and called Logan. Logan's cold dread gave way to black rage.

Dear gods, he was a complete blind fool. He'd tumbled into Matt's trap like a sucker. He'd run up here the instant he'd heard Nadia's plea for help, her desperation. He'd rescued her, held her, kissed her, had sex with her, and told her he loved her.

You stupid, stupid moron.

Matt must be laughing his ass off.

He swung open the door, letting the chill air slice through the room. Nadia still lay sleeping on the bed and didn't stir.

The wolf in him snarled. How easy it would be to become the werewolf, rip the covers from Nadia's body, and tear into her. She lay asleep, trusting him like he'd trusted her.

He'd even let her take his life essence, weakening himself for her. And he'd smiled and said, *I love you.*

This is what demons did. Nadia had once worked a demon club where she'd smiled at the clientele and gave them the thrill of being with a demon. All Nadia had to do was claim she'd walked away from that life, that she'd only done it because she had no choice, and he'd fallen for every word.

Logan felt his face start to change, his teeth sharpen, his face elongate into that of the wolf. He forced himself to stay human. He didn't want to kill her. He wanted to look her in the face and demand to know why she'd gone along with Matt's plan.

He strode back into the bathroom and snapped on the faucet at the sink, splashing cold water on his face. Wolf's eyes looked back at him in the mirror, yellow and angry, and he splashed more water until he calmed down a little.

When he went back out into the bedroom Nadia was still asleep, still beautiful. Her hair curled against her forehead, her cheek rested on one slim hand.

As soon as Logan woke her, the illusion he'd carried of her for seven months would be ruined. The illusion that she was brave and beautiful and that they could somehow be together.

Logan dragged in a breath and jerked the covers from her body.

Nadia stirred and blinked sleepily. She put one hand up to rub her eyes, then stretched, her toes curling.

"Logan?" she asked muzzily. "Has something happened?"

For answer, Logan held the list of phone calls in front of her face, Matt's phone number sharp and clear.

It took Nadia a few sleep-drenched seconds to figure out what she was looking at. Logan held the piece of paper rock steady in front of her face, and she saw the evidence of her phone call at the bottom of the list of numbers.

"Logan."

His eyes were glittering gold and impossibly still.

"Get up and get dressed, and then get the hell out of my life."

Nadia pulled the bed's dingy coverlet over her bare breasts. "Logan, he didn't give me a choice."

"You told him where I am. When will he show up?"

"He already knew. The front desk clerk told him."

Logan's expression remained like flint. "What do you get out of this? Money? Or the satisfaction of taking down a werewolf? Or was it my life essence you were after?"

Nadia sat frozen, tears trickling down her face. She'd done what she had to do and had known she'd lose Logan for it. But she hadn't realized how much it would hurt. Her daydreams about finding a happy ending with him evaporated like the smoke they were.

"I was eighteen," she began.

"When you met Matt?"

"No, when I got pregnant."

Logan turned away. He was already dressed, the bag on the other side of the room half packed.

"I don't want to hear your life story. I'll read it in your police file."

Nadia wiped her eyes with the heel of her hand. "I'm telling you for a reason. When I was eighteen I fell in love with a human called Terry Snyder. I met him at a department store in Westwood, where I worked. They liked demon girls because we could make ourselves look good and entice in human customers. I knew demon males could impregnate human women, but I didn't know it could happen the other way around—I was naive. I had Terry's baby, a son. Joel is ten now."

She broke off, swallowing her grief. It was difficult to talk about it, but Logan needed to understand. He might still hate her, but at least he'd understand.

Logan tossed loose clothes into his duffel bag. He wouldn't look at her, made no indication he was listening.

"Terry didn't want Joel," Nadia said. "And he didn't want me, not the real me. My family is very conservative. They don't think demons should mix with other races for any reason, and they refuse to acknowledge Joel. He lives with his human grandparents now. The Snyders are good people, ashamed of the way their son treated us."

Logan continued to silently pack, his movements jerky.

"I worked to support him—I wasn't about to make Terry's parents pay for everything, and Terry left. He was always driving around in flashy cars, and one day he killed himself in a wreck. I'm pretty sure it was just an accident, none of my demon clan taking revenge or anything. The entire clan had shut me out by then."

Logan finally turned around, but his face was forbidding. "What the hell has all this got to do with Matt?"

"You were right that Matt had someone spy on you until he figured out every person you got close to in LA. He knows how fond you are of Samantha, but he wasn't stupid enough to use the matriarch of a powerful demon clan to trap you. Besides, he heard about Tain and decided it was a bad idea to piss off an Immortal." She felt herself almost smile, but her heart was empty. "There was no one to care what happened to me. Matt decided I was the most vulnerable."

"I figured out most of Matt's plans by myself," Logan said tightly. "What you've left out is why you helped him."

Tears slid unheeded from her eyes. "Don't you get it? He threatened Joel. Matt said that if I didn't get you up here, he'd murder Joel. He has some of his own people following Joel, waiting for the order to kill him. All Matt has to do is make a phone call, telling them either to go ahead or call it off. If I do what Matt tells me, Joel will never even know he was in danger."

Logan's expression didn't change. "So the hunt through the woods, your capture, was all a fraud?"

She shook her head. "No, it was real. I hitchhiked and took the bus, like I told you. The van met me. When I woke up from the tranquilizer, Matt pushed me out of the van and told me to run. My fear had to be real, he said, or you'd know something was wrong."

Logan turned away again, a muscle in his back jerking. "So, it was more like reality TV then."

Nadia studied the blanket, her voice subdued. "Matt forced me to choose between you and Joel. I had to pick Joel."

She fell silent, drained of words and emotion. Logan continued to stare at nothing, his black T-shirt tight against his back.

He'd said he loved her. And she loved him back.

"Why didn't you tell me?" he grated.

"Please don't ask me that. I couldn't tell you."

"You damn well could have." Logan swung around, eyes blazing. "Did you think I'd hate you for having a child? For Matt using you? He's a twisted bastard who'd use his own mother to get his way, and he has. Or is everything you told me bullshit, so I'd feel sorry for you?"

"It's all true." Nadia dragged herself up, letting anger give her strength. "I've never lied to you."

"Omitting big chunks of truth is the same as lying. You still haven't answered me—why didn't you tell me? Did you think I wouldn't try to keep your son safe?"

"I don't know what I thought. I only know that if I told you and you went after Matt or back to help Joel, Joel would die. Matt said that once he had you he'd tell his men to leave Joel alone. But if they *don't* get Matt's call by tomorrow morning, they'll kill my son. He promised that. He told me I had to keep you here and a long way from help."

Logan sighed. He raked his hand through his hair, looking tired. "So you called Matt while I was in the shower and told him where we were. And then did your best to keep me here. Your technique was very effective." His voice was bitter, and the look in his eyes broke her heart.

"That's not why I made love to you," she said.

"Wasn't it? But that wasn't enough. You decided to drink my life essence in attempt to weaken me further."

Nadia got to her knees, the covers still around her. "I swear to you, that had nothing to do with Matt."

"Sorry, sweetheart, I don't believe you."

He gave her a grim smile, then turned back to his duffel bag. Anger flowed from him in waves, rage at her betrayal, at Matt, at himself.

He hated her now. Nadia hated that she'd had to choose, but she couldn't have sacrificed her own son.

"I hope you know I don't plan on letting Matt kill me," Logan said calmly, but she heard the strain in his voice. "I thought that when I walked away from my pack, that would be it, but I guess not."

"Why didn't you fight him before? I wish you would have, so I'd never have met him."

"I walked away because I knew I'd kill him. Then the pack would either have to accept me as leader or destroy me for killing Matt. That's what Kayla wanted, and I wasn't about to give her the satisfaction."

The deadness in his voice hurt her worse than his anger. "Logan, I'm so sorry."

"It's not your fault you got caught up in my joke of a life." Logan turned away from her again, heading for the window. "It's not your fault you did what you could to keep your son safe. I'm only pissed at you for not trusting me."

"How could I? You're a werewolf, a life-magic creature, my natural enemy. Besides, you're a cop, and I'm a demon who used to work the clubs. I can't *imagine* why I didn't automatically trust you."

"I thought we were friends. I thought, when we went out together and I could talk to you about anything, that we could be close. Stupid of me, wasn't it? You never even mentioned Joel."

"Hot guys don't always want to go out with single moms," she shot back. "I wanted to get to know you better first."

Logan looked at her over his shoulder. "I thought we were building a relationship. Getting close. I guess that was my wishful thinking."

"I could have said nothing, you know, could have let Matt take you by surprise."

Logan's mouth flattened to a hard line. "You only told me now because you got caught."

Nadia fell silent. He was too angry to listen, and it wouldn't matter what she said. She tossed back the covers and reached for her underwear.

Logan didn't look at her. No enticing him with her body—not that she wanted to do that or believed it would work.

"Get dressed," he said tersely. "I'm taking you back to LA."

"Didn't you hear me? Matt wants . . ."

"Screw what Matt wants." Logan swung around. His eyes had changed to wolf eyes, and his canines elongated. "He won't keep his side of the bargain, darling. Werewolves don't have levels of oaths or any respect for demons. They're very direct."

Her heart thumped with fear. "Logan. Please. This is my son, a little boy who has nothing to do with this."

"That's why we're going back to LA, Nadia." Logan's face looked more human, but his eyes still blazed with rage. "To save your son from Matt. After that, what you want to do is up to you."

Logan made two phone calls while Nadia dressed. She pulled on her clothes right there in front of him, but he deliberately didn't look at her.

As they raced away from the motel to the highway on the Harley, he felt her body warm against his back. But too much rage boiled through him to appreciate it. It was all he could do to stay human and ride.

Nadia had betrayed him, but Matt would betray her. That's what Matt did—used people up and discarded them. If Matt fought Logan and won, he'd kill Joel and Nadia because he could. A werewolf victor was allowed to do whatever he liked with his rival's women, children, and possessions. Even in these more enlightened days, the human police probably wouldn't look too hard at the deaths of a demon and her half-demon get.

Logan was a good rider. He managed to eat up speed on the back highways without alerting any local law enforcement. They made it to the southbound freeway in a couple of hours.

It was past midnight when he finally saw the glow of Los Angeles on the horizon, the city that had long since flowed around its barrier of mountains and out into the desert. Because it was the middle of the night, the traffic was only slightly maddening as they rushed from the 405 to the 101 and west.

Nadia directed Logan through the streets of Thousand Oaks, until they pulled up in front of a moderate-sized residence with all the lights on.

Nadia felt the presence of too many life-magic creatures as she raced up the driveway to the house. "Joel?"

A huge hand grabbed her and jerked her back. Nadia gasped and looked up into the face of the most frightening man she'd ever seen.

He had red hair cut short, a face scarred with fighting, and a patch over one eye. The other eye was piercingly blue, and two wicked-looking swords stuck out from sheaths in his belt. An overwhelming wave of life-magic rolled off him.

"Tain," Nadia breathed, relieved and alarmed at the same time.

"What's going on in there?" Logan came up beside them.

Tain's blue gaze raked over Nadia, and she read pity in his face. "They're holding everyone hostage inside the house," he said. "Waiting for you, Logan. I'd have taken them down, but Samantha is afraid they'll kill the boy. I think she's right."

Nadia stood still, her heart freezing as her worst fears assailed her.

"No," she whispered, and darted forward again.

CHAPTER THIRTEEN

Logan grabbed Nadia and yanked her back.

"Where do you think you're going?" he demanded. "Those are werewolves ready for a dominance fight, and you aren't going anywhere near them."

"Joel is in there," Nadia said, white-faced.

Tain studied the house. "This Pack Leader of yours brought wolves loyal to him, ones he's promised to promote. Forming a new pack, maybe? If the old one is split?"

"Maybe," Logan growled. "What better way to prove he's still strong enough to be Pack Leader than taking out a Pack-master? Damn werewolves."

"Inconvenient," Tain agreed.

"That's my son in there," Nadia snapped. "Don't you dare say it's 'inconvenient.' "

Tain turned a quiet gaze on her, not offended. "Samantha is waiting over there." He pointed at a dark SUV in front of the next house. "Why don't you go sit with her?" His accent bore an unusual lilt. Welsh, Tain always said it was, but Logan knew it came from a time long before Wales had been its own entity. Tain was an Immortal warrior, born nearly two millennia ago.

"I'm not leaving," Nadia said.

Logan wanted to demand she go wait with Samantha, but he knew he'd waste his breath. Unless he knocked Nadia unconscious and tied her up in the back of the SUV, she wouldn't stay there. Plus, Samantha herself would join them as soon as there was any action. She'd been a good cop, and she wouldn't let her friends enter a fray without being at their backs.

He sensed many more people in the dark than the shadows revealed. Some had black auras, demons. Others had powerful life magic, and still others were human. Tain and Tony Nez had been busy.

"Let me talk to them," Logan said.

Tain gazed at the darkened windows, and Logan felt a tightening in his brain. "Speak in a normal voice. They'll hear you."

"I'm here," Logan began without bothering to ask Tain what he'd done. "I'll come in alone, but only if you let the little boy and his grandparents out first."

There was a silence. Nadia stood tense at his side, her fists clenched.

A front window opened. "You come in first," someone called to him. "Leave your weapons."

Logan recognized the voice, one of the wolves that had been Matt's sycophants.

"Where's Matt?"

"Waiting for you." The wolf sounded smug.

"All right. I come in, you let them out."

Tain gave Logan a look and shook his head slightly, but Logan knew these wolves would only be happy if they could rip into Logan. They didn't really care what happened to Joel and his grandparents.

Logan stripped off his fleece coat, no longer needed in balmy LA, and removed his shoulder holster with its pistol. He slid the leg of his jeans upward and took out the witch-spelled blade. He handed both weapons to Nadia.

"That's all of it," he said to the house. "I'm coming in."

Nadia gave him a scared look. Logan brushed his hand over her cheek and kissed her. She looked surprised, and Logan turned away.

"Tain, don't do *anything* until Joel makes it to Nadia," he said.

Tain gave him a nod. "Don't worry. Get the boy out the door, and I'll take care of it."

Logan knew that Tain had the power to blow the roof off the house and destroy everyone inside. He was glad that the man worried about hurting the innocents. Tain had come a long way since arriving in LA, half crazed and dangerous, the year before.

Logan squared his shoulders and strode down the walk to the front door.

The house had been built about thirty years ago, and the front entrance was a double door with solid panels on the bottom and crosshatch panes on the upper half. The panes were covered with sheer shades for privacy, but Logan didn't need to see inside. He could easily smell the powerful musk of werewolves ready to kill.

Four of them, all angry to the point of insanity, and Matt. Three of his wolves were still in their human forms; one had already changed. Logan could hear him snarling, as well as the quick breathing of the three humans they'd trapped.

Logan tapped gently on the window glass. "It's Logan. Let them out."

A werewolf wrenched open the door. His eyes were flat wolf-yellow, his teeth already elongating. "Put your hands on the wall and spread your legs."

Logan gritted his teeth, but he assumed the position, placing his hands on the stucco of the outside wall. The werewolf patted him down, then before he turned away, slammed his forearm upward into Logan's balls.

Through the sudden pain, Logan heard him hiss, "He's clean."

"Send the kid out," Logan repeated, his jaw clenched.

"Sure, whatever." The werewolf jerked Logan inside.

The slate-floored foyer gave way to a living room sunk down one step from the rest of the house. A scared man and woman in their fifties sat in separate armchairs, each with a werewolf guarding them. The werewolves had semiautomatic pistols.

The fourth was in wolf form, a large gray beast that guarded a little boy who had Nadia's eyes. Joel was standing in a corner, the wolf's huge body blocking him from the rest of the room.

Joel looked afraid, but not petrified. Logan sensed death magic in him, not very strong, his human side dampening most of it.

The werewolf who'd let Logan in jerked his chin at the two guarding the man and woman. The werewolves backed a few steps from the captives but didn't put away their pistols.

"Out," the first werewolf said.

The woman looked at Joel. The wolf in front of the little boy snarled and continued to pace.

"I'll take care of him," Logan said. "Go to Nadia."

The woman nodded, but he read anger, frustration, and fear in her eyes. She walked with her husband out the door the first werewolf held open. The remaining werewolves trained their pistols on Logan.

"And Joel," Logan said.

"The kid stays," the first werewolf said.

"That wasn't the bargain."

"It's the bargain now. Either the kid stays or we shoot his grandparents on the sidewalk. How's that?"

Logan corralled his anger with effort. "If you guarantee Joel's safety, I won't kill you."

The first werewolf chuckled. "You're out of your territory, Packmaster. You don't get any guarantees."

Joel looked over the wolf's back at Logan. "Is my mom okay?" he asked in a steady voice.

"She's fine," Logan said. "Worried about you, but fine."

Joel looked relieved. "She always worries about me."

"You being held hostage by a pack of idiot werewolves is a worry, wouldn't you say?"

Joel grinned. He was afraid, but mastering it. "That's a good point."

"Don't push it, Logan."

Matt Lewis leaned against the doorframe to the back hall. He was naked, his muscles tight and gleaming. His eyes glowed yellow when Logan faced him. Matt was big, the largest wolf in the pack, and he had a bully's personality to match.

Logan held his gaze. "I accept the Challenge," he said. "But you have to send Joel out before it starts."

"Challenge?" Matt laughed. "Do you think I'd let you have the honor of the Challenge? I'm just going to kill you."

"I don't really give a shit what you plan. Joel is leaving first."

"No," Matt said. "What I'm going to do is sit you down and shoot you in the head with a couple of silver bullets. That's what we do to pack traitors. It's either that or we kill the boy. So what's it going to be?"

Logan calculated the distance between himself and the two werewolves with weapons. But even if he took them down, the wolf could kill Joel with a swipe of his paw.

"Fine, shoot me. Just call off the wolf and let the kid out of the corner. Let Joel walk across the room and out the door to his mother without stopping him, and you can shoot me all you want to."

Matt looked slightly surprised. "You'd die for a half-demon kid?"

"He has nothing to do with this. This is your game, not his."

"It's not a game, Logan."

Logan shook his head. "Not anymore. You leave pack law behind, you've lost your hold on the pack."

"I haven't lost my hold on the pack." Matt bristled. "The most dominant female is my mate, and I've chosen a new Packmaster."

Logan's gaze went to the wolf guarding Joel. "That's him? What's his name—Karl?"

"He's a hell of a better Packmaster than you were. He obeys me."

"That's not the Packmaster's job. Packmasters uphold the law of the pack, not the leader's whims."

"You always had a fucking big mouth, you know that? The kid, is he yours?"

"You'd know if he were part werewolf."

"But he's the spawn of your demon lover. You betray your own kind, starting the bond with a death-magic demon. You make me sick."

"I spared your life," Logan said. "And gave you Kayla."

"You ran away from the Challenge because you're a coward."

"I admit I made a mistake," Logan said quietly. "I thought I was helping the pack by leaving, but if I'd killed you then, the pack wouldn't be tearing itself apart now."

"It isn't tearing itself apart. I'm still the Pack Leader. It's just a few assholes who want more than their share."

"Kayla sounded scared."

Matt's eyes took on a red glint, and he came at Logan. "If you touched Kayla . . ."

"I talked to her on the phone. She believes I can kill you. She begged me not to."

"Bitch." Matt nearly changed, the stink of his hatred permeating the room. "Here's what we'll do. You call your 'mate' in here. Then I fuck the demon whore and let her kid go."

"No deal." The wolf in Logan snarled in black rage, but Logan the human tamped it down. The second his wolf leapt at Matt, one of his werewolves would shoot Logan or maybe Joel. He had to be careful.

"Then I get the kid," Matt said. "And I try to turn him. Wonder if it would work with a demon-spawn?"

Logan went cold. Werewolves had evolved over the centuries to be able to breed with other werewolves, and nowadays, most werewolves were born, not made. A human could still be turned by other werewolves, but it was unusual, excruciatingly painful, and most often ended in the death of the would-be werewolf. Logan had never heard of a werewolf trying to turn a child.

"Fight me," Logan said in a hard voice. "If you want to stay Pack Leader so bad, face the Challenge."

"And have your warrior friend take me out the minute we start fighting? I want a guarantee I can get away, and that guarantee is the little demon boy."

Logan wanted to rip into him. "I'll tell them to give you and your wolves safe passage out. Leave Joel alone."

"Right, like I'm going to trust you." Matt gave Joel a possessive look. "I've already bitten the kid once."

Logan looked at Joel, and the boy nodded slowly, putting his hand under his left armpit. There was no blood on his shirt, which meant Matt hadn't been trying to savage. He'd been claiming a prize.

"Why do you want him?" Logan asked.

"Souvenir."

"Can't you and Kayla have kids?"

From the rage on Matt's face, Logan knew he'd guessed right.

"Adopt from the pack, then," Logan said. "A half-demon couldn't take over as leader anyway."

"No, but he'd be *mine*." Matt ended on a wolf growl, and his face changed. Lips rippled back from his huge teeth, and he swung toward Joel.

"Joel," Logan said rapidly. "Lie flat on the ground and put your hands over your head."

Joel unquestioningly lay facedown on the floor. Matt ran in a half crouch to the boy, stood over him, growling.

"Get on your knees," one of the other werewolves instructed Logan. He cocked his pistol

Matt snarled at the wolf guarding Joel, his human speech returning. "Packmaster. Execute."

The big wolf morphed into a large man with a shaved head. He picked up a sword from the floor, the silver Packmaster's sword Logan had once carried.

"I thought you were going to shoot me," Logan said.

The new Packmaster looked at him with grim purpose. "Sword's the better way."

"Do it. Or the kid dies," Matt demanded.

Joel was going to die anyway, Logan knew. There wouldn't be time for Tain to get Joel out before Matt was on him.

Logan sank slowly to his knees, his heart beating swiftly. He deliberately suppressed his wolf, knowing the others would sense his change if he started it. As Packmaster he'd always been calm and cool, never betraying his emotions. That calm was a long way from him now, but he managed to fake it.

The cold edge of the sword pressed Logan's neck, the silver stinging. The Packmaster lifted the sword high and brought it down.

But Logan wasn't there. He rolled, his vision going red as he changed. His clothes ripped from his body, but he didn't notice the pain as he leapt at Matt. Matt became wolf as they hit the floor, and they rolled over and over each other, teeth and claws ripping.

Dimly Logan heard the other wolves cursing, then the sudden roar of a gun. Pain bit deep into Logan's back along with the fiery burn of silver.

CHAPTER FOURTEEN

Nadia heard the gunshot. "Joel!" she screamed.

The demon in her glowed white hot, and her wings unfurled, tearing the shirt Logan had bought her. She heard Samantha call her back, but Nadia swooped toward the house on outstretched wings, her demon fury bursting loose.

"Nadia, get down," Samantha shouted, and Nadia felt a huge wave of life magic pour past her.

She fell facedown on the lawn, then lifted her head to see the windows and doors of the house explode outward. Tain stood behind her, his swords out, snakes of electricity sparking up and down the blades.

"Joel," Nadia cried.

Then she heard his answering shriek. *"Mom!"*

Nadia started running and launched herself into the air, her demon wings carrying her straight into the house.

Logan fought Matt hard, the two wolves meeting in a frenzy of fur and fang.

He lost track of Joel, but hoped the boy would run outside to safety. Logan felt teeth ripping his flesh, claws sinking deep. The bullet in his back burned like fire. It hadn't struck an organ, but the silver weakened him and would kill him before long.

He fought hard, landing punishing blows, trying to lock his mouth around Matt's throat. Matt reeked of wolf anger, his claws scrabbling to rip Logan's underbelly.

The other wolves had backed off. Logan saw the Packmaster out of the corner of his eye simply waiting, his silver sword raised between the other wolves and Matt and Logan. This would be the Challenge, a fight to the death. This was pack law in action.

Something bright white slammed into the room, death magic power flowing from it. The werewolves cringed, but Matt, in a blood frenzy, didn't notice.

Nadia's black wings snapped against her white body, and she struck, feet first, against one of the wolves. He turned and attacked her, only to meet Tain's sword. The warrior crossed his twin blades, and white-hot magic sparked through the air.

"Where's Joel?" Nadia screamed.

Dimly Logan heard Samantha's voice and Nez's reply, both of them fully in cop mode. "Let's contain this," Nez said to his uniforms.

Silver nets slung through the air, trapping the werewolves. The Packmaster fought, but he went down with his wolves. The smell of silver made Matt snarl, and Logan's nostrils burned.

"No," the Packmaster shouted. "Let them fight it out. There has to be a clear winner, or we do this all over again."

"Screw that," Nadia said.

Her bare feet connected with Matt, her demon strength bowling between him and Logan. Matt didn't stop tearing, his wolf fighting for his life and his place in the pack. Killing Nadia, Logan's mate, would give Matt a huge advantage.

Logan felt himself weakening, the silver bullet doing its damage. Nadia was at full strength, having imbibed Logan's life essence. Her demon turned savage, claws ripping at Matt, fur and blood erupting everywhere.

If Matt killed her, Logan would want to die. The mate bond had sealed when he'd made love to Nadia, binding her absolutely to him. He could feel her fury, the dark magic inside her, her joy when her claws tore open Matt's flesh.

Nadia kicked away from Matt and rolled to her feet. She

snatched up a pistol one of the werewolves had dropped and shoved it into Matt's face. "You hurt my son," she grated. "You dared."

Matt snarled, his razor-sharp claws going for Logan's throat. His face flattened to human long enough for him to say to Nadia, "I've killed your mate, bitch. That means you turn that gun on yourself."

"I'm a demon," Nadia said. "Not a werewolf." And she pulled the trigger.

The moment the silver bullet entered Matt's brain, all the werewolves in the room, Logan included, lifted their heads and howled. The sound shrieked through the air, sending the humans to their knees. Only Tain remained standing, his face pale. Nadia dropped the gun and clapped her hands over her ears.

Logan felt a wrench of unspeakable sorrow before his rational mind kicked in again. He morphed back to human form, panting heavily, his back killing him.

"The Pack Leader is dead," he rasped.

"Do you claim the pack?" Karl the Packmaster asked, his voice hoarse.

Logan shook his head. "I didn't kill him."

"You and your mate did," Karl said. "Together. Do you claim the pack?"

"No." Logan turned bleary eyes to Karl. "It's yours unless someone wants to Challenge."

"Who gives a shit?" Nadia said. "Where's Joel?"

"He ran out the back," Samantha said. "I sent a patrolman to watch him."

Nadia touched Logan's shoulder, anguish on her white demon face.

"Go," Logan gasped. Nadia caressed his face, then turned and ran, her wings giving her speed.

The dark face of his Navajo partner appeared in Logan's field of vision. "You all right, man?" Nez asked.

"I've been shot with a silver bullet. What do you think?"

"Tain," Samantha said quietly.

The huge warrior knelt next to Logan and placed his hand between Logan's shoulder blades. "This might hurt."

It couldn't hurt more than all the gashes and bites Matt had given him. Or maybe it could. Logan gasped as he felt the bullet travel backward, leaving a raw trail. The gasp turned to a groan as a burst of white magic entered him, cleansing his blood and closing the wound.

"Hell," Logan said. "Remind me to stop getting hurt around you."

A brief smile touched Tain's mouth. Tain had healed him before, at a time when Tain had been half dead himself. "I was in a hurry."

"You always are."

"Want me to read these guys their rights?" Nez asked as Logan sat up. "Or do you want to do the honor?"

"Right now I want to find Nadia."

Samantha reached a slim but strong hand down and helped Logan to stand. She didn't pay any attention to his nakedness, having gotten used to him changing from human to wolf and back again when they'd been partners. "You look awful," she said. "But I'm glad to see you still breathing."

Logan shot her a shaky grin, then left Nez to make the arrests and ran through to the kitchen and out the back door.

The house had a wide yard behind it with a lawn running down a gentle slope to a cement-block wall. Logan saw movement off to his left, but his enhanced sense of smell told him it was more human police plus a few of Samantha's most trusted demons. On the path not far from him lay the crumpled body of a uniformed LAPD officer.

Logan stopped, his heart pounding in painful beats. Nadia's scent ran straight down the hill, overlaying that of her son. But blanketing both Nadia's and Joel's scents was the powerful smell of wolf.

"Damn it." Logan sprinted after them. Matt must have had backup, wolves waiting on the fringes to come in if Matt went down.

The lights from the house didn't reach the corners of the yard, and none of the outside lights were on. Logan heard the struggle before he reached it, the sound of beating wings, of a soft cry from Nadia, the snarl of a wolf.

A growl rumbled in Logan's throat. He rushed into the darkness and saw the werewolf, his body halfway between man's and wolf's, with his arms hard around Joel. The wolf-man lifted the little boy and began to squeeze, while Nadia, still in demon form, desperately clawed at him.

Logan sprang. The wolf went down with Logan on him, releasing Joel on the way.

Logan felt the Packmaster rise within him. He was the sword of justice—the pack's judge, jury, and executioner. The wolf he fought had been doing his best to kill Joel for no other reason than to hurt Logan.

Logan pinned the werewolf down and reached for his throat. The wolf scrabbled away in fear, tearing huge chunks of lawn with his claws. He squirmed out from under Logan and leapt, not for freedom, but straight at Nadia and Joel in her arms.

His jaws were wide, his curved-razor claws spread. Joel's eyes widened as he stared at certain death, but at the last minute, Nadia turned to take the brunt of the blow.

The wolf hit Nadia. She went down screaming, with the wolf on top of her, shredding her back and wings to the bone.

At the same time, Logan landed on the wolf, jamming his jaws around the wolf's neck. He yanked the wolf off Nadia and shook him once. The werewolf yelped, and then his neck snapped and he went limp.

Nadia was on the grass, Joel under her. Logan shifted back to human as he gently turned her over. "Nadia."

"Logan," she mumbled.

Joel scrambled up, panting, his eyes wide as he looked down at his mother.

Logan gathered Nadia in his arms. Her blood was hot, her broken wings soft against his skin.

"Thank you," she said to him, touching his face. "Thank you for saving my boy."

"And you," Logan said fiercely. "I saved you too. I'm not losing you."

Nadia smiled. "I didn't tell you before, back at the motel." Her eyes closed, her expression creasing with pain as she slid back into her human form. "I love you."

Logan leaned down and kissed her. "Help is coming."

Nadia didn't answer. Joel grabbed her hand and pressed it between his small ones. "Hang on, Mom."

Logan kissed her again. "I love you too," he breathed against her lips, but he wasn't certain she heard.

CHAPTER FIFTEEN

Nadia walked out of the house a week later to see Logan explaining the finer points of throwing a baseball to Joel. Sun gleamed off Logan's tawny hair as he bent to show Joel exactly how to place his fingers.

Joel wore a small LAPD T-shirt Logan had given him, which had become his favorite. He'd started talking about being a cop when he grew up.

Nadia had stayed in bed for five days, recovering from the deep gouges the werewolf had torn into her back. Tain had begun the healing process, but recovery was slow.

Joel's grandparents had been wonderful about taking care of her and of Joel, and they seemed happy with Logan, who visited every day. Trust the gorgeous Logan to soothe them after the traumatic event of a werewolf battle in their living room.

Nadia paused in the sun, self-consciously straightening the sleeveless dress she'd bought herself as a reward for surviving. It bared her arms and legs and covered the hideous scars on her back that Tain told her she'd have for life.

If not for Logan, she'd be dead, and probably Joel would be too.

Logan raised his head and saw her. He stilled.

Joel smiled and waved at her. Then he nonchalantly moved to the corner of the yard where he started practice throws against the fence.

Logan waited. Nadia walked across the grass, liking the cool tickle of it around her sandals.

"You've been here every day." Nadia folded her arms and suppressed a shiver as she stopped close to him. "Keeping an eye on things?"

"I wanted to make sure none of the pack tried revenge," Logan said, his tone neutral. "I thought Kayla might, but it sounds like she's trying for Pack Leader."

"Can female werewolves be Pack Leader?"

"They never have before, but times change. Besides, the Packmaster and Matt's most loyal wolves are in jail awaiting trial for kidnapping and assault."

"Good," Nadia said darkly. "I hope they get life."

"Not in a human court. But they'll be tried by the new Pack Leader. They broke a lot of pack laws, foremost of which is interfering with the Challenge. Matt should have just issued it and met me, not tried to corner and murder me."

"He did it that way because you'd have kicked his ass in a straight Challenge," Nadia said. "And he knew it. He had to shoot you before he could even fight you."

"Matt was always a cheater."

"And now he's dead." Nadia searched within herself for remorse, but her demon had killed to protect her young, and it didn't care. "Will the new Pack Leader want to try me?"

"No. You were defending your mate, and Matt violated the Challenge."

"Werewolf law?"

"Yes."

"Never studied it, sorry." Nadia looked him over, taking in his tall body, his wide shoulders, the tawny eyes that flicked to her. "You've come to see Joel every day."

Logan shrugged. "To keep an eye on him. And to show him not all werewolves are bad."

"They're not?" Nadia asked in an innocent voice.

"Not even all the ones in my pack are bad. Some are still my friends."

She lost her smile. "I don't want to meet them. Not right now."

"Maybe later. Definitely when we go to Minnesota to visit. I'll wait until things simmer down, but we need to go. I'm still part of the pack, and there are rules."

Nadia blinked. "Back up a minute. What do you mean when *we* go? Who are you taking with you?"

The heat in Logan's eyes was incandescent. "I'm taking you with me, and Joel if he wants to go. I need to present my mate to the pack."

Nadia's heart tripped in strange, fast beats. "That talk about me being your mate was just bullshit for Matt's benefit."

"No, it wasn't."

She dragged in a panicked breath. "But he's right. I'm demon. Death magic. You're life magic. We'll cancel each other out."

Logan seemed to suddenly be closer to her. "Samantha married Tain."

"She's only half demon, and he's a freak of nature."

"You need life essence, and I'm not letting you take it from anyone but me."

"Maybe you're just addicted to demons," she said desperately. "Did you ever think of that?"

Logan's arms went around her, pulling her against his hard body. She felt the warmth of his chest, the rough of his jeans against her bare legs. "I'm not. I've only given life essence to one other demon, and I never craved her. I didn't give life essence to you until last week, and I've wanted you in my bed since I met you."

"Why? You have a thing for crime victims?"

"I have a thing for you, Nadia." He gathered her close and pressed his face to her hair. "You're brave, and strong, and *beautiful*. I love your prickliness and how I can surprise you into smiling. I love your dark eyes and your black hair, and I love how you groan when I make love to you."

"What I tried to do . . . Matt could have killed you."

"Matt had you cornered, and you were right. If you'd told me, and I went on a rampage, he'd have killed Joel without waiting. You keep on protecting your son. Only you won't have to do it alone anymore."

"What about my demon form? Could you love that?"

Logan stroked her hair from her face. "I've never seen anything so beautiful."

She smiled, shyly pleased. "You and your wolf aren't bad either." She slid her hand between them. "My, what a big"— *squeeze*—"you have."

Logan laughed, turning his body to block Joel's view, but her son was playing, not watching them. "All the better to love you with, my dear," he said softly. "I like your wings. I keep thinking of them brushing over my naked body."

Nadia's insides tightened. "I could arrange that."

The teasing look fled Logan's eyes. "Gods, Nadia. I love you and want you in my life. How can I prove that to you?"

She pretended to think. "By taking me home and screwing me senseless?"

Logan chuckled, then slanted a hard, hot kiss across her mouth. "I could arrange that," he said, breath brushing her lips. "And then I'm arranging for you to marry me. I'm not letting you out of my sight again."

Nadia shuddered, the heat suddenly leaving her. "Are you sure you want to do that? I'm not really the kind of girl you take home."

"You're the kind of girl I marry." Logan's arms enclosed her, and his lips scalded her temple. "You never have to worry again, baby. I'll take care of you and Joel. When a wolf takes a mate, it's for life, and we protect what's ours."

"I don't want to be imprisoned," she whispered. "From what I've seen, werewolves, especially Packmasters, are overprotective."

"Like I could ever keep you from doing something you really wanted to. I know you better than that. You're strong and resilient and independent. All I ask is that you share that strength and independent spirit with me."

Nadia pressed her hand to his strong cheek. "Being independent is one thing. Being alone all the time is another. I'd rather be with you. I've always wanted to be with you."

"That's settled then," Logan murmured.

He kissed her, his strong lips opening hers. Nadia let herself sink into the kiss, tasting his spice, feeling the spark of his life essence.

"One thing first," she whispered.

"Mmm?" Logan was reluctant to release her, but she turned in his arms.

"Joel, honey, what would you say if Logan wanted to marry me?"

Joel caught the ball he'd bounced off the wall. He glanced once at Logan and Nadia standing together then turned back to his game. "I'd say it's about time. He's in love with you, Mom. Everyone knows that."

He spoke with the quiet wisdom of a ten-year-old who knew what was important.

"That really settles it." Nadia turned back to Logan, letting her hands steal to his tight, very satisfying ass. "Now what about my request for you to screw me senseless?"

Logan grinned and bent to her mouth. "You got it, my love. My wife." His kiss turned dark, and the fiery taste of his life essence slid into her mouth. "My *mate*."

JOY NASH

BLOOD DEBT

To Leah, Jennifer, and Robin . . .
Thanks for making the Immortals series one wild ride!

CHAPTER ONE

The Eternal City.

When all was said and done, it was a fitting place for a vampire.

Arthur Jackson Cabot IV swirled the ruby contents of his wineglass. The heat of the day lingered in the iron of the balcony rail, but somehow the warmth did not transfer to his bare forearms.

The sun was gone. From his hotel's perch atop a lofty hill behind Vatican City, Jackson watched twilight sigh into surrender. Church domes faded into ink-dark sky. Wary lights winked to life, one by one, an offering spread at his feet.

Night had come.

Night. His refuge and his torment.

Hunger gnawed Jackson's gut. His hand shook, causing the red liquid in his wineglass to tremble. He rubbed his eyes against the sting left by the harsh lights suspended above the Colosseum, more than three miles distant. He'd heard news of a charity concert in the ancient arena. A cadre of international rock stars, raising money to aid vampire addicts. Jackson's bitter laugh was low, and unamused.

The night was overly warm, and humid. His linen shirt clung to his chest, glued to his skin by a sheen of sweat tainted by city pollution. Jackson shifted his shoulders, trying to dislodge a feeling of uncleanliness. But the fabric only clung that much more.

His throat burned. The sensation had gone beyond subtle

irritation and now approached real pain. He could not ignore the thirst much longer, no matter how much he despised the craving. Summer bloodthirst was especially loathsome. Summer days were too long, summer nights too hot. Summer brought memories. It had been summer when death came for him.

It came, but had not succeeded in taking.

He peered into his glass. Contemplated taking a sip, then rejected the notion. With a subtle twist of his wrist, he poured the liquid over the balcony railing into the garden below. Call it an offering to a vengeful god. A poor offering, at that.

It was only wine, after all.

The balcony door scraped open.

"Monsieur Cabot?"

He closed his eyes. His steward's blind loyalty was yet another punishment. Solange was far too young for the thankless job she'd inherited. Why did she stay? If the tables had been turned, Jackson would have fled.

"Monsieur?" she said again. "Are you . . . well?"

He turned. Silhouetted in the doorway, Solange met his gaze with steady purpose. Even as a child, she'd been solemn. Lately, she'd been even more so.

"Will you roam tonight?"

The question was offered with deference, but it did not hide the worried beat of her heart. He could hear the organ, beating swiftly against her ribs. Her left hand fluttered, lamplight glinting off the plain gold band she still wore. Had only three months passed since Jean-Claude had coaxed a smile to his wife's eyes? It seemed like an eternity.

"The moon waxes. You must . . ." Her voice trailed off. A steward did not challenge her master. At least, not directly.

He handed her his glass. "Do not worry. I will drink tonight."

Relief rippled through her. "That is good."

"But I will not roam. The hotel can provide what I need."

"That too, is good." The young witch stepped back

through the balcony door. "Legrand's minions are sniffing about. The bastard knows you are here in Rome."

He followed her, his bare toes sinking into plush carpet.

"It is nothing I did not expect. The endgame approaches."

Solange's nostrils flared. "It is too soon. You cannot be certain you will win. Not yet. You should go into hiding. Until we are sure you are strong enough."

Jackson set his wineglass on the bar. The base cracked under the pressure of his frustration. He'd waited so long. Now, with the end in sight, it was imperative he proceed carefully. But how he wished he could end it. Tonight.

He glanced toward the window.

"Please," Solange whispered. "I beg of you. Let us not linger here. We must go to ground. Before the sun rises. We cannot risk—"

He raised his brows.

She flushed, but did not avert her eyes. "I apologize, monsieur, for my forward speech. But I am . . . concerned."

Her concern was prudent. Solange may be young, but her instincts were excellent. Jackson didn't want to heed her advice—the illusion of humanity he maintained as a guest in a human hotel was as potent as a lover's kiss. Pragmatism was a much less seductive mistress.

Ah, well. When it came to self-denial, Jackson was a master. He inclined his head. "As you wish. We will depart one hour before dawn. Inform the others."

Solange turned to pick up the pieces of his broken glass. "Very good."

Jackson strode to his bedroom, stripped off his damp clothing and dressed anew. When he again entered the sitting room, Solange stood waiting, the fingers of her right hand twisting the gold band on her left. She wasn't aware of the habit, he thought. Or perhaps she was.

"There is a fete on the terrace," she informed him. "Wine flows, lovers stroll in the gardens beyond the swimming pool. Enzo and Gunter are already in attendance. You will easily find what you need."

Jackson nodded, already heading toward the door. By now his craving had grown desperate, displacing even his guilt at what came next.

His fangs elongated, cutting the inside of his lip. Blood touched his tongue. Stolen blood, its life essence all but depleted. His throat was raw.

His thirst burned.

Somehow he managed to turn, hand on the doorknob, and speak in a normal tone. "I won't be long. Do not wait for me. Go to your room and get some sleep."

His steward inclined her head, and Jackson took his leave.

Solange had been right, as she most often was. The party on the terrace provided easy hunting. Enzo and Gunter roamed the edges of the glittering crowd, laughing and exchanging shallow pleasantries with the guests. Each vampire escorted a stunningly beautiful human woman.

Jackson's eyes narrowed, but he knew the living females would come to no permanent harm from his minions' feedings. Nor would the women's bodies be violated—no, not even if they begged for it. Neither Enzo nor Gunter would dare disobey Jackson's express orders.

He plucked a wineglass from a tray, but did not drink. Deftly, he mingled with the hotel's wealthy, multinational revelers, switching from Italian to French to English with ease. His youthful lessons in language and deportment had proven useful once again, just as his Boston Brahman grandmother had predicted.

He made his selection quickly, the burning in his gut escalating. Females, all. Feeding on men unearthed memories best left buried. He lured the first victim into the lush greenery beyond the terrace. The vivacious model from Milan did not realize how close to danger she ventured. The first bite was always the most difficult to control, especially after denying himself for so long. Exercising iron control, he lifted his head after just three sips.

She stumbled away, dazed. Immediately, he lured another

victim. Blonde. British. Her escort's brow creased as she made her excuses and slipped from his arms.

And so the evening progressed, with sips from a dozen veins pulsing in a dozen slender necks. Life—intoxicating life—flooded Jackson's body. With life came lust, weighting and warming his loins. Exercising long-practiced willpower, Jackson denied his body's demands. He closed each victim's wound and erased the pain from her mind, leaving only a vague impression of pleasure. Call it a payment of sorts. Yet Jackson felt every bit the dirty thief that he was.

"Vorresti andare alla mia camera?"

Would you like to go to my room? His final victim pursed her full lips.

Jackson's heart, pumping its stolen blood, thudded against his ribs. This one had red hair.

His body clenched. Pure fire flowed into his erection. Several seconds passed before he trusted himself to voice a rejection. *"Mi dispiace, bella, ma no."*

The woman pouted and gave him her back. Jackson stared at the sleek fall of her hair until she disappeared into the crowd. Sated, disgusted, aroused almost beyond bearing, Jackson fled to the elevator.

Solange had extinguished the lights in his suite. Jackson dropped onto the leather couch in front of a blank television screen. On his feet again within moments, he paced.

God in heaven. Red hair. And it hadn't come from a bottle, either.

His erection throbbed. Visions of the unnamed redhead—naked, lying on white satin, arms flung overhead—blended with the image of another red-haired siren. A woman from long ago.

Striding to the bar, he passed over the wine in the decanter and opted for whiskey. He poured it, unwatered, down his throat. The glass cracked in his hand as he fought to master his breathing. He chanted a mantra; the syllables provided a measure of calm. He grasped at the peace. Tried to pull it inside.

The urge to utter a prayer—for strength, for forgiveness—was all but overwhelming. He resisted it. An old Harvard drinking toast claimed the Boston Cabots talked only to God, but Jackson had withdrawn from that futile conversation over a century ago.

Slowly, surely, he mastered his demons, his memories, his painful lust. And was rewarded with a surge of power. Magic blazed through his veins—blinding, glorious. Like the sun he could no longer look upon.

A few moments later, his breathing was quiet, his body relaxed. He settled anew on the sofa, his long legs crossed and propped on the cocktail table in front of him. Absently, he picked up the remote and pointed it at the television.

He scanned several channels, then paused when coverage of the charity concert at the Colosseum illuminated the screen. The international effort sported the usual collection of do-good musical superstars. Bono, Sting, Springsteen, McCartney, Manannán. A large-breasted reporter discharged rapid Italian commentary near the backstage entrance, where fifty or more hysterical females mobbed a line of police barriers.

He was about to change the channel when a sleek black limo, escorted by four *polizia* mounted on flag-adorned motorcycles, slowed before the ancient stone archway. Jackson lowered the remote as the limo door opened.

Out sprang Manannán mac Lir, the Celtic musician and demigod, a wide grin on his handsome face as he greeted his adoring public. Several figures spilled from the limo behind him. A pair of tall Sidhe males, two dark-haired human females, and a large, disgruntled-looking man wearing a tuxedo. Jackson recognized the last as the Immortal, Kalen, hero to the human race and obscenely rich patron of the arts.

Manannán turned and offered a hand to the last occupant of the limo. Jackson found himself riveted by a pair of long, exquisite legs. The rest of the woman emerged from the vehicle, piece by piece, like candy spilling from a bag. Curvaceous hips. Tiny waist. Lush breasts. A classically beautiful profile.

Pointed Sidhe ears peeked through her red hair.

"My *gods*."

Jackson's feet slid off the table, hitting the ground with a force that made the picture on the screen shake. His cock hardened with such sudden, painful intensity that he heard himself gasp. His mind blanked on a rush of white-hot lust.

And red-hot anger.

One hundred years might have passed, but it would take much longer than a mere century to erase this particular redhead from his mind and his soul.

He'd thought she'd be dead by now. Or at the very least, older. But no. She was as alive, as young, and as beautiful as he remembered—and still consorting with artistic talent and vast wealth.

Just as she had all those years ago in Paris.

He'd worshiped this woman. In return, she'd whispered words of devotion and left him for dead. But Jackson hadn't died—or at least, not quite as completely as she'd expected.

It was a mistake she would soon regret. Dearly.

He stood.

It seemed he was meant to roam tonight, after all.

CHAPTER TWO

Leanna's handsome half brother sent her a grin brilliant enough to charm an ogre from its den.

"Ah, come now, love, you can't mean to retire so early. The night's barely got started. The clubs are waiting." Pumped from his stage performance, Mac radiated more life energy than should be legal in the human world.

"Yes, but—" Leanna began.

"But nothing, little sister. Rome needs you."

Artemis, Mac's wife, rolled her eyes. "Listen, Mac, we can't stay out too long. I need to get back in time for Cameron's four A.M. feeding."

"Then we best get going quickly, no? Come now, Leanna. You can't let Artemis and me dance alone."

"I don't think—"

"Mac," Artemis broke in, "Can't you take a hint? Leanna doesn't want to go clubbing. Leave her be. You didn't say a word when Kalen and Christine left for the hotel after the last curtain call."

"Kalen's a bloody old man," Mac said without heat. "He hates crowds, and Christine, bless her soul, thinks Ellie will give Pearl too much of a fuss." He snorted. "As if there's anything that old biddy can't handle."

Leanna hid a smile. Kalen's mixed-blood halfling/gnome housekeeper did have a special talent with children—even such magical imps as Kalen's immortal daughter, Mac's semidivine firstborn, and Artemis's magical older son.

Mac's green eyes narrowed on Leanna. "What's wrong, love? You're always good for a late-night jaunt. Not ill, are you?"

"No, nothing like that. I'm just tired." *And melancholy.* "You and Artemis go on and have fun. I'll take a taxi back to the hotel."

"Not a chance. We'll have the limo drop you off. I've just got a few fans to greet at the back gate . . ."

A "few" fans turned into ten, then twenty. By the time Mac and Artemis dropped Leanna at her hotel at the top of the Spanish Steps, two A.M. had come and gone. Muted voices and the strains of a guitar drifted from a knot of tourists lingering on the famed Baroque stairway. Leanna didn't look over. She'd sat on those steps years ago, laughing and flirting with a young poet named John Keats, in the shadow of the house where he'd died not long after.

Leanna had killed him.

Oh, all right, maybe technically it hadn't been murder. Keats had surrendered his life of his own free will, just as all Leanna's doomed lovers had. Desperate artists, they'd begged for the inspiration her sex magic could provide. To a man, the poets, painters, and musicians had willingly traded their life essence for the fame and fortune they craved more than life itself.

It had been each man's choice to die. Or at least, that's how Leanna, a Celtic *leannan-sidhe*, or love muse, had rationalized her ruthless magic for more than two hundred years.

She couldn't lie anymore. Not even to herself. The agonizing year she'd spent in the death realms, a slave to demons, had stripped her of all illusion. She'd been trapped in Hell, facing an eternity of death and darkness. It had been a pure miracle that Mac had stumbled on Leanna while searching for Artemis in that horrible place. A second miracle had occurred when Mac had decided his sister's miserable arse was worth saving.

Now, having spent the better part of a year with Mac in the Celtic Otherworld, healing the damage Hell had done to their souls, Leanna and her brother were something she'd never dreamed they'd be. Friends.

Mac gave a final wave as his limo pulled away. Leanna drew a breath, but mere oxygen wasn't enough to fill the hollow sensation in her chest. In the past year, Mac had conquered his inner demons, married his true love, and fathered a child. In contrast, Leanna had done . . . nothing. Nothing at all.

She neared the front desk. The night clerk was handsome and young, with olive skin and bedroom eyes. And he was, as fate would have it, an artist.

A sketchbook lay open before him; a pencil graced his elegant, long-fingered hand. He greeted her with a smile. Before she quite knew what she was doing, a tendril of muse magic escaped. The pulse caused him to go still, then swallow thickly. Leanna had no doubt that behind the desk something else was thickening as well.

Gods. How long had it been since she'd bedded an artist? Almost two years. And the ugly truth was, Leanna missed her muse magic. The heady exchange of inspiration and life, delivered at the precise moment of orgasm, was a mind-blowing high, one she'd reveled in for two centuries, while her conscience slept.

Right here, right now, she wanted this boy, fiercely. She could lose herself in him, at least for one night. It wouldn't be a one-sided exchange. There was much she could offer him. She could give him his fondest dream. Under the influence of her magic, he would create a brilliant work of art. His fame would be instant. The world would throw itself at his feet. Worship him like a god.

And then he would die.

Leanna yanked her magic back. What was she thinking? She couldn't chance taking this young man to bed. The boy could very well be so hungry for fame and fortune that he would destroy himself to get it. That was the problem with artists. One could never tell how desperate they were, until it was too late.

That was why, during her recent stay in Annwyn, she'd renounced her muse magic. While it wasn't death magic, strictly speaking, it was a path to darkness. She'd renounced death magic as well, in all its forms. She wouldn't—*couldn't*—give herself to darkness again.

She nodded briefly at the clerk and passed by without speaking. Perhaps he would never be a great artist, but at least he would have a chance for a long and happy life.

The elevator doors swished closed, leaving her alone in the cab. When would she ever grow accustomed to keeping her own company? Never, she suspected. She hated being alone in the night. But every night since she'd escaped Hell, she'd been just that.

Her hotel room was quiet, shrouded in darkness. She didn't bother to turn on the light as she shed her dress, shoes, stockings, and bra. Wearing just her thong, she slid between the sheets. Her head sank onto a stack of downy pillows, but her eyes remained open. Despite what she'd told Mac, she wasn't tired at all.

The lace curtains at the window fluttered; the hazy light from the street danced across the coverlet.

A sudden shadow fell across the bed. She blinked. She didn't at first understand what was happening.

A man's voice broke the velvet darkness.

"*Bonsoir*, Leanna. Or at this hour, perhaps I should say *bon matin?*"

She sucked in a breath.

She wasn't alone, after all.

CHAPTER THREE

Elflight lifted from Leanna's palm to hover over her head. The intruder was tall, with a broad chest and long, powerful legs. Death magic radiated from his body. Leanna suspected the potency she sensed was only a drop in the vast reservoir of his power. He wore a dark suit jacket over a black shirt, open at the neck. His hair, a glossy nut-brown touched by moonlight, shone. She should have been afraid, but oddly, she wasn't.

He looked familiar.

"Do I know you?" she ventured.

He smiled, a quick glint of white teeth that was anything but mirthful.

"Is your memory fading, Leanna? And here you promised never to forget me. But then, when you've known so many men, I suppose it's hard to keep us all straight in your mind."

He took a single step forward. Elflight bathed his features.

Leanna stared. Her hand crept toward her throat, her palm flattening on the pounding of her heart. Her lips parted, but no sound emerged.

He snorted. "Speechless? I can hardly believe it. As I recall, you were never at a loss for words."

She swallowed. The reflex was painful. When her voice finally emerged from her throat, it was as a scratchy whisper.

"*Jackson?* Jackson Cabot?"

He bowed, a swift, graceful angling of the waist. So elegant. So much like the man she remembered.

But Jackson was . . . dead.

"You're . . ." She cleared her throat and began again. "You're not a ghost."

"No," he agreed.

He stepped closer, almost to the foot of the bed. Elflight shone full in his face, illuminating his beauty. His angled cheekbones, patrician nose, and high forehead hadn't changed at all. But his hazel eyes glinted with a cynical light that was wholly foreign to the man she'd once loved. And his complexion . . . it wasn't right. The Jackson she'd known spent every free moment in the sun. This man before her . . . he had none of Jackson's tanned, healthy glow.

Horror oozed through her veins. "You're . . . vampire."

Jackson planted both hands on the high mattress and leaned toward her. "And you, Leanna, are still a very beautiful woman."

His gaze left her face and traveled . . . lower.

She inched the blanket higher.

"Modest?" His tone was hard, completely lacking the teasing lilt Leanna associated with her memories of Jackson. "I confess, I'm surprised. What are you about, returning to your hotel unaccompanied? The last thing I expected was to find you climbing into this bed alone." He straightened. "What happened to your latest conquest?"

She stared up at him, his mocking tone flowing over her as she struggled to wrap her mind around the fact that this was Jackson, *her* Jackson. Here. In her bedroom. Speaking to her. It wasn't a dream. Or a nightmare.

Then his words registered. "Conquest? What are you talking about?"

His jaw tightened. "Manannán mac Lir, the musician. I saw you with him on the television."

"You saw Mac and me on the telly?" Inane reply. Her brain refused to operate properly.

"I did. Tell me, where did you screw him? In his limo? Or in his hotel room? Was he good?"

Shock caused the air to puff from her lungs. "*What?* You think . . . Mac and I—"

"Manannán's fame has exploded in the past year. And now I find that he's traveling with you. You're a sex muse. You can't tell me your magic hasn't played a part in his—"

"Mac's success had nothing to do with my magic. For the love of all the gods in Annwyn, Jackson, Mac is my *brother!*"

He snorted. "Oh, really? I don't recall you ever mentioning a divine brother."

"Mac's my half brother. We have the same mother. I never told you about him because Mac and I weren't speaking when you and I . . . when we were . . ." She lost her words. Her throat closed. Her lashes were wet.

"Were in love?" Jackson prompted with more than a little sarcasm.

She met his gaze evenly. "Yes. When we were in love."

"Love." He spat the word. "I thought it was love, Leanna, but I soon learned how deadly your particular brand of that emotion is, didn't I?"

He paced the room. "A good novelist could live off the irony of our affair for years. I never wanted you for your magic, as your other lovers did. I'd been in Paris only two days when I realized my meager talent was nothing compared to the art of the great masters. I was resigned to the fact that Paris was to be just a pleasant interlude, after which I fully intended to return to Boston and take up the reins of my father's manufacturing empire." Turning abruptly, he faced her. "And then I found you."

"We found each other," Leanna whispered.

Jackson dragged a hand over his face. "I wanted you for my wife. I knew there was every chance you would refuse. What I didn't expect, Leanna, was that you would kill me."

The hoarse emotion in his voice sent a tremor through Leanna's body. How many times had she lain in Jackson's arms, ear pressed to the low rumble of his chest as he told her of his life, his love, his dreams?

"But . . . you weren't dead when I left you! I didn't want

to kill you—I just didn't want you to follow me. I made sure you had enough life essence left to recover. I thought . . . I assumed you'd awakened the next morning. And returned to your family in Boston . . ."

"A fine rationalization, even for you. You knew far better than I what sort of scum roamed the alleys in Paris in those days."

Gods help her, she did.

Another ruthless glint of teeth. "Really, Leanna, you left me too soon. You should have made sure I was completely dead. Loose ends come back to strangle, sooner or later."

For the first time, she felt a glimmer of fear. "What . . . what happened to you that night, Jackson? I left a warding spell to protect you. No one could have broken it."

He crossed his arms. "Armand Legrand did."

"Oh, gods." *Armand Legrand* had been—was still—the oldest and most ruthless vampire on the European continent.

"I provided Legrand with a fine meal. All my blood intact, and so little energy with which to fight. Legrand was so pleased he decided to keep me. I woke the next day, newly turned. Newly enslaved."

Leanna shuddered. Legrand's brutality was legendary. The humiliation and sexual perversions the vampire master forced on his newly turned minions were known to be . . .

Her stomach heaved. "I'm . . . I'm so sorry, Jackson."

"Not sorry enough," he said softly. "Yet."

Fear closed her throat. Several moments passed before she realized the bedcovers had slipped from her numb fingers, and that Jackson's unfeeling gaze had traveled to her bare breasts.

She snatched at the cotton.

"No," he said thickly. "Leave it."

She tugged it higher, all the way to her neck. Her gaze flicked past him, to the door. Mac wouldn't have returned yet, but Kalen's room was just down the hall. If she screamed . . .

Jackson's eyes flicked to her face, his anger silencing her more effectively than a gag. When had she ever seen him angry? Rarely. The Jackson Cabot she'd once known had been a lighthearted, smiling man.

He was not smiling now.

"Make no mistake, Leanna. You will not escape. Not until I decide to let you go."

His eyes changed, the brown irises growing darker, as dark as the pit of Hell. She tried to blink; her eyelids remained open. She tried to look away. Impossible. Jackson's vampire mesmerism was stronger than any she'd encountered. That made no sense. A vampire's power increased with age. Jackson had been turned just a century ago. Leanna's Sidhe magic should have easily overcome such a newly made vampire. It didn't. Jackson controlled her as easily as a puppet on a string.

Irresistible pressure, like an invisible hand gripping her wrist, inched her arm downward. The bedcovers, clutched in her fingers, went with it. Cool cotton slithered over her chest.

She gasped a spell—life magic, the most powerful she could muster. The words fell dead, a meaningless jumble of syllables. The bedsheet crested the pearled tips of her breasts; the fabric whispered to her waist. Jackson's fierce, hot gaze followed.

He devoured her with his eyes. He'd often done the same, during their time in Paris. Just looking. Not speaking. Not touching. The silent foreplay had never failed to arouse her. Now, her body remembered. Her skin heated, her heart pounded. The tips of her breasts itched. There was a pulling, aching sensation, like a slow fall from a high place. It caught in her belly and did not let go.

She couldn't look away from his eyes. The irises were almost black now, shining with death and death magic. These were not the eyes she'd known a century ago. Those eyes had been filled with good humor and mischief. Blazing with desire. Flooded with awe and tenderness. Or—and this had been the worst—filled with something akin to pity.

It had been all too easy to confide in him. Once she did,

Leanna had felt like a wild animal trapped in a cage. Lust she could handle. Laughter, too. It had been Jackson's sympathy and understanding that had caused her to bolt.

The bedsheet inched past her navel. Another desperately whispered Sidhe spell failed to halt its descent. One hundred and ten years ago, Jackson had been heir to a vast fortune and a talented artist besides, but he'd been a mundane human. He hadn't possessed even a drop of magic.

Now he was stronger than she; she was trapped within his power. Dark emotion poured from his body. The sharp inhale of his breath, the flare of his nostrils, the clench of his jaw—all transmitted his anger. The bulge in his trousers blatantly announced his lust.

She wasn't sure which of his warring emotions aroused her more.

The sour scent of death magic radiated from his body. It should have disgusted her. Instead, it turned her on. This was *Jackson*, the man she'd once loved with frightening intensity. She thought he'd grown old. Thought he had died. That he was standing here before her was nothing short of a miracle. She didn't care if the miracle came wrapped in death magic and vampire power. She wanted him still.

The sheet continued its downward path, tugged by her own shaking hands. The top edge skimmed her hip bones, then dropped to her thighs. Her thong, a thin scrap of silk, was all that protected her from Jackson's consuming gaze.

His eyes flared with heat as the sheet fell away. She felt his desire like a knife thrust into her gut. Her belly quivered, her thighs grew slick with longing. Jackson had been a gentle lover in Paris, sweet and playful. She sensed he wouldn't be gentle now. He'd use her roughly, slaking a century of rage on her body. And she wouldn't fight him, even if she could. She would give this bitter, wounded man whatever he required of her.

Would he demand only sex? Or would he drink her blood, too? He could easily drain her veins, leeching every last drop of blood and life. The one thing he could not do, however, was make her become like him. Sidhe magic would not allow one of their own to be turned vampire.

Jackson's heavy footfalls rounded the bed. Fear and desire snaked through Leanna as he approached. It was perverse, humiliating, this dark wanting. She understood it too well—the yearning was akin to the fatal craving she had inspired in her artist lovers. The sins of her past had returned with a vengeance to demand their reckoning.

Jackson's shadow fell dark on her pale skin. His black gaze consumed her. He smelled of fury and magic. A sheen of sweat glistened on his jaw. The lock of brown hair that had fallen across his eyes looked softer than moonlight. She longed to reach out and stroke it.

She didn't dare.

She lay tense, waiting for his move. Excruciating moments passed.

He didn't touch her.

And yet he didn't move away.

She wet her lips with her tongue. "What . . . what do you want from me, Jackson?"

He seemed not to hear. He reached out, as if he meant to touch her. Her belly clenched, dreading and craving the contact.

His hand dropped to his side and curled into a fist.

"You look just the same," he said at last, more to himself than to her. "How is that possible? Sidhe age slowly, but not that slowly. Not when half their essence is human."

"I've spent the last year in Annwyn. The magic of the Otherworld . . . it gave me back my youth."

Surprise flickered in his eyes. "Annwyn? You told me once you weren't welcome there. That your Sidhe mother refused to acknowledge you."

Her cheeks flamed. He knew too much. He knew that her mother, the queen of Annwyn, had abandoned her half-human daughter. He also knew that Leanna's human father had been a drunken fool who hadn't been able to control his carnal urges when his pubescent daughter's Sidhe sex magic

had first made itself known. She had whispered those humiliating confessions to Jackson in the darkness one night and
immediately regretted it. His pity had made her burn with
shame.

His eyes were far too knowing. She wanted to look away,
but Jackson didn't allow it. He held her pinned, body and
soul, like a live butterfly impaled on a naturalist's board.

"Mac—my brother—he convinced my mother to let me
into Annwyn." Somehow Leanna managed to speak. "I'd . . .
I'd spent a year in the death realms. I was in need of healing."

"And now you're young again. Beautiful and deadly. Free
to beguile. Free to kill."

"No, I—"

He rounded the bed and leaned over her, his face hovering scant inches above hers. His right hand came down over
her mouth, smothering her words.

"Silence. Lie still."

She sensed him waging some inner battle. After several
tense moments, a rush of breath left his lips, and his shoulders collapsed a fraction. It seemed like he'd accepted a defeat of some kind, but exactly what had conquered him, she
couldn't imagine. Jackson clearly was the one holding all
the power in this encounter.

His right hand still covered her mouth. Now his left hand
touched her—first one breast, then the other. Had she expected harshness? His handling of her wasn't abrupt or angry
at all. He stroked her with consummate delicacy. She was reminded of the afternoon she'd come to his studio overlook-
ing the Seine. His soft-bristled brush had swept over her
breasts in just the same way.

On that long-ago evening, after his lovemaking had left
her languid and sated, she'd watched as Jackson anointed
that same brush with paint. He'd teased images onto canvas
like God calling Eden into being.

Now he applied that same artist's skill to the canvas of
her body.

His fingertips brushed her nipples. Stroked her belly.

Circled her navel. He drew a line downward, sketching the rise and fall of her Venus mound. He paused—too delicately—at the place that throbbed for him.

Her thighs parted—whether at his silent command or in response to her own yearning, she didn't know. His fingers explored between her legs, stroking either side of the damp fabric of her thong. She moaned and arched shamelessly, offering herself to his hand.

He watched her closely as he touched her. She blinked up, looked into his face. Fear rushed to do battle with her lust. Jackson's expression had darkened. His brows were drawn, and his eyes burned. His hand, still clamped over her mouth, flexed. A cold knot of fear formed in Leanna's belly and tightened.

Slowly he withdrew one hand from her lips, the other from her body. He planted both palms on her pillow, one on each side of her head. His breath rasped; his chest heaved.

Their gazes remained locked. A metallic scent—like death, like blood, wrapped her like a noose. Her body responded; she couldn't help it. She'd been a practitioner of death magic. She'd endured a year as a demonwhore in the death realms. It didn't matter that she'd finally been welcomed in Annwyn. Didn't matter that she'd forsworn death magic, had dedicated herself to light and life magic.

She craved darkness. Craved death magic. And that hunger, she knew, would never go away. It was part of her soul. And Jackson, with his vampire power, his vampire magic, knew it.

He lowered himself to the bed. His long, powerful body stretched out along her right side, his torso supported on his elbow. The mattress dipped under his weight, causing her to roll toward him, until every part of her softening body was pressed against hard, unyielding muscle.

She felt his erection thickening against her belly. "Jackson—"

"Silence."

He captured her chin in his fingers, peering intently into her eyes. She lay still, silent as he'd commanded. Chaotic sensations racked her body. She wet her lips, and his eyes darkened dangerously.

"Temptress," he whispered. "Siren. Whore."

The words dropped like pebbles into a taut pool of anticipation. Ripples radiated to every corner of her soul. Jackson's body trembled, almost as violently as her own.

"You will destroy me once again."

"No, never! I—"

"Silence!"

Her protest died in her throat. Her heart pounded in her chest, as she waited for him to act. For several long moments, he didn't move, leaving Leanna to wonder what held him back.

And then nothing held him back.

CHAPTER FOUR

Jackson, in his vast pride, had believed his control unshakable.

He found, to his eternal humiliation, that it was not. Leanna's lips were soft and tasted faintly of cherries.

Taste begat scent; scent begat sensation and images. Memories assaulted his brain. He recalled the evening he'd first set eyes on her, at a party given by a mutual friend. Her red hair shone in candlelight, her pointed ears delicate and impossibly erotic. She'd seemed so fragile and somehow inexpressibly sad.

His fingers had brushed hers when he'd presented her with a flute of champagne. He'd asked her to dance. She'd refused. Her faint Scots accent had intrigued him.

He'd asked her a second time. And a third.

Finally, he'd made her laugh, and she'd accepted.

Their first dance was a waltz. Afterward they'd strolled through their host's garden. From then on, they were inseparable. They'd wandered the streets of Montmartre, joined the crowds at the Moulin Rouge. They'd ascended Gustave Eiffel's folly, and marveled at Paris laid out at their feet.

In the darkest hours of the early morning, they'd made love . . .

His palm grazed her breast, riding on memories. Fingers tightened on soft flesh. His kiss turned urgent. This was dangerous, he knew. He was falling again—too far, too fast. If he didn't pull away in time . . .

He needed to remember why he'd come to her. Not for this. She was to be his tool, not his destruction.

He gathered his resolve. He almost put his good sense into motion. But then Leanna whimpered against his mouth, and arched into his hand, her nipple pebbling in his palm. The helpless sound she made was not fear, but desire.

Lust burned through him like lightning. The magic that kept his heart beating—death magic—reared its ugly head. Hunger, sexual hunger, too long repressed, battered his defenses. His tongue invaded her mouth; his fangs erupted. Shuddering, he fought the urge to bite hard and bite deep. The sheer effort blanked his mind.

She should have been fighting him. She wasn't. Just the opposite—her arms stole around him, stroking, kneading, entwining about his neck, wrapping her legs around his hips. He shook with the strength of his need. It had been more than seven decades since he'd had a woman. Too long, by any man's reckoning. Far too long.

She licked his ear. Her legs encircled his torso. Magic— *life magic*—washed over him.

It was like a bucket of ice thrown on a raging fire. Abruptly, his sanity snapped into place.

What in God's name was he doing? He tore his lips from hers. He grabbed her calves and wrenched her legs from around his waist. He thrust himself off her body to stand at her bedside, staring down at her beauty, his chest heaving painfully. She gazed up at him, flushed and panting. Bewildered, but willing. Very willing.

God help him. He closed his eyes, clenched his fists, and concentrated on his most difficult mantra.

"Jackson—" Her voice was no more than a whisper of breath.

He opened his eyes, and immediately regretted it. She was so beautiful; gazing on her hurt something deep in his chest. Her red hair was much shorter than it had been in Paris, but the gloss, the luxurious texture of it—that hadn't changed. Thick lashes fringed clear gray eyes, wet with tears.

She was trembling.

And so was he.

He repressed a rush of sympathy, replacing it with anger. He'd seen Leanna's tears. Seen her use them as weapons. A sharpened sword couldn't cut a man to shreds with more efficiency than the feminine grief she manufactured so easily. She'd cried that last night in Paris. Only moments before she drained his soul.

If he wasn't careful, she would lure him to ruin. Again.

She reached for him. "Jackson? What's wrong?"

"You will find," he said tersely, "that I am no longer the fool I once was."

"You were never a fool, Jackson."

He grabbed for the bedpost, steadying himself. "Get dressed. Your body no longer interests me."

He ignored the flash of hurt in her eyes. Turning, he paced to the window, where he looked to the street below, seeing nothing but the scenes flashing through his own mind. The bed creaked; Leanna's footsteps padded across the carpet. A drawer opened. He heard the whisper of fabric on skin.

Her silent obedience brought him a measure of satisfaction. He imagined her on her knees, obeying him in other ways, her rosy, pouting lips opening . . .

God*damn* it. He shut his eyes, called his mantra, willed his raging erection to wilt. Slowly, it did. He sensed Leanna behind him, watching. Calmer now, but not yet ready to face her, he opened his eyes and peered once more through the glass. A lone figure paced the cobblestones. Gunter. He sensed Enzo and Solange nearby as well.

He willed his minion to glance up at the window. Gunter's gaze lifted immediately. A flick of Jackson's fingers, a thought directed to the young vampire's mind, was all that was needed to communicate his orders.

Gunter nodded and moved out of sight.

Jackson turned to face Leanna. He would not allow her to distract him from his purpose. She had destroyed his past. It was only fitting that he use her to ensure his future.

He didn't immediately speak. Instead, he watched her grow increasingly uncertain in the face of his silence. She'd donned a simple knit dress. Off-white. Clinging. The hem fell demurely to her knees. Her unbound breasts looked even more tantalizing covered than they had bare.

She'd stepped into low-heeled sandals. Her fingers twisted together, and her pulse skittered. Her face was very pale.

"Jackson, why did you come here?"

He told her the truth. "To take you with me."

Her gray eyes widened. "Where? Why?"

"You'll find out soon enough."

"And if I don't want to go?"

He laughed, harshly. "I'm afraid you have no choice. As I've demonstrated, mine is the greater power. I can make you dance like a marionette."

He lifted a hand, fingers spread, and captured her gaze. He unleashed a small tendril of his vampire mesmerism and allowed his power to strike.

Leanna's body jerked.

He willed her to walk across the room.

Her limbs responded instantly. She resisted his command, she threw all her magic into the effort. He toyed with her, relaxing his will and letting her believe she'd broken his control, then swiftly overpowering her again. Bowing to his greater might, she sank to her knees.

Illicit fantasies exploded in his brain. With a curse, he jerked her back to her feet, more roughly than he'd intended. In that instant his self-hatred burned more fiercely than perhaps it ever had.

Humiliation flushed her face. Her shoulders shook. "Jackson, please. Don't. Don't do this. I'll come with you willingly. Only . . . tell me why." She drew a breath. "Do you mean to kill me?"

"No."

"What, then? Please, tell—"

She broke off as the door leading to the hallway swung open. Gunter entered, Enzo on his heels. Solange crossed the threshold last, and closed the door behind her. Leanna's gaze flew to the other woman. For several seconds, the two females stood motionless, assessing each other.

Enzo and Gunter looked at him expectantly.

"Take her," Jackson told them.

When Leanna woke, she couldn't move.

Her arms were numb and tied behind her back. Her ankles were bound as well. Her thoughts fuzzed around the edges of her mind. Even prying her eyelids open took supreme effort.

Wherever she was, it was dark. She didn't remember her arrival—her most recent memories were hopelessly mud-dled. Vampire magic. The undead regularly toyed with the minds of the living. A vampire could compel humans to do things they would never do under their own free will.

Leanna had known many vampires in her long life. Thank-fully, Armand Legrand had not been one of them. To date, Jackson was the most powerful vampire she'd encountered.

She blinked into stygian darkness. She lay on a soft surface—a bed, perhaps. Her clothing, thankfully, was intact. Nothing hurt, other than the ache in her stretched arms, but the sheer vulnerability of her position infused her with dread.

She sniffed the air. Damp. Musty. The flat smell of an-cient death lingered. She tried, unsuccessfully, to suppress a shiver.

Fighting the haze in her mind, she searched for her magic. The power was there, but far away. Touching it was like stretching her arm across a chasm. The flicker of elflight she managed to call was weak. But it was better than nothing.

The illumination spread just below a rocky ceiling. Shad-ows resolved into shapes. Her prison seemed to be a narrow cave. A silk carpet hugged the ground; velvet fabric draped the walls. The edges of the wall hangings touched bare rock. About fifteen feet from the foot of the bed, a tapestry hung the width of the space, shielding the makeshift room from whatever lay beyond.

Furnishings were sparse. A table, two straight-backed

chairs, one deep leather armchair. With a start, Leanna realized the latter was occupied. By the young woman Jackson had admitted to Leanna's hotel room.

The woman spoke. "Ah, so you are awake. At last."

She was young and lovely, with long glossy hair. She spoke English with a French accent. She rose with catlike grace, inclining her head in Leanna's direction, as if they'd just been introduced at a party. Leanna scrutinized her aura. She was human, and powerful. Alive, not vampire. A witch.

"Who are you? Where is Jackson?"

The witch clasped her hands before her. "The sun shines; the master sleeps. He commanded me to watch over you."

"You are . . . ?"

"The master's steward, of course."

The explanation caused Leanna to tense. Most vampires employed magical human stewards—to safeguard their sleeping places and perform various daylight tasks. Many vampires also used their stewards sexually, but this woman was so young. Barely out of her teens, Leanna guessed. Surely Jackson wasn't physically intimate with her. Then again, what did she really know of the man Jackson had become?

"Solange." As if called from her thoughts, Jackson's voice intruded. "You may leave us now."

Immediately, Solange turned and bowed. "Oui, monsieur." She rounded the edge of the tapestry and disappeared.

Jackson stepped into the elfglow. Leanna studied him. His features were stark, and his skin very pale. The expression in his eyes was completely devoid of emotion.

A tear trickled down her cheek. She'd turned him into what he was. Of all the many sins she'd committed in her life, what she'd done to Jackson was perhaps the worst. Because he'd loved her so much. Perhaps as much as he hated her now.

"Crying, Leanna?" His tone was mocking. "You? You surprise me."

She blinked, shocked to find him standing beside the bed,

his dark gaze raking her body. He'd crossed the room so quickly and silently she hadn't perceived his motion at all.

She swallowed the lump in her throat. She wished she could wipe her damp cheek.

"Jackson. What is this place? Where are we?"

He didn't immediately answer. Instead, he bent his head over her ankles, releasing the restraints. He unbound her wrists, then stepped back and raised his brows.

She tried to move, tensing her muscles and struggling with all her might to reach an upright position. She couldn't do it. The ropes had been for the benefit of Jackson's steward. Jackson had no need of them. His death magic held her captive.

With no more than a nod, he released the mesmerism. But his point had been well made. She could not escape him. She sat up, watching him warily.

"We're hidden," he told her. "My minions stand guard. No one's coming to rescue you, Leanna, if that's what you're hoping."

He turned and lifted the velvet wall hanging nearest the bed. Deep shelves pierced the cave wall, each just long and deep enough to support a human body. In fact, several berths did contain corpses, wrapped in rotting linen.

"This is a crypt," she said.

"Yes. An undiscovered tributary of the Catacombs of St. Domitilla, to be precise."

He let the velvet fall. "Just think, Leanna. Above our heads, living humans go about their daily tasks, blessedly ignorant of the abomination of death lurking beneath the rock they trod. Life essence and life magic abound. For them, the sky is blue. For them, the sun shines." He exhaled. "The sun. I have not seen it for more than one hundred years. I live in darkness, Leanna. Because of you."

"Oh, Jackson." A tear dripped across her cheek and ran along her jaw. Another followed it. "I am sorry for that. More than you know." She fought to remain calm. "Why did you bring me here, Jackson? I don't understand."

He didn't immediately answer. His heated gaze was bold on her body, lingering on her breasts, and the V between her thighs. She drew up her knees, and wrapped her arms around them.

"Modesty, Leanna? I did not think the word was in your vocabulary."

"I won't fight you, if that's what you think. I know you're the wronged party here."

Shadows draped his lower body; she couldn't tell whether he was aroused. Gods help her, she was. Dark longing twisted in her belly, and moisture flooded her thighs. Jackson's nostrils flared; his eyes narrowed. She was sure he sensed how soft and ready she was, for whatever he chose to do. And yet, he did not touch her.

Instead he laughed. "You would like for me to climb into that bed, wouldn't you? Do you think you can command me to service you? Ah, no, Leanna, I think not. Do you think I would offer you a chance to destroy me a second time?"

"No, Jackson, you have it wrong. I would never hurt you . . ."

"How could you not, Leanna? Your magic is my downfall. Its allure taints the air I breathe, inflames the blood pumping through my body. Even if you wished to, you couldn't stop yourself from destroying me. You can't divorce yourself from your magic. It's the very nature of your soul." His jaw tightened. "If you have a soul, that is."

She shook her head. But her denial was a lie; Jackson's accusation was as accurate as an arrow to the heart. How many nights had she lain awake in Annwyn, faced with the awful truth: her magic was flawed, an aberration to light and life. Her worst fear was that she would never conquer the part of her soul that craved death and death magic.

Jackson's eyes were intent, lit with dangerous light. Fear wrapped tendrils of dread around her heart.

"What do you want of me, Jackson?"

"Haven't you guessed yet? I want your magic, Leanna. The worst of it. Nothing less."

She was aghast. "You want to die?"

He smiled slightly, and for a brief instant Leanna caught the glimpse of the man she'd once loved. Her heart caught.

"Perhaps I do want to die, Leanna. But that would be impossible. A vampire's instinct for survival is too great. No, it is not my own existence I wish to obliterate with your magic, but another's."

She inhaled sharply. "You . . . want me to kill someone?"

His lips drew back, baring even white teeth. She saw no hint of fangs. "Yes. A simple task, to drain the life essence from a lover. After all, you've done it often, and thoroughly, in the past. You will do it again, for me. Afterward, I will release you."

"No, Jackson." Her voice trembled. "Not that. I can't do it. I . . . I've renounced my muse magic. I won't use it to kill anyone, not ever again. Not even for you."

He snorted. "You will do as I command." He leaned forward, his pose deceptively casual. "I will compel you. You'll have no choice but to obey."

She looked into his eyes and knew he spoke the truth. He would force her. If he could. She fought the urge to shrink away from him.

"You don't understand," she said. "I spent a year in the death realms, enslaved to demons and death magic. When Mac brought me to Annwyn, I swore I would never kill again."

"A pity, then, that you will have to break your vow."

"No. I won't." She swallowed. "How long do you think you'll be able to keep me hidden? My brother is vastly powerful—more so even than you. When Mac realizes I'm missing—"

"He'll find the message you left on his voice mail. You've told him not to worry. You've decided a few days at a spa in Tuscany will do you a world of good." He mocked her surprise. "What? You've forgotten? How strange."

"That won't work. Not for long."

"I won't need your services for long," he replied. "One

night is all I require. This evening, you'll visit Armand Legrand at his club in the city center. You'll open your thighs and beg him to violate you.

And then you will kill him."

CHAPTER FIVE

Jackson watched Leanna's throat flex. The flutter of her pulse—just *there*, beneath her sweet, tender skin—tormented him. Unbidden, his fangs erupted, the points scraping the inside of his mouth. Damn it all to hell. He'd fed only scant hours before, but now the burning thirst had scraped his throat raw. He was as ravenous as if he'd gone without blood for months.

He had not thirsted for a woman so fiercely in the seventy long years of his self-imposed celibacy.

It would be so easy to drink from her. To nip the rapid pulses at her neck, her wrist, her groin. She would taste like sunshine. And Jackson had been living in darkness for so very long.

Could he allow himself the indulgence? One small sip? Taking Leanna's blood wouldn't dim his own power. Just the opposite—her Sidhe blood, so potent with life essence, would strengthen him. The danger lay in the near-certainty that the bite would lead to more. To physical carnality. Plunging his cock into Leanna's ripe body, breaking his long-held vows, would drain his power. And if she managed to unleash her muse magic on him as well . . .

She could destroy him.

He was heavy with need, the blood pulsing slow and hard in his loins. Leanna rubbed her bare arms, causing the knit fabric of her dress to stretch across her breasts. His eyes followed the movement, his groin tightening. It was too arousing, having her here in his lair. In his bed. He could not let himself forget how very dangerous she was.

She was afraid of him. He had made her so. Part of him— the part that clung to his humanity—hated that fear. The man he'd once been would never have tormented a woman this way. Especially this woman. Once, he'd wanted nothing more than to hold her in his arms and protect her from the sadness that only he seemed to see in her eyes. Perhaps it had been an illusion, after all. Perhaps he'd only dreamed of her vulnerability. But no. When he looked at her now, he saw that the sadness still remained a part of her. He still wanted to banish it.

He was a fool.

He dared not do so much as lay a finger on her. Because even after all the time that had passed, even after what her betrayal had cost him, he still burned for her. If he touched her, it would not stop at that. Decades of waiting, of plotting his vengeance on Legrand, would go up in flames.

With a power born of long, agonizing practice, he battered his sexual hunger into submission. Only when he'd brought his appetite under some semblance of control did he allow himself to look at her.

Her eyes were wide, gray, and utterly horrified.

She licked dry lips and spoke. "You want me to . . . to whore for Legrand? And then . . . kill him with my magic?"

"Don't think of it as killing. Legrand is vampire. He is already dead."

"You want me to destroy him. It amounts to the same thing."

He nodded once, grimly. "Do it, and I will free you."

"Please Jackson, just let me go. Nothing good can come of this."

He averted his eyes. "You won't be alone when you go to him, if that's what you fear. My minions will protect you." He paused and looked back at her. "*I* will protect you."

"But . . . your plan is insane. Even if I did approach Legrand—you forget that Legrand and I both lived in Paris for decades. We never met face-to-face—I wasn't so foolish in those days as to confront him—but he certainly knew of me, and of my muse magic. He would never willingly take me to his bed."

"It will be little trouble for you to fool him. Cast a glamour. Play the human whore. A vamp addict, looking for a blood high."

Her dusky auburn lashes swept downward. "I can't do it, Jackson. I can't break the vows I made in Annwyn. Don't you understand? I swore on Annwyn's tree of life! I swore on my soul!"

"And what of my soul, Leanna? The one you doomed to an eternity of waking death?"

"I wronged you, I know. I'm so sorry for that. If there were any way to undo what I did that night . . . I'd give my life to change the past. But please, don't ask me to kill for you. I can't do it."

His jaw clenched so tightly, pain spiked into his ear. He found himself wanting to pardon her sins, no matter that she was the one who had condemned him to his dark, depraved existence. He summoned the image of Legrand's face, twisted in perverted pleasure, and found the courage to go on. "I'm not asking you to kill Legrand, Leanna. I am commanding you."

"Do you really have that much power, Jackson? I think . . . you're conning me. You can make me have sex with Legrand—I know that much is true. But can you really force me to use my Sidhe magic against him? You're powerful, yes, but are you *that* powerful?"

His gaze narrowed. She was too astute. It was true, Sidhe magic was not like human magic. He was not certain any vampire could control Sidhe magic, no matter how strong his powers of mesmerism.

"Even if I were willing to help you," she went on. "I doubt if my magic could kill a creature as old as Legrand. He must be hoarding several millennia of life essence. Too much for my magic to drain completely."

"Then there's the solution to your moral dilemma," Jackson said evenly. "You needn't kill Legrand. All you need to do is weaken him, and I will gladly finish him off." He placed his palms on the edge of the bed and leaned toward her. "You owe me that, at least, Leanna."

He was all too aware a note of supplication had crept into his voice, and he hated it. Almost as much as he hated the thought of Leanna giving her body to Legrand. But God help him, with her help, it could be over tonight. Legrand could be dust by the time the sun rose. He was willing to sacrifice anything for that boon.

Scant inches separated his lips from her skin. He could hear her Sidhe blood, so strong, so sweet, so alive, pulsing through her veins. He wanted it. He wanted *her*.

She regarded him with shadowed eyes. Slowly, she unfolded her body from its defensive pose. When she rose on her knees and reached for him, placing one small hand on his forearm, he flinched.

"I can . . . imagine . . . what you suffered at Legrand's hands. And now you want vengeance. I understand the desire for vengeance, Jackson, more than you know. But revenge won't make you whole. It would be better just to walk away. You escaped Legrand's influence years ago—why have you stayed in his territory all this time? Why not go home, to Boston? Why not forget Legrand, and make a new life?"

"Run, like a beaten dog? I think not."

"Don't think of it as defeat. Think of it as the start of a new life. You could come with me to Scotland. Legrand's influence doesn't reach as far as the Highlands. You would be safe there."

Safe? In a world that included Legrand? It was not possible. The vampire master had burned his putrid essence into the marrow of Jackson's soul. The pain, the humiliation, the insanity of being slave to that monster would never fade. The horror of Jackson's first kill, the shame he felt in draining and using the victim Legrand had chosen, the sexual perversions he had forced on innocents—and those that

Legrand had forced on him—the rancid memories of what he'd been would never leave him. He was tainted, dirty. Sometimes his rage at what he'd endured, what he'd become, was so profound he wondered how his body could contain it. He would never be clean, never have peace—not as long as Legrand survived.

And then there was Jean-Claude's fate to consider. Jackson could not have loved a son of his own flesh more. Solange's husband had been taken by Legrand's minions. Had they killed him? Or was Jean-Claude even now suffering the same horrors Jackson had endured as a newly turned vampire? He couldn't rest until he knew.

"I vowed to destroy Legrand," he said quietly. "I will use any weapon at my disposal. Even you, Leanna."

"Oh, Jackson." Her disappointment made him feel unclean. "It doesn't have to be like that."

She rose from the bed. Her hips swayed—seductive, hypnotic. She moved toward him, releasing tendrils of life magic. They felt like warm, fresh air. Like sunshine.

He clenched his fists so he wouldn't reach for her.

She stepped close, raising her slender arms and linking them around his neck. Her head tilted back. Her scent filled his nostrils. Green grass in the sun. A clear, sparkling stream, diamond light reflecting on the water. White clouds, floating on a blue sky. All the things he would never see again.

He could hear her heart beating. The organ pumped swiftly, propelling life blood through her veins. He wanted to taste it, drink deep, take it into his body and into his soul. But if he did, he'd lose himself, his hard-won strength. And Legrand would win.

Before he quite knew what she intended, she went up on tiptoe and kissed him.

"No—" The protest died in his throat as she pressed her body against his—her softness melting into the hard planes of his chest, his stomach, his thighs. The sensation was like a drug, clouding his mind and his purpose. Her thighs cradled his rampant erection. Her siren seduction called. Ruin raced toward him at light speed. He couldn't turn away.

He was lost to Leanna's magic.

Again.

CHAPTER SIX

Jackson's low curse reverberated in Leanna's ear. Her body responded with a need so great, it was impossible to hold back her magic. She tightened her arms around his neck. Rubbed her breasts against his chest. She wanted to crawl inside his skin. Gods help her, she craved the death magic that kept the flames of his existence burning.

"That young witch. Solange. Is she your lover?" she whispered against his neck.

He stiffened, and drew back. "God, no. Solange is like a daughter to me. Her grandfather—a powerful sorcerer—was my steward for nearly fifty years. Solange assumed the role when he died."

"She's so young."

"Another of my many sins. I shouldn't have allowed her to become my steward. The danger is far too great. My defection angered Legrand—he's been hunting me for over seventy years. But Solange was a powerful witch, even at eighteen, and she knew the risks. She would not accept my refusal. But I was very glad when Jean-Claude joined us."

"Jean-Claude?"

"A young sorcerer I encountered in Marseilles. I got him out of a tight spot with Legrand. In gratitude, he pledged his service to me. When he and Solange fell in love, I was content. I knew Jean-Claude would protect her with his life." He swallowed. "And he did. Three months ago, when Legrand's minions attacked, Jean-Claude made sure Solange escaped to safety. But he himself was taken."

"Is he dead?"

"Dead, or worse. He could be vampire now. I don't know. If so, Legrand's death will free him from slavery, at least. But he is no longer the husband Solange knew. What woman wants to be wed to a monster?"

"If she loves him, it won't matter," Leanna said.

"You cannot know that."

"I can." She drew a breath. "I know because . . . it doesn't matter to me."

"It should."

She cupped the side of his face "Jackson . . ."

"Leanna, no." He covered her hand, his eyes flaring dark.

"Jackson, I know you despise my magic. With good cause. But if you believe anything, believe me when I tell you that I would never turn it against you. Please, don't push me away. If . . . if I'm to help you, if I'm to whore for you . . ."

His grip tightened. "Then you agree? You will use your muse magic against Legrand?"

She closed her eyes and offered a silent prayer for forgiveness to all the gods in Annwyn. Jackson's heady vampire power overwhelmed her senses. The scent of death was like a drug. She'd tried to suppress her craving since emerging from Hell a year ago—had even, for a time, succeeded. But now, with Jackson in her arms, with his death magic wrapping her like a soft, dangerous cloak, she was ready to abandon her soul. To Jackson. He was everything she'd rejected in Annwyn. And everything she desired, right here and right now.

She loved him.

"I'll try to drain Legrand," she said. "But, Jackson, before I do, I need . . . I need to be with *you*, first."

He jerked backward. "No. That's not possible."

She tried to hide her dismay at his swift rejection. "You don't trust me. You think I'm going to betray you . . ."

"No. That's not it." He straightened, taking another step

back and shoving his hands in his pockets. "Listen to me, Leanna. We cannot have sex."

Her gaze dropped to where the fabric of his trousers was drawn tight over his erection. Her lips curved.

"Yes," she said softly. "Yes, we can."

His lips drew back, revealing fully extended incisors. His eyes bled midnight darkness. A wave of numbness swept over her mind.

"Be careful what you ask for, Leanna. Sex with a vampire invariably ends in blood."

"I want that, too, Jackson." Gods help her, it was true. Like the most pathetic addict, she craved his bite. She wanted to belong to him in every way possible.

"You don't know what you're saying. I'm not the man you knew in Paris. I'm not a man at all. I'm a monster."

"I don't care. I want you. As you are."

"Hell."

He yanked his hands from his pockets and advanced on her so quickly she had no chance at retreat. Gripping her shoulders, he dragged her body against his. His arms wrapped her like a vise.

She went very still as he lowered his head, his lips grazing her neck. He nipped at her. His fangs scraped, but didn't break her skin.

"You should not want me, Leanna. You don't know what I have become."

"Show me, then."

He hesitated. Then, with a low growl, he gathered her dress in his hands, yanking the fabric up to her waist. Cold hands roamed her heated skin. When he explored between her thighs, she moaned at the contact. She was slick, so ready for him. He grunted, a low, guttural sound, barely human. For the first time, waves of trepidation overtook Leanna. She swiftly banished her doubts. This was Jackson. She had to believe he wouldn't hurt her. When his hand moved again, she parted her legs.

Moving. Turning. Falling. Somehow she ended up with her spine pressed to the bed. Jackson stood over her, his handsome face shadowed—strained—filling her vision. She lifted her arms to him. He didn't move. He held himself rigid at the foot of the bed, holding himself apart from her. His breathing was ragged. His hands were fisted, his knuckles white.

She stared up at him, panting, needing, wanting him so badly. She was ready to do anything for him, even damn her own soul. He stood over her, motionless, his gaze so hot and desperate it seared her skin.

His body trembled. He wanted her, she knew, though perhaps he didn't want to need her. *I love you,* she longed to say. But she knew he'd never believe it. And so she lay still, and silent, as he held himself apart and devoured her with his eyes.

His gaze lit a trail of fire down her body, pausing at her most sensitive spots. Every pulse point became a throbbing center of pleasure. Her neck, her wrists, the inside of her elbows. The back of her knees. The crease at the top of her thighs. The dark place between her legs.

The aching sensations pulsed together, lifting her, opening her. It took a moment for her to realize that as much as she wanted him, this blissful torment wasn't entirely natural. It was magic. Dark magic. Jackson was creating this dark need, this humiliating want, this craving to debase herself in dark surrender. It was, after all, what vampires did.

Her gaze jerked to his. The vulnerability she'd thought she'd glimpsed there had vanished. A chill cascaded down her spine.

He smiled grimly. "This is what I am, Leanna. Unliving. Unfeeling. I take what I want. I give death in return."

A terrifying wave of longing swept over her. Death magic. How she craved it. Her stomach turned sour. The sensations Jackson was forcing on her had nothing to do with love, and everything to do with power. The lust tearing through her body was no different than the degrading craving that any vampire addict experienced, in any seedy back room of any vampire club in any city in the world. Need. Addiction. Humiliation. Complete and utter surrender.

She'd wanted to believe what she felt for Jackson was different. Once, they'd shared a great love. But that was in the past. Right now, Jackson was not even bothering to provide the illusion of love that most vampires cultivated for their victims. His eyes were hard. Blank, and bitter. The eyes of a predator, a creature of death.

Leanna felt ill.

She tried to close her legs. He wouldn't allow it. Her hips, riding on the wave of his death magic, lifted toward him. Her body was weeping for him, wanting him inside. Craving death. Craving *him*. The man he once had been; the man she loved.

The man she had killed. And yet, she could not bring herself to believe that man was completely gone.

The wet silk of her thong felt raw against the dark, building pleasure. Grim satisfaction shone in Jackson's eyes. "Do you see now, Leanna? This is what I am. How does it feel, to surrender control of your body, your mind, your very soul, to a vampire?"

"Like heaven," she whispered. "Like heaven and hell, together."

"Damn you . . ."

Pleasure fell on her body like a jailer's whip. Jackson flogged her with bliss, over and over. There was nothing but shame in this kind of punishment, but the deeper Leanna fell, the less she cared. Wicked yearning pounded her, drenched her, pulled her apart. She was the shore to Jackson's angry ocean. She did not try to resist. The shore did not run from the sea.

The tide of sensation lifted her, tossed her, used her. She writhed, her palms flat on the mattress near her hips, as if someone held them pinned. All the time she kept her eyes open, staring up at Jackson.

He still hadn't so much as laid a finger on her.

His breathing was harsh. Beads of sweat formed on his forehead, ran down his face. His fangs shone in the faint light. She had never seen anything so beautiful.

She was close to climax, so close, but the peak eluded her. "Jackson. Please. Touch me. Come inside me."

His jaw clenched so tightly she thought it would snap. A vein pulsed in his temple. Yearning—deep, elemental longing—flashed in his eyes.

"Damn you," he repeated. "Damn you to Hell."

He moved, but not to touch her. He tore open his own trousers instead. His cock sprang, red and huge, into his hand. He gripped it so hard Leanna was sure he'd caused himself pain. But the harsh moan that tore from his throat told of a different kind of agony.

She watched him stroke himself. For her. The thought ratcheted up her own arousal. Her hips canted forward. Her gasps mingled with his ragged breath. The sight of his self-pleasure, the hard planes of his body, the taut lines of his face as he milked his shaft, was so beautiful, beyond erotic. But gods, how she wanted him closer.

And then he was kneeling over her, on the bed. So close. Bliss.

He stroked himself with one hand, touched her with the other. He explored her body almost angrily, igniting fire on her skin. She tried to reach for him. He held himself back: her fingers clutched air. She arched her spine, offering her body. He kneaded her breasts, clawed past her belly, ground the heel of his hand into her mound. Slipped cool fingers inside her.

It was too much. Her orgasm shattered, a dam blown apart by a swollen river. Jackson's body went tense; his shout fell on her ears. His seed spurted, bathing her thighs.

It was dead seed. Seed that would never grow.

But somehow, the wet heat of it felt like new life.

CHAPTER SEVEN

The shout that erupted from Jackson's lips at the instant of his release was equal parts bliss and rage. The orgasm—his first in nearly three-quarters of a century—ripped through his brain with the vicious strength of a ravening beast. Seven decades of ruthless self-control, obliterated in one long groan of ecstasy.

Seven decades of hoarded power seeped through the rapidly widening cracks in the shield of death magic he'd constructed around his soul.

He looked down at Leanna. Her beautiful face bore an expression of pure wonder. His dead heart clenched, painfully. Life, love, purpose—had he thought a century of death had erased the memory of those things? Had obliterated his feelings for this woman? It had not. He'd loved Leanna. And—God help him—he loved her still. And he would destroy himself on her altar, once again.

He felt his power slipping away through the bliss. The sensation snapped him back to the present. Wrenching his mind from the blinding pleasure, he clamped down on his liberated emotions, pulling back whatever power he could reach. Some of it was already irretrievable. He wouldn't escape this encounter unscathed. How much had he lost? A year's potency? Ten years? More? He'd doomed himself to another decade of waiting and hiding. Because he knew now that he could never go through with his plan to use Leanna as his weapon.

Caught as he was between the sharp edge of pleasure and the sickening knowledge of what he'd lost, Jackson didn't notice the trembling of the cavern walls until Leanna's startled cry jerked his attention back to his surroundings. A loud crack split the air. A chunk of rock, then a shower of pebbles and grit, rained down all around.

Leanna coughed, scrambling upright, shoving her dress down. "Gods. The roof—"

Jackson looked up and saw cracks, lengthening and widening before his eyes. "Son of a—"

He grabbed Leanna's arm and yanked her off the bed. An instant later, a section of the catacomb ceiling crashed onto the mattress where they'd lain just seconds before. He lost control of their backward momentum; they landed together on the carpet in a tangle of limbs. Instinctively, he rolled, sheltering Leanna with his body as more debris cascaded from the shattered ceiling.

Something struck his arm, clung, and burned. Biting back a curse, his eyes shot toward the pain. He expected to see flames, but his arm wasn't on fire at all.

It was bathed in sunlight.

His gaze jerked upward. Blue sky gaped through a yawning hole in the catacomb ceiling. The edges of the gap were still crumbling, admitting even more destructive light. Jackson lay at the edge of a brilliant pool of daylight.

"Damnation." He scrambled out of the sun's path, dragging a senseless Leanna with him. Her eyes were closed. Blood trickled from a gash on her forehead. He froze for an instant, staring at the jagged crimson line. He wanted, more than anything, to drag his tongue through that wet stream of life.

Instead he forced himself to crawl to darkness. Once clear of the sun, Jackson sat for a moment, cradling Leanna in his lap, breathing through the pain of his burned arm. His eyes were drawn backward, toward the glorious shaft of light he'd fled. It pierced the gloom of the catacomb like an avenging angel's sword. Swirls of white dust danced on the blade.

Apprehension bled into his gut. Solange had been above ground, guarding his sanctuary. If the cave-in had been natural, she would have already appeared in the light, looking for him. That she had not was a very bad sign.

He would have given much to have been able to leap into the sun and call to his steward. But that was impossible. He cursed his impotence. He could feel his face reddening, just from the ambient light. His wounded arm burned. His eyes stung.

Even worse was how the sun had churned his emotions. The kiss of sunlight had stripped his soul bare. He felt as weak and naked as a newly made vampire, cowering in agony before a single slender candle.

The memory of Legrand's laughter echoed in his skull. Legrand had enjoyed his slave's suffering.

Don't think of the past. Think of here and now.

His arms tightened on the woman in his arms.

"Leanna?"

No answer; she was still unconscious. He half carried, half dragged her farther from the light. The movement woke her. Thank the gods. Her eyelids fluttered open.

She focused on his face with dazed eyes. "What . . . happened?"

"The catacomb ceiling caved in. A chunk of it hit you on the head."

"I feel . . . dizzy."

"Don't worry. I'll take care of you." Jackson's knees shook as he rose; he was grateful his legs didn't buckle entirely. Slogging through rubble, he made his way toward the tapestry that formed the far wall of his ruined sanctuary. If he could just get to the other side, where the sun couldn't follow, he might be able to quell his rising panic long enough to consider his next move.

He feared Legrand's human minions had engineered the cave's collapse. Had the bastards harmed Solange? Had they taken her? He couldn't bear the thought. And what of Enzo and Gunter? Jackson's vampires were stationed deeper in the catacomb. They should have been at his side by now. Unless they'd met with an attack of their own.

He shoved the tapestry aside with one shoulder and ducked behind it. His blood froze at the sound of a harsh Gallic voice. Jackson went rigid, his eyes fixed on the figure stepping from the shadows.

"*Bonjour*, Monsieur Cabot." A glint of white teeth accompanied the greeting. "At last, I have cornered the rabbit in his lair. He now faces the sharp jaws of the fox. The master will be most pleased."

Jackson's jaw clenched. "Xaviere."

Legrand's deputy advanced. Xaviere was a tall, skeletal vampire, almost as old as his master. Sharp nails tipped his bony fingers. Another step and his face came into view.

He was as ugly as Jackson remembered.

Leanna twisted in his arms. He lowered her to the ground gently, setting her on her feet.

"Go. Escape. He can't follow you into the light."

She didn't move.

Xaviere's small eyes flicked over Leanna, then returned to Jackson. The vampire smiled thinly.

"You are surprised, *mon ami*, that I would hunt you while the sun shines? Ah, but you should not be. Night has not provided good hunting where you are concerned. You are far too clever for your tender years. But your minions . . . the two in the tunnels? They are young and foolish. And now they are . . . gone."

"You lie."

"Do I?" Xaviere opened his fist. A slow stream of ash poured through his fingers.

Jackson caught a fleeting whiff of Gunter's scent, then Enzo's. He closed his eyes briefly on a surge of grief.

"Your young steward on the surface, she is cleverer," the vampire continued. "But not, more's the pity, clever enough. She gave her best, but . . ." His shoulders lifted and fell. "*C'est la vie*, no? Or perhaps, more accurately . . . *c'est la mort*?"

Jackson felt ill. "You will pay, Xaviere."

Xaviere's fangs flashed. "I think not, *mon jeune ami*. But I tell you this: your servant fought bravely and died nobly, protecting her master. But do not worry. She is not gone forever. She will wake soon, in the master's presence. Legrand will enjoy her reunion with the vampire who was once her husband—"

Jean-Claude. "You bastard," Jackson spit.

"Come now, Cabot. Do you not weary of this game? You cannot win. You cannot hide from Legrand forever. Sooner or later, he will drive you to your knees." The vampire laughed. "You have been there before. If you beg sweetly and perform well, the master may tolerate your continued existence."

Jackson barely heard the taunts. His mind burned with the image of Solange, drained of blood, helpless, enslaved. All because of her loyalty to Jackson. Why had he allowed her to serve him? He should have sent her away when her grandfather died.

But he had not.

Leanna touched his arm. He felt her surge of empathy. He didn't want to turn, didn't want to look at her. Would his pride, his pitiful craving for human contact, destroy her as it had Solange? Damn it, why wouldn't she run? He angled his body, shielding her from Xaviere's view.

The vampire's amused gaze slipped to a spot below Jackson's waist. Belatedly, Jackson realized his trousers were still undone from his encounter with Leanna. With a muttered curse, he jerked up the zipper.

Xaviere's teeth glinted. "I admit, I did not expect you to be . . . entertaining . . . when I came for you. Did you imagine your sanctuary to be inviolate? Your power may be far beyond what a vampire of your years should wield, Cabot, but soon you will know your rightful place. Legrand will render you weak as a cub."

"Legrand can go to Hell."

"Undoubtedly, he will. Eventually. But not, I think, today. Today belongs to you." Xaviere paced a step closer. "You may believe yourself to be a match for me, but I am far older, far stronger. Your game is up, Cabot. I am here to crush you."

And he just might succeed. Jackson struggled to mask the deadening fatigue dragging at his limbs. His knees were trembling. The orgasm had drained his magic. How much, he could not be sure. But one thing was certain. Xaviere had made note of his adversary's weakness. A small smile played on the vampire's lips.

Jackson contemplated his chances of surviving a duel with the vampire. Xaviere was not as powerful as Legrand. An hour before, Jackson would have defeated the deputy. Now he wasn't sure he could hold his own.

As if sensing the direction of his thoughts, Leanna stepped from behind him to stand at his side. Xaviere's cool gaze slid over her.

"A Sidhe," he said. "How interesting. The master will enjoy draining her."

The taunt snapped Jackson's control. He lunged at the vampire's sneering face. The sudden attack caught Xaviere by surprise. Jackson slammed the vampire's skull into the wall behind him. His fingers found Xaviere's throat and squeezed.

But the precious seconds of advantage didn't last. Cursing, Xaviere threw Jackson back. Jackson kept his grip on the vampire's throat, dragging Xaviere with him. The pair staggered in a grotesque dance, spinning, then lurching heavily against a free-hanging tapestry. The billowing carpet broke their fall.

Jackson grabbed one edge of the heavy rug as he fell. The tapestry tore from its ceiling hooks, falling amid a shower of dusty grit. Jackson went down. Xaviere fell atop him. The vampire's knee cracked against Jackson's sternum, driving the air from his lungs.

Jackson choked as his foe sprang to his feet. Xaviere grabbed the front of Jackson's shirt, lifting him, one-handed, into the air. With a brutal heave, he flung Jackson in the direction of the sunlight.

Jackson grabbed the edge of a table just in time to halt his deadly forward momentum. The heavy furniture toppled; Jackson ducked behind it. As he dropped to his knees, he caught a glimpse of Leanna, scrambling over the debris piled atop his shattered bed. She entered the light. Her pale dress shone like an angel's robe.

Go, he urged silently. *Escape.*

She paused near the gap in the cavern roof. She was a short jump to freedom—why was she stopping?

An instant later, Jackson understood. Two hulking figures were climbing through the opening, framed by daylight. Legrand's human minions. Leanna hadn't been bent on escape. God in heaven. She was defending Jackson.

She uttered a stream of words in a strange language. It sounded like a battle cry. Her fingers traced a pattern in the air. Elfshot exploded. A man's howling cry told Jackson she'd hit her mark. His large body fell, impacting the cavern floor with a resounding thud.

Then Xaviere loomed large, blocking Jackson's view of Leanna's battle. The vampire slashed; his claws whistled. Jackson's defensive move didn't come quickly enough. Sharp nails opened a gash on his throat.

Blood spurted; life energy hemorrhaged. Crimson puddled on the cavern floor.

Laughing, Xaviere closed his fingers around Jackson's neck. More blood splashed. Xaviere's claws twisted, and Jackson gagged. Vertebrae in his neck popped.

He pulled desperately at Xaviere's hands. When the iron claws wouldn't bend, he tried to get his own fingers around the vampire's neck. But Xaviere was taller, his arms longer. Jackson couldn't get enough leverage.

Xaviere's eyes flashed dark with satisfaction. "*C'est finis*, Cabot. The end. My only regret is that the master is not here to witness your destruction."

"I'm sure you will console him," Jackson choked out. "I'm sure you will bend over and offer Legrand your—"

He gagged as Xaviere's fist crushed his windpipe. Oxygen

ceased to flow into Jackson's lungs. It was an odd sensation, not breathing. But hardly fatal. A vampire did not need to breathe.

But a vampire did need blood, and Jackson's body was leaking copious amounts of that precious commodity. The edge of his vision went fuzzy. Raw survival instinct kicked in; he lashed out with all his strength. But all his strength wasn't good enough.

Xaviere was stronger. And for that, Jackson had only himself to blame.

He could no longer see Leanna—had she defeated the other human minions and fled to safety? He fervently hoped so. If she was safe, he could die with a measure of peace.

Peace. At last.

He closed his eyes and offered a prayer for his damned soul. He did not think God would hear him, much less answer, but the habits of childhood died hard.

Xaviere's laugh echoed. His grip on Jackson's neck tightened, Jackson's stolen blood pumped into the dirt. There was an odd sound, a ringing in his ears, a strange melody he'd never before heard. Light flashed into his vision.

The end had come. He only hoped it would be swift.

CHAPTER EIGHT

Leanna's spell slammed Xaviere right between the shoulder blades.

It was perhaps the most powerful binding charm she'd ever crafted. The result was swift and supremely satisfying. The vampire's body went rigid. His legs stiffened; his knees locked. His fingers snapped open, and his arms flung wide. He teetered for one long second before toppling, face first, onto the ground.

The bind was a life-magic spell, unable to kill. But with sunlight streaming through the shattered catacomb ceiling and Xaviere unable to move, it would be easy enough to drag him into the light and finish him off. So much for the vows she'd made in Annwyn. Her promises, her good intentions for the future, had gone up in flames. Three of Legrand's human stewards already lay dead. Leanna shoved her guilt to the back of her mind. She'd examine her crimes later.

After she finished committing them.

She scrambled down the pile of rocks on the bed, half sliding, half falling, scraping her shin in her haste to reach Jackson's side. He lay in a puddle of blood, his neck bearing a cruel slash and the deep imprint of Xaviere's fingers. He wasn't breathing, and she couldn't find a pulse. If he were mortal, he'd be dead. But Jackson was vampire. He'd died long ago. The normal rules didn't apply.

Dirt trickled onto her head. Startled, she looked up. A clump of grass—and a dead man's limp arm—hung over the edge of the hole, framed by a patch of blue sky. She held her breath, but there was no shout, no sound other than the distant hum of traffic from the road across the field. But surely there were more of Legrand's minions about.

If she was going to escape, now was the time.

She rejected the thought even as it formed. Jackson had urged her to run, but she had no intention of leaving him. She eyed Xaviere's motionless form. First things first.

Grabbing the vampire's ankles, she tugged his body toward the light. He was heavy; she conjured a spell to assist. Even so, she grunted as she heaved the undead corpse onto the pool of daylight on Jackson's carpet.

Bright sun bathed Xaviere's face. In an instant, his skin reddened to lobster hue, then darkened to the color of fresh blood. Leanna watched in horror as the blistered skin turned black, curled away from the white skull beneath, and crumbled like ash. Muscles and bones deteriorated next, causing shirt and trousers to deflate like a leaking balloon. In the end, all that was left of Xaviere was dust, a puff of smoke, and a sound like a human sigh.

Leanna averted her eyes. She tried to draw air into her lungs; the breath was painful. It was all too easy to imagine Jackson's beautiful body meeting the same horrible end. Turning, she made her way back to his side.

He lay just beyond the farthest reaches of the sun. His normally pale skin was red and blistered. Gods, the sun. The angle of the beam had changed, moving the shaft of light across the floor in Jackson's direction. Hooking her hands under his armpits, she dragged him deeper into the catacombs, scattering debris as she went. Navigating a dim corridor flanked by ancient tombs and moldy corpses, she didn't stop until she'd turned a sharp corner and the sun was no longer visible.

She illuminated the space with a ball of elflight. Immediately, she wished she hadn't. She'd dragged Jackson through piles of broken bones, many marked by rodent teeth. The trail was slick with Jackson's blood. A sheen of white dust coated his clothes and face.

He lay as motionless as a corpse. Panic battered Leanna's ribs; she swallowed it back. Jackson wasn't dead. Or rather, he was dead, but he hadn't left her. A vampire had phenomenal powers of healing, as long as his undead heart remained beating. Jackson would awaken. But when? She sent nervous glances up and down the corridor. More of Legrand's minions could attack at any moment. Living stewards from the surface. Vampires from the depths of the catacombs.

"Jackson."

She laid a hand on the side of his face. His skin was cold. The burn caused by the sun was already fading. She told herself his pallor was a good sign.

"Jackson, can you hear me? Wake up. Please."

No answer, but she thought his chest might have moved. She laid her palm on it and held her breath.

His ribs expanded. Contracted. Ever so slightly. His next inhale was deeper. The next exhale longer. She felt a weak thump against her palm. His heart, still pumping. She watched, stunned, as the raw edges of his neck wound drew together, until the slash was little more than a thin red line.

Leanna released the air from her lungs in a long, heartfelt sigh.

Seconds passed. Jackson's eyelids fluttered open. His eyes were glassy, his gaze uncomprehending. Lines creased his forehead.

"Leanna." He licked his lips. "You're . . . still here." He paused. Swallowed thickly. "Why?"

"Because this is where I want to be. With you."

"Xaviere?"

Leanna drew a sharp breath. "He . . . the sun hit him. He's . . . gone."

"The sun . . . you should have left me. You should have escaped."

She blinked back tears. "I will never escape you, Jackson. Never."

He tried to lift his head, winced, and laid it back down again, stirring a puff of dust.

"Legrand's stewards? On the surface?"

"I . . . killed them."

Some of the tension seeped from Jackson's body. "Good."

"More will come."

"Yes, certainly."

"We have to get out of here. Can you stand, do you think?"

"I can try." Jackson levered himself onto one elbow. His arm shook. "God, I'm weak."

With effort, he shoved himself into a sitting position. Once upright, he put his head between his knees and groaned.

Leanna watched him closely. "Are you all right?"

"Yes. Comparatively speaking. But I'm weak." He looked up at her, his expression pained. "It's been a long time since I felt so drained. Not since the last time I—" He averted his gaze. "It will take some time for me to regain my strength."

"I'll stay with you."

"No, you—" He cut off abruptly. His next words were spoken so quietly she almost missed them. "How many lovers have you had since our time in Paris, Leanna?"

The non sequitur took Leanna aback. Heat rushed to her cheeks. "I . . . I don't know."

He closed his eyes. "Too many to count, I imagine."

It was an accurate assessment. Leanna had had many, many men in the last century. Most had been artists. She'd provided them with magical inspiration; they'd given up their life magic. But somehow, their offerings hadn't made her feel alive. Only Jackson had done that.

"What about you, Jackson? Vampires are hardly famous for their sexual restraint. You must have had hundreds of women in the past century."

"There were many in my early years as a vampire. Legrand chose each one, and I could not refuse. I used them and, more often than not, killed them afterward." His voice sounded infinitely weary. "There is so much blood on my hands, Leanna. A new vampire's craving . . . you cannot imagine how it twists the mind. I would have done anything for blood in those years. Anything. The crimes I committed will land me in Hell for all eternity."

"You had no choice."

"Not at first, no. But then . . . my vampire power started to grow. More and more, I was able to assert my own will. Choose the time, the place, the victim. My crimes became my own. For years, I did not let myself feel the full horror of what I had become. But then, one night, I *did* feel it. And it nearly destroyed me."

"Oh, Jackson."

"Twenty-some years after my turning, I was no better than Legrand's worst minions. And then . . . I found the courage to forge my own path."

"How?"

His eyes fixed on a point beyond her right shoulder. "It was May. I remember that most clearly. Springtime in Paris, with lilacs blooming everywhere. I could see them only at night, of course, when the light was gone and colors muted, but the scent . . . it haunted me. My grandmother had grown lilacs in her garden. It was that spring, when the lilacs were in full bloom, that I received word that she had died."

His lips twisted. "I'd hired an investigator to bring me news of my family. They believed me dead. As indeed I was. I was my grandmother's favorite. She never fully recovered from my loss. The day after I learned of her death, as I slept in Legrand's cellar, I dreamed of her. The image was so vivid. So real. So . . . *alive*. When I woke, I felt almost . . . human. That night, when the time came to roam, to rape . . . I did not. I took blood, yes—I could not reject the bloodthirst without destroying myself. But I drank only a little from each woman, took only as much as I needed. Afterward, I made sure my victim forgot what had happened. But as for my carnal needs—I did not fulfill them. I returned to my coffin at dawn, still wanting."

His laugh was weak. "The next evening I woke much stronger than the evening before. After a month of abstinence, I became a thousand times more powerful. I realized then that sexual energy was a form of life essence—life essence a vampire typically wastes. I wondered if, in repressing my cravings for sex, I could horde that energy, and use it to strengthen my power. All around me, other vampires squandered their sexual essence. Legrand most of all. His vast sexual appetite kept his power from growing, but he did not notice—or perhaps, he didn't care. Legrand is the oldest in Europe—his power was vast, and it had been decades since he'd crushed his final challenger. But that same night, I vowed I would destroy him."

"How long ago was that?"

"Seventy-three years."

"And in all that time—?" Leanna's whispered question hung between them.

"I haven't had a woman. I hadn't even allowed myself release, until today. With you."

Horrified understanding dawned. "And our . . . encounter. Did it drain your power?"

"It did." He grimaced. "And all the blood I've lost hasn't helped matters." His gaze traveled the crimson path on the cavern floor. "It will take some time for me to gather enough energy to leave this place."

"You would heal faster if you drank blood."

He did not meet her gaze. "Yes."

Yes.

How, Leanna wondered, could one spoken word convey such depths of bitterness. Of self-loathing? Of pure self-disgust?

Her heart nearly broke. With that single syllable, Jackson had revealed more of himself and his undead existence than she suspected he'd meant to. He hated what he was. Utterly. And yet there was no escape.

"You have nothing to be ashamed of, Jackson."

"You think not? I beg to differ. Leave me, Leanna. Leave now."

"I'll do no such—" She broke off as a tendril of death magic snaked through the air, lodging in her chest as an uncomfortable pressure. Someone—something—was approaching. She cocked her head, listening. Feeling with her magic. Ominous vibrations traveled from the ground into her body.

Jackson's breath was harsh, his tone urgent. He'd felt the intruder, too. "Vampires. Legrand's minions. They'll be on us soon, Leanna. Turn and run. There's still time for you to escape."

"What about you?"

"I can hold them off until you reach daylight."

"Forget it." Leanna was already on her feet. "When Sidhe don't want to be seen, they're not. I can hide us. They'll never know we're here."

Deftly, she wove the strands of a glamour spell, and cast it around Jackson and herself. Sinking to her knees by his side, she commanded the elflight around them to fade into darkness.

"Don't move," she cautioned. "Don't speak."

She felt Jackson's pride prickle. He didn't want to hide from his enemies; despite his weakened state, he wanted to fight them. She wrapped the magical protection tighter and pressed her body against his. He was so cold. So very cold. Her own heart froze with dread.

Three dark shapes appeared at the end of the passage. Eyes glowing with dark light, they muttered among themselves in French as they made their way toward Jackson and Leanna's hiding place.

"The bastard's got to be here. We've blocked all the exits. Xaviere staked Cabot's two pathetic minions—"

Jackson tensed. Leanna tightened her arms around him.

"There's nowhere for him to hide," a second voice muttered. "We've searched every passage. This one is a dead end."

"And yet . . . he's eluded us. And Xaviere has disappeared as well."

"Perhaps he's captured Cabot."

"And taken him where? Into the light?"

The trio passed within inches of Leanna's right foot, still

muttering. They paused at the turn in the passageway, peering toward the sun. Then the lead vampire jumped back, as if stung.

"Dust," he said. "Ash."

"Cabot?" One of his companions rasped.

The leader advanced a few cautious steps, sniffing the air. A low growl emerged from his throat. "*Merde.* No, not Cabot. Xaviere."

Curses pierced the gloom.

"The master will hold us responsible." Fear was palpable in the rear vampire's rising tone.

"The master may be appeased," the leader muttered, "if we bring Cabot to him."

"But how? The bastard's gone."

"Not far. Look. There's a trail of blood . . ."

Leanna's head jerked up as the vampires approached. She fed the glamour, strengthening the shielding with all her magic. Legrand's minions drew up short, not three steps from their hiding place.

"The blood stops here. Completely."

The leader made a sound of frustration. "What foul magic is this? Damn Cabot. He's slipperier than an eel."

The trio lingered, trading opinions and curses. Eventually, they moved off. Several minutes passed before Leanna dared speak.

"They're gone."

Jackson didn't answer. He shifted away from her, until their bodies were no longer touching. Cautiously, Leanna sparked a glow of elflight within the protection of the glamour.

Jackson sat with his back against the cave wall, his forearms resting on his bent knees. Just above his bowed head, a corpse lay in its tomb. The linen strips binding its skeleton had begun to unravel.

When she met his gaze, what she saw in his eyes wasn't human, but vampire. Her heart stuttered.

Hunger. Stark, raw hunger.

His lips drew back in a snarl, exposing his fangs. She couldn't look away from his gleaming incisors. Couldn't help longing to feel them on her skin. Was it his vampire mesmerism causing the sudden flood of heat between her legs? Or her own craving for death magic?

"Jackson." She swallowed. "What's wrong? What's happening to you? To me?"

His voice was a low rasp. "I warned you to escape while you could. You didn't listen. Being this close to you . . . here in the darkness . . . with thirst clawing at my throat . . ." He swallowed, thickly. "Your blood. I can smell it, Leanna. Did you know that? The scent of it is so sweet . . ."

His exhale was a harsh moan. "Only the thinnest thread of humanity prevents me from sinking my fangs into your sweet neck and draining every last drop of blood from your body. Leave me, Leanna. Flee into the sun. Now, before it's too late."

"No."

The word was on her lips before she even willed it. Even so, she didn't regret it. "I won't go, Jackson. Don't ask me. I'm here for you."

She laid her hand on his chest. His heartbeat was so faint she couldn't feel it. "You don't have to steal my blood. I'm more than willing to give it to you."

"Why debase yourself? I have nothing to offer you but death magic. Obsession. Destruction. You don't want that, Leanna."

"I know what death magic is," Leanna said quietly. "I've practiced death magic. I summoned a demon, an Old One. In my arrogance, I thought I could bend its evil to my will. Instead, I became its slave. My soul is already tainted. A vampire's bite could hardly make it blacker. My blood is yours, Jackson. Take it. Please."

"Leanna—"

He gripped her head between his palms, roughly, and forced her to look at him. What she saw in his eyes made her mouth go dry with terror. He was a death creature. Ravenous. Unforgiving. How could the man she loved live be-hind those dead, burning eyes?

Somehow, she believed he did still live. He had to. She would not accept anything less. She forced herself to speak.

"I love you, Jackson. I always have, and I always will. There's nothing you could do, nothing you could *be*, that would change that."

"Damn it, Leanna. Do you know how many humans I've killed? How many innocents I've turned into undead monsters?"

"No. And I don't want to know. Don't tell me. It doesn't matter. I know who you are."

"Do you? Then you know more than I do."

She touched his cheek. So pale. Tears crowded her eyes. She reached for the man he once had been.

"Do you remember the evening we met?"

He closed his eyes briefly, but she didn't miss the flicker of humanity he tried to hide. "How could I not remember? You were standing at the bottom of the stair. I was coming out of the ballroom. You were surrounded by men, but I did not think you saw any of them. You looked . . . lost."

"No one else noticed how unhappy I was that night. No one cared what I was feeling. Especially not the artists hanging on my every word. They were too busy lusting after my magic. And ogling my bust."

"All I wanted to do was to make you laugh."

Leanna smiled. "And you did."

A reluctant amusement softened his features. "Toppling a waiter carrying a full tray of wineglasses wasn't part of any grand plan to provide for your amusement, I assure you."

"But when the merlot spilled into Mrs. Emerson's cleavage—"

Jackson chuckled. Leanna's heart leapt. "I thanked God and heaven she didn't recognize me," he said. "She would have written my father. He would have demanded I cease my foolishness and return to Boston."

As quickly as Leanna's elation had risen, it fled. Her chest went hollow. "You never did go home. Because of me."

His smile faded. "Because I fell in love with you. I wanted to stay by your side. Make you laugh, for as long as you wanted."

"A part of me wanted that, too. I loved you so very much."

"Did you really, Leanna? For a time I thought that might be true. During that long summer, every time I made you laugh. Every time we made love. And that night I painted your portrait."

Gods. Her portrait.

He paused, his throat working. "That painting is here in Rome. It hangs in the Galleria Nazionale. Did you know?"

"No, I didn't," Leanna said quietly. "But I'm not surprised. It was a true masterpiece."

"But it wasn't my masterpiece. It was your magic that created that portrait."

"It was what you came to Paris for, wasn't it? To create a work of great genius?"

"It was, until Paris showed me that what I thought was my great talent was in reality nothing more than dabblings of a dilettante. But then I met you, and it didn't matter. All I wanted was your love."

"My love wasn't the prize you thought it was," Leanna said sadly. "My feelings for you—they were too frightening. I couldn't quite make myself believe you weren't lusting after the inspiration my magic could provide. I forced myself to treat you as I did the others. I told myself that if you accepted my magic, if you painted a true masterpiece, it meant you didn't truly love me." She paused. "And you did paint that masterpiece, Jackson."

He stared at her, clearly stunned. "That is why you left me?"

She nodded.

"Ah, Leanna. If only I had known, I would have burned that canvas to ashes."

"I'm not sure even that would have convinced me. No

man had ever wanted me for myself. Only for my magic, and my body. Even my own father . . ." She blinked back hot, shameful tears. "I couldn't imagine anything different."

Jackson shut his eyes and did not answer. His breathing had roughened, she noted with some alarm. And his hands—they were shaking. His face had gone white as chalk. When he opened his eyes, it was clear his vision had lost its focus.

"You're getting weaker," Leanna said, dread curdling in her stomach. "You need blood. Take mine, Jackson. Please."

He wet his lips with his tongue. "Don't . . . don't tempt me."

"Why not? There's no danger. Sidhe can't turn vampire."

"But they can die. I thirst . . . so strongly. I could suck you dry in an instant."

She shifted so she was kneeling in front of him, and took his hands in hers. "You won't. I trust you."

His hands found her waist, his fingers flexing. "You shouldn't, Leanna. God knows I don't trust myself."

"Then I'll trust enough for both of us."

He tensed—she thought he would push her away. Then his fingers bit into her waist.

She leaned into his embrace and brushed her lips across his. "Jackson . . ."

"Leanna, don't."

She ignored his plea. Opening her mouth, she ran her tongue along the seam of his lips. When she licked the point of his fang, a profound shudder washed through him.

With a surrendering moan, he dragged her into his lap. Her arms encircled his neck. She pressed her body flush against his, her breasts squashed against his chest, her legs straddling his thighs. He was cold, so cold. She wanted more than anything to give him all the fire, all the life, in her soul.

His kisses sent drugging pleasure into her veins. Vampire magic? Or was she addicted to the man himself? His hands roamed her body, molding her breasts, cupping her arse, dragging up the hem of her dress. She felt his cool palm on the heated skin of her inner thigh.

She kissed a fervent line along his jaw, then scraped her cheek against his stubbled chin, stretching her neck, making herself vulnerable. He inhaled sharply as the point of his incisors scraped her throat's pulse. His erection pressed, hard and insistent, against her hip. A wave of aching lust took her breath. Her blood coursed in her veins, for him. Only for him.

The wanting cut like a knife. It sliced at her soul, carving it into thousands upon thousands of yearning pieces. And more. It was as if Jackson had released every atom from her body, allowing them to float free, into the atmosphere. And then had recaptured and enslaved every particle of her being.

He cursed, his voice hoarse. "Leanna. You don't want this. You can't—"

Not want it? At that moment, she would have willingly died for his bite. She gasped a sound that was half laugh, half moan.

"Gods, Jackson, I want you more than I want my next breath. Do it, Jackson. For you. For me."

For a long, heart-stopping moment, she thought he'd master his need of her. Perhaps it was a sign of how much the battle with Xaviere had cost him that his resistance lasted only a few heartbeats. Then his big body shook. She felt the damp of tears on her cheek.

She laid her hand on his head, threading her fingers through his hair.

He kissed her neck.

"Leanna."

He exhaled her name, his voice slipping into dark bliss. His body sank into his bite. His teeth stung, but the pain was gone almost before she'd felt it.

The pull of his lips on her neck roused a shifting, writhing emotion in her heart. His teeth seated themselves more deeply in her flesh. Her response was a tide of sensation, unlike anything she'd ever known.

Pleasure. She'd expected that, of course. If vampires weren't masters of pleasure, humans wouldn't sell their souls for the privilege of submitting to undead fangs. The bliss was intense, but not unmanageable. She knew pleasure. She'd had it in so many ways, for so many years, from so many men, in light and in darkness.

But pleasure was only the beginning.

There was fear, too. A building sense of panic that somehow only augmented the erotic suction of Jackson's bite. Fear for her life, as blood pumped from her heart into his body. She felt as though her soul were traveling with it.

She couldn't move. Like a plump fly caught in a spider's jaw, she was paralyzed. He could see into her soul, into her mind, into her darkest desires. She was vulnerable to whatever he chose to take from her. Or to give.

But she could not see into his soul, his mind, his desire.

The one-sided intimacy he forced on her was nearly unbearable. Leanna was skilled in hiding the essential aspects of her soul. She was used to separating her mind from her body when her emotions became too intense to face. She'd learned the technique as a girl just entering womanhood. It was the only way to endure her human father's hands on her body.

For years, even after she'd come into the fullness of her Sidhe power and fled the Highlands, her sordid adolescence had colored every interaction she'd had with men. She'd never revealed her true soul to her lovers. She'd always remained hidden.

But now, with Jackson, she couldn't hide. He'd stripped her bare, laid out her soul in the sunlight for his leisurely perusal. For his complete possession. Jackson's vampire bite did more than touch her soul. It shredded it. Inhaled it. Consumed it.

And all she could do was accept it.

The bite seemed to stretch on and on, pleasure and pain

spinning into eternity. She felt her blood flowing into him. It was an exquisite sensation. If he lost control, if he drained her, she wouldn't even protest. When he pulled back at last, she cried out, and tried to prevent him from leaving her.

The room swayed. She'd lost her hold on the elflight, and the spell had begun to flash like a strobe. Jackson's handsome face flickered in and out of darkness. His fangs, tinged with her blood, glinted. She licked her own lips, almost expecting to taste it.

His eyes focused on the slight movement, going dark and darker still. They were now so black she thought she might plunge into their velvet depths and never emerge.

His lids lowered. Finally, she managed to draw a breath. Then he bent his head, his lips again seeking her neck.

She arched to receive him. But the sting didn't come. His tongue flicked gently over her wound, the only sensation a pleasant tingle. The lingering pain of the puncture disappeared. When she brought her fingers to her neck, she felt only unbroken skin.

His tone was self-mocking. "This is when I usually wipe a victim's memory along with her wound. I could do the same to you, if you'd like."

"No," Leanna whispered, blushing. A part of her desperately wanted to erase those agonizing seconds of raw vulnerability, but the thought of Jackson remembering, while she forgot, was too much to bear. "No, please don't."

He nodded and stood, propping one shoulder against a solid section of wall between two tiers of tombs, his back half turned to her. Leanna drew her legs up to her chest, hugging them. Watching him. As the seconds ticked by, she became more aware of her body. Oddly, she didn't feel dirty and drained, as a vampire's victim usually did after a bite. Instead she felt . . . clean. Calm.

Almost peaceful.

"Did . . . did you take enough? I thought you might have . . . stopped too quickly."

He glanced down at her, and then away.

"I took what I needed. You have Sidhe blood, after all."

From his tone, she couldn't tell if that was a good thing. Slowly, she stood.

"Is Sidhe blood a problem?"

"Far from it. Your blood is much more alive than a full human's." He exhaled and turned, pressing his shoulder blades flat against the cave wall. "That sip from your veins . . . I think it replaced most of what I'd lost before, when we . . ." He trailed off.

She blushed. "I'm glad." A thought occurred to her. "Will another sip make you even stronger? Strong enough to destroy Legrand? I'll . . . I'm willing to give you more of my blood, Jackson. Whatever you need."

"No, Leanna."

The finality of his tone chilled her to the bone. "But—"

"You won't give me anything more. Not blood, not comfort, not aid." He dragged a hand over his face and she realized he was shaking. He gestured toward his groin. Leanna took in the size of the bulge in his pants and drew a sharp breath.

He laughed, crudely. "Do you honestly think I could drink more from your sweet neck without ripping that pitiful scrap of a dress right off your body? Without wrenching your thighs open and plunging inside? Without pounding myself inside you, using you, defiling you, until long after you scream for me to stop?"

The raw erotic images his words painted in her mind nearly buckled her knees. She couldn't seem to gasp enough air.

"I wouldn't beg for you to stop, Jackson. I'd beg for you to make it last forever."

His lips pressed together briefly, as if in pain. When he spoke, his eyes were flat and dead, and his voice was low. His words vibrated with ruthless resolve.

"You don't know what you're saying. You don't know what it would mean, being chained to me for eternity. That is, if you even survived my lust. You cannot imagine how close I am to losing all control. That is why you are going to turn around, and walk into the light behind the tapestry. You will climb into the sun and go back to your life. And you will not look back."

"No, I won't. I—"

"I don't need you any longer. Leanna. And I don't want you, either."

His words hurt. She told herself that they were lies, that he was protecting her the only way he knew. Somehow, that didn't make the pain of his rejection any easier to bear.

"If I go, what will you do?"

He didn't answer.

"You're going to confront Legrand, aren't you? You're going to challenge Europe's master. Tonight, as soon as the sun sets. Even though you know you're not really sure you're strong enough to win. And you won't take more of my blood, when you know it would give you the advantage."

"Leanna . . . don't. I feel my strength returning . . . Perhaps I'm even stronger than before I came to your hotel room. I believe I can defeat Legrand. Leave, Leanna. You've given me what I need."

"It's not enough. Jackson, don't turn me away now. I want to help you."

"You've helped me enough already." His eyes seemed to soften.

"I want to help more! Just hours ago, you were ready to force me to fight Legrand."

"That was before I realized I—" Abruptly, he crossed his arms. "That was before, when I was angry. My rage seems to have burned itself out. Now, I want only for you to leave me. Now, Leanna. I won't have your life on my conscience."

"That's your pride speaking."

"Pride?" He laughed. "Hardly. I lost whatever pride I once had long ago. Guilt, perhaps? Now that, I admit, I have in abundance." A shadow crossed his features. "Solange—she was above ground, guarding my lair. Now she's been taken. Killed. As Jean-Claude was." His shoulders slumped. "They are vampire now. I've failed both of them. I won't rest until I free them from Legrand's clutches."

"Which is exactly why you need my help! What good will it do if you die trying to rescue them?"

"Die? You forget, Leanna." His eyes went flat. "I'm already dead."

CHAPTER NINE

Not six months earlier, Leanna had sworn on the sacred silver branches of Annwyn's ancient tree of life that she would never kill again.

Unfortunately, she'd broken her sacred oath. She'd killed Legrand's human minions. She'd destroyed Xaviere. And it had felt good to kill that monster. She repressed a shudder. What did that say about her soul? She wasn't willing to stop and think about it. There was more killing yet to accomplish.

The sun had all but set, casting long shadows into the dense warren of medieval buildings that formed Rome's historic center. Emerging from a twisting alley into a blaze of light, Leanna paused. Piazza Navona buzzed with activity—mimes and magicians, café chatter, peddlers selling their wares. Tourists, mostly, but a few locals, as well. No one noticed she was dressed like a whore; a strong glamour shielded her from prying eyes. Careful of her spiked heels on the uneven cobbles, Leanna picked her way across the piazza, drawn by its central fountain. Maybe the life magic of the cascading water would dampen her rising anxiety.

It didn't.

Clasping her small evening bag to her stomach, she stared at the fountain's sculpted figures. She'd forgotten, she'd been here just a week ago with Kalen and Christine. She stared at the nearest sculpture, a man lying on his side, one arm upraised as if shielding his eyes from the church facade looming above him. Kalen had explained that the fountain's sculptor had been a rival of the church's architect, and had sculpted this figure to mock his adversary. At the time, she'd barely given the story a thought. Now, the long-dead artist's contempt for his rival, frozen in stone for eternity, chilled her to the bone.

Hate could last so very, very long.

She thought of her last glimpse of Jackson, before she'd finally obeyed him, turning and climbing out of the catacombs without a backward glance. His eyes had been flat, his jaw rigid. He wouldn't accept her help. He didn't want her blood. He'd closed his mind and his heart to her. His entire being had been focused on his hatred of Legrand.

Yes, hate endured, long after love was gone.

The last rays of the setting sun burnished the piazza's stuccoed buildings to rich amber, then to deep chocolate. As daylight faded, Leanna left the fountain. Slipping around a large group of German tourists, she made her way to an alley at the far end of the piazza.

The passage existed in gloom. Canyonlike walls loomed high on either side. The buzz of the crowd faded as she moved farther into the shadows. After several twists and turns she halted before a doorway framed by a chiseled stone arch. The entrance was unexceptional and bore no sign other than the number 6 etched on a brass plate. The door knocker was fashioned in the shape of a cat's head. The eyes were ruby-red stones, glowing faintly.

For the hundredth time, she wondered if she was doing the right thing, coming alone to this place. She'd dodged her brother and her friends at the hotel, not wanting them to know she'd been with a vampire. Maybe she should have come clean to Mac and begged for his help. But she hadn't been at all sure that he would have given it. Mac despised vampires. Not only would he have refused to enter a vampire club, it was very likely he would have prevented her coming here on her own. She hadn't wanted to chance that.

So she'd slipped into her hotel room under heavy glamour, gathered what she needed, and left the premises, with Mac and the rest none the wiser. Let them believe she was lounging in a Tuscan spa. It was safer that way.

She drew a deep breath, executing a meticulous scan of her glamour magic even though she'd checked it not five minutes earlier. And five minutes before that. Legrand was an Old One; her magic had to be perfect. He would be suspicious of a Sidhe voluntarily seeking out a vampire, and worse, he might even connect her with the Sidhe muse who had once blazed a wide path through the Parisian demimonde. A path that had been littered with the corpses of handsome artists. As she'd told Jackson, she and Legrand had never met face to face, but the vampire master certainly knew of her. And knew what she was capable of.

Steeling herself, she lifted the knocker and let it fall. A thud reverberated in the hollow space beyond.

Mere heartbeats later, the door opened.

The spidery-looking doorman was vampire, recently turned. The youth's jerking, mechanical movements coupled with the wild panic in his eyes told the sordid story. His features were twisted with equal parts hopelessness and revulsion. He was a slave. No—less than a slave. A slave, at least had the hope of escape. A newly made vampire did not.

Leanna struggled to imagine Jackson in the pathetic youth's place. She couldn't. Even flat on his back, drained and wounded, Jackson exuded power. Raw, angry magic. A force that Leanna could almost believe had a chance against Legrand's endless evil.

But she wouldn't take the chance that he might fail.

She crossed over the threshold and brushed past the doorman. He made no protest. She entered a long, dark hallway that narrowed like a funnel. It ended at a linen-draped table. A pallid female vampire flicked undead eyes over Leanna.

Leanna knew what the vamp saw: a beautiful human female with round ears and long blonde hair. Her ample breasts were barely trussed into a lace corset, her lush round arse sparsely covered by a fluttering black skirt. Delicate chains dangling from her garters supported the sheer stockings covering her long, shapely legs. Her stiletto heels were long enough and sharp enough to impale, but—thankfully—the attendant didn't seem unduly concerned.

"Five hundred euros. Cash," was all she said.

Leanna snapped open her clutch and extracted the bills. The vamp snatched the money and, with a jerk of her head, indicated a solid black door.

The doorknob was hot. Leanna's heart pounded as she stepped through the door and closed it behind her. She found herself on the edge of a crowded dance floor, in a room that was almost as dark as Jackson's catacomb. Music vomited from hidden speakers, so loud it seemed as though it was coming from inside Leanna's skull.

Her heart skipped a beat in an effort to match the aberrant rhythm. The notes were laced with death magic, strong enough to make Leanna feel ill. Writhing bodies crammed the dance floor. Human throats stretched for their undead partners. She looked away as an ancient vamp sunk rotting fangs into a teenage girl's neck.

She advanced a few steps, her eyes adjusting to the thick, smoky atmosphere, barely brightened by anemic wall sconces. Someone shoved a glass in her hand. The metallic odor of its contents caused her stomach to spasm. Blood. She looked up to find a pale vamp watching her, his lip stained red. When she caught his gaze, he lifted his glass to her. His lips drew back, exposing his fangs.

She felt her gorge rise.

Turning abruptly, she threaded her way through the crowd, pressing her full glass into the first pair of empty hands she saw. The edges of the room were dark, and darker still where the main space faded into semiprivate alcoves. Human shadows wrestled and pulsed in the niches, amid sighs and groans of rancid pleasure.

The erotic symphony disgusted Leanna. The dance room was a waste of her time. She knew how vamp clubs operated—the owners rarely mingled with riffraff off the street. Legrand would be ensconced in a private parlor, entertaining victims handpicked by his most trusted minions. She noted a handful of those elite guards pacing the perimeter of the dance floor, silently watching.

A stair in the corner of the room led to rooms on the upper levels, where humans and vamps could exchange sex along with blood. Leanna considered the possibility that Legrand was in one of those rooms, then almost as quickly rejected the notion. An Old One would not tolerate a berth above ground. The master would be below.

Should she approach one of his minions and offer herself for the master's pleasure? It was all too likely one of the brutes would decide to keep her for himself. No, better if she employed a bit of Sidhe stealth, and searched for Legrand on her own terms.

She spotted the down staircase, nestled behind the bar. Two vampires stood guard. One male, one female. Not newly turned, but for all the power bristling around them, they were hardly on their most alert behavior. The pair looked extremely bored.

Good.

It was easy enough to enhance her glamour with a look-away spell that made her nearly invisible. It was harder, however, to move through the crowd undetected—the club's patrons were packed tight, thigh to chest. Leanna made slow progress toward the stair.

Eventually, she reached the pair of vamp sentinels. Neither the male nor the female glanced her way as she slipped past them onto the stair. Leanna breathed a sigh of relief as she rounded the first landing.

The stair ended in a short corridor and a heavy door. The lock, surprisingly, was nothing more than a mundane mortise affair. A concentrated blast of elfshot dissolved it quite easily. Behind the door, the twisted descent of yet another stair gave out to a parlor of sorts. The carpet was lush, the furniture upholstered in leather. The walls were bare and ancient. The cellar was a Roman-era ruin, its diamond-shaped stone bricks forming a pattern reminiscent of a net. The space seemed to be deserted, but the air of menace was unmistakable. Cool dampness chilled the bare skin above Leanna's stockings, and raised goose bumps on her arms and the back of her neck. She tried her best to ignore the sensation of being lured into a snare.

A single exit pierced the opposite wall. A horizontal slash of light shone beneath it. As Leanna approached, she became aware of the sounds slithering beneath the portal. The whistle and crack of a whip, a man's sharp cry, a guttural groan, a sigh of bliss. Her stomach turned. She swallowed the bile in her throat and put her hand on the door frame.

The door sported an iron latch, and a single old-fashioned keyhole. Kneeling, she pressed her eye to the hole. What she saw in that narrow field of vision caused her gorge to rise anew.

Leanna had been a slave in the demon realms, had even descended into the pit of Hell itself. She'd seen things, awful things, that haunted her dreams still. But this? This somehow was worse. Because she knew what she was witnessing had been Jackson's fate long ago. A fate to which Leanna had delivered him.

She wanted to run. Instead, she summoned every ounce of her once-famous audacity and pushed the door open. She strode boldly into the light of a hundred dancing candles.

The illumination was unwelcome. If the dungeon room had been dark, the massive width of Legrand's bare shoulders, flexing as he whipped a naked youth manacled to an X-shaped wooden frame, would have been nothing more than a shadow. The angry stripes crisscrossing the victim's shoulders and back, and the blood smeared over his buttocks would have been invisible. But even in the dark Leanna would have heard the whistle of the metal-tipped flogger, and the sharp, agonized cry of the vampire master's victim.

The young male was far too pale to be a living man; he was vampire, most likely newly made. He was not the only vamp slave in the room—a woman lay pale and still on a velvet upholstered chaise. Two deep puncture marks marring the smooth white skin of her neck told of a recent vampire bite. Long, dark hair spilled over the edge of the couch. A cold sense of inevitability settled on Leanna as she crept close and peered at the woman's face.

Solange.

Dead, but not gone. Sleeping off the effects of her first bite. When she woke, she would be vampire.

Legrand paused in his flogging, his head cocked. He'd sensed her. Slowly he turned. For a moment he said nothing while he assessed the newcomer. His bloody whip dangled from his long fingers.

Leanna lifted her chin, thrust out her chest, and met the vampire's gaze with silent, provocative challenge. Inside her fears churned. Europe's vampire master was a large man, close to seven feet tall. His massive chest and arms, bared to view, bulged with muscle. Legrand had been in his prime when he'd died. Two millennia had done little to mar his physical perfection.

He brought his whip hand to his face and shoved a long hank of black hair from his eyes. Sweat shone on his forehead; his leather pants—his only garment—hung undone, crudely revealing yet another physical trait that fit his grandiose name.

The scent of sexual ecstasy, extracted from his suffering victim, clung to him like dung. A low, wretched sound spilled from the young man's lips. A determined chill stiffened Leanna's spine. Legrand was truly a monster. This undead aberration must be destroyed.

And she would be glad to do it.

Casually, she laid her evening bag on a low table.

"Ah. What have we here?" Legrand's nimble tongue flicked over bloodstained lips. His eyes raked her body, sending a sensation like a scurry of insect legs across her skin. For one heart-stopping instant, she feared he'd seen through her glamour. But no, he was only assessing his latest plaything.

"Remy has sent a delicious new morsel." The vampire's

accent carried a hint of the aristocratic; his features, Leanna
thought, had once been handsome.

"So he has," she murmured.

"My minion has done well, as always, anticipating his
master's needs." Legrand flicked his whip toward his bound
slave, opening a new slash and raising a hiss from the man's
throat. "I grow bored with this one. He will be much more
amusing when my newest slave awakens." His smiling gaze
traveled to Solange. "I'm looking forward to uniting this
worm with his newly undead wife."

Leanna had suspected as much. The young vampire was
Jackson's missing steward. Jean-Claude was dead, as Jackson
had feared. And vampire. Again, as Jackson had feared.

Solange's husband strained against his bonds, eyes blazing. "Damn you to Hell, Legrand."

"Silence!"

The vampire spun and landed a vicious blow to Jean-
Claude's torn and bloody skin. The prisoner's spine arched,
a cry choking in his throat. On the second blow, he went
slack and silent. His head lolled to one side.

"Finally, peace. Ah, well, this one is young, and stubborn.
It will take some time yet to break him. Until then . . ."
Legrand smiled, showing his fangs. "New blood as sweet as
yours is always welcome."

It took all Leanna's self-control to keep her revulsion
from showing on her face.

Legrand's gaze crawled down her body. "Remy chose well,
yes, but he should have removed your clothing before
sending you to me. Strip now, and be quick about it."

Leanna froze.

Legrand's eyes narrowed. His grip shifted on the whip
handle.

Leanna forced her shaking hands to the top hook of her
corset. No sense in resisting Legrand's command. This was
what she'd come for, after all. The quicker begun, the
quicker done. She popped open the top hook. Her breasts
strained. Legrand's gaze slithered to her cleavage.

"Very nice," he murmured. "Go on."

She dropped her arms to her sides and took one careful step toward him. "But . . ." she protested in silky French. "That would be so . . . ordinary. Surely you don't wish to take me as you do your other . . . lovers."

He seemed amused. "And why not? In two thousand years of existence, I've learned my own desires."

She moved closer, on silent feet, until she stood less than an arm's length away from the monster. "Give me a chance to prove I can give you something new. Something . . . unique. I came to Rome only for you, after all."

"That is nothing new. Many seek me out."

"None of them are like me."

She was taking a grave risk, but she had to chance it. Legrand was even more brutal, more depraved than she'd imagined, and he was an Old One. She could feel his power humming, reaching for her. If she wanted to throw him off-balance, she had to capture his curiosity. Now. But she was well aware of the fine line she walked. She must not reveal too much.

She inhaled, thrusting her breasts forward as she lifted her arms and smoothed her hair back from her face. She let her glamour drop, just a little. Enough to reveal delicate, pointed ears.

The vampire's surprise was evident. "But what is this? A Sidhe?"

"No, I'm human. Mostly. But I have a little Sidhe blood. Enough to interest you, I hope." Leanna tensed, waiting for Legrand to see through her ruse.

He reached out, grasping her chin in his fingers. She tried not to gasp. He smiled indulgently. She forced herself to relax. Thank the gods, he didn't seem to recognize how danger-ous she was.

"Your life essence is very strong," he said.

"I will give it to you. Gladly. For a taste of your death magic."

He released her chin and moved his hand to her neck. He

wrapped his fingers around the slender column and flexed them with gentle menace.

"What game do you play? The Sidhe abhor death magic."

Leanna's pulse beat against his thumb. "But humans do not. My human desires far overwhelm my Sidhe nature. Here," she whispered. "I'll show you."

Before she could change her mind, she opened her soul. Digging deep, she touched the dark stain on her life essence that would never be completely cleansed, not even if she lived in Annwyn for a thousand years. Red lights spun in her vision, and her head grew light. She nearly gagged at the foulness of what she'd been, of what she'd done in her past. Choking back revulsion, she brought her eternal shame forward, and let it seep into Legrand's mind.

She watched his smile spread as the filth of what she'd once been washed through him. His brows rose. A greedy gleam leaped into his eyes.

He licked his lips. "You are demonwhore."

"I was. No more. My masters met defeat at the hands of their enemies, and I escaped the death realms. Since then I've tried to erase the death magic from my soul, but I found . . . that wasn't possible. Death is part of me. I think of it, I dream of it. I crave it."

Shameful heat crept up her neck. Her words were not the lies she wished they were.

"And so," she whispered, "I've come to you. Death's master. My master."

"My slave." His gaze, his touch, his breath—they were grimy fingers picking over her body, her mind, her soul. He smiled, showing large teeth, slightly yellowed, stained around the edges with fresh blood.

The mesmerizing touch of his mind slid into her brain. She didn't resist—couldn't resist—as he walked her backward. The backs of her knees bumped a cushioned surface. An armchair. She sat. Legrand loomed large above her, his muscular legs spreading her thighs. Leaning forward, he released a foul tide of dark magic. It burned every inch of her skin.

"Lift your arms over your head."

She obeyed without hesitation. Indeed, there was no way to resist. His magic was strong; far stronger, she realized, than Jackson's. Had Jackson truly believed he could destroy Legrand? Leanna knew that he could not.

But she could. At the moment Legrand climaxed inside her, she would release her muse magic and drain every last drop of stolen life essence from his damned soul. The thought of taking him inside her body left a bitter residue in her throat. She swallowed hard and tried to expand her tightening ribs.

She was terrified. But her fear for herself, for what she was about to do, was nothing compared to her fear for Jackson. Jackson was strong, but Legrand was stronger. A battle between the two could only end in Jackson's obliteration. She would not allow that to happen.

His hands were on her. His long fingernails scraped painfully, shredding her corset to ribbons until it fell away, baring her breasts. He continued stroking. Dark pleasure trailed in lines of fire over her skin. It was false pleasure, she knew—a vampire's illusion. But it felt all too real. She gasped at the brazen intimacy of it and tried not to think of Jackson. He would not want to touch her ever again, once Legrand had defiled her. But that didn't matter. As long as Legrand was dead, and Jackson was safe.

"Look at me," Legrand commanded.

She did. His eyes were dark, completely so. No variation showed between iris and pupil. The orbs shone with deadly light. Leanna wished with all her heart that she could summon the strength to look away.

A fingernail traced up the inside of her leg, pausing high on her inner thigh. "You were not lying when you promised uniqueness. I can smell your blood. It's sweeter than anything I've known."

He went down on his knees and yanked off her shoes. Ripped her stockings. She tensed as he bent his head over her foot, teeth scraping each of her toes in turn. His tongue, like flame, licked at her soles.

Leanna felt a pinch, felt him lick away a drop of her life essence. Drugging weakness weighted her limbs. He didn't seem to be in any hurry to have sex. She wanted to move, to encourage him, but her limbs would not obey. Trapped like a puppet on his string, she spun slowly, slowly, into shameful pleasure. Darkness rushed her brain; fear alone kept her from losing consciousness. Gods. Did Legrand want her senseless before he used her? If she succumbed to his drugging fog, she wouldn't be able to cast her magic.

"Sweet," he mused. "So sweet."

His breath was hot on the arch of her foot. Was he contemplating another nip? How long would he toy with her before he sank his fangs into her pulse and drank deeply? How much could she endure before blacking out?

She would not let him win this encounter. She lifted her head and captured his gaze. His brows raised.

"Come inside me," she said.

He showed his fangs. "Patience, my pet."

"No. I can't wait. I need you." She begged him like the whore she'd once been. "I'll go mad if you don't take me now."

"Madness has its own pleasures. You may find you prefer it to sanity."

"Please . . ."

He stroked her calf. Death magic emanated from the pores of his fingers. Foul. Familiar. Her vision went fuzzy. It was all she could do to keep the rolling darkness at bay.

"Inside me. Now. Please."

Legrand's hands left her. He stood, looking down at her in the chair. His gaze was fixed on the pulse point of her neck; his magic was holding her motionless. She could barely breathe. If he chose to drain her blood before entering her body, her magic would be useless.

She waited, suspended on a knife's edge of terror. His hands fell to his groin, stroking.

"As you wish, *ma cherie*. Stand and remove what is left of your clothing."

She rose and put some distance between them. Her every instinct recoiled from his command, but there was no use in resisting. Her muse magic could only be released at the moment of his climax. She prayed it would not take long. She fixed her mind on the point in the very near future when Legrand would lay senseless, drained of his life essence. The instant his eyes closed, she would snatch up her shoe and drive the stiletto heel straight through his heart.

Her hands shook as she slid the zipper on her skirt. It hit the floor, leaving her clad only in her thong.

Yes, very soon, Legrand would lie at her feet. His evil would never rise again.

It was a good plan. It might even have worked.

If Jackson Cabot hadn't chosen that precise moment to enter his enemy's lair.

CHAPTER TEN

The shock of seeing Jean-Claude strapped to Legrand's flogging frame was bad enough. The sight of Solange's pale, still body was even worse. But finding Leanna standing before Legrand, all but naked . . .

Pure rage boiled in Jackson's veins, evaporating every rational thought. His vision bled red with rage. He flashed across the room. She screamed as he flung her behind him and spun to face his adversary.

"You idiot!" Leanna hissed behind him.

He didn't glance back at her. Legrand was rapidly recovering from the shock of Jackson's unexpected appearance in his private sanctuary.

Casually, Legrand rose, adjusted his cock, and buttoned it back into his trousers.

"Cabot. *Quelle surprise.* Apparently my minions have gone lax." He glanced at Leanna. "Was this one yours? You must have left her sorely dissatisfied, or she would not have come to me."

Leanna shoved past Jackson, as if trying to protect him. Was the woman insane? Jackson grabbed her upper arm and thrust her behind him.

"Jackson—"

"Shut up. And stay back."

Legrand's lips curled in a smile. "No need to growl, Cabot. In fact, you're more than welcome to join us." He opened his arms wide, in a gesture that encompassed Jean-Claude and

Solange. "Indeed, once your former stewards awaken, all five of us could—"

"Bastard. You know why I'm here. It's time. I challenge you, Legrand. We fight. Here. Now. To the end."

"A duel, Cabot? Most unwise. You cannot defeat me."

"We shall see."

His lot was cast. He would win or die. Completely, this time. Revenge, or oblivion, would be his. He tried not to think of what his defeat would mean for the others in this dungeon. Failure here would haunt him in Hell for all eternity.

Legrand's eyes flashed bright with good humor as he strolled to the whipping frame. He stroked a slow hand across Jean-Claude's bloody buttocks. Jackson's stomach turned.

"How long has it been since I took this one from you? Two months? Three? You'll be pleased to know he fought me well. I was vastly entertained."

Legrand turned and paced to the chaise. Jackson's eyes followed him.

"This one will fight as ferociously, I am sure. But your Sidhe mongrel?" His eyes found Leanna. "She does not fight at all. She begs for my cock. I am surprised, Cabot. Such a minion is not in keeping with your usual standards."

Jackson's jaw set. "Nevertheless, she is mine."

"Ah, but that is where you are wrong. She is mine, body and soul. And I will use her to the utmost." He paused, smiling. "After I destroy you."

Jackson flexed his fists. "There will be no *after*. Not for you."

Legrand smiled. "We shall see."

Jackson and Legrand circled slowly, eyes locked, an aura of death rising between them. Leanna threw power into the churning magic, intent on bolstering Jackson's cause. Her spell slammed up against a psychic wall. She barely managed to duck the rebound.

"It's no use." Jean-Claude's hoarse voice intruded. Her head whipped around. She hadn't realized the vampire had regained consciousness. Bound facedown on the flogging frame, he twisted his neck to look at her. "No one may interfere with two vampires dueling for dominance."

"But—there must be some way to help."

"No. I am sorry."

A sound like fingernails on a blackboard snapped Leanna's attention back to the battle. Legrand, moving so quickly his body was no more than a blur, hurtled toward Jackson. Jackson's body fuzzed as he dodged the impact. Legrand smashed against the wall. The room shook. Candles in the sconces flickered wildly. One fell to the floor, smoldering. Leanna dashed over and beat it out with a quick spell.

Legrand sprang to his feet, growling. Blood streaked down his temple.

Jackson crouched at the ready. "Feeling your age, Legrand?"

Legrand snarled, the fingernails of his clenched hands lengthening into claws. His body blurred a second time. This time, his assault struck its mark. Leanna's lungs seized as Jackson and his foe collided, then fell in a heap onto the armchair. The chair's legs snapped. Rolling violently onto the floor, the combatants veered toward Solange. Jean-Claude cried out, desperately twisting in his bonds, then slumping when the vampires narrowly missed smashing into the chaise where his wife lay.

Leanna dashed toward the young vamp. It took several moments to fashion a spell to open the first manacle, but at last the lock gave way with a blessed click. The youth hissed as the iron sprang open, revealing a ring of macerated flesh. Grimly aware of the duel crashing behind her, Leanna worked the remaining shackles.

Jean-Claude's knees buckled as he stumbled free. Leanna tried to catch him, but his weight threw her off balance and they tumbled to the floor. He righted himself quickly, wincing as he rose into a crouch. He held himself motionless for a long moment, his sharp eyes intent on the blur of movement in the center of the room. Waves of death energy radiated from the duel.

She crouched beside him. "Can you tell what's going on? Who's winning?"

"No. Jackson was eager to issue this challenge, but Solange and I . . ." He shot a grim glance toward his wife's unconscious body. "We feared he was not ready. We wanted him to wait another year, at least . . ."

Jean-Claude stood, moving swiftly to his wife's side. The deep slashes inflicted by Legrand's whip were already starting to close. Bending over Solange, he cupped her pale cheek.

"Solange. Can you hear me?"

There was no response.

"Too soon," he muttered.

The battling vampires crashed into the flogging frame. The heavy piece skidded across the floor, exploded against the wall, and splintered into a hundred pieces. Leanna ducked behind the chaise as debris showered over her. A smoking candle struck the upholstery. Quickly, Leanna spoke a spell to extinguish the flame. Jean-Claude hunched his shoulders over his wife, shielding her the best he could.

Leanna peered over the back of the chaise. Damn. Several more small fires smoldered, smoke seeping into the air. "This can't go on much longer. There must be some way to help Jackson."

"There is not. It will be a fight to the death." Jean-Claude lifted Solange into his arms. "We should flee."

"Run away? Are you insane? We can't just abandon him!"

"Jackson would command it, if he could," he said. But reluctance shadowed his eyes. "If Jackson wins the duel, he will rule Europe, and all will be well. If he loses . . ." His arms flexed around his wife's limp body. "Solange needs care. A head start will increase her chance of survival."

Leanna could only nod. "I understand. Go. Take her to safety. But I'm staying."

"But there is nothing you can do here."

"I can't accept that. I have magic. Strong magic. There must be some way I can help Jackson."

Jean-Claude met her gaze for a long moment, then nodded. He turned toward the door without another word.

Standing very still, Leanna stared into the shimmering energy at the center of the room. If only she could tell who was winning. Frustrated, she shot a blast of elfshot over the battle. The bolt ricocheted around the room like trapped lightning.

As the blurred movement of the sizzling green elfshot fire dissipated, the haze in the center of the room cleared. Legrand, bloody and battered, stood amid the smoke and detritus of his ruined dungeon. His bulging forearm was clamped around Jackson's neck from behind, pinning him to his chest. Jackson was struggling to free himself, to no avail. Leanna's heart lurched as Jackson surrendered to Legrand's greater strength.

His body sagged like a rag doll's. His eyes glazed, but did not close.

"Gods, no," Leanna whispered.

Legrand showed his fangs. "Should I snap his neck now?" He seemed to consider. "But no, that is too merciful. There is a more pleasant way to destroy a traitor."

With a dark laugh, Legrand heaved Jackson into the air. He hit the wall, skull cracking against the stone in an impact that would have killed a living man. Jackson slid to the floor, eyes glazed, head lolling.

Rage, pure and raw, rose in Leanna's throat. She thought she screamed; she couldn't be sure. The surge of her magic blotted out her mundane senses. Raising both hands, she flung a double blast of elfshot at Legrand's head.

The vampire met the assault with one upraised hand, absorbing the green sparks into his palm with practiced ease. His fangs flashed a sneer. Leanna found herself stumbling backward, her brain once again captive to the vampire master's will. The back of her knees hit the chaise. She stumbled and fell. Out of the corner of her eye, she saw that Jean-Claude had set Solange on the floor. The young vampire clawed at the dungeon door, but the oak slab didn't budge.

"On your feet," Legrand barked at Leanna.

Leanna's limbs lurched. Calmly, Legrand bent and retrieved a long shard of wood, a remnant of the flogging frame. With deliberate malice, the vampire approached and pressed the weapon into Leanna's hand. Her fingers closed around it.

"*You* will destroy him. Lay Cabot on the floor. Then stake him through the heart."

Leanna tried to force a refusal past her lips. They would not move. She tried to swallow. Her throat was paralyzed.

But the rest of her body was not. Clutching the stake to her chest, she stumbled toward Jackson. His chest heaved; his dull eyes tracked her. He didn't resist as she set the stake on the ground and crouched to grab his ankles.

She dragged him away from the wall. The back of his head hit the ground. His limbs were limp, his body unmoving except for the harsh rise and fall of his chest. His eyes, however, were open and fully lucid. He knew what she was doing.

He knew she was going to destroy him.

Blindly, propelled by dark magic she couldn't begin to fight, Leanna picked up the stake. Legrand gave a grunt of satisfaction as she lurched to her feet and raised the splintered shaft high over her head. The jagged point poised over Jackson's heart, suspended for the fatal blow.

Dark waves of magic swept over her. The urge to strike was overwhelming.

No! Leanna's mind screamed in silent horror. *No!*

Her arms tensed; her shoulders flexed.

No. This couldn't happen. She couldn't kill Jackson. Not again.

With gut-wrenching effort, Leanna reached for her strongest magic. It was hidden beneath the darkest part of her soul, behind a wounded, ugly place that frightened her so badly she couldn't bear to open it to the light. The ugly stain inside her meant she would never be whole, no matter how long she lived, no matter how hard she tried. The deepest part of herself bore permanent scars, inflicted by her Sidhe mother, her human father. By all the men who had ever used her for her magic. By her time in Hell. But the most painful wounds were the ones Leanna had inflicted on herself—those caused by her willing acts of dark magic.

But beneath the scars—ah, there was a place of pure life. A place where risk was still possible. A place where love was true.

The stake, driven by Legrand's will, whipped downward. Leanna grasped at the magic in that long forgotten corner of her soul. She had no time to form the power she called. No time to refine her intentions into a coherent spell. She could only fling the pure magic, messily, just as the stake pierced Jackson's flesh.

His torso jumped, as if shocked by live wires.

And then he lay still.

Horror tightened iron bands around Leanna's chest. She couldn't breathe, couldn't cry out. She could only stare at the stake sunk deep into Jackson's chest. At her own numb fingers, clenched like claws around the splintered wood. She couldn't let go, even as Jackson's blood bubbled up around the hideous wound.

She knelt motionless in the spreading crimson puddle.

She'd failed.

CHAPTER ELEVEN

Legrand threw back his head and laughed.

And laughed and laughed and laughed.

Leanna's world contracted until it was filled with nothing but that soulless mirth. Nothing but Legrand's handsome, twisted face. Nothing but his flat, evil eyes.

Nothing but her hands, ripping the bloody stake from Jackson's chest.

Nothing but her body, slowly pivoting.

Moving. Lunging.

Nothing but the blow she struck, straight into Legrand's heart.

Nothing but the flash of shocked understanding in Legrand's eyes.

Nothing but his slow, openmouthed fall to the ground.

Nothing but blood and death and bitter, bitter regret.

CHAPTER TWELVE

Leanna nearly fell onto Legrand's blood-soaked body. Jean-Claude caught her as she went down, and yanked her upright. The vampire's long-dead corpse, its undead heart spilling the last of its stolen blood, turned a sick shade of gray. Leanna's living heart hammered a thousand fists inside her chest as the ancient human shell darkened and shriveled before her eyes.

Gods. Jackson, lying behind her, had met the same fate. She had done that to him. She couldn't bear to look. She stared at her bloody hands instead.

"Get me out of here, Jean-Claude."

The young vampire gripped her shoulders. "Leanna—"

"*Now!*"

"No, you don't understand . . ."

"Get. Me. Out!" She balled up her fists and pounded his chest. Pain shot up her arms. It was nothing compared to the pain in her ripped and bleeding heart.

"I can't bear it. I can't stay here. I can't look at him . . ."

Jean-Claude shook her, hard enough to whip her head forward and back. "Leanna. Listen to me. Jackson . . . he's not gone."

Leanna stilled. "What did you say?"

"Jackson is not gone."

Gently, Jean-Claude turned her. Jackson's body lay on the floor, motionless and pale. The bloody wound in his chest gaped. His arms were flung wide; his eyes were open and staring at the ceiling. He looked like the dead man he was.

A trickle of blood pulsed from his chest.

Leanna lurched out of Jean-Claude's grip. Falling on her knees, she placed both her palms over the hole in Jackson's chest. The faintest of pulses beat against her hand.

"Gods in Annwyn," she breathed. "His heart . . . it's still beating."

She looked up. Jean-Claude was standing over her, his outline blurry through her tears.

"My magic . . ." she whispered. "It must have deflected the blow."

"Yes. If his heart had been pierced, he'd be nothing but dust. But even so . . . it will be some time before he can move on his own. We have to get him out of here, before—" He broke off with a curse as a muffled shout sounded behind the oak door. "*They are here.*"

Leanna looked up. "Who?

Heavy fists pounded on the door. The iron latch rattled. Angry voices sounded. "*Ouvrez!*" Open.

"Jean-Claude, what is it? What's happening?"

The young vampire ran to the door and stooped to gather Solange into his arms. Slowly, he backed away. "Legrand's minions know he is gone. They will break down the door to get to us. *Mon Dieu!* How can we fight so many?"

"But why? Legrand is gone. We mean them no harm. Why should any of them want to destroy us?"

"Because one vampire must rule Europe. Jackson Cabot was second in power to Legrand. Now he is first. But he is in no condition to defend his rank."

"You mean—any vampire who wants to be Europe's master must destroy Jackson first?"

"Or chase him off the Continent."

"That should be no problem," Leanna said. "Jackson will be more than ready to leave."

The door shuddered on its hinges. "He will not get the

chance. Not when that door gives way. They will rip him to shreds."

"Then we've got to get out of here before that happens! Is there a back way out of this place?" She scanned the room, peering through smoke and flames. There was no second door that she could see. "A secret passage?"

"No. At least, in the three months I've been prisoner here, I have never seen evidence of it."

A mighty crash shook the door. The iron hinges groaned. Tendrils of vampire magic curled under the door, reaching for the minds within.

Jean-Claude laid Solange's body in the shelter of a heavy armoire, bending to smooth her hair from her face and place a gentle kiss on her brow before returning to stand beside Leanna. "Jackson saved my life. I will die defending him."

"Not if I can help it," Leanna muttered.

Constructing a quick barrier spell, she threw it over the door. It wouldn't hold indefinitely, not against vampire magic, but it would buy some time. Enough time, she hoped.

She turned and scanned the room, hunting through smoke and detritus, flinging dousing spells at several small fires. At last, she spied a flash of silver. Her clutch purse. Snatching it up, she fumbled inside for the cell phone she'd hidden there.

Jean-Claude tracked her movements. "What are you doing?"

"Calling for help."

Angry voices growled on the other side of the door. "*Un, duex, trios . . .*" A thundering crash shook the room. Leanna stifled a cry. Dark magic and brute strength would soon shatter her barrier spell. She stabbed the phone's power button.

"What help? There is no time!"

Leanna, her gaze intent on the phone's display, didn't answer. "Come on . . ."

Searching for satellite . . .

No service.

"Ballocks." She waved the phone in the air. "Damn. Damn, damn, *damn*. We're too far below ground." Gods, maybe Jean-Claude was right. Maybe they *were* doomed.

The door shook.

"There is a telephone," Jean-Claude said suddenly.

Leanna's gaze snapped to the vampire. "*What?*"

"A telephone. Behind that panel by the door. I don't know what good it will do, but—"

"Gods in Annwyn," Leanna gasped, lunging for the life-line. "Why didn't you say that in the first place?"

She snatched the receiver off the hook just as the door's top hinge cracked.

CHAPTER THIRTEEN

Leanna bypassed Mac's number and went straight to Christine's. It was Kalen's magic she needed, but she knew the Immortal would rather be roasted alive than carry a cell phone. Thankfully, his wife answered hers on the first ring.

"Leanna? Goddess, what's wrong? We thought you'd gone to a spa in Tuscany . . ."

Kalen arrived within seconds of Leanna's terse explanation of her predicament, his broad form materializing out of the smoky dungeon air. Immediately the room seemed smaller.

Jean-Claude's eyes nearly bugged out of his head.

The Immortal took a quick survey of the room. Leanna winced, imagining the scene through his eyes. It looked bad, very bad. Death and death magic. Blood. Vampires. And she was naked except for her thong.

Kalen fixed her with a baleful glare. "Leanna—"

He broke off as a crash splintered a corner of the door. Leanna's barrier spell spiderwebbed. Scowling fiercely, Kalen held up one hand, reinforcing Leanna's magic.

"Just what kind of trouble have you gotten yourself into this time?"

Jean-Claude made a choking sound. "*Mon Dieu.* You're . . . you're . . ."

"The Immortal Kalen," Leanna told him. "He can get us out. One at a time. Solange can go fir—"

Kalen's voice dripped warning. "Leanna. Surely you are not offering my magical services to vampires."

"Yes, Kalen, that's exactly what I'm doing. There's no time to explain. Just trust me—"

"To do what? Stay away from death magic? Stay out of vamp clubs? What the hell happened to the vows you took in Annwyn? Were they nothing but a pack of lies? No—" He cut off her reply with a raised hand. "Don't even bother answering. It's Mac you'll need to explain yourself to."

Gods. She wasn't sure what frightened her more—the thought of facing her brother, or the ferocious growls on the other side of the dungeon door. Jean-Claude went paler than the pale he already was. The broken hinges creaked ominously.

"Kalen," Leanna ground out. "Shut up! There's no time."

The Immortal grabbed her wrist. "All right. Let's get out of here before whatever's behind that door gets in."

She twisted out of his grasp. "No! I mean—yes, we need to get out, but . . . you've got to take the others out first."

"You mean these vampires? You have got to be kidding me. This is their world. Let them deal with it."

"No. You don't understand. This isn't just any vampire club. It belongs—belonged—to Armand Legrand."

Kalen inhaled sharply. "Europe's vampire master?"

"The same." She jerked her chin to the dusty pile of leather on the floor. "That's all that's left of him."

"Legrand destroyed? How?"

"I staked him."

The Immortal's brows shot up. "How the hell did you manage that?"

"These vampires—they helped me get rid of him. So can you please just get them all out of here? *Now?*"

"Solange first," Jean-Claude said as the cracks in the door splintered and widened. He thrust his wife into Kalen's arms. His shoulders went back as he met the Immortal's gaze. "Please. She is my wife."

Kalen muttered something under his breath and winked out of sight, taking Solange with him.

Leanna's shoulders sagged. "Thank the gods."

She threw all her magic into holding the door. In the space of half a dozen heartbeats, Kalen was back.

"Christine's speechless," he reported. "And believe me, that doesn't happen often. As for Mac . . . well, I'd rather not repeat what Mac said."

"Jean-Claude next," was all Leanna said.

Kalen placed his hand on the young vampire's shoulder and disappeared a second time. Leanna's gaze found Jackson. He hadn't moved an inch. He looked so pale, so still. So . . . dead.

He *was* dead. He was vampire. He'd never be otherwise.

Kalen reappeared at her elbow.

"You next."

"No. Take Jackson," she said, blinking back tears.

Kalen's charcoal-gray eyes rested briefly on the wounded man. "Who is he?"

"A . . . friend. I knew him a century ago. When he was still alive."

"You care for him."

"Yes. I did then, and I do now."

"Leanna. He's a vampire. A dead man. A death creature."

"Damn it, Kalen, don't you think I know that?" The room shook with death magic, causing Leanna to clutch Kalen's arm for support. Gods. Legrand's minions would take the whole building down at this rate.

"Just get him out of here!"

Kalen nodded. Kneeling, he placed his hand on Jackson's arm. "I'll be back in five seconds."

An instant later, they were gone. Leanna released a long stream of air from her lungs.

Before she could draw her next breath, the dungeon door shattered.

CHAPTER FOURTEEN

"Gods damn it, that was too close."

Kalen uttered another few choice words as he dumped Leanna on a chair in the sitting room of his hotel suite. "If I had arrived one second later, you'd have been nothing but a collection of bloody body parts strewn across the floor."

Leanna, eyes squeezed shut, could only nod at Kalen's rage. Her heart was racing, and her lungs were in the midst of a hard spasm. A verbal reply was totally beyond possibility.

A second angry male voice intruded. "Bloody hell, Leanna. What in the name of Annwyn were you doing in Armand Legrand's club?"

"Mac, back off. Can't you see she's in shock?" The admonition came from Mac's wife, Artemis.

Artemis tugged her to her feet. Leanna stumbled after her. Dimly, she was aware of her sister-in-law pushing her into the shower and washing her like a child. Stepping out of the water, she felt a whisper of silk descend on her shoulders. A robe. She wrapped it around her body and pulled the sash tight.

When she stepped back into the sitting room, the first thing she saw was Mac. Gods. Her brother looked angry enough to tear someone limb from limb. Leanna had no doubt that she was on the top of his list of candidates.

Artemis blocked his approach. "Now, Mac, get a grip . . ."

"Grip, nothing! She deserves a good shaking. Kalen found her just about stark naked, up to her ears in death magic."

The disappointment in Mac's eyes hurt Leanna like hell. Gods, there was so much to answer for. And she would answer. But right now . . .

"Where's Jackson?"

Mac swore.

"All three vampires are in the master suite," Kalen, standing by the window, cut in. "Christine is with them. I warned her not to waste too much of her magic on them. They'll heal fast enough on their own."

Leanna rose on shaky feet and headed toward the closed door Kalen indicated. Mac stepped up, blocking her path.

"You swore to me, Leanna. You swore to Niniane. You swore on Annwyn's silver tree of life that you would give up death magic."

"I'm sorry, Mac. But . . . I couldn't turn away. Not from Jackson."

"What is this vamp to you, Leanna?"

"Please. I'll explain it all later. Right now—I just need to see him."

Artemis none-too-subtly tugged Mac out of Leanna's way. "Let your sister be. Can't you see how upset she is? Whoever—whatever—the man is, she's in love with him."

Mac frowned as Leanna shoved passed him. Christine, her blue eyes grave, slipped from the bedroom as Leanna approached the door.

"Good luck," she mouthed as she caught Leanna's eye.

Leanna steeled herself and opened the door. The room was dark, the heavy drapes drawn against the encroaching dawn. Jackson lay in the center of the large bed, eyes closed, his face almost as pale as the bed linens. His chest was bare. The ugly wound she'd inflicted on him gaped open. The jagged skin around it was ripped and raw.

"He is weak," a woman's low voice said. "He needs blood to heal. But he will survive."

Leanna's gaze swung to Solange. She sat in a deep arm-chair, awake and alert, and clad in a white terry cloth robe that matched her face's pallor. Jean-Claude, newly showered and similarly garbed, stood behind her.

"Thank the gods for that," Leanna said.

"Jackson may curse those same gods, when he awakens," Solange replied.

"But why? Legrand is gone."

Solange shivered and looked away. Jean-Claude regarded Leanna with sober eyes. "My wife means to say that . . . our master's existence, for so long, has been fed by little more than his hatred of Legrand. Now that Legrand is gone . . ." The vampire spread his hands in a gesture of helplessness. "We cannot say what Jackson will be. What he will do. How he will live."

"Whatever happens," Leanna said, "He won't have to face it alone. I'll be with him."

"Be careful what you promise," Jean-Claude said. "It is not easy, being the living companion of a vampire."

"I never imagined it was. But someone will have to take the job, now that you and Solange are vampires. The three of you will need a steward with very powerful magic."

"Are you offering yourself for the role?" Solange demanded.

"Yes. Yes, I am." Her gaze strayed back to Jackson. "Do you think he will agree?"

Solange shrugged and looked away.

"Your life-magic friends will shun you," Jean-Claude said.

Leanna rubbed her arms. "Likely, that's true. But I don't care. I love Jackson."

"Do you? Solange and I . . . we know who you are. We know what you did to the master long ago, in Paris. You are the reason Jackson is vampire." He paused. "He has hated you for a very long time."

"I know I have much to atone for, if only he'll let me." She blinked back a blur of tears. "Please. May I . . . may I be alone with Jackson for a while?"

Reluctantly, Jean-Claude helped Solange to her feet. "But

of course," he said. Then he let out a reluctant chuckle, and Leanna caught a glimpse of the living man he'd once been.

"In the meantime," he said, "my wife and I will entertain your astonished friends."

"Jackson? Can you hear me?"

The woman's voice was low and sweet, and sounded like a dream he wished would never end. Jackson muttered a non-committal sound and slipped deeper into velvet darkness.

Wet heat on his cheek. Soft lips, caressing his temple.

The woman spoke again. She was closer now. Trembling. For him?

"Jackson, please. Wake up."

He struggled to understand. He thought the voice came from his past—a past he tried never to think about. Such thoughts were too painful. They had the power to destroy. For years, decades, a century, he'd locked them away. Why had this siren come to awaken those fatal yearnings?

The voice moved away. The woman's heat retreated, leaving him chilled. He suppressed the urge to call her back. He didn't deserve her. He—

Cold, wet shock assaulted him. Icy water, like a slap across his face. He sputtered, jerking upright, gasping for breath. His eyes snapped open, just in time to be blinded by a second liquid assault.

"Thank the gods," she said. "That's much better."

He wiped the back of his hand across his eyes, blinking furiously. He lay back on a wide, soft bed; he was naked beneath the cool linens. His chest ached. How had he gotten here? The last thing he remembered was Leanna looming over him, driving a wooden stake into his heart.

She loomed over him again now. This time, her weapon of choice was a chilled bottle of mineral water.

He shoved aside the soaked sheet and swung his legs over the side of the bed. The room lurched unpleasantly.

He glared at her. "Why the hell are you trying to drown me?"

She set the bottle on the nightstand with a dull thud. Belatedly, he realized her hand was shaking. And that tears were leaking from her eyes.

She dashed them away with the back of her hand. "I'm sorry, Jackson. But . . . seeing you so pale and still, with that ugly hole in your chest . . . Gods. You looked . . . dead."

"I am dead."

She hugged her torso. "You know what I mean."

He peered down at his wound. The movement of his eyes caused black squiggles to dance in his vision. He felt lightheaded. Weak as a newborn kitten. And hungry. Ravenous, in fact. His wound cried for blood. Healing, nourishing blood.

And the sweetest meal he'd ever had was within arm's reach.

He couldn't let himself think about that.

He lifted a hand and pointed to the hole in his chest. "Your aim is pathetic. My heart is at least an inch to the left."

She didn't laugh. "I know that! Oh, gods, Jackson, I tried so hard to miss entirely. One inch was all my magic could do."

"It was enough, it seems."

"But you lost so much blood. It was everywhere. And now . . . you need more before you'll begin to heal."

Blood.

His gaze lifted, seeking and finding the delicate pulse point on Leanna's neck. He could hear her Sidhe blood, vibrant with life, rushing through her veins. Despite his weakened state, lust stirred. He curled his fingers on the edge of the mattress so he wouldn't reach for her.

Scowling, he looked around the room for the first time. "Where are we?"

"My hotel. This is Kalen and Christine's suite, actually. Mac and Kalen—and their wives—are in the next room. I called Kalen from Legrand's club. He's able to translocate at will. He got us out, brought us here. You, me, Solange, Jean-Claude . . ."

Jackson's memories of recent events were elusive.

"Solange . . . she was sleeping off Legrand's bite. Is she awake?"

"Yes, awake, and adjusting to her vampire state, I imagine. But she seems strong enough. Jean-Claude is with her, of course. I think he gave her blood. They're in the other room." She grimaced. "With Mac and Kalen."

"Jean-Claude has recovered?"

"He looks well enough, even after what he went through . . ."

Regrettably, the scene in Legrand's dungeon was becoming clearer in Jackson's mind. He nodded grimly. "Vampires are a strong breed, and you needn't fear we will hide behind you and your friends. The three of us will leave this place at sunset. Legrand will surely be searching—"

"Legrand isn't searching. He's . . . he's nothing but dust now."

It took a moment for her statement to register in his mind. When it did, for a moment he could do nothing but stare.

"Dust?" Jackson said finally. "But how? Did Kalen . . . ?"

"No. It happened before he came. It was me, Jackson. I destroyed Legrand."

"You, Leanna?" Jackson felt as though he'd been punched in the gut. "God damn it, did you have sex with that monster after all? While I lay unconscious at your feet?"

"No!" she said quickly. "Gods, no. I swear. I got rid of Legrand the old-fashioned way. I staked him. With the same stake I drove through your chest, actually."

"How? Legrand's power . . ."

"I'm not sure how I did it. After I impaled you, Legrand stood there laughing, gloating. It was horrible—I thought I'd pierced your heart. I thought you were gone. My mind blanked—I went insane, I think, with rage. I barely remember what happened after that, but somehow I yanked the stake from your body and lunged at Legrand. I . . . I must have caught him by surprise. The stake went clean through his heart."

"My God." Legrand, destroyed? At Leanna's hand? After all Jackson's years of carnal self-deprivation and careful planning? An ironic twist indeed. He fell silent, absorbing the enormity of the notion. Legrand. Gone.

It would take some time to get used to.

He felt Leanna's gaze drop to the hole in his chest.

"Does it hurt?"

"It will heal," he said.

She sighed and sank down next to him on the bed. She was too close. His fingers were just inches from her pulse. If he moved his hand slightly, he could grasp her wrist and bring it to his lips.

Blood-hunger gnawed his gut. He ached to bury his fangs in her sweet flesh. Bury his hard cock in her body. Fool that he was, he didn't even care that only a flimsy door separated him from the combined wrath of a demigod, an Immortal warrior, and their two witchy wives.

Damn it. Didn't Leanna realize the danger he represented?

He spoke through gritted teeth. "You may leave me now. I'm fine."

Leanna's brows rose. "Fine? Who are you kidding? Fine is the last thing you look. Death warmed over is a more apt description." She bit her lip.

The innocent, erotic nibble went straight to his groin. He stifled a groan.

She gasped. "Jackson? What is it? Are you ill? Do you need blood?"

"No," he ground out. "No. I don't need blood. Not your blood, at any rate. I only need you to leave me alone. Get out of here, Leanna. Go back to your life-magic friends."

The perverse woman didn't obey. Instead, she laid her delicate hand on his chest, her palm covering his wound. His fingers closed on her wrist. God help him, he didn't have the strength to push her away.

Her mouth brushed his jaw.

"Leanna. Don't do this. You'll regret it."

"I won't."

She nuzzled him with her cheek. Stretching her neck, she offered her pulse to him. Her blood beat against his lips. Tantalizing. Forbidden.

Hunger and lust exploded; his fangs emerged. He opened his mouth to mutter a soft curse. The tips of his incisors scored her skin.

"I'm willing, Jackson, and you can't turn me vampire. Why hesitate?"

"I could kill you. Easily. Drain you dry. If I lose control—"

"You won't lose control. I trust you, Jackson. Utterly. I love you, Jackson. My blood is yours. Whatever you need from me, I'm ready to give."

Gods. She just didn't understand. She was light and life; he was death. They didn't belong together. Nevertheless, his throat burned with painful need; his cock throbbed mercilessly. Her pulse beat against his lips. One bite, and she would be his. Forever.

"Make love to me," she whispered.

"Leanna . . ."

She lifted her head from his shoulder. He felt the loss of contact keenly, but didn't pull her back.

"Is it because you think you'll lose the power you worked so long to gain? Because if—"

"No. Not that," he said. "I gathered that magic for one purpose. To defeat Legrand. Now that he is gone . . ."

"There's no reason to push me away."

He expelled a rush of air from his lungs. "Leanna, you don't know what you're offering! Do you honestly think that if I make love to you now, drink your blood, that I could ever let you go? If I take you now, I'd never be strong enough to set you free."

She smiled with all the brilliance of the sun he'd not seen in a century. "I don't want to be free of you. I want to stay by your side, always. I'm the perfect choice for your new steward. You'll be needing one, after all. Solange and Jean-Claude, too."

He stared at her. "You can't mean that! You're Sidhe, Leanna. Your kind doesn't consort with vampires. Sidhe are creatures of daylight."

She snorted. "Actually, I'm more of a night person."

"Don't joke. I'm serious. It's preposterous. A Sidhe cannot be a vampire's steward."

"Why not?" She placed a kiss on his jaw.

He groaned. He couldn't seem to stop himself from reaching for her. Her blood called to him, filling his ears with a low, deep buzz. He struggled to form a coherent sentence.

"You'd have to live in caves. Caverns. Dank cellars."

She kissed him again. "Sidhe love the earth."

"Vampire society is highly territorial. We'll never be left in peace. I'll be threatened by rivals, always. You'll be in constant battle with their stewards."

Her lips grazed the corner of his mouth. "My magic is up to the challenge, I believe."

"Your brother . . . your friends . . . they'll be horrified."

"True," she agreed. "In fact, they already are. But I don't care."

She nibbled his lips. Her ample breasts squashed between their bodies. He swept his hand up her side and filled his palm with her soft, yielding bounty.

She licked him, the tip of her tongue scraping from his chin to his ear. "Gods, Jackson, you taste so good."

It was too much. With a groan of surrender, he rolled her beneath him on the bed and plundered her mouth. His fangs scraped her lip, slid over her jaw. He scored a thin line down her neck, then pressed his incisors to her throbbing pulse.

Her robe fell open. Gods, she was naked beneath it. She wrapped her legs around his waist. The fullness of his erection slid between her thighs.

"Come into me, Jackson."

Even if he'd wanted to, he couldn't have stopped himself from obeying her command. Dragging in a breath, he bit deep, his fangs sinking into her neck at the exact instant he pushed himself into her body. Her blood was sweet on his tongue; her inner muscles clenched his shaft in an intoxicating embrace.

He fed as he moved inside her. Euphoria beyond imagining tossed him high. Leanna's blood was potent, magical; her love was his renewal. Life essence and life magic spread through his limbs, into his veins, his muscle, his sinew. He felt the wound in his chest close completely as he filled his hands with her body and his heart and soul with her love.

They exploded together, in a shower of peace so profound that when the world stopped spinning and Jackson's sanity finally returned, he found his face wet with tears.

"You've done it now," he whispered, his arms tightening around her. "I'll never let you go."

Leanna snuggled closer, smiling. She didn't open her eyes. "Good," she said.

EPILOGUE

The nice thing about February on the north coast of Scotland was that the sun barely rose above the horizon, and then only for scant hours each day. That happy fact of nature made the Immortal Kalen's island castle the perfect vampire winter home.

Leanna, wineglass in hand, glanced across the library at Jackson. A casual observer would never guess he was vampire. In the six months since they'd left Rome, Jackson had lost much of the pallor most people associated with vampires. Her rich Sidhe blood had done that for him. Her husband no longer hunted human blood.

As for Jackson's vampire power—true, his magic wasn't increasing at the same amazing rate it had during his years of celibacy, but it wasn't draining, either, as they'd feared. Leanna had discovered she was able to offer Jackson the inspirational benefits of her muse magic along with her blood, without claiming his life essence in return. Jackson had resumed his long-abandoned artistic explorations. He painted and sculpted almost every spare moment he wasn't worshipping Leanna in bed.

Against all odds, Jackson had found something he thought was impossible. Happiness. He'd regained the exuberant good humor that had drawn Leanna to him in Paris. He teased her, and laughed often. In a few months, when the Scottish summer days began to stretch to unmanageable lengths, they would travel south and spend a blissfully dark winter in Patagonia. Leanna was looking forward to the trip. She'd never seen a penguin in its natural habitat.

She sent her husband a nervous smile. He paused in his conversation with Kalen—they were deeply engrossed in a discussion of Impressionism—and sent a quick grin back at her. A warm flush spread over her. It was almost enough to dispel the cold knot of anxiety in her chest.

Almost.

She took a deep, almost desperate sip of merlot.

"Gods," she muttered under her breath. "What I really need is a good whiskey."

Mac, standing at her elbow, chuckled. "That's precisely why Kalen locked up his Glenfiddich."

Christine and Artemis exchanged amused glances. Leanna scowled.

"Don't worry." Christine, ever the peacemaker, patted Leanna's arm. "I'm sure everything will be fine."

"Fine?" Leanna demanded. "Fine? How could it possibly be fine?" She poked a finger at Mac. "This is *not* a good idea. I can't believe I let you talk me into it."

"Relax, love." Mac looked calm enough, his arm casually draped over his wife's shoulders, but Leanna could tell he was nearly as keyed up as she was.

"It's only our mother, after all," he said wryly. "And you must admit, Niniane does have the right to meet her only son-in-law."

"She's going to explode," Leanna said flatly.

Mac grinned. "Likely. But look at the bright side. Mum will be forced to admit Artemis isn't the worst thing to happen to the family. A vampire is clearly worse than a reformed death witch."

Artemis rolled her eyes. "Thanks, Mac."

"Go ahead," Leanna said darkly. "Make jokes. It won't save you when Niniane gets here."

Niniane may have acknowledged Leanna at last, but it had only been at Mac's insistence. Leanna's relationship with her mother was shaky at best. And now that Leanna had broken the vows she'd made in Annwyn, and married a vampire to boot . . .

She sent a worried glance toward the far side of the library, where Artemis's older son, Zander, sprawled on the floor with his infant half brother, Cameron, and Christine's and Kalen's immortal toddler, Ellie.

"I'm not sure it's safe, having the children in here when Niniane arrives. Maybe you should have Pearl watch them somewhere else."

"It'll be safer with them here, actually," Mac replied, his gaze resting fondly on his firstborn, who at the moment was sprawled on his pudgy stomach, nearsightedly surveying Kalen's Persian carpet for edible lint. "Niniane wouldn't dare endanger her only grandson."

"Where is Niniane, anyway? She should have been here by now."

Mac laughed. "So now you're anxious for old mum to arrive?"

"I'm anxious for her to come and go," Leanna muttered. "As quickly as possible."

She drew a sharp inhale as Kalen's stout halfling/gnome housekeeper, Pearl, waddled into the library doorway. The expression on her hairy face could not have been more sour.

"May I present—"

Pearl's voice dripped with more sarcasm than Leanna thought could safely fit into the room.

"—Her Royal Highness, Sidhe Queen of Annwyn, Revered Keeper of Celtic Mysteries, High Counselor of the Sidhe Court, Honored Protector of Celtic Lore, Most Beautiful and Benevolent Benefactress of Celtic Creatures in Annwyn and in the Human World . . ."

Mac snorted under his breath, then covered the laugh with a cough when Artemis elbowed him in the ribs.

". . . Niniane the Exquisite!"

Pearl looked like she wanted to vomit.

Leanna thought she might spew as well.

Instead, she held her breath and pasted a smile on her face as Niniane glided through the door. Her mother's youthful beauty was, as always, stunning. The Sidhe queen may have been well over a thousand years old, but she looked no older than a twenty-two-year-old human female. Her gown, a stunning confection woven from silver leaves, dewdrops, and pink petals, draped a perfect, dainty body. Platinum blonde hair, braided into a regal crown atop her head, accented her long, graceful neck and delicately pointed ears.

Dimly, Leanna was aware of Jackson moving to her side, and cupping her elbow. "Don't forget to breathe," he whispered.

Leanna inhaled.

Mac reached Niniane first. Bending, he kissed her cheek. "Hullo, Mum. You're looking lovely, as always. So glad you could make it."

"Where is he, Mackie?" Niniane demanded, her eyes sweeping the library. "Where is this"—she gave a delicate shudder—"*vampire* your sister's married?"

Icy fingers of apprehension clutched Leanna's throat and squeezed. This was an exceedingly bad idea. Niniane was liable to eviscerate Jackson. She was more than capable of doing it, right here in Kalen's library, without harming a hair on the children's heads.

Jackson shook off the death grip Leanna had on his arm. Smiling, he approached Niniane, and bowed.

"Arthur Jackson Cabot IV, at your service, your Highness."

Niniane's mulish expression didn't flicker as she gave Jackson a blatant once-over.

She huffed and met Leanna's gaze across the room. "This man hardly looks like a vampire."

"He's—" Leanna began.

"It's your lovely daughter's influence that keeps me so . . . alive," Jackson cut in. "Nevertheless, I assure you, I am vampire."

"And I don't have a glamour on him, either," Leanna said.

Jackson graced his mother-in-law with a flash of his fangs.

Niniane gazed at him a moment, then sniffed and continued to address her daughter.

"So he looks like a living human. That hardly matters. It's just not *natural*, a Sidhe married to a death creature. It was bad enough Mac took up with a mixed-race death witch—"

"Mother—" Mac cut in, his tone ominous.

Niniane huffed. "—but at least my *darling* daughter-in-law is *alive*, and practices only life magic now." She sent a brilliant smile toward the children. "I must admit, Artemis has given me a lovely grandson. But vampires? They're pure death, Leanna. And they can't reproduce."

"My apologies, your Highness," Jackson said mildly.

Niniane ignored him.

Leanna let out a huff. Handing her wineglass to Christine, she stalked to Jackson's side.

"Mother, stop it. Right now. I won't tolerate you being rude to my husband."

"Leanna. I know I treated you poorly for most of your life. But I thought we'd gotten past that. I accepted you into Annwyn. I acknowledged you as my daughter. In return, you swore you would abandon death magic forever. And *this* is how you repay me? With an undead son-in-law?"

"It had nothing to do with you, Mother! I married Jackson because I love him."

"Your Highness," Jackson interjected. "May I speak?"

Niniane's brows arched toward her hairline. She turned and fixed Jackson with a baleful stare.

Leanna held her breath at her husband's breach of Sidhe etiquette. Humans, even undead ones, did not pose direct, uninvited questions to Sidhe royalty. A long pause ensued, in which even Mac shifted nervously. Then Kalen cleared his throat in subtle warning, and Niniane gave a brief nod.

"Speak."

Leanna let out a long breath.

"I love your daughter," Jackson began. "And she loves me. Her life magic balances my death magic, and I will honor and defend her with every breath in my unfortunately undead body. There is only one flaw in our happiness. Leanna wishes her mother's blessing on our union. Please, will you give it?"

For a long moment, the room breathed in silence. Even the babies ceased babbling. The only sound came from the ormolu clock on the mantle. The precise ticking fell on Leanna's ears like blows of a hammer on an anvil.

Her heart nearly seized when Jackson reached for Niniane's hand. A warning spark of elfshot fired from the queen's fingers. Jackson smiled as if he hadn't noticed.

Bowing, he brushed a kiss across the backs of Niniane's fingers. "Please, my lady. Give Leanna your blessing. Her happiness will be as perfect as you are."

Mac made a choking sound. "Laying it on a bit thick, no?" Leanna heard her brother whisper to his wife.

"Shut up," Artemis hissed back at him.

Niniane tilted her head back and examined Jackson's face. "You are a charming devil, aren't you? And handsome, too. No wonder Leanna tossed her better judgment to the four winds."

"Quite right," Jackson replied.

The queen's perfect bosom rose and fell in an exaggerated sigh. "My standards, I find, are dropping to new depths. I suppose I should count myself lucky Leanna didn't bring home a demon. At least you *used* to be alive."

Jackson quirked his most endearing smile. "Does this mean we have your blessing?"

Niniane made an impatient gesture. "Yes, all right, you may have it. All I want is my daughter's happiness, after all."

"Brava, Mum," Mac murmured. "You do have a heart, after all. Who'd have thought?"

"Oh, Mother . . ." Leanna could hardly get the words past the sudden lump burning in her throat. She wiped away a tear. "Thank you. Thank you so much."

"Yes," Jackson echoed, his arm tight around Leanna's waist. "Thank you, dear Mother."

Niniane's eyes widened in pure horror. "*What* did you call me?"

Jackson grinned. "'Mother,' of course. You don't mind, do you? 'Your Highness' seems far too formal for family."

The expression on Niniane's face was priceless.

"Now, let's not get carried away! My standards haven't plummeted *quite* so far as all that . . ."

Absurdly, Leanna began to laugh.

Mac's chuckle joined her. A moment later, Kalen, Christine, and Artemis joined in. The babies giggled. Pearl added a husky guffaw.

Eventually, even Niniane smiled.

"Well done, Mum," Mac said, wrapping his mother in a tight hug. "See? That wasn't so hard, was it?"

"You have no idea," Niniane muttered. "Thank the gods I only had two children. Now," she added, looking toward the children. "I want to hold Cameron."

Jackson kissed Leanna soundly on the lips as Niniane glided toward her grandson. "See? I told you everything would be perfect."

"Hmm . . ." Leanna tilted her head and pretended to consider the situation. "You did, didn't you?"

He nodded. "Most certainly."

Leanna smiled up at Jackson.

His eyes laughed down at her.

And the moment was, indeed, perfect.

ROBIN T. POPP

BEYOND THE MIST

To you.

ACKNOWLEDGMENTS

I would like to thank:

Marlaine Loftin—for being such a good friend, plotting partner and proofreader. Not everyone is willing or able to discuss fictional characters and situations *ad nauseum* and still have fun with it. I appreciate that you can.

Janette Weaver—for using various versions of this story on which to practice her copyediting skills; I certainly benefited from your efforts and feedback.

Mary Baxter—for sharing with me a moment of creative genius which became the Well of Lost Souls. (This acknowledgment appeared at the front of *Immortals: The Haunting* and if you (the reader) saw it and thought it made no sense, you were right, but even writers get confused on what book they're working on at the moment and while I was drafting the dedication for The Haunting, I was up to my Lost Well in *Beyond the Mist*, so to speak. This acknowledgment will make sense now.)

Leah Hultenschmidt—for being such a terrific editor. It's always a pleasure to work with you, Leah.

Jennifer Ashley and Joy Nash—for all their hard work and effort on the entire Immortals series which extended beyond the writing of their respective books. I hate to see it all come to an end.

CHAPTER ONE

"Do you want some help?" Jenna Renfield asked. "I know sometimes the longer words get to be a little tricky."

Dave Runningbear didn't bother to look up from his *Iron Man: Legacy of Doom* comic book. He lounged sideways in the recliner with one leg draped casually over the arm. "We can't all be scholars like you, Jenna."

"I'm not a scholar. I just happen to read books that don't have pictures in them." She turned her attention back to scrubbing the kitchen counter. "How come you didn't go with Mai and Nick to the party? I know you were invited."

He shrugged, but kept reading. She wondered whether Mai and Nick, still concerned about her state of mind after the death of her sister, had left Dave to babysit. "You don't have to stay with me, you know. I'm not a child."

He lowered his comic to peer at her, his gaze slowly ravishing her body. His coppery brown eyes sparkled with amusement. "Believe me. I would never mistake you for a child—ever."

Jenna had to remind herself that he didn't mean anything by it. Flirting came as naturally to Dave as breathing.

"As it happens," he continued, "I didn't go because I'd already made plans." He turned his attention back to his comic book, clearly having no intention of sharing the details of those plans with her—though she could guess.

She'd been living with Mai, Nick and Dave since before

Mai and Nick were married, just over two months now and she'd come to know Dave fairly well. A spirit walker and shape-shifting chameleon just like Nick, he did personal protection work for Nick's security agency. When he wasn't off working some assignment, he was playing host to a steady stream of female visitors who mostly looked like they worked at the local nightclubs.

Deciding she really didn't want to know his plans, she went back to her work in the kitchen. She'd just about finished when the intercom buzzed. Before she could even think about going to answer it, Dave flipped his comic book aside and hopped out of his chair. He moved across the room with the smooth ease of a natural athlete. His muscle shirt and loose cotton sports pants showed off his body to great advantage. He might be a jerk sometimes, but even Jenna had to admit he was a hot jerk.

He pressed the intercom button and spoke into the box. "Yes?"

"Dave? It's me," a bubbly female voice announced.

"Come on up." He pressed the button that gave his caller access to the penthouse's private elevator.

"How nice for you," Jenna said dryly. "You scheduled a play date."

"Yes, I did. And if you ask real nice, I'll let you play with us."

"A threesome?" she asked, pretending to be shocked.

"Just you, me and Tiffany." He waggled his eyebrows at her like a silent-movie villain might, coaxing a smile to her lips.

"Tempting—and yet I find myself completely turned off. Sorry."

"You don't know what you're missing," he teased just as the elevator chimed its arrival.

"No. *You* don't know what *you're* missing," she told him and, setting down the sponge, she walked from the kitchen to her bedroom, closing the door behind her.

She threw herself on her bed, fighting a sudden but familiar wave of loneliness. She wished her sister were around.

Sarah.

The name echoed in her head like a mournful cry. Sarah had been kidnapped by an evil genie three months ago and if Jenna had shown better control of her magic, Sarah might still be alive. With her death had gone Jenna's primary purpose in life. Now she faced a future that lay bleak and dismal before her.

It had been a long, full day in Ravenscroft and though the sun had gone down hours ago, the birthday celebration continued. Mai finished singing "Happy Birthday," and smiled down at her godson as he grinned at the adults gathered around him. Where had the time gone? It wasn't that long ago that she and Lexi had been single and the greatest excitement in their lives was a night at the local club. One Immortal warrior, an ancient demon, a battle of apocalyptic proportions, a missing woman, a haunted apartment, an evil genie and a devilishly handsome spirit-walker later, she and Lexi were both married to the men of their dreams and Lexi had a child. Life was good.

She glanced at Nick standing beside her. As if feeling her gaze, he looked down. The sparkle in his eyes was hard to resist when he wrapped his arm around her shoulders and pulled her to his side.

"What do you think?" he whispered. "It wouldn't be so bad having a little one running around the house."

"No, it wouldn't, except we don't live in a house. We live in a large apartment, which sometimes I think we're already sharing with two children. We might want to wait a little longer before we add to that confusion."

"Jenna and Dave still not getting along?" Darius asked as his son devoured the slice of birthday cake Lexi had placed on the tray of his highchair.

"Who can't get along with Dave?" Sekhmet interrupted. "He's perfectly charming."

Darius rolled his eyes at his mother. "You only think that because he flirts with you."

"What's this?" Darius's father asked, raising an eyebrow as he turned to his wife, a goddess once feared by many for her fiery temper. "Who dares to flirt with you? Perhaps I should teach him some manners."

Sekhmet, who despite being a grandmother looked like she was twenty-something, smiled at Wesley affectionately. "It is nothing, love. There is no need to be jealous. I only have eyes for you."

Wesley pulled her to him and kissed her. "As I for you."

At that moment, Zach let out an irritated scream. He'd pushed his cake away and was holding both arms in the air, impatiently opening and closing his tiny fists.

"All right, all right," Lexi said in a placating tone as she grabbed a cloth to wipe the sticky remains of cake from his face and hands. Once he was reasonably clean, she lifted him out of his high chair and carried him into the family room.

The rest of the adults followed and Mai took a seat beside Nick on the couch while Sekhmet and Wesley claimed the twin recliners. Darius sat opposite his parents in a large stuffed chair.

"How's Jenna doing?" Darius asked.

"It's hard to know," Mai said. "I didn't know her very well before Sarah disappeared, so I don't know what she was like before. She seems depressed and carries around a lot of guilt. She tries to hide it from the rest of us, but I think she has bad days and worse days."

"That's sad," Lexi said, going to perch on the arm of Darius's chair now that Zach seemed to be happily entertaining himself with his new toys. "But maybe that's why she and Dave don't get along. He's not exactly Mr. Sensitive."

"I don't think that's it," Nick said. "I actually think he likes her. And it's not like Jenna is the kind to sit around and mope. She gives back as good as she gets. And while those two are at one another, she isn't thinking about her parents or Sarah, which is why I think Dave teases her."

"I know about Sarah," Sekhmet said. "But what happened to her parents?"

Mai shot Nick a worried look before meeting the goddess's gaze. "We're not sure exactly. When Jenna was in the hospital in that catatonic state, Nick and I entered her dreams hoping to help her. We found her in the middle of a memory. She was a teenager arguing with her parents because she misused her magic. During their argument, she must have been drawing on her power without realizing it because when she shouted at her parents to go away, they just disappeared; vanished into thin air."

"She killed her own parents?" Lexi asked, sounding aghast.

"We can't be sure that what we saw was an actual memory," Nick cautioned. "All we know is that she blames herself for her parents' and Sarah's deaths."

"I feel bad for her," Mai said. "I just don't know how else to help her."

"Seems like you're doing plenty to help already," Sekhmet commented. "You're letting her live with you, making sure she eats."

"It's only until she gets back on her feet," Mai said. "She was in the hospital for so long after Sarah's death that she lost the two jobs she was working to put Sarah through school. Right now, she's got no income to pay for rent, food or anything else. Nick and I, well, we wanted to help. After all, the genie was after me when he took Sarah by mistake. That makes us feel responsible, in a way."

At that moment, Zachary tossed his toy aside. Like his father, he was covered with tattoos and he tapped one of them on his young chest. As he pulled his hand away, a dragon the size of a baby alligator rose into the air and started flying about the room, emitting tiny bursts of fire that singed whatever they struck.

Mai and the others jumped to their feet and raced after it, trying to capture the creature. Zach's peals of laughter mingled with a litany of oaths as chaos ensued in the palatial great room.

* * *

Sekhmet raised her hands, about to use her power to restore peace and quiet, when suddenly everyone stopped moving and the room grew eerily quiet.

Only another god could wield such power in her private domain, and she knew exactly who dared to do so now. For the last year, she'd dreaded this moment. Now that it was here, trepidation filled her.

"Poseidon. To what do I owe this pleasure?" She kept her tone casual but cool.

A large, powerfully built man with long, flowing white hair, mustache and beard materialized before her. He surveyed the frozen figures in a leisurely manner before turning his attention to Sekhmet. "Someone's having a birthday party, I see. One year old already?"

"Yes, he's Mai and Nick's child," she lied. "They're friends of Darius and Lexi. We wanted to do something special so we're having the party here in Ravenscroft." She gestured to Mai and Nick. "His parents. I think he looks just like his father, don't you?"

Poseidon scowled at her. "Please. You and I both know this is Darius's child, but the truth is, I didn't come here under my own power." He held out his hand, palm up, and a scroll appeared. "This brought me. You remember our contract, don't you? Sealed by our combined magic?"

Mistaking her horror-struck silence as a refusal to admit she knew what he was talking about, he undid the leather strap around the scroll and, using both hands, unrolled it. "Now, let's see." His eyes scanned the writing. "Ah. Here it is. In return for extracting Darius's immortal soul from his body and storing it in an amulet, I, Sekhmet, Eye of Ra, do hereby agree to surrender the life and soul of my firstborn grandchild to Poseidon within a year of his or her birth."

Sekhmet didn't need him to read the words to her. She knew them by heart because they'd haunted her every day for the last year.

Thinking back to the day she'd made the deal, it hadn't

seemed like such a heavy price to pay. After watching her sister Cerridwen suffer over the disappearance of her son, Tain, Sekhmet had been desperate to find a way to keep Darius from a similar fate. The only solution had been to confine him to Ravenscroft and for that, she'd needed help.

Poseidon's price for helping her was what he charged every deity who sought his help. After centuries of fathering infertile children, Poseidon's only recourse to get the grandchild he so longed for was to take someone else's.

Sekhmet knew that if she ever had a grandchild, she'd never be able to give him or her up. At the time, though, she'd had none and if her plan worked as intended, then Darius would never leave Ravenscroft, never fall in love and never father a child.

In her mind, she'd had nothing to lose and everything to gain, so she'd agreed to Poseidon's terms. He'd given her the spell she'd needed to remove Darius's immortal soul and place it in an amulet for safekeeping, making it impossible for Darius to leave Ravenscroft. And she'd told no one that Poseidon had helped her or that there'd been a price to pay. For seven hundred years, all had gone as planned.

Then last year, Darius had outmaneuvered her, taking back his soul so he could go back into the world and fight an ancient demon threatening to destroy the world. At the time, she'd been more worried about his safety than whether he would fall in love. Before she knew it, Darius was married with a child on the way.

She'd lived every day since Zachary's birth anticipating the moment Poseidon appeared to claim payment—and praying it would never come.

Her gaze flew to her grandson, frozen in place, his small hands pressed together in a delighted clap, his lips curled up in a happy smile. She felt heartsick. Zachary looked so much like Darius had when he was young. She remembered his first birthday party and how her friend Hathor had—

Her thoughts came to a screeching halt and she turned to glare at Poseidon. "You don't need my grandson. You already have a grandchild—and not someone else's. Your own, thanks to Hathor's fertility spell." She moved closer to the big man, angry now. "She told me all about it."

"It's true. Hathor paid her debt to me by using her power of fertility to help my daughter conceive a child," he admitted. "That's why I thought to ignore our agreement, but it seems the magic used to seal our contract is more powerful than either of us and it has brought me here to execute its terms. Before this day is out, your grandchild's soul will be mine unless we can agree to alternate payment."

"What would you like?" She tried to think what she could offer him. "I have many fine gemstones. Or perhaps your grandchild would like a living tattoo like the ones I've given Darius and Zachary."

"No. Payment must be made in kind: a soul for a soul."

She knew he was right, but who was she willing to sacrifice? Desperate, she looked about the room. These were the people she loved. She couldn't give up one of them.

"Time is running out," Poseidon warned her. "At midnight, the magic we used to seal our contract will rip your grandson's soul from his body—and there's not a damn thing you or I can do about it." He rolled up the scroll and, with a wave of his hand, caused it to disappear. "All I need by way of payment is another soul, Sekhmet."

She was desperate. "I may know of someone. She would fit in with your . . . collection."

Poseidon eyed her carefully. "In what way?"

"She may have used her magic to kill her parents."

"All right," he said. "But I need a name, Sekhmet. Give me a name. I'll take care of the rest."

She closed her eyes. "Jenna Renfield."

No sooner had the words been uttered than a flash of light and clap of thunder rendered the contract paid in full—and sealed the fate of the unsuspecting woman.

CHAPTER TWO

It was noon the next day when Jenna saw Dave again. She was standing in front of the refrigerator, trying to decide what she wanted for lunch, when his door opened.

He stepped out of his room, bare to the waist, and ran his fingers through his tousled hair. She longed to feel the silky strands for herself, run her hands across his broad chest. More than that, she wanted to be wrapped in his strong arms until she felt warm, safe and not so terribly alone in this world. Despite—or maybe because of—his constant teasing, Dave was the closest thing she had to a friend. Was it so wrong to want that friendship to be something more? Not wrong, she thought, but it wouldn't be smart. And she was always smart.

Turning back to the contents of the refrigerator, she studiously ignored him.

"Morning, sunshine," he said, strolling into the kitchen. "Did you make coffee?"

"Good *afternoon*," she said pointedly, "and yes I did, but that was hours ago and I've since drunk it all—and what I didn't drink, I poured out."

He grabbed the empty carafe off the warming plate and held it upside down. "Damn. Not a drop left."

"How about a sandwich instead," she offered, taking sliced turkey and Swiss cheese from the fridge.

"Are *you* offering to make *me* a sandwich?"

The look he gave her made her heart skip a beat. "Only

because I'm making myself one. Don't get used to it." He leaned against the counter next to her as she worked. "What about your sleepover buddy?" She tried not to sound too curious.

"What about her?"

"Should I fix her a sandwich as well?" She really didn't want to, but felt obligated to offer.

"No. She left early."

Jenna shook her head, amazed. "I don't know how you can do it."

"Years of practice," he said with a grin. "Builds the stamina."

"I wasn't complimenting you," she snapped. "Do you care about any of them?"

"Of course I care." He sounded irritated. "What kind of man do you think I am?"

"The kind who sees women only as sexual objects."

He grabbed one of the finished sandwiches off the counter and tipped it to her in mock salute. "Then you'll be happy to know that I don't see *you* that way."

She considered throwing something at him. A knife, maybe. "You have no respect for women."

"That's not true," he objected, going to sit on the couch. "I have a great deal of respect for women. I *love* women. You think I'm taking advantage of them, is that it? That they come over here thinking about china patterns and starting a family and then I cast them aside along with their broken hearts?"

She didn't answer because that was exactly what she thought.

He gave a labored sigh. "I'm totally honest with these women. They know up front that I'm not interested in commitment. It's all about having fun."

Jenna gave a disgusted snort.

"You want to know what your problem is?" he continued. "It's not that you don't know how to have fun. It's that you won't *let* yourself have fun." His tone turned gentle. "And I understand why, but you're wrong. Now that you know how precious life is, you should embrace it, live it to its fullest. Don't beat yourself up because you're still alive and your sister isn't."

His words caught her so off guard, she wasn't sure what to say or how to react. Fortunately, the intercom buzzed, giving her time to collect her thoughts as she went to answer it.

"Certified delivery for Jenna Renfield," a man's voice replied.

She pressed the button to give the man access to the elevator, all too aware of Dave, who'd come to stand beside her as she waited.

When the doors opened, a young man stood there. "Jenna Renfield?"

"Yes." Stepping forward, she took the proffered clipboard and signed for the delivery, then took the envelope he handed her. Studying its return address, she barely noticed the man's departure.

"Who's it from?" Dave asked, coming to stand beside her.

"Poseidon Cruise Lines." She opened the envelope, pulled out the letter and started reading.

"It's a scam," Dave, who'd been reading over her shoulder, pronounced a minute later.

"Not necessarily." Jenna pulled out the ticket that had been included. "It says free tickets are part of their promotional campaign."

"No one wins a ticket for a free four-day, all-expense-paid cruise—at least not to anyplace nice," he said, taking the letter from her so he could examine it more closely. "And what's with just one ticket? They expect a single woman to travel by herself? Look at this." He pointed to a date on the back. "They don't even give you a choice of when to sail. And they sure as hell don't give you adequate time to prepare. This cruise leaves tomorrow." He handed the letter back to her, dismissing it, and went to sit on the couch. "I bet it's not even legit. Go ahead. Log onto the Internet and see what you find. The only thing you'll get if you take that cruise is a small four-by-four room in the underbelly of a nasty old freighter, and the four days is how long it takes to reach a remote part of South America where you'll be sold into slavery."

She stared at him aghast. "You're unbelievable." Her sandwich forgotten, she headed for her bedroom.

"Where are you going?" he asked.

She stared up at him defiantly. "To my room—to pack."

"Don't do it, Jenna. It's a big mistake." His tone was very serious now.

"I disagree. It might be fun and you said yourself that I need to embrace life."

He got up from the couch and took hold of her upper arms so she couldn't avoid looking into his face. "Truce. Please."

She frowned, not sure what his angle was.

"You want to have fun? We'll do dinner and a movie tonight, you and me. If you don't want to go out, we can pick up dinner and rent a movie.

"I wouldn't want to get in the way of your other plans."

He shook his head. "I didn't make plans for tonight."

"No play dates?"

He shook his head. "No. Tonight, you're the only play date I have."

She gave him a sharp, distrustful look that had him holding up both hands in a gesture of surrender. "Just dinner and a movie, I promise."

She hated to admit it, but it did sound like a nice change. "Okay. Dinner and a movie sound good. But *only* dinner and a movie."

That evening, Dave congratulated himself. It had taken two months, but Jenna had finally agreed to go out with him. Of course, it was hard to consider it a real date when all they were doing was staying at home, eating pizza and watching a movie, but Dave would take what he could get.

When he'd first met Jenna, there'd been something about her that piqued his interest—something besides her classic good looks. He'd tried at Mai and Nick's wedding reception to get to know her better, but she'd run from him like a rabbit from a hound and he'd known then that if he ever wanted to know her better, he'd have to take things slow. Painfully slow.

"Jenna," he called out, slipping the first of the Bourne movies into the DVD player. "Movie's ready."

The door to her bedroom opened and their eyes met briefly. He took in her short shirt, dance pants and bare feet. With her long dark hair looking a bit mussed, her pixielike features and the dark circles under her deep blue eyes, she looked like a lost waif. A surge of protectiveness unexpectedly rose in him.

"We did say this was a casual dress occasion, didn't we?" She sounded both nervous and a little breathless, and he realized it was because he'd been staring at her.

"Yup. Want to get started? We can pause the movie when the pizza gets here. Have a seat while I get the beers."

He had just pulled two chilled Coronas from the refrigerator when the intercom buzzed. Holding both bottles in one hand, he pushed the button.

"Pizza," a male voice announced.

Dave buzzed him in, then carried the beer to the coffee table before walking back to the elevator.

As soon as the doors opened, Dave knew his perfect evening was over. Standing next to the pizza deliveryman was Mandi.

"Dave, honey," she cooed, looking like pure sex in her spandex aerobics outfit. Sidling up to him, she gave him a quick but very thorough kiss and pushed her way past him into the apartment.

Dave automatically handed the money to the deliveryman and took the pizzas, desperately trying to think of a way to get rid of Mandi and salvage his evening with Jenna. By the time the elevator doors closed, he still hadn't thought of anything. Turning around, he saw Jenna's shell-shocked face and no sign of Mandi.

He walked over to the coffee table and set the pizza boxes down. "I'm sorry," he said quietly, urgently. "Give me five minutes. I'll find out what she wants and get rid of her." He glanced at his closed bedroom door with unease. "Maybe ten."

He knew Jenna didn't believe he intended to send Mandi home, but he was determined to prove her wrong. Crossing to his bedroom, he opened the door and found Mandi kneeling on his bed, completely nude, looking like a center-fold spread in Penthouse.

"Come to mama," she said in a deep, throaty voice.

He groaned and closed the door behind him. Picking her clothes up off the floor, he handed them to her. "I can't. Not tonight."

Her eyes went round in stunned disbelief. "You don't want to have a little fun?"

He did—just not with her. His gaze flickered to the door.

"So it's like that," Mandi said in a knowing tone of voice as she started pulling on her clothes. She didn't sound mad, for which Dave was grateful.

"I'm sorry."

"Hey, my fault. I should have called first."

"I'm not just talking about that."

She looked confused for a moment, then figured it out and waved his apology aside. "Forget it. We knew this day was coming for one of us sooner or later." She paused, giving him a teasing smile. "Who'd have figured you'd trade me in for the Ice Bitch, though, eh?"

Dave frowned. "Don't call her that anymore, okay?"

She laughed. Dressed now, she sat on the edge of the bed. "Before you kick me out, would you do me a quick favor—for old time's sake?" She dug in her oversized purse and after a few seconds, pulled out a spiral notebook. "Could you tell me how to work this problem?" She flipped through the pages until she reached the one she wanted. "Number seventeen."

Mandi was taking online classes in her spare time, trying to get her undergraduate degree. "I can't teach aerobics the rest of my life," she'd told him when she'd first enrolled. That had been two years ago and this wasn't the first time he'd helped her with homework.

Glancing at his watch, he saw that he was well past his five or ten minutes, but he didn't want to take the time to go out and explain to Jenna what was taking so long. She wouldn't have believed him anyway. Better to just help Mandi so she could leave. Then he'd have the rest of the evening to make it up to Jenna.

He took the notebook and studied the problem. "Okay, when you're working with two unknowns, you first have to solve the equation for one of the unknowns in terms of the second. Understand?"

She got that deer-in-the-headlights look and he resigned himself to spending a little more time explaining the basic tenets of algebra. He'd known Mandi for years and in a sense, she was one of his closest friends. She deserved better than to be sent away when she needed his help. So he started over, this time working through the equation more slowly.

Jenna sat on the couch, watching *The Bourne Identity*. Matt Damon would never be so rude as to have sex with one woman when he was supposed to be on a date with another, she thought, casting a wistful glance toward Dave's door. She turned her attention back to the television and tried not to think about what was happening behind that closed door.

One beer, two pieces of pizza and half a movie later, she finally accepted that Dave didn't want to be with her. Putting the leftover pizza in the fridge, she went to her room.

There, her gaze fell on the envelope from Poseidon Cruise Lines sitting on her dresser. Maybe a cruise wasn't such a bad idea after all.

CHAPTER THREE

It was late when Dave finally said good-bye to Mandi and found himself staring at Jenna's door, wondering if he should try to apologize now or wait until morning. He hadn't expected the homework to take so long and now Jenna was probably asleep.

Rubbing a hand down his face, he meant to go back to his room, but something in him yearned to see her once more. He reached for her doorknob and found it unlocked. He eased open the door just enough for him to see her still form lying in the bed. He knew she had a strong spirit, but in her sleep, she appeared soft and fragile. Another wave of protectiveness rose up in him, but he squelched it. It wasn't his place or his right to be her protector.

About to close the door and go back to his room, he spotted the white envelope on her dresser. The cruise ticket.

He'd moved into the room and grabbed the envelope before he realized his intentions. It would be just like Jenna to go on the cruise—to spite him, he thought.

Back in his room, he considered the best place to hide the envelope. It wouldn't take her long to figure out he'd "borrowed" it. With a smile, he slipped it beneath his pillow. At the very least, they could find themselves in an interesting situation if she tried to retrieve the ticket while he was still asleep.

Then he stripped out of his clothes, turned off the light and went to bed.

* * *

When Dave woke the next morning, he estimated from the sunlight streaming into the room that it was going on noon. He rolled over, not yet ready to get out of bed, and heard the crinkle of paper. Remembering the envelope, he felt smug for having outsmarted Jenna. He climbed out of bed, pulled on a pair of boxers and left his room.

Expecting to find Jenna already in the kitchen, he was surprised to find the room dark and empty. He went to her door and knocked, not caring if he woke her. When she didn't answer, he opened it and looked inside. Her room was empty. He searched Mai and Nick's suite as well as the extra one. She wasn't in either.

It left only one possibility. She'd gone out. The question was—where?

It would be easy enough to follow her out of the building because one of the advantages to his being a spirit walker was being able to track the residual energy patterns people left behind as they moved from one place to another. Spirit walkers saw these patterns as colored wisps of clouds. The more vibrant the cloud, the more recently the person had been in that area.

Dave released his spirit from his body and moved about in the spiritual plane. He found traces of Jenna's deep purple energy all over the apartment, but the darkest, most recent trail led to the elevator.

After returning to his body, he went back to his room and was pulling on a pair of jeans when he spied the corner of the envelope peeking out from under his pillow. A horrible thought crossed his mind. He'd just assumed the ticket was inside.

Grabbing the envelope, he opened it—and felt cold sweat break out across his brow.

Jenna sat on the full-size bed in the surprisingly spacious cabin assigned to her on the cruise ship, and wondered if she might be making a mistake. Taking the cruise was an impetuous thing to do, but she'd been so hurt and angry last night that she hadn't cared if the cruise was a bit suspect. She'd wanted to prove to Dave that she could have fun without him. In order to be gone before he woke, she'd packed last night while he was still in with that woman, and slipped the ticket into her purse, leaving the envelope on the dresser.

The next morning, he was sure to realize she was gone, but if he looked for her, he'd see the envelope lying there and assume she'd just run an errand. He'd eventually figure out the truth, but she was hoping to be long gone by then.

The ship's horn let out a long blast, letting her know they were leaving dock. Finally. She sighed with relief and tried to look forward to her impromptu vacation. Everything would be fine. This would be fun.

She had just finished hanging up her last outfit when she heard a knock at her door. Surprised, she went to open it.

"What are you doing here?" Jenna demanded when she saw Dave standing there.

"I came to see if I could talk you out of this nonsense," Dave told her.

"Are you crazy? How'd you even get on the ship?"

"You'd be amazed at how easy it was. The security on this ship sucks, which is another reason why I think you should come back to the apartment with me—"

"No thanks. I'm not leaving."

He sighed. "I thought that's how you'd feel. Okay, then."

The blast of the ship's horn sounded again. "You'd better hurry," she said. "You don't want to get stuck on board."

"I think it's already too late, but that's okay." He leaned down to grab something and Jenna saw it was his khaki green duffel bag. Before she could ask why he had it, he was pushing past her into the room, looking all around. "Very nice. Bed's a bit small, but I suppose we can make it work." He plopped his duffel bag onto the bed and gave her a smile. "This cruise might not be half bad—up until they hit us over the head and sell us into human slavery."

"That's not going to happen," she chastised him. "Hey, what are you doing?" He'd unzipped his bag.

"Unpacking."

"Oh no, you're not." She went over to the bag and pulled the zipper closed again. "Get your own room."

"Can't. Don't have a ticket." With a grand gesture, he unzipped his bag again.

"This isn't going to work. Either you leave or I'm calling security."

Crossing his arms, he turned to her. "I'm not leaving you alone on the ship, Jenna, so if you want to call security and try to have me thrown off, you're welcome to try."

She stared at him defiantly. "You don't think I'll do it?" His knowing smile was the only response she got. "Watch me." She stormed out of the room.

Despite her anger, as she made her way down the hallway to the elevator banks, she was struck by how much the inside of the ship reminded her of a Las Vegas resort hotel. There was so much to see and do, it could take days to experience it all.

Exiting the elevator on the Lido deck, she walked around, smiling and nodding to the people she passed as she searched for someone to help her. There was a group gathered in the open area near the main pool, so Jenna stopped to see what was going on.

At the center of the group, a uniformed woman was talking. After listening a few minutes, Jenna realized the woman was the cruise director and she was outlining the rules of a game. Soon the crowd broke into teams of two, each holding a burlap bag. Standing side by side, each member of the team placed their inside leg into the bag. At the whistle, the teams raced for the finish line, cheered on by the assembled spectators. Jenna, caught up in the excitement, didn't notice the man who came to stand beside her until he spoke.

"Looks like fun, don't you think?"

She turned to him and offered what she hoped was a polite smile. "Yes, it does." The man was considerably taller than she was, with a ghostly pale complexion. He had porcelain-fine features and a decidedly aristocratic air. His platinum blond hair was buzzed close to his head and had it not been for his odd pale green eyes, she would have thought him an albino.

A sense of uneasiness crept over her, and she casually stepped away from him under the pretense of trying to get a better view of the next race. He moved closer, appearing just as casual.

"You're Jenna Renfield, aren't you?"

"I'm sorry, have we met?" She tried to hide her surprise that he knew her name.

"No, but I expect we'll be getting to know each other better." He gave a tight smile that sent a chill up her back. "My name is Conrad Davis." He held out his hand and waited for her to take it. Touching him was the last thing she wanted to do, but she didn't know how to get out of the handshake gracefully, so she placed her hand in his.

His hand closed over hers, overwhelming hers with its size. It was biting cold and she fought the urge to snatch back her hand. After a quick shake, he released her from his grip, but not his intense gaze.

"Would you like to go to the bar and get a drink?"

What had she done to make him think she was interested? "I'm sorry, but I'm supposed to be meeting someone." She glanced at her wrist, hoping he wouldn't notice the absence of a watch. "I should run. Bye."

She hurried off, pretending not to hear him when he called her name. She was halfway across the deck before she stopped to look back. There was no sign of Conrad. With luck, she'd lost him.

Feeling immensely better, she continued at a much slower pace. When she came across a row of lounge chairs looking out over the ocean, she decided to stop and enjoy the view.

Without land in sight on this side of the ship, it was easy to imagine being in the middle of the sea, surrounded by blue-green water. It had the effect of making her feel very small and alone in an otherwise huge, populated world. The scrape of a nearby chair disrupted her quiet reflections and she looked over to see who the newcomer was. Her heart stopped at the sight of Conrad easing his long frame onto the lounger beside her.

She tried to ignore him, but his presence loomed large beside her, making it impossible. "Mind if I keep you company—at least until your friend shows up? I assume this is where you're meeting him? Her?"

"Him," she croaked, her voice suddenly dry. Why was he following her? "I was just checking out the view one last time before going inside. It's such a lovely day." She scrambled up from her chair. "I'd better run."

This time, she didn't even bid him good-bye before hurrying off to find the elevators. She'd go back to her room and hope Conrad found someone else to bother.

She took the elevator down to her floor and was nearly to the last turn in the hallway that would take her to her room when she heard the ding of the next elevator's arrival. The hairs on the back of her neck began to prickle, causing her to look back just in time to see Conrad step off.

Terror shot through her. Convinced the man was stalking her, she hurriedly turned the corner, hoping he hadn't seen her, and raced to her room, pulling her key card out of her pocket as she did. Nerves caused her fingers to fumble with the card and she nearly dropped it. Then she was at her room and inserting the card to unlock the door.

As soon as she was inside, she slammed the door shut and threw the dead bolt. She didn't think it would keep a man as big as Conrad out if he was determined to get in, but she hoped it would slow him down. She looked around the room, wondering where Dave had disappeared to. The one time she needed him, he wasn't around. Anxiously, she waited, her eyes glued to the door, ears listening for any sound coming from the hallway. Several minutes went by before someone knocked. Then the door handle twisted like someone trying to get in. She cried out in alarm and jumped back.

"Jenna? Are you in there? Open the door."

It took a second for the voice to register and then she flew to the door to unlock it. "Dave?" She was so glad to see him standing there, she almost threw herself into his arms. It was with supreme effort that she resisted the temptation.

"Are you all right?" he asked, closely watching her. "I thought I heard you cry out."

She sighed and waved his concern aside. "I met a kind of creepy guy up on deck who knew my name and seemed to be following me. When you knocked on the door, I thought it was him." She forced a small laugh. "It's silly. Really."

He continued to closely watch her face. "You're sure you're okay?"

"Fine. Where did you go?" she asked, wanting to change the subject.

He didn't look as though he was satisfied with her answer, but didn't press her for further explanation. "When you didn't come back right away, I got worried, so I went to look for you."

"Oh." She struggled not to let him see the comfort she'd found in his explanation.

He looked around. "So, where's the security detail that's going to toss me overboard?"

The encounter with the stranger had made her forget why she'd gone on deck in the first place. Now she wasn't so sure she wanted to be alone. "I changed my mind. You can share the room with me."

"Don't sound so glum. It'll be fun." He winked at her and proceeded to dump the contents of his duffel bag onto the bed.

"What did you do? Pack your bag from your dirty clothes hamper?"

"These? No, they're clean. Why? Do they smell?" He grabbed several items and held them to his nose. "Yep, clean." He carried them to the dresser and pulled out a drawer. Finding it full, he pulled open another and then another until he'd checked them all and found them full.

Receiving a dark look from him, she capitulated and scooped up the contents of one of the drawers so he'd have space for his things, all the while mentally shaking her head at the irony of her situation. She'd taken the cruise to get away from him!

CHAPTER FOUR

"Are you decent?"

"If you mean am I dressed, then the answer is yes," Dave said from the bedroom.

Jenna rolled her eyes. Why did the man have to be a tease all the time? They'd spent the remainder of the afternoon walking around the ship and had more or less gotten along well. When the sun started to set, they'd visited one of the many onboard shops to purchase appropriate attire for the formal evening meals. Then they'd taken their new clothes back to the room to dress.

Jenna took another look at her reflection in the bathroom mirror. Turning first to one side and then the other, she studied herself critically. She'd curled her hair and pulled it back in quarter-inch strands, which she'd pinned in place for a cascade effect. She wore a pearlescent beige, off-the-shoulder gown that clung to her body in all the right places. She wondered if Dave would think she looked nice, but then silently chastised herself for even caring. What he thought shouldn't make a difference.

"I'm coming out." With a firm hold on her emotions, she opened the bathroom door.

Dave, in a black suit, light charcoal shirt and a burgundy tie, stood waiting for her. He looked stunning, very GQ.

"You look nice," she said a little shyly, trying to ignore the way he slowly walked around her, studying her from head to toe.

"Damn." He stopped in front of her and it was hard to read the expression in his eyes. "You are a vision tonight."

"Thank you." Despite her vow not to care, she took pleasure in his compliment.

"Ready to go?" He held the door for her as they left. Once in the passageway, he placed a hand at the small of her bare back to guide her forward. His warm touch made her feel safe, as though someone was looking after her. She'd looked after Sarah for so long, she'd forgotten what it was like to have someone take care of her. A girl could get used to this, she thought, though she'd be smarter not to.

They reached the dining room and stepped through the large double doors. The room was huge, easily filled with a hundred cloth-covered tables already set for the evening meal. The thousands of small glittering lights running across the ceiling two stories above cast a soft romantic glow over an otherwise dark room.

In addition to the tables, there was a live band playing, and couples on the dance floor. Jenna had never experienced anything like it. She was barely aware of Dave guiding her through the crowded room and probably would have walked past their assigned table if he hadn't stopped her. He held her chair while she sat, then took the seat beside her.

"It's beautiful," she gasped.

"Gorgeous." Something in his tone caught her attention and she looked over at him. His gaze was focused on her instead of the room and the realization made her blush.

At that moment, a waiter came over to take their drink orders and Jenna used the interruption to pull herself together. After he left, she became conscious of a prickling sensation running along her arms. She rubbed her hands up and down her arms to rid herself of it.

"You cold? You can have my coat." Dave started to shrug out of it, but she stopped him.

"I'm not really cold, but there's something . . . do you feel it?"

He grew very still, but then shook his head. "Not really. I mean, I feel a lot of energy in the room, but other than that . . . nothing."

Something familiar about the sensation disturbed her. *Death magic.* The words echoed through her head, sending a chill racing down her spine. Looking around the room now, the warm, cozy atmosphere took on ominous undertones.

"You okay?" Dave placed a hand on her shoulder and peered into her face. "You're pale as a ghost."

"There's something about this place," she started to explain. "I think—"

"Hello."

Jenna stopped talking and looked up to see an Audrey Hepburn-type woman and a distinguished-looking man taking seats across the table from them.

"Hello." Dave stood to shake hands with the man. They exchanged pleasantries and Jenna decided it would be better to wait until they were alone to tell Dave what she'd felt. Soon others joined them at the table and for the next several hours, they enjoyed great food and lively conversation. Jenna couldn't help admiring the way Dave seemed at ease around these people. He had a gift for getting along with everyone, it seemed.

Hours later, as they finished their meal, couples moved onto the dance floor.

"Let's dance," Dave suggested, pushing back his chair.

"I don't know," she hesitated. "I'm not very good at it."

"Don't worry," he told her, flashing a grin. "I'm a great partner."

Jenna smiled back as he led her onto the dance floor and pulled her into his arms. She hadn't danced with a man since high school. Not only was she worried about tripping over her own feet, she was keenly aware of the hard male body pressed up against her. The body alone would have left her breathless, but knowing it was Dave made her so self-conscious, she could barely function.

"Relax," he whispered in her ear. "Close your eyes and focus on the music. It's okay. I've got you. I'm not going to let anything happen to you."

His words washed over her, soothing her. She let the rest of the world slip away until he became the center of her universe. Her body melded into his until they were one. When he moved, she moved. When he stepped, she stepped. When he stopped, she stopped.

Abruptly brought back to reality, she wondered why they had stopped. Then she heard a familiar voice. "Excuse me, mind if I cut in? I'd like to dance with Jenna."

Jenna's gaze shot to Dave's face, praying he wouldn't do the polite thing and let Conrad cut in.

It was on her lips to refuse to dance with the man when Dave spoke.

"Sorry, pal," he said. "Not tonight." He spun Jenna around and they moved off in the opposite direction.

"Friend of yours?" he asked her.

"No," she replied adamantly. "I'd never seen him before today, but somehow he seems to know my name." She told him the story and watched his features grow serious. This was how she imagined him at work: alert, dangerous—even deadly, if need be.

"It might be best to avoid him altogether."

Jenna groaned. "That might be easier said than done. Here he comes again."

She watched as Conrad picked his way through the crowd toward them. Dave turned her so he could face Conrad, but Jenna had no trouble knowing when Conrad reached them. It was like running into a brick wall.

Dave looked up at him. "Something you wanted?"

"I'd like to dance with Jenna," Conrad said.

"Look, buddy," Dave said, stepping in front of Jenna protectively. "Jenna and I are here as a couple and I'm not sharing her. Go find someone else."

Conrad remained standing where he was just long enough that Jenna thought there was going to be trouble, but then he moved off into the crowd.

Dave pulled her back into his arms and dipped his head. "I think he got the message." His warm breath brushed across her neck and along her bared shoulder, sending delicious shivers down her spine.

"Thank you."

She moved as if in a dream and when Dave slowed their dancing until they were barely moving, she raised her head to look at him.

He was staring down at her, his eyes lit with heated intensity. He slowly lowered his head and she couldn't look away, couldn't move. She was mesmerized, eager to feel the touch of his lips against hers.

How long had she waited for this moment? Too long.

Then an image of Dave kissing Tiffany came to mind, quickly followed by an image of Dave kissing Mandi and Donna and Patricia and . . .

The list went on and on and now, at the bottom, would be her name.

She pulled out of his arms, shaken. "I'm sorry," she said. "I can't do this." She heard the panic in her voice and wasn't surprised when Dave gave her a questioning look. She couldn't possibly explain, so she didn't try.

With a muttered excuse, she hurried from the room. Worried that Dave would follow, she quickened her pace and reached the elevators just as the doors were starting to close. Squeezing through, she relaxed a little, knowing that she had the length of this elevator ride to be alone and pull herself together before facing Dave again. He had no doubt caught one of the other elevators and was following her back to their room.

She closed her eyes and tried to think. She must be crazy to even consider getting involved with Dave. It would be fabulous while it lasted, but what happened when he lost interest? She was in no position to move out of Mai and Nick's apartment, and watching him with other women was already so hard. It would be a constant reminder that she'd not been anything special, just one more in a long line.

The elevator doors opened and Jenna stepped out. She'd rounded the corner before noticing she was on the wrong floor. Disgusted with herself for not paying attention, she went back to the still-open elevator and pushed the correct button for her floor.

The doors remained open. Jenna pressed the button again, but with the same lack of results. She selected another floor, but nothing happened.

Frustrated, she got off and tried to call another elevator. None would come.

Forcing herself not to panic, she decided to go look for another bank of elevators, maybe at the far end of the ship. Or perhaps she could find stairs leading up to the next floor. She started down the passageway, noticing that unlike the rest of the ship, the interior here looked old and worn. It was almost as though she'd slipped through a time warp. Ancient globe lanterns gave off a dull yellow glow while their erratic flickering created shadows that jumped about on the walls.

From the end of the passageway, behind the only door, she thought she heard the sound of voices. Anyplace there were people would be better than where she was now. Maybe they could help her get back to her floor.

She started toward the sounds and as she got closer, what she'd first mistaken as singing took on a mournful quality.

Dave's theory of the South American slavery ring came back with harsh clarity, turning the sounds into cries of pain.

Fear pulsed through her veins. She was not a brave woman, but neither would she turn her back on people in need. Moving as silently as she could, she neared the door. She was almost to it when she noticed a prickling across her skin like thousands of roaches were crawling over her. *Magic.*

Nervous, she looked around. She was still alone in the passageway. She took hold of the door handle and exerted the slightest pressure. She expected to meet the resistance of a locked door and was surprised when it opened easily.

So much for the theory that there were captives on the other side. She wanted to laugh for letting her imagination run away with her. It was probably nothing more than a storage room.

Still, some sixth sense cautioned her to proceed slowly. She eased the door open just a crack, barely wide enough to see through, then she peered through the slim opening.

She fought to stifle her horrified gasp. What she saw made no sense.

Dozens of dirty, emaciated men and women sat in pairs down the length of a large room. Dressed in rags, each one gripped a large wooden pole with both hands. The pole stretched out horizontally with one end extending through a hole in the side of the ship.

She was trying to understand why no water was pouring in through the holes when a shrill whistle sounded, causing her to jump. At the sound, the men and women leaned forward, pushing their poles before them. At the next whistle blast, they leaned back, this time pulling the poles toward them. The whistle sounded again and again and each time, the men and women moved as one, forward, backward. Forward. Backward. Over and over.

They were rowing, Jenna realized with shock. The sound of grating metal drew her gaze to the chains securing the steel cuffs around each person's ankle to ringbolts on the floor.

Someone gave an angry shout, startling her. She stepped back, ready to make a run for it, but no one came. Daring to push the door open a hair wider, she saw a large man sauntering up and down the aisle between the rowers, blowing the whistle and shouting for them to "row harder." In one hand, he carried a large whip that, from time to time, he cracked indiscriminately against the back of a man or woman. The staccato sound reverberated loudly and was followed by the rower's tortured cry of pain. It was this sound that had first drawn Jenna's attention.

Horrified, she backed away, not even bothering to close the door. Soon she was racing back down the passageway toward the elevators, her heart hammering.

She pressed the call button several times, as if that would

make the elevator come faster. At any second, she expected to see the man with the whip suddenly appear behind her. The ding announcing an elevator's arrival startled her. As soon as the doors opened, she rushed inside—only to slam up against something tall and hard. Fingers gripped her arms like iron bands and when Jenna looked up, she saw Conrad's familiar white hair—and screamed.

CHAPTER FIVE

"Jenna. Calm down. It's me." Dave's voice pierced through her cries and she stopped fighting long enough to take another look at who was holding her.

"Dave?" Her relief was so great, she moved into his arms, feeling safe within their shelter. "I'm so glad to see you." In her fright, she'd mistaken the elevator's dome light, which from her angle of looking up, seemed to be sitting on top of his head, as Conrad's white hair.

"What are you doing down here?" he asked.

"I don't know. I must have pushed a wrong button, but wait until you hear what I found." She quickly told him about the magic and the room of prisoners. When she was done, she waited for him to tell her she was mistaken.

"Show me," he said, stepping out of the elevator with her before the doors could close.

Feeling more confident now that he was with her, she led him to the passageway and gestured to the door at the end. "Behind there," she whispered.

Dave moved past her toward the door. The deafening silence should have struck her as strange, but her attention was focused on the door. It was still ajar, just as she'd left it.

Hanging back a little to give him room, she waited breathlessly as he peered through the opening. Time seem to drag as she watched for his reaction.

After a minute, he glanced at her. "You're sure this is the right place?" he whispered.

She nodded, too afraid to make any noise.

Before she could stop him, Dave grabbed the knob and pulled open the door. Jenna gasped as adrenaline shot through her system. She didn't know if she should get ready to fight or run for her life.

But the room was empty.

There were no oarsmen. No rows of benches. No slave master. Not even a prickle of magic. "But it was all here," she said, disbelieving. "I don't understand." She moved back into the hallway and looked around. "Maybe we have the wrong room."

Retracing her steps to the elevator, she started over again, Dave following quietly behind her. They ended up at the same empty room.

Dave came up to her and put his arm around her shoulders. "Let's go back to our cabin. It's late and we both need our sleep."

Confused and disheartened, she allowed him to lead her back to the elevators.

"It doesn't work," she said when he pulled her inside the car and pressed the button for their level. To her amazement, the elevator doors closed and the elevator started its upward climb. Why did it work now but not earlier?

"You think I'm crazy," she said miserably once they reached their room.

"I don't think you're crazy." He offered her a reassuring smile. "I just wish you hadn't gone exploring on your own. It's dangerous."

Jenna heaved a sigh. "I didn't intend to go exploring on my own. The elevator wasn't working properly. No matter which button I pressed, it took me down to the bottom and wouldn't bring me back up. What was I supposed to do?" As she grew frustrated, her voice rose in pitch.

"Okay. I understand." He paused, like he was trying to control his own frustration. "Look, next time something like that happens and I'm not with you, use your magic to make the elevator work. I know you have talent. Mai and Nick told me you do. You don't have to be the victim in a situation like the one you just experienced."

She was already shaking her head. "My so-called magical talent is a curse and if I never use it again, it'll be too soon. Nothing good comes from using magic."

"If it's a matter of learning control—"

"It's not." She cut him off, turning her back on him and walking into the bathroom before he could ask her anything else. She refused to use her magic again, for any reason. And while he probably deserved an explanation, her reasons were nobody's business but her own.

"Look, I'm sorry that I upset you," Dave said to her through the bathroom door. "I didn't mean to."

She wiped at the unwelcomed moisture in her eyes. "I'm fine."

"Okay. Good." There was a pause and then he cleared his throat. "Look, it's late. I'm just going to go up on deck and enjoy a bit of the night air for a couple of minutes. Give you time to get ready for bed. I'll be back in a bit."

Then he was gone and she was staring at her own reflection in the mirror. Thoughts of the eerie room and what she'd seen stayed with her as she readied for bed and then later, when she tried to fall asleep. She found it impossible to relax without Dave around. The longer he was gone, the more worried she became that something might have happened to him.

It was nearly three A.M. before he returned to the cabin.

"You're still awake?" he asked, stepping into the room and seeing her sitting up in bed.

She gave him a rueful smile. "I was worried. Did you see anything . . . unusual?"

"No. Everything looked normal." He threw the dead bolt on the door before shrugging out of his coat.

"I know what I saw," she said around a huge yawn. Now that he was back, she was suddenly so tired, she could barely keep her eyes open.

"Let's talk about it in the morning." He walked into the bathroom and shut the door.

She wondered if he intended to share the bed with her, wondered if she wanted him to. And if they did share a bed, would he expect other things as well?

She tried to keep her eyes open as she waited for him to come out, feeling like they should set a few boundaries, but he was taking so damn long . . . .

Dave quietly opened the bathroom door and saw that Jenna had fallen asleep. Finally. Knowing how tired she was, he'd purposely taken his time getting ready in the hopes of avoiding that awkward moment when they had to decide who slept where. He'd already decided he wasn't sleeping with her—not because he didn't want to, but because he *did* want to. And if he'd crawled in bed with her, she'd know just how much he wanted to.

Jenna, however, wasn't the kind of woman to have casual sex—but she *was* a woman and if he'd told her he had no intention of sleeping with her, then she'd somehow interpret that to be a negative reflection on her. Dave understood women just enough to know there was no understanding the way a woman thought. So he'd taken his time, hoping she'd fall asleep.

He stared at her, trying to resist the temptation. She'd kicked off the covers and her nightgown was bunched up around her thighs, exposing nicely toned legs. He'd taken two steps toward the bed before he stopped and clenched his hands into fists to keep them from running along that long length of smooth skin.

"What are you doing to me?" he muttered under his breath. His every fiber vibrated with awareness of her.

Why was he so attracted to her? She wasn't like the other women he dated, willing to keep the relationship casual and uncomplicated. Jenna was the kind of woman who wanted commitment, and Dave wasn't sure he was ready for that.

He'd tried it once long ago and it had been disastrous. On the other hand, the thought of Jenna with any other man was nearly intolerable. The smart thing, he knew, was to keep it casual. End things before it was too late.

Ignoring the small voice that told him it was already too late, he shifted to a more comfortable form and settled down on the floor where he willed himself to sleep.

As sleep took him, Dave separated his spirit from his body and entered the spirit realm. Blurs of residual energy patterns were everywhere, like a time-lapse photo of Times Square at night.

He lifted his spirit higher and entered the dream realm. There was an unwritten rule about respecting the privacy of others, so he made it a point to not intrude on the dreams he encountered.

At first, he thought his movements through the realm were random, but gradually he became aware of a growing sense of purpose, as if he were being beckoned. By what, he didn't know.

He let the feeling guide his footsteps, passing close to dreams as he went. Sometimes the dreamer's emotions swept over him, adding clarity and definition to the dreams until Dave "saw" what the dreamer saw, but as a spectator, not a participant.

The more dreams he passed, the more puzzled he became by the overriding sense of gloom and horror. Not at all like the dreams of people on vacation. One dream, in particular, caught his attention.

A forty-something man stood at a kitchen sink, holding a prescription bottle in his hand. When he turned his head, Dave followed the direction of his gaze to the next room, to an elderly man. He was thin to the point of emaciation and his skin was nearly translucent with age.

At the sound of running water, Dave turned back to the younger man in time to see him dump a handful of pills into a glass of water.

"Drink this, Dad," the man said, handing the glass to his father.

The older man held it with difficulty in his palsied grip and slowly raised the cup to his lips.

Dave knew from the son's emotional projections that the pills would kill the old man—and that the son considered it a mercy killing, though Dave thought it looked more like murder.

Just dreams, he reminded himself as he continued, led by a growing certainty that he was nearing his destination.

Next he came upon a man and woman dancing. She wore a flowing, silvery gown and Dave sensed something familiar about her. He moved closer until he could see her face. Jenna.

It never occurred to him to turn around and leave, to give her privacy to dream. Seeing her in the arms of another man drove him forward, determined to see her dreampartner.

The couple turned and Dave found himself looking into his own face.

He was stunned—and pleased—and in so much more trouble than he'd first thought.

He should leave her to her dream, get out while he could; but he knew he wouldn't. With the ease of an experienced spirit walker, he slipped into her dream, taking his own place.

"I've wanted to dance with you ever since Mai and Nick's wedding," he said, pulling her a little closer as he slowed their movements. With a thought, he changed their surroundings until they were at the reception.

She was looking up at him, clearly puzzled, and so he kissed her. It was what he'd longed to do all night. To his delight, she kissed him back.

When they broke from the kiss, they were in the room on the ship. Even knowing this was a dream, he fumbled with the straps of her dress, wanting to feel her creamy, smooth skin. As the dress slipped to the floor, he gazed at her bared form with longing.

He tried to rein in his imagination, knowing that what he

"saw" was a product of his own creation and not reality, but he was too far gone to care about the difference.

White-hot desire shot through him. "I want to make love to you," he told her, knowing that she'd never realize how much he meant it.

"I'd like that." She spoke softly.

If this had been happening for real, Dave would have taken things slower, but this was a dream—Jenna's dream—and his ability to control it was limited.

In the space of a breath, they went from standing with clothes to lying naked in bed with Dave between her legs. He kissed her again and when they finally came up for air, she sighed. "Dave."

The sound of his name tore him from the dream and he raised his head to look at her, still asleep in bed. She sighed again, his name escaping on a soft rush of air.

It was everything he could do not to slip back into the dream, but he knew better than to risk it. He was already in danger of losing control.

He lowered his head and listened to the sound of her breathing, letting it lull him to sleep.

Just before he drifted off, he thought he heard a distant keening cry in the night, so faint it could only be the wind.

CHAPTER SIX

Jenna's dreams turned from erotic to frightening in a heartbeat. One minute, she was dreaming of making love to Dave, and the next she found herself racing through the dark corridors of the ship, lost and confused. Wailing voices called to her. "You belong with us," they cried.

She ran faster until a vaporous, ghostly light appeared, blocking her escape.

"He's waiting for you," the apparition moaned. "Beyond the mist."

The specter came at her, wrapping its ghostly tendrils around her until she couldn't move. She fought for breath, but the tendrils were squeezing the air from her lungs. Fear made it impossible to think of anything but the cold death that waited. She opened her mouth, trying to give voice to a scream. It echoed silently in the night.

Jenna lurched upright in bed, covered in sweat. Frantically, she looked around, fearing the apparition might still be after her, but she was alone—and it was morning. Rays of bright sunshine were pouring through the open curtains to fill the cabin with a cheery glow, helping to chase away the lingering vestiges of her nightmare.

She wasn't surprised she'd had the nightmare, not after finding that creepy room downstairs, but why couldn't her subconscious have just continued with the first dream?

She looked at the empty spot beside her in the bed. Dream

sex might be the only sex she ever had with Dave. It seemed a shame to cut it short.

She wondered where he was. When she heard the sound of breathing, she threw back the covers and crawled to the foot of the bed, where she froze. Lying on the floor was a large black panther.

She gasped in surprise, and the sound woke the panther. He opened his eyes and lazily turned his head to look up at her. Jenna's heart started pounding so hard, her entire body shook.

The large cat blinked and she realized there was something familiar about its coppery brown eyes. "Dave?" Her voice came out barely above a whisper.

The cat blinked again before gracefully rising to its feet. Jenna scooted back, waiting expectantly.

The air around the cat began to shimmer and the cat's features blurred. The colors of its black coat and brown eyes ran together like a sidewalk chalk drawing in the rain before finally turning to a light bronze.

Then the image elongated and took on definition. Soon, Dave stood before her, tall, majestic—and nude.

Her hand flew up to cover her eyes. "For cripes sake, put on some clothes," she said.

She heard the sound of movement followed by the rustle of fabric. "Okay, I'm decent," he announced a minute later.

"That still remains debatable," she muttered, as she opened her eyes to peek at him through cracked fingers. When she'd verified he was dressed, she lowered her hand.

"You almost gave me heart failure," she exclaimed. "I keep forgetting you're a chameleon."

"Sorry I scared you," he said, stretching.

"You didn't." Her gaze drank in the muscled definition of his upper arms and chest, and the way his cotton pants hung loose on his hips.

"You all right?" he asked, interrupting her musings.

She looked up guiltily to meet his gaze, hoping he hadn't noticed the way she'd been staring at him. "Um, yes. Fine, thanks. And you?"

"I'm good."

Jenna nodded. "Good." What had they been talking about? "Why did you sleep on the floor?"

"I thought it safer not to assume we were sharing the bed. That pretty much left the floor, which, I find as I get older, isn't as comfortable as it used to be. At least, not in my human form."

"So you chose a panther? Why not, say, a cute poodle? I wouldn't have been frightened of a poodle."

"Right," he said with a small degree of irritation in his tone. "Neither would anyone else. After what we've seen on this cruise, I thought it best to be prepared for anything. If someone broke into our room while we slept, running into a panther would make them think twice about staying."

It bothered her that he felt the need to protect them. "Do you think we're in danger?"

"I don't know, but it never hurts to be cautious. On the other hand, I don't think we need to hide out in our room for the rest of the trip. Let's do whatever it is most people do on a cruise—only let's keep our eyes open, okay?"

She nodded, still not one hundred percent reassured.

"Are you hungry? Because I'm starving. Changing forms burns a lot of calories."

At the thought of food, her stomach growled. "You want to check out the breakfast buffet?"

"Works for me," he said. "Out of curiosity, what are our plans today?"

"*Our* plans?" She had trouble believing he *wanted* to spend time with her, which meant he thought she was in danger and needed protecting—whether from others or herself, she didn't know. "You don't have to spend your vacation time with me. I'll be fine by myself."

"I know you will," he replied without any hint that he was patronizing her. "As it happens, I want to spend this time with you. Is that so surprising?"

"Actually? A little."

"Well, it shouldn't be." He smiled and she couldn't stop

the little thrill of excitement that ran through her at the thought of spending the day with him. An echo of her dream—nothing more. "So—what are our plans?"

"Well, they're pretty exciting." Her tone was heavy with sarcasm to mask the relief she felt. She knew she wasn't crazy, which meant strange things were happening on this ship. She didn't want to be alone. "We'll be sunbathing."

"Sounds great." Jenna waited for him to try to talk her into doing something he might enjoy more, but he didn't. "You can have the bathroom again to dress while I change into my bathing suit out here. We can grab a bite to eat on our way to the Lido deck. How's that sound?"

"Great." And it did. Climbing off the bed, she grabbed her clothes and went to change.

Ten minutes later, she stared at herself in the mirror. There was a lot less to her bikini than she'd remembered. She might as well be wearing nothing at all, she thought, eyeing herself critically. Briefly she considered telling Dave she'd changed her mind, but then realized she was being silly. Compared to Tiffany and Mandi, Dave wouldn't give her a second look.

Pulling on the kimono, she opened the door.

Dave had already changed into his suit and stood waiting. "Ready?"

"Let's go," she said. She slipped her feet into sandals and opened the door. She was about to step out when she remembered towels.

Turning suddenly to go back in, she ran full body into Dave, who grabbed her by the arms to steady her.

"Towels?" she mumbled weakly, much too conscious of where his body touched hers.

"They have extras on deck. I saw them yesterday."

He spun her around playfully and followed her into the passageway.

They entered the dining hall a few minutes later to find an elaborate buffet. As they helped themselves to food, Jenna couldn't help looking around for anything that might appear out of place. But everything seemed normal.

After they finished eating, they went to the Lido deck, where they were met with clear blue skies and bright sunshine. Finding a secluded spot not far from the smaller of the two pools, Jenna busied herself covering her chair with one of the towels they'd picked up. Then, with a quick glance at Dave to make sure he wasn't watching, she shed the kimono.

"Holy fu—"

Jenna spun around at Dave's uttered curse to find him staring at her. He tore his gaze away from her body, with effort it seemed, and met her gaze. "Sorry," he said, clearing his throat. "You look . . . uh . . . really nice."

"Thank you." Feeling self-conscious, but pleased by his reaction, Jenna stretched out on the lounge chair. She pulled a bottle of sunscreen from her bag and started applying it to her arms and legs, trying to ignore the way Dave watched her. When she finished, she held the lotion out to him. "You're welcome to use this if you want."

"Thanks." He sounded a little surprised, but took the bottle from her and spread lotion over his arms and chest. Jenna was tempted to watch but didn't dare. Instead, she closed her eyes and let her thoughts drift as the warm sun soaked into her skin.

She had no idea how long she lay there before Dave's voice roused her from her daydreams. "You might want to turn over."

She cracked open an eye to look at him. The sun was bright and she had to shield her face to see him. "What?"

He was sitting on the edge of his lounger and she had the impression he'd been sitting that way for several minutes. Had he just been staring at her?

"We've been out here almost twenty minutes and your skin is starting to turn red," he explained. "If you want to tan evenly, you might want to flip over."

Jenna held out her arms and looked at them. He was right. They were just starting to turn pink. "Thanks."

As gracefully as she could, she turned onto her stomach

and had just closed her eyes again when she sensed Dave standing over her. "What are you doing?"

"Relax," he said. "I'm just going to put lotion on your back."

"You don't need to." The last thing she wanted was his hands on her. Actually, that wasn't true, but her dream was still too fresh in her mind and she was afraid she might do something embarrassing—like moan from the pleasure of his touch. He didn't listen to her and before she could stop him, he'd squeezed lotion into the palm of his hand and rubbed it over her.

The lotion was cold, but his large hands were warm as they ran over her skin. She fought to keep her breathing even, hoping he wouldn't notice how her heart pounded in her chest. She was in agony. Sweet, sweet agony and as much as she wanted him to stop, she wanted him to never stop.

Dave spread his fingers and slid them up Jenna's back, knowing beyond a shadow of a doubt that he was making a huge mistake. He was still half jazzed after their dream encounter, and her skin felt so soft and smooth. He could practically span her waist with his hands and when he envisioned doing it, his gaze drifted to her hips and butt.

Thank you, Mother Goddess, for bikinis, he thought. He would have loved to see her in a thong, but it was probably just as well that she wasn't wearing one.

"You don't have to do my legs," she said when he started running his hands down them. He noticed the breathless quality of her voice. Maybe she wasn't as unaffected as she'd wanted him to think.

"No problem," he assured her. "I'm almost done. There." He rubbed the excess lotion across the top of his legs and moved a bit awkwardly back to his lounge chair, taking care not to stand too straight.

For another twenty minutes, they sunbathed in silence. Finally, Dave had had enough. He was hot—in more ways than one—and needed a cool dip in the pool. He looked over at Jenna. Her head was turned toward him, but her eyes were closed. He stared at her for a minute, just enjoying the view. Why had he never noticed before how beautiful she was?

He knew why Nick had warned him away from her. She was in a vulnerable state and he wasn't known for long-term, meaningful relationships. Jenna had enough troubles; she didn't need someone like him playing with her emotions. Yet he wasn't sure he could leave her alone.

"I'm going for a swim." He pushed himself off the lounger, no longer able to lie beside her alone with his thoughts. "Want to join me?"

Jenna raised her head to look over at the pool. "I don't know."

"Come on," he encouraged. "Let's go cool off and then we can come back." He saw from her expression that she was tempted. "The pool's empty," he added. "You won't have to worry about kids jumping in and splashing you or anything. But it's up to you."

He went over to the pool's edge and tested the water with his foot.

"How is it?" Jenna called over to him.

"It's nice. Cool but not cold." He dove in and began plowing through the water with long, even strokes. When he reached the far end, he executed a flip and started back. By the time he reached the other end, Jenna was in the water, standing on the bottom step.

"You're right," she said. "It does feel good." She looked around the empty deck. "I wonder why there aren't more people out here enjoying it."

He looked down at the clear blue water. "I don't know. You think there's something wrong with the water? It feels . . ."

His words trailed off as a peculiar expression came over his face.

"Is something wrong?" Jenna asked, growing concerned.

"My hand feels funny." She heard the alarm in his voice and her gaze flew to the hand he lifted out of the water. At nearly twice its normal size, it was swelling at an alarming rate. When he raised his other hand, she saw that it, too, had started to swell.

Horrified, she started toward him, intent on helping.

"Stay back," he hollered. "I think it's spreading. My back . . ." He tried to reach behind him, but his swollen arm was useless and all he did was turn in place.

When she saw his back, she gasped. A huge piece of swollen flesh protruded from the center. It looked like a—fin? She stared at it a bit longer and then started to laugh. "Cute."

He turned and gave her a big grin before diving under the water. He swam to the deep end of the pool and then shot into the air, fully transformed into a dolphin, executed a flip and dove back into the water.

He swam to her and then reared out of the water, swimming backwards. She clapped her hands in delight and moved to stand in the shallow end. When he brushed against her, she reached out to touch him. Somehow she ended up holding onto his fin and letting him pull her the length of the pool and back.

She laughed despite herself, only to quickly close her mouth to avoid swallowing water. After their third lap around the pool, she let go and went to sit on the steps. "I had no idea you were so talented," she said when he morphed back into himself.

"Please," he scoffed, treading water. "I've got mad skills. Turning into a dolphin's just a parlor trick. Check this out."

He sank into the water and shifted into a great white shark. Slowly, he circled the edge of the pool, looking enough like the real thing that she scrambled up the steps and out of the pool, preferring to watch from a safe distance.

The shark—she had a hard time thinking of it as Dave—passed in front of her and then swam to the deep end.

"Oh!" Startled, she jumped back when a large serpent's head burst from the water. Covered with scales in shades of sapphire and emerald, the creature's body filled the entire deep end. It moved toward her and she had to tip her head back to look up at him. Her breath caught in her throat. "Magnificent."

The serpent's form blurred and the air around it shimmered. When everything came back into focus, Dave, once more in his human form, stood in the shallow end.

"I think you forgot something," she said, her cheeks heating.

"Oops." He gave her a wicked grin. "Be right back." Turning, he gave Jenna a momentary view of his bare buttocks before diving into the water. She saw him swim to the deep end and retrieve something off the bottom. When he reappeared, he was once again wearing his bathing suit.

"That was amazing," she said as he came to sit beside her on the steps. "Your ability to change into different forms, that is. Not that other display, although . . ." She laughed at the shocked expression on his face. "What?"

"Did you just crack a joke?" he teased.

She shrugged. "What can I say? I'm full of surprises."

"I'm beginning to see that," he replied in mock seriousness.

She enjoyed this playful exchange, but her happiness was quickly followed by guilt. What right did she have to be happy when Sarah's chance at happiness had been brutally taken away? Her smile died on her lips.

"Did I say something wrong?"

Jenna shook her head. "No."

He leaned into her, gently nudging her shoulder with his. "It's not your fault."

"What?"

"Sarah's death."

She wasn't surprised that he knew what she was thinking. "I had a chance to save her and I failed. That makes it my fault. Maybe if I'd tried harder . . ."

Dave watched her eyes tear up and draped an arm across her shoulders. She didn't try to pull away. "From what Mai and Nick told me, you did everything you could. The genie holding Sarah hostage was stronger than anyone expected."

She wanted so badly to believe that—to be absolved of her guilt—but she couldn't let his explanation blind her to the truth. "That's not what killed her. She died because I used magic."

"What? That's absurd. Who told you that?"

Jenna shook her head. "No, it's true. Someone *always* dies when I use magic." A small cry of despair escaped when she exhaled.

"What do you mean? Other than Sarah, who else has died?"

"My parents."

CHAPTER SEVEN

Dave was stunned by the confession. Was it really possible that she'd killed her parents with magic?

No. He refused to believe it. Jenna wasn't a murderer. "Tell me what happened," he gently coaxed her.

"I was the only one in my family born a witch," she began. "My parents didn't understand what it was like to have such talent. They couldn't teach me how to use it and they certainly didn't know how to help me control it."

Dave tensed, trying to mentally prepare for whatever she was about to tell him.

"When I turned eighteen, I no longer needed my parents' permission to study witchcraft, so I contacted the local coven and started lessons." She sighed. "It was wonderful. These people didn't think of me as a freak because they were just like me. They taught me the fundamentals of spell casting and I was a good student."

Dave thought he caught a hint of a long-ago excitement in her tone.

"It was tough for a while, going to school and secretly attending night courses at the coven. I thought it would get easier once I graduated, but then my folks started pressuring me to attend college. To appease them, I enrolled in community college, but I hardly ever went to class."

She paused and Dave knew she was finally getting to the hard part of her story. "On the day my parents died, I'd spent the entire day practicing magic in my room. It was the first time since starting my studies at the coven that I was using magic without another witch present to supervise. I got so caught up in what I was doing that I forgot that my parents had asked me to pick up Sarah from school that day. We were going to have a family portrait taken and they wanted everyone home early enough to get dressed.

"When my folks got home and realized Sarah wasn't there, they blew a gasket. There was a chance that Sarah would catch the late bus home when no one showed up for her at school, but rather than take that chance, they went to get her."

Her tone grew somber. "As it turned out, Sarah did catch the late bus, thank the goddess. Otherwise, she would have been in the car with my parents when an eighteen-wheeler ran a red light and T-boned them. The police later told me that they died on impact."

She started to cry and Dave wrapped his other arm around her, offering her what comfort he could. "Jenna, I'm so sorry."

"If I had just done what they asked me to do, they wouldn't have been killed," she sobbed against his chest. "It's my fault they're dead."

"No," he said firmly. "It was the truck driver's fault. If he hadn't run the light, your parents would have gone to the school, seen that your sister had caught the bus and returned home. You weren't responsible for their deaths any more than you are for Sarah's. That genie was extremely powerful. You can't blame yourself."

She shook her head and he knew that it would take much more than his saying so before she'd forgive herself. All he could do was stay with her and console her as best he could. He would hold her forever, if it took that—and he found his willingness to do so odd. He wasn't really the kind of man who enjoyed cuddling.

Finally, Jenna pulled back to wipe her eyes. "Thank you for letting me cry all over you," she said softly, not quite meeting his gaze. "And for talking to me. I've never told anyone about what happened that day."

His expression was tender as he used his thumb to wipe away a tear trailing down her cheek. "I'm glad you told me." They reached an uncomfortable moment of quiet and Dave refused to let it linger. "It's almost lunchtime. Let's go get something to eat."

She nodded and after gathering their things, they headed back.

During lunch, things between them were different, Jenna thought. Their constant teasing had taken on a lighter tone and there was a growing camaraderie accompanied by something more, something exciting and forbidden. Jenna had to work hard to concentrate on their conversation while they ate because while the words they exchanged were friendly, the looks were smoldering and fraught with sexual tension.

"I'm glad I decided not to let you take this cruise alone," Dave told her after they'd both been quiet for a bit.

She smiled, warmed by his words. "I'm glad you did, too."

"Please don't take this the wrong way, but I really enjoy being with you. I can't believe you've been living with me for three months and I'm just now discovering this."

"Well, I'm not exactly living *with* you," she clarified. "And you've been . . . busy."

"Work," he explained.

Jenna gave a ladylike snort of laughter. "Yeah, right. Unless by work you mean Tiffany, Mandi, Sondra, Bambi—"

He laughed. "I don't know anyone named Bambi, but I concede your point." He sobered. "You don't approve of the women I see."

"It's not the women," she clarified. "It's the number of women." She sighed, knowing she was at risk of ruining the tone of their new relationship, but unable to stop herself from asking. "Why so many?"

He stared at her hard for a minute. "The truth?"

She nodded, almost holding her breath.

"You know that my people believe in spirit mates. That for each of us there exists that one special someone with whom we can share the deep bond of true love." He hesitated, drawing a breath. "Well, I found mine several years ago."

The news left her feeling suddenly adrift. She didn't like hearing that he'd already found his one true love; it meant it would never be her. Not that that was even a possibility, she quickly told herself.

"In the way most spirit mates find one another, she came to me in my dreams," he continued, seemingly lost in the retelling of the story. "I was surprised to discover she was someone I knew, though at the time, I didn't know her well. Anyway, we met in person and it wasn't long before we started dating. Within a week, we were engaged and a year later was our wedding."

Jenna gasped. "You're married?"

He shook his head. "She left me standing at the altar. It never occurred to me that she'd run off with someone else. I thought she was having last-minute wedding jitters, or worse, had had an accident driving to the church. I went to look for her, thinking to comfort her, and found her in the arms of another man. In that moment, I realized she'd been lying to me all along."

"But she was your spirit mate," Jenna said, incredulous.

"Turned out that was a lie, too. Like me, she was a spirit walker. She purposely entered my dreams and made me think I'd found my spirit mate."

"Why would she do that?"

"Money, I suppose. Or maybe status. My family was one of the few in the village with money." He shrugged. "Needless to say, we didn't get married after that. Nick's the only one who knows what really happened that day."

Jenna thought she understood now. To keep from getting hurt again, he'd made it a practice to casually date as many women as he could so as not to become too attached to any of them. "Thank you for telling me."

He nodded and looked pointedly at her empty plate. "You finished eating? If so, I've got a surprise for you."

"What?" she asked, laying her folded napkin beside her plate and pushing away from the table.

"Not here."

Jenna loved surprises, though she hated waiting to have them be revealed. She pestered Dave the entire walk back to their room, but he refused to say anything. Finally inside their room, she turned to him expectantly and waited.

"I've been thinking about what you told me earlier," he began. "About how every time you use your magic, someone dies. We both know that's an exaggeration. I think it's also an excuse to not use magic anymore."

She stared at him dumbfounded.

He didn't give her time to protest. "Your power frightens you because you never learned to control it. So I'm going to teach you."

"How would you know anything about casting spells?" she asked, forcing her stunned brain to form coherent thoughts.

"My mother's a witch. I grew up watching her practice and sort of picked up a few things here and there." He took her hands in his. "Do you trust me?"

She studied his eyes and then slowly nodded.

"Okay then. Let's get started." He turned her hands so the palms faced up. "Now relax and focus your thoughts. Try to form a simple ball of power."

She nodded and stared at her hands. "Mother goddess, hear my plea. Grant the power I ask of thee—"

"Stop," Dave ordered.

"Why?" The air above her hands had started to shimmer, a sign that her magic was gathering.

"My mother never spoke spells out loud. She said that words and spells are good if you have a group of witches trying to work together, but when you're practicing alone, words are too limiting. For instance, think of the sunset we saw last night. When I say go, try to remember all the different colors. Go." A few seconds ticked by. "Stop. How many colors did you remember?"

"I don't know. Maybe a dozen or more."

"A dozen different colors in a fraction of a second? Okay. Now when I say go, I want you to give me the names of the exact shades you saw. Don't say orange if the color was tangerine, understand?" She nodded. "Go."

"Mauve, gold, tanger—"

"Stop." He cocked an eyebrow. "What happened? I gave you the same amount of time. I even gave you one of the colors and yet you only gave me two of the dozen or more colors you saw. My point here is that the mind is a powerful tool, with infinite possibilities. Use it to control your magic."

"I'm not sure I know how," she admitted.

"By concentrating. Now try again."

She held her hands in front of her, palms up. She started to open her mouth to chant, but snapped it shut and instead used her thoughts to call the magic.

To her amazement, the air above her hands began to shimmer with power. She concentrated harder, but the ball began to fade.

"Don't force it," Dave coached. "Let it come."

She relaxed and tried again. Above her open palms, the shimmering air began to form a ball. She kept her breathing steady, but the ball continued to grow larger. Suddenly, she had visions of the ball filling the room or blowing a hole in the side of the ship. Who knew what devastation that much magic could do?

"Jenna." Dave's sharp voice brought her back to the present. Her hands were shaking and the ball of magic was shimmering like a gigantic bowl of golden Jell-O. "Relax. In your mind, visualize the ball growing smaller and the magic subsiding. You can do it. You have to believe in yourself."

Jenna let go of her fears and concentrated on what he'd said. It meant so much that he believed in her. As she focused on that one thought, the magic began to shrink. Soon it was once more the size of a golf ball. She was nearly giddy with excitement, but she kept her thoughts and emotions under control.

Feeling the drain of having used magic, she let the ball vanish completely. She'd done it. She couldn't believe it. Overcome with happiness, she threw herself into Dave's arms and kissed him.

When she realized what she'd done, she tried to pull away, but his arms tightened around her like steel bands. He angled his head and kissed her, drinking from her lips like he was a dying man and she was the well of life.

She lost awareness of everything except for this man holding her in his arms. When he finally ended the kiss, she stepped back awkwardly.

"I could definitely get used to that," he said. Then he took a breath, as if he needed to clear his head. "You're more powerful than I thought," he continued a minute later. "You'll need to practice, of course. When we get back home, I'll take you to meet my mom. She'd be glad to talk to you about magic. I'm sure there are a lot of things I don't know about the craft that she could help you with."

Jenna could hardly believe it. "You'd really do that? Introduce me to your mother?"

He smiled. "Sure. I think you'd get along well."

CHAPTER EIGHT

Jenna practiced for several more hours before she begged Dave to let her stop. Using magic was draining and she was exhausted.

"There are a couple of hours before dinner. I'll leave you alone to rest," he told her.

She didn't want him to leave, but was too tired to argue. "All right," she agreed. "But I don't want to sleep so long I can't fall asleep tonight."

"Okay. I'll be back in two hours to check on you, deal?"

"Deal." She lay down, her eyelids suddenly too heavy to keep open.

"Get some sleep, Jenna."

She heard the click of the door opening. "Dave?"

"Yeah?"

"Please be careful." She was asleep before the door had closed.

Dave was glad she hadn't asked where he was going. He didn't want to lie to her, but the truth would only worry her.

He walked to the elevators and pressed the button that would take him to the floor where he'd found Jenna in such a state of panic. Though he had no real expectation of finding a room full of chained oarsmen, he was going to look anyway.

It didn't take him long to find the room at the end of the passageway and he was just considering whether or not he should simply open the door or try a subtler approach when he heard the sound of footsteps coming from the other side of the door.

Surprised, he backed hurriedly down the passageway and around the corner, where he stopped to listen. The door opened and he caught the sound of voices, one of which sounded familiar.

". . . talked to him last night and he's not happy about the situation," said the man Jenna had called Conrad.

"So what?" the other man argued. "She brought a friend. I don't understand the problem. Why not take him, too?"

"You know it doesn't work that way."

"But to kill him?" The second man sounded surprised. "Are you sure that's what the boss wants us to do?"

"That's what *I'm* telling you to do. On this side of the curtain, *I* give the orders. Remember, we're not dealing with an ordinary human. He's a spirit walker. They're harder to kill."

"What about the woman?"

"We leave her for the boss to deal with."

Their voices were louder now, and to avoid being caught, Dave moved to the end of the passageway. He needed to figure out a way to get himself and Jenna off the ship as soon as possible.

The voices stopped and the sudden silence set alarm bells pealing in Dave's mind. He turned, intent on making a quick run for the elevators, only to stop dead in his tracks.

Conrad stood there, a massive tower of hostility. Dave didn't even have time to wonder how the man had slipped past him. Conrad's meaty fists slammed into Dave's face and stomach with inhuman force. Dave doubled over in pain. He looked up in time to see the next blow coming and just managed to block it with his arm.

He heard the sound of bone cracking and felt the pain radiate along his arm. Fear for Jenna's safety enabled him to keep fighting back.

Conrad's lips split when Dave punched him in the face, though Dave thought he'd sustained more damage to his own hand. He refused to back down, though, and was in the act of launching his next attack when it occurred to him that he'd not seen the other man.

No sooner had he finished the thought than the man appeared, wielding a broken piece of wood like a club. Part of an oar, Dave thought absently as the man's arm came down.

The force of the blow was so hard it nearly split his skull. Pain lanced through his brain, and he dropped to his knees, fighting to stay conscious.

The next blow caught him before he'd recovered from the first and Dave slumped to the floor, unconscious.

The first thing he noticed as he came around was that he was freezing. His entire body felt numb, which wasn't a good sign, he knew, but at least he wasn't feeling any pain. He assumed his broken arm was a hairline fracture since he saw no distortion of the arm and no bone poking out. It, like his various other cuts and bruises, would heal by themselves—in time.

Time, however, was something he didn't have. Cracking open an eye, he looked around. He was lying on a hard floor surrounded by empty frost-covered shelves. Turning his head, he saw another set of shelves on the far side.

There was only one place he could be—the ship's freezer.

It seemed an odd choice for a prison cell. Of course, maybe they weren't expecting him to survive his imprisonment. Perhaps the plan was for him to stay in here until he froze to death. Whatever they had in store for him, he had no intention of sticking around for it.

He tried to sit up, but his body responded sluggishly. The cold had seeped into his muscles, making them stiff. He rolled over and pushed himself to his hands and knees. After pausing to catch his breath, he managed to stand.

He couldn't feel his arms and legs, so he had to focus on each step he took to keep from toppling over. It took forever to cross the distance to the freezer door, even though it was only a couple of feet away.

His thrill of accomplishment when he reached the door vanished when he saw there was no inside handle. There was no way to open the door. He would have thought that a basic safety feature like an inside handle was standard freezer design, but he had to remind himself that this wasn't a typical cruise ship.

Eyeing the thick layer of frost covering the inside of the metal door, he knew he couldn't try to push against the door with his bare hands. Even if it opened, his hands would freeze to the metal. So instead, he raised his foot, with difficulty, and kicked at the door.

It didn't budge.

He considered kicking it again, but it seemed futile—at least in his current form. A polar bear might have better luck. Dave focused on assuming the form of the large bear, but it was difficult to concentrate when he was so cold. He put more energy into the effort, but his body refused to cooperate. It was as if he were too frozen to shift.

He wondered if his captors had known this would happen. Then he recalled the bit of conversation he'd overheard. *Jenna.* He needed to warn her.

He could think of only one way to do it and hoped she was still asleep.

Eyeing the cold floor with distaste, Dave eased himself down. As he stretched out across it, the cold seeped into his body and he wondered if he'd ever feel warm again.

Closing his eyes, he released his spirit and hoped for the best.

Jenna was dreaming of sandy beaches and crystal blue waters rolling onto the beach in gentle waves. She turned to Dave sitting beside her, enjoying the heated look in his eyes. When he leaned in to kiss her, she found herself waiting in breathless anticipation. She wanted this.

His lips were warm and demanding as they pressed against hers. They ignited a hunger deep inside her, and wrapping her arms around his neck, she gave free rein to her feelings.

Still kissing her, he eased her back onto the sand, coming to lie on top of her. His tongue swept into her mouth, stirring such heady sensations she grew drunk on them. Then he started trailing those kisses down her throat to the swell of her breast. She reached up to untie her top, pulling it down to bare her breasts to his hungry gaze.

His mouth latched on to her nipple and tugged, sending delicious waves of heat licking down her body to the sweet spot between her legs. She moaned and arched into him.

Then she felt him grow still. "What's wrong?"

"Jenna?" He sounded confused and she smiled up at him reassuringly. His gaze dipped to her bared breasts and lingered before he finally raised his eyes to look at her again. He seemed surprised. With a groan, he dipped his head again to take her nipple with his tongue while he molded her breasts with his hands.

She was lost in a torrent of sensations when he pulled his head up again. "I'm sorry," he said, sounding breathless. "I shouldn't be taking advantage . . . I mean . . ." He rubbed a hand down his face. "Lousy timing." He dropped a quick kiss on her lips and pushed himself off her, getting to his feet before helping her up.

"Jenna, I need you to listen to me. I need you to focus—" His gaze dropped to her bared breasts once more and in a seemingly irritated move, he grabbed the ties of her bikini top and pulled her suit back into place, tying it securely.

Once she was covered, he seemed to relax a little until she looped her arms around his neck and nuzzled it. She liked the way his entire body shivered from her touch.

"Jenna!" He pulled her arms down and set her away from him. "I need you to pay attention. This is not a dream. I'm in trouble. I'm locked in the ship's freezer. You have to get me out."

They weren't the words of love and adoration she'd been expecting. Moving restlessly in the bed, she forced her mind to replay the dream and once again found herself lying on the beach kissing Dave.

He kissed her with the heat and passion she'd been search-

ing for, but pulled away from her long before she was ready
for the kiss to end.

"You sure as hell are making this hard on me," he swore.
Once again, he climbed off her and pulled her to her feet.
"Listen to me. There are dangerous men on the ship, so be
careful. But come quickly, Jenna. I don't know how long I've
been in here."

She stared at him, trying to make sense of his words.
"You're not a fun date."

"Jenna!" he shouted. "Are you listening? Wake up!"

Jenna awoke instantly, her heart racing. "Dave?" She
could have sworn she'd heard him call her name, but looking
around the darkened room, she didn't see him. Of course,
she couldn't see much of anything because no light was coming in through the porthole curtain.

She glanced at the clock on the nightstand. Instead of
letting her sleep for two hours, Dave had let her sleep for a
good six hours.

Damn it. Why hadn't he come back for her? What could
he be doing that would keep him so preoccupied, she wondered?

Swinging her legs over the side of the bed, she sat up and
rubbed the back of her neck. Wispy fragments of her dream
floated around in her head, and she mentally swatted at
them like she might a bothersome gnat.

She went to the bathroom and splashed water on her face
to wake up. Then she did a quick repair of her makeup before going back into the bedroom to wait for Dave. She
glanced at the clock again, unable to shake the feeling that
something was wrong.

As she waited, she found her thoughts returning to the
dream she'd had. What had Dave said? *I'm in trouble. I'm
locked in the ship's freezer. You have to get me out.*

CHAPTER NINE

If Dave really was in the freezer, she was willing to bet that he hadn't trapped himself. Who would do such a thing to him? Her first thought was Conrad, but just because she'd found the guy creepy didn't necessarily make him the guilty party.

Unable to wait any longer in the room, Jenna left, her only thought now to reach the ship's kitchen as quickly as possible. She hurried down the passageway, undaunted by the cleaning staff's cart that practically blocked her way, and reached the elevator. This whole thing could be a wild goose chase, she reminded herself, stepping into the elevator and jabbing the button for the Fiesta deck. As her concern for Dave escalated, she became more impatient. When the elevator dinged less than a minute later, she practically clawed the doors open and raced off.

She moved unnoticed past the people milling through the passageway. Entering the dining hall, she was struck by all the noise; people talking, the band playing. Careful not to walk too fast, she made her way past the tables to the side door through which the wait staff kept coming and going. It would be difficult to walk in without being noticed, but she had no intention of sneaking in. She was going to storm into the galley and demand to speak to the head chef. She would explain the situation to him and insist he open the freezer at once.

If she found Dave inside as she suspected she would, then they'd report the entire incident to the captain. If Dave wasn't inside, well, she'd deal with that later.

With no time to talk herself out of it, she pushed through the door.

It should have been a madhouse of activity, with wait staff rushing around, dropping off orders and picking up food. Instead, the galley was empty. The stoves stood polished and unused, the stainless steel gleaming dully in the dim lighting.

Jenna moved into the room, confused. Where was everyone? She would have sworn she saw a waiter come out with a food tray not two minutes ago. She turned back to the door and watched it swing open. A waiter walked in—then simply vanished.

She stared at the spot, dumbfounded. Where had he gone? She looked around, but there was no sign of him. Too stunned to move, she stood watching the point where he'd disappeared, jumping when the door swung out for no apparent reason. As it started to close, Jenna stared out into the dining hall where hundreds of passengers still sat at their tables. Then her view was obstructed by the sudden appearance of a waitress carrying a tray of food.

The door had no sooner closed than it swung in again and another waiter strode into the galley, heading directly for her. He was walking fast, his gaze focused elsewhere, as if he didn't see her. He walked past her and she turned to watch him when suddenly he stopped and looked directly at her. Her breath caught, but before she could even think what to do, he vanished.

Totally unnerved, Jenna hurried to the large metal doors along the far wall. One of these had to be a freezer. With no one to stop her, she started pulling them open, finding each one empty and warm. If the ship had no food, what were the passengers eating?

She tried not to think about it because there was no logical explanation. Instead, she focused on the two remaining doors. She tried the first one and found it wouldn't open. She pulled on it several more times before she realized it wasn't stuck—it was locked. Why would a ship with no food and disappearing wait staff need to lock a freezer? Were they trying to keep someone from getting in? Or keep someone from getting out?

She summoned her magic just as Dave had taught her, intent on blowing open the door, but then hesitated. Whoever locked him inside was sure to come check on him. If they found the door as they'd left it—that is, without a huge gaping hole blown through it—they might not open it—at least, not right away. The longer it took them to discover Dave was gone, the more time she and Dave had to figure out a way to get off this ship.

She noticed that the freezer's top edge stuck out from the wall about an inch, and ran her fingers along it. Her first pass uncovered nothing, but on the second, her fingers touched a piece of metal.

Bingo, she thought. A key.

As she swung the heavy door open, at first she didn't see him. He was curled into a tight ball, eyes closed. "Dave!" She hurried to his side, afraid he was dead.

Kneeling beside him, she touched his face. His skin was ice cold and she wondered why he hadn't assumed the shape of an animal better suited for cold weather. Placing her hand on his chest, she felt it rise ever so slightly and gave thanks. He was still alive. "Dave, it's Jenna. Can you hear me?"

"So . . . so . . . c . . . co," he muttered so softly, she almost couldn't hear the words. "C . . . can't . . . see." Icicles had formed along his eyelashes, sealing his eyes shut.

"Hang on, I can help with that." Summoning her magic again, she focused on creating heat. Then she placed her palms over his eyes and held them there for a second. When she pulled her hands away, the ice had melted and he was able to open his eyes a crack. Summoning her magic again, she generated more heat between her hands and ran them along his arms and legs. "Do you think you can stand?" she asked. "We need to get out of here."

"Helb . . . meuh."

His speech was slurring and he wasn't shivering: two symptoms of advanced hypothermia. She had to get him someplace warm and dry, and she had to get him there fast.

Stepping behind him, she levered him into a sitting position. Helping him stand was a bit trickier because he was so much bigger than she was, but somehow they managed. Then, with his arm slung over her shoulder, they took their first tentative steps for the door. Dave shuffled along and Jenna hoped that the movement would get the blood pumping through his body and warm him up.

They left the freezer and Jenna closed the door, making sure to lock it and replace the key.

They went through the back entrance to the kitchen to avoid the main dining room, and headed for the nearest elevator bank. Out in the warm air, Dave's frozen clothes began to thaw and as they thawed, they grew damp. Dave started to shiver. By the time they rode the elevator to their floor and got out, he was shaking so badly, the few people they passed in the passageway stopped to stare. Jenna ignored them, her only goal to get Dave back to their room before his shivering got so bad he could no longer hold himself up.

The cleaning staff's cart had moved several doors closer to their room, and the sight of it made Jenna stop. If they went back to their room, they'd be sitting ducks. She glanced at Dave. He wasn't going to be strong enough to race around the ship looking for a better hiding spot.

Then she remembered an open room she'd passed earlier. It had been clearly unoccupied and was just what they needed.

"Can you stand here a second?" She propped him against the wall, hoping that despite his violent shivering, he could remain standing while she hurried down the hall to the cleaning cart.

There was no sign of the cleaning staff but a master key card was still lying on top. Snatching it up, she hurried back to Dave, ducking under his arm so she could support his weight once more.

She helped him back down the passageway to the room

she knew was unoccupied, using the master key card to open it.

"We'll be safer here, I think," she told him, helping him inside.

A quick look around reassured her that the room really wasn't occupied by passengers. "Be right back," she told him. Grabbing a towel from the bathroom, she rolled it up, then opened the door to peak outside. Seeing no one, she went into the hallway, jamming the doorway with the towel to keep the door from closing. She quickly returned the key card to the cart and hurried back to the room, locking the door behind her. If no one noticed the key missing, no one would think to look for them in another room.

She went over to Dave, who was still standing, his arms wrapped around him as his entire body shook. "I'm sorry," she told him, pulling the covers back on the bed and then starting to undo the buttons of his shirt. "I need to get you out of these damp clothes and under some blankets."

"S'all . . . right." His teeth were chattering hard enough that she worried he might bite his tongue.

She peeled the damp shirt off his shoulders and down his arms, fighting the sudden rush of heat in her face. How often had she fantasized about doing this very thing—but under other circumstances? Now she couldn't even take the time to enjoy the moment.

Dropping the shirt to the floor, she turned her attention to his jeans. His hands were already fumbling with the waistband, so she let him try to undo the snap himself.

"Let me help you with those," she said after a second, shoving his hands out of the way.

"Been wa . . . waiting to hear yo . . . you say that . . . for long time."

She looked up and saw he was smiling at her. She smiled back. "Careful, big guy. I've got you at my mercy here. Don't give me any ideas." She unzipped his pants and tried to ignore the boxer briefs underneath when she pulled the jeans down past his hips. "I need you to sit on the bed."

"What about . . ." He reached for the waistband of his boxers, but she gently swatted his hand away.

"Give me a break, will you? I'm way out of my comfort zone here." She placed her hand on his chest and shoved, knocking him off balance enough to make him sit.

She had to remove his shoes and socks before she could get his jeans off. Then she lifted his legs and turned him so he was lying down.

"Let's see if we can get you warm." She covered him with the blankets, even folding the bedspread over on itself to double the layers, but he was still shaking badly. "Are you feeling any warmer?"

"N . . . n . . . no."

Damn. "Okay. Let me see if I can find more blankets." She searched the closet and dresser drawers. Nothing. Going into the bathroom, she grabbed all the large bath towels and piled them on top of him.

Going to stand beside him, she brushed a strand of hair from his forehead. It didn't look like his shivering had eased any.

She listened to his teeth chatter, feeling helpless. She considered running a tepid bath, but had read somewhere that it could do more harm than good. She was out of options. There was only one thing more she could do to raise his body temperature.

She turned out the room lights and there was still enough moonlight filtering into the room for her to see where she was walking. Going back to the bed, she took off her clothes, leaving on only her bra and panties. Though she'd worn less to sunbathe, she felt exposed and vulnerable.

"I can't believe I'm doing this," she muttered as she pulled back the covers and crawled into the bed from the opposite side.

He'd been watching her and now looked surprised. "Wh . . . what are you do . . . doing?"

"I'm saving your life," she told him. "Don't make me regret it."

Lying beside him wasn't going to do the trick, she knew. She was going to have to press her body against his. The prospect was both frightening and exhilarating. She knew if she thought about it any longer, she'd lose her nerve, so she moved over beside him and draped her leg over his.

"Argh!" She gasped, reacting to his icy cold skin.

"I w . . . wish I could fe . . . feel you," he groaned. "I'm so . . . cold, my body is . . . nu . . . numb."

"It's probably just as well," she said, stretching her arm across his waist as she laid her head on his chest. She was glad to hear her voice sounded so relaxed, because she was anything but. He might not be able to feel her, but she could feel him. If she hadn't been so concerned with his welfare, she'd have been enjoying every second.

They lay there for what seemed an hour before she noticed that his shivering seemed less pronounced. "How are you feeling?" she asked.

"Better," he replied, able now to speak without his teeth chattering. He moved his arms, wrapping them around her to hold her close. "Thank you."

She smiled to herself. "You're welcome."

He was going to be okay, to her immense relief. The adrenaline pumping through her system since the moment she'd stepped into the galley finally burned out. She relaxed and listened to his steady breathing. In. Out. In. Out. The rhythm lulled her into a drowsy state and her eyelids grew heavy. Unable to stay awake, she crashed.

How long she slept, she had no idea, but when she woke, she was still lying with her head on Dave's chest and she was toasty warm. Raising her head to peer up at him, she was surprised to see his eyes were open.

He smiled at her. "Good morning."

She glanced at the porthole window and saw the barest hint of light just starting to show. A yawn she couldn't suppress stole over her. "I'm sorry. I didn't mean to fall asleep on you. How are you feeling?"

"I feel great," he said, giving her a grin. "A little stiff."

"I'm sorry," she said chagrined, thinking of him stuck beneath her for hours while she slept. She tried to push herself off him, but he grabbed her by the arms and rolled so he ended up on top of her.

"That's not what I meant." He pressed his hips into her and she felt the long, hard length of him against her abdomen.

"Oh," she said, too stunned to come up with anything else.

"I've been lying here for hours with nothing but my fantasies to occupy my thoughts while you slept. I've wanted to make love to you for so long, I can't even begin to tell you how bad I want you."

"You hid your feelings well," she said, thinking of the women she'd seen him with.

"Distractions to take my mind off you. Believe me, if you'd given me the slightest hint you were interested, the only woman you would have seen me with is you."

"Really?" She found she wanted so badly to believe him.

"Really," he assured her. "And now I have you right where I've wanted you. Only I keep thinking that I owe it to you for saving my life to be a gentleman and behave, but you know what I've decided?"

She stared up at him, her heart in her throat. "No, what?"

His head loomed above her as he stared intently into her face. "Fuck being a gentleman." He lowered his head and his warm lips touched hers.

CHAPTER TEN

Need rocketed through her, and Jenna returned the kiss with unabashed enthusiasm. When Dave's tongue ran along the seam of her lips, she opened her mouth, inviting him in. Tentatively, she mimicked his moves and felt his answering shudder. Soon their tongues were engaged in a primal dance that had Jenna's pulse racing.

The hand cupping her cheek moved down her neck to her shoulder and along her arm until it grazed the side of her breast. She waited in eager anticipation for his next move. He didn't make her wait long.

Reaching behind her, he undid the hooks of her bra and pushed the fabric out of the way, freeing her breasts to brush against the hard planes of his chest. Reaching between them, he massaged her fullness before brushing her nipple with his thumb until it stiffened to a hard peak. With each stroke, the sweet tension inside her built. Longing pooled between her legs and she squirmed, trying to ease the ache.

She ran her hands along his arms, chest and shoulders, savoring the feel of his powerful, well-muscled body.

"Jenna." He breathed out her name. "If you don't want this, tell me now."

The sensations rippling through her made it impossible to think. She knew if she told him to stop, he would end this delicious torture—and she would regret it the rest of her life. "I want this," she gasped.

He paused long enough to look deep into her eyes. "Are you sure?"

She smiled hesitantly. "Yes."

He caught her lips in a hungry assault that left her head spinning. She was barely aware of him ripping off her panties, conscious only of the blunt head of him pressing against her. She felt a moment's panic as he pushed into her. The pressure of him filling her was unlike anything she'd experienced, and she worried that he wouldn't fit.

"You're so tight. It feels so good. I don't know how long—" He stopped talking, stopped moving and stared down at her in what could only have been shock. "You're a virgin?" Small tremors shook his body as his muscles strained to keep him from moving.

She felt her face heat as she nodded. "Wait," she pleaded when he began to pull out. "This doesn't change anything."

"Yeah, it does."

"No, it doesn't." Her emotions were in turmoil. Lack of opportunity didn't make her a prude. If he left her in this state, she would be mortified. Though she tried to keep it in, a small cry escaped. "Please, Dave. Don't make me beg you to have sex with me."

"Oh, baby," he said gently, bending down to brush another kiss across her lips. "I just thought you'd want your first time to be with someone special."

"It *is* with someone special."

He looked surprised but then smiled. "If you're sure."

"I am."

"Okay." He still hesitated, like he was trying to wrap his mind around the idea of being her first. "It might hurt a little, but afterwards, I promise I'll make it better."

She nodded. This wasn't the dark ages where she didn't know what to expect.

Slowly he eased back into her until once again, he'd hit the thin membrane of her maidenhead. He dipped his head to capture her lips in a kiss so electrifying that she forgot everything else. He pushed past the barrier and she felt the small burn, but knew it would pass.

He ended the kiss and gazed tenderly into her face. "You all right?"

"Yes," she gasped, riding the wave of delicious tension building inside her. It was too much effort to form a complete thought, much less a sentence.

"Good." His voice sounded strained. He eased himself out and then slowly pushed back into her. She felt the slick thickness of him rubbing against her, heard his moan. The earlier pain vanished and there was only the heady rush of pleasure growing stronger every second.

"Yes," she gasped.

He increased the speed and force of his penetration, caught up in the moment just as she was. The combination of pleasure and pain had her digging her fingernails into his back, begging for more.

He growled and surged into her. Faster. Harder. Over and over. Jenna was no longer conscious of anything but the exquisite tension building inside her. She was close now and locked her legs around his hips, trapping him against her. He groaned again and grabbed the top of her shoulders, holding her down as he drove himself forward. One. Last. Time.

Her climax broke like a tidal wave, crashing over her, drowning everything except the rush of heady sensation. She was barely conscious of Dave's primal roar as he found his own release.

Long minutes later, he eased himself out of her and rolled to his side, gathering her close. She basked in the afterglow of their lovemaking, feeling sated and content.

Dave listened to Jenna's steady breathing as she fell back to sleep. He hadn't expected her to be a virgin, and knowing that he'd been her first made what they'd shared that much more special to him. He didn't like that it should have happened on a night when they were hiding from people trying to kill them. He vowed that he'd get them out of this mess one way or another, starting with putting out an SOS to Nick.

Dave released his spirit and allowed it to soar. For the first time in a long while, he felt free. "Nick." He sent the name forth, surprised when it echoed back to him a second later. He tried it again with the same results. Sending his spirit soaring upward, he got another surprise as he ran into some type of barrier.

Perplexed, he tried to go around it, but no matter how far he searched in any direction, he couldn't find a way to circumvent it.

Frustrated, he was about to return to his body when he spotted another spirit. Like Dave, she appeared as a reflection of her corporeal being—a petite blonde with a head full of Shirley Temple curls. He knew instinctively that she wasn't a spirit walker because she lacked the aura of residual energy that existed with living creatures. Her residual energy had faded a long time ago, which meant that Dave was looking at a ghost, a soul trapped without a living body.

"You must be new," she said. "I don't remember seeing you before. I'm Laura."

"I'm Dave."

"Dave." She seemed to test the sound of his name. "Been here long?"

He looked around. "Where's here, exactly?"

She looked startled by his question. "The ship, of course."

"I've been here long enough. Listen, I don't suppose you know how I can get off the ship, do you?"

"You don't get off. None of us do. Ever." She must have seen that he didn't understand. "You have to pay for your sins," she explained.

"By taking a cruise?" It didn't seem like much of a punishment to him.

"Wait until you've made the same trip a couple of hundred times, pretending to still be alive and everything's fine when all you really want to do is warn the poor sucker who won a free ticket to run for their life before they end up like you."

"I guess it doesn't sound all that good," he admitted.

She shrugged. "If you're up here, then the worst of it is over—unless you do something stupid, like try to escape."

"The worst part?"

"Yeah, the rowing."

He thought of the room Jenna had described to him. "Right."

"Look," she said. "I need to go now. The boss will be looking for me."

Before he could stop her, she disappeared. Spooked, Dave returned to his body and prepared to break the bad news to Jenna.

Jenna was sleeping soundly when she felt someone touch her shoulder. Her eyes flew open as she came instantly awake, a scream lodging in her throat only to die when she realized it was Dave.

"Sorry," he said softly. "I tried calling your name, but you were really out of it."

She took a couple of deep breaths to steady her nerves. "Everything okay?" she asked, rubbing her eyes. She was acutely aware of how close he was.

"I thought I'd try to contact Nick," he began. "Using the spirit realm."

"Yeah?"

His eyes clouded over. "I didn't have much luck. It's like there's a barrier around the ship I can't get past. But I did learn something interesting."

He quickly told her about meeting the ghost Laura.

Depression settled over her. "I'm the one they want," she said when he finished. "Because of what happened to Sarah and my parents." She was more frightened than she wanted him to know. "You shouldn't be here," she told him. "Whoever *they* are, they don't want you. Maybe you should leave . . . somehow," she finished lamely, not sure how either one of them could escape this mess.

"I'm not going to leave you," he reassured her, brushing a

strand of hair from her face. "And the gods willing, I won't let anyone harm you."

His confidence made her smile. "I bet you say that to all the girls."

He stared down into her face, looking very serious. "You're not just another one of the girls, Jenna. You're the only one I want to be with from now on." He bent his head and kissed her with the same heat and passion he'd kissed her with earlier.

Jenna knew it was too late to protect her heart. She'd been attracted to him from the start and what she felt for him now was so much stronger. It frightened her to know that once again, she'd let someone else come to mean so much to her.

When the kiss ended, Jenna continued to hold on to him, wanting to make the moment last as long as possible. Slowly reality forced its way back in. "What are we going to do?" she whispered.

"We're going to get off this ship," Dave said.

"How?"

"We're going to go up on deck and walk around, just like all the other passengers. We're going to find a lifeboat and paddle as far away from the ship as we can. Eventually, we'll make it far enough that I'll be able to summon Nick's help. Then it'll just be a matter of waiting for him to pick us up. What do you think?"

Jenna wasn't sure, but she nodded. "Beats sitting around waiting for the boss and his men to figure out where we are." She sighed. "Now that I think about it, the South American slavers would have been easier to deal with."

He gave a soft laugh and pulled the covers back so he could climb out of bed. Jenna's gaze hungrily drank in his nude form. My man, she thought, appreciating the defined strength that characterized every inch of him. She wanted to believe him when he said he was only interested in being with her.

Tearing her gaze away, she climbed out of bed and had to

search the tangled sheets to find her bra and panties. The bra was still wearable but the panties were nothing more than torn fabric now. Her face heated at the memory of how they'd come to be that way. Feeling Dave's gaze on her, she looked up to see his knowing smile with not an ounce of regret in his expression.

She quickly pulled on her jeans and was trying to fasten the back hook of her bra when she felt Dave wrap his arms around her waist and hug her from behind. "I wish we were back in the apartment," he whispered in her ear. "I would take my time showing you just how I feel about you."

"I'd like that," she told him sincerely.

He gave her a final hug and left her alone to finish dressing. By the time she was done, Dave was also fully dressed.

He held out his hand to her and she took it. "Let me just slip outside and see what's going on," Dave said. The air around his body started to shimmer and his expression turned blank. Jenna knew he'd freed his spirit so he could look around. He was back before she could wonder what to do if he didn't return.

The passageway was empty, so they made their way to the elevator. They didn't run into anyone until they exited the elevator a few minutes later on the Promenade deck and began to walk around.

Jenna tried not to stare at the passengers she saw, but it was hard not to. Were all these people ghosts, she wondered?

Suddenly, Dave stopped walking, pulling her to a stop beside him. "What's the matter?" she asked. He gestured with his head for her to look up. "What? I don't see anything."

"Exactly. No lifeboats."

"There have to be." She looked up and down the length of the ship. "Maybe we're in the wrong spot."

"Maybe." He didn't sound like he believed it, but they started walking again, quickening their pace. "Let's finish checking this deck."

It took about ten minutes to reach the other side and discover there were no lifeboats there either. Dave pointed to the deck above them. "Let's check up there."

"Passengers aren't allowed up there."

"Says who?" Dave asked, frowning.

"I read it in the brochure left in the room that first night. Someone's sure to spot us if we go up there."

"Okay." He stepped to the railing and leaned out over the side. "Grab my hand," he told her. When she did, he leaned out even farther, twisting his body until he was looking up.

Then everything happened at once. One second she was holding Dave's hand, and the next, huge arms grabbed her from behind. A meaty hand hammered down on hers where she still clutched at Dave's hand and she lost her grip.

As the man holding her lifted her out of the way, two other men she'd never seen before grabbed Dave by the legs and pitched him overboard.

Jenna screamed and began kicking at her captor's legs, clawing with her nails at the big arms holding her tight, twisting this way and that. Anything to free herself. None of it worked. She would have thought ghosts wouldn't feel so real, but they did.

Her captor held her tighter, making it even harder for her to catch her breath. She started to grow faint and her vision began to tunnel. Her efforts to free herself grew pathetically weak until she could hardly lift her hand.

As she slipped into the darkness, she wondered if she'd wake up again. Maybe they meant to kill her now, and that would be okay. Without Dave, she had nothing left to live for.

CHAPTER ELEVEN

When Jenna came to, she was lying on a bed in one of the cabins. It wasn't the one assigned to her and it wasn't the one she and Dave had slept in the night before, but it could have been. It looked the same.

She sat up and rubbed her forehead, trying to ease the ache. It was nothing compared to the pain in her chest. Dave was gone. She didn't know how it was possible for her to survive the loss of yet another person she loved.

Seeing that she was alone in the room, she climbed out of the bed. Her muscles were sore from fighting, but she welcomed the reminder of what these men had done to her; what they'd done to Dave. She would not let them take her again so easily. As soon as she got the opportunity, she would make them pay for what they'd done.

She tested the doorknob. Not surprisingly, she found it locked. She tried to summon her magic, but she was having trouble focusing her attention. When she finally managed to form a ball large enough, she hurled it at the door.

There was a burst of light and a loud explosion, but the door looked untouched. No burn marks on the surface, and it was cool to the touch.

She fought her momentary attack of self-pity that nothing was going her way, and turned her energy to searching every inch of the room for a way out. She found nothing. The walls were as solid as the door, and the porthole was too small to squeeze through. There wasn't even an air shaft.

She wasn't going to escape from the room, but that didn't mean she'd give up. Eventually, someone would come for her and she would test her magic on them.

Going to the far side of the room, opposite the door, she sat on the floor with her back against the wall. Focusing on her magic, she practiced forming balls of power. The energy it took to use magic wore on her, so once she was sure she could summon her magic at will, she rested.

It seemed that only an hour had passed before she heard movement outside her door. Tensing, she summoned her power and held it in her hands. The doorknob rattled like someone was trying to open it and she wondered if they were simply toying with her.

Then with a loud, splintering sound, the door crashed inward. Jenna yelped in surprise and hurled her ball of magic. She saw a figure dive out of the way and heard a muffled curse in a voice she recognized.

Jumping to her feet, she raced over to the prone figure. "Dave?" She could hardly believe her eyes. "I thought . . . that is, I wasn't sure." She didn't want to tell him that despite his amazing magical talents, she'd thought the worst. "How did you get here?" She ran her hands along his arms and chest, needing to touch him and prove he was really there. Tears ran unchecked down her cheeks. "Are you okay?"

"I'm fine." He struggled to sit up and then pulled her into his arms. "Are *you* okay?" he mumbled into her hair. "I was so afraid I wouldn't get back here in time. Did they hurt you?"

"No, I'm fine. I passed out and when I woke up, I was in this room. You're the first person I've seen. I'm sorry about the magic. I guess it's a good thing my aim is so lousy."

He pushed her away from him so he could look into her face. "Your aim is terrific. Fortunately, after I tried the doorknob, I came in as a spirit to make sure you were really in here. That's when I saw you against the wall with the magic and figured out what you were planning. I called your name to let you know it was me, but I guess you didn't hear me.

Anyway, here I am and I'm thinking we should get out of here. Unless you wanted to stay?"

She helped him to his feet and he pulled her to him. Their kiss was brief because there wasn't time for more. "I'm so glad to see you. How did you survive?"

"I've got mad skills, remember? As soon as I realized I was falling, I morphed into an eagle and flew away."

"You should have kept going," she said.

He cupped her face with his hands, looking deep into her eyes. "I would never leave you. So let's get going."

"Where to?"

"Off this ship. There aren't any lifeboats—while I was an eagle, I checked—so we're going to have to swim."

She shook her head. "I don't know how far away land is, but I know I can't swim that far."

"You won't have to. I'll change into a dolphin and tow you."

She thought about it. There really was no other option. "All right."

"That's my girl." He gave her a quick kiss and, taking her by the hand, pulled her toward the door.

They left the room and made their way to the nearest outside deck without anyone trying to stop them. The ghosts continued their performance of being passengers, giving Jenna and Dave polite smiles as they passed.

Once outside, Dave led her over to the side and was just about to help her over the railing when they both heard footsteps behind them and turned.

"Conrad!" Jenna gasped.

Dave moved forward, placing himself protectively in front of her. "We're getting out of here and you're not stopping us."

"It's too late," Conrad said. "We're already there." He pointed out to sea, where a massive curtain of white mist stretched out in all directions as far as the eye could see.

"What the . . ." Jenna had never seen anything like it. She turned to face Conrad, hoping for some explanation, but the other man only smiled. Then he ran to the railing and jumped overboard.

Stunned, both Dave and Jenna leaned over the side. There was no sign of Conrad. Neither wanted to say what they were both thinking—that Conrad would rather kill himself than pass through that curtain of mist.

There was no point in trying to escape now. They couldn't outswim the mist. It loomed before them. Brilliant. Impenetrable. Ominous.

Then it was upon them. As the bow of the ship touched the mist, Jenna stumbled back to get away from it, pulling Dave along with her. Her skin prickled like it had before. There was magic here—powerful magic.

Dave grabbed her hand and they raced along the deck toward the stern of the ship, away from the mist. Her legs pumped furiously as she struggled to keep up.

She cast a quick look back the way they'd come, and it was enough to make her heart pound even faster. A third of the ship had disappeared into the mist.

The prickle of magic was worse than ever now. Too soon, they reached the end of the ship. As she leaned against the railing, trying to catch her breath, she saw only the long drop down and water everywhere. There was no place else to run.

She looked back over her shoulder. Only half the ship remained visible; the rest was lost behind the mist. An unnatural hush was settling all around as passengers on the lower decks started disappearing. Were she and Dave to be next?

"What do we do?"

"Damn it," Dave swore. "I can't shift." He was clearly frustrated.

"Maybe I can do something . . ." She lifted her hands out in front of her, focusing her thoughts as she tried to summon her magic. Sweat broke out across her forehead as she tried to concentrate—or perhaps the moisture was from the mist.

Most of the ship had disappeared behind the curtain now.

Only the last small section of the stern remained. Jenna gave up. The magic at work here was far stronger than either hers or Dave's.

Dave opened his arms to her and she went to him. "Whatever happens, we face it together."

She was numb with fear and yet so grateful he was with her.

He caught her jaw with his hand. "I love you."

"I love you, too," she gasped.

Their voices were unusually loud in the deafening quiet. Not even the sound of the ocean could be heard now, only the sound of their pounding hearts. Dave dipped his head and kissed her with fierce, possessive finality.

Then they turned to face whatever lay beyond the mist.

CHAPTER TWELVE

The thick wall of mist closed over them. Jenna, expecting to be hit by a blast of icy water so thick she'd have to struggle to breathe, was surprised to feel a rather anticlimactic cool spray.

The sky, once sunny and clear, became filled with ominous dark storm clouds—and it wasn't the only thing to change. The modern cruise ship they'd boarded a few days ago had been replaced by an ancient sea vessel that invoked images of Vikings—or pirates.

More disturbing than either the sky or the ship's appearance was the noticeable absence of any other living creature. She and Dave were all alone on an empty deck in the middle of the ocean on a ship that wasn't moving.

"Now what?" Jenna asked.

"I guess we wait and see?"

"For how long?"

A loud, awful grating noise started, rattling the entire ship.

"I'm thinking not long," Dave said dryly. He looked around the deck. "Where's it coming from?"

He went to look over the railing. "There," he shouted, pointing to two enormous chains dropping into the water from twin openings in the hull.

At first, she thought they might be anchors and wondered who was lowering them. Then the ocean water began to bubble, giving her something new to worry about.

"Merpeople," Dave said softly.

Surprised, she took another look and this time, the bubbling ocean resolved itself into what seemed to be hundreds of fish tails churning the water as merpeople grabbed the chains and started swimming. As more of them joined in, their combined strength gradually dragged the ship forward. "They're towing us," she exclaimed.

"But to where?"

"Maybe they're saving us," Jenna said.

Dave sighed. "I doubt it." Putting his arm around her, he hugged her tight. "Guess we'll find out."

As it turned out, Jenna would have liked the merpeople to have taken more time. All too soon, they felt the ship slow down. Looking over the side, they saw that the chains had been released and now hung along the front of the ship, their ends dangling in the water.

When the ship came to a complete stop, they were still in the middle of the ocean with no land in sight. Jenna wondered whether they'd be stranded here, but then she heard the sound of grating wood. Tracking down the noise, they found a section of railing where a gangplank was being extended down to the water's surface.

A mermaid rose out of the ocean as if lifted by invisible hands. She had long, greenish-blonde hair and her skin was the color of pearls. She wore no clothes and appeared to be human from the waist up, though just how close the resemblance was Jenna couldn't tell because the woman's long hair hung strategically down her front in two thick curtains.

The lower half of her body was a fish tail covered with dark green scales, but as she cleared the water, the tail divided into two shapely legs.

"Hello," she said in a beautiful voice that was pure and melodious; not at all what Jenna expected to hear from a creature about to kill them. "My name is Dolphene."

Dave and Jenna exchanged wary glances. "Why are we here?" Dave asked.

"It is not for me to explain," she replied, sounding apologetic. "But if you come with me, you'll get your answers."

Jenna looked around. "Go with you where?"

"Below, of course," Dolphene said.

"Beneath the water?" Dave started shaking his head. "No way."

"You'll be perfectly safe, I assure you."

"I know *I* will, but Jenna can't breathe underwater. So, I think we'll stay here."

"The ship is leaving," Dolphene told them. "And where it goes, you can't. But please don't worry. Our magic is strong, and we would not let anything happen to you."

Jenna slipped her hand into Dave's. "It's not like we have a lot of choice," she pointed out.

He seemed to consider it, then nodded.

Dolphene gave them a friendly smile and started down the gangplank. Dave followed, with Jenna a few steps behind. When they reached the bottom, Jenna saw that Dolphene was standing on a small platform floating at the base of the gangplank. As soon as they joined her, it gave a quiet shudder and began to descend into the ocean. Dave put his arm around Jenna and pulled her close.

"Please," Dolphene said. "You will be fine. See?" She pointed to the bottom of the platform, which was now about a foot underwater. To Jenna's surprise, water was not rushing in. Instead, it was as though invisible walls held it back.

The platform continued downward and the ocean rose on all sides, forming an air-filled box. If she hadn't been so worried about what lay ahead of them, Jenna might have enjoyed the view. It reminded her of being in Sea World's tunnel beneath the aquarium where huge fish swam so close, it felt like she could reach out and touch them.

Soon they were so far below the ocean that if the magic failed to hold back the water, she would die before she could swim to the surface. It was an unsettling feeling.

The water grew darker, and she noticed sparkling lights

coming from deep below. As they continued to descend, the lights became buildings and the buildings became a city.

"Atlantis," Jenna breathed in awe.

Dolphene gave a delicate laugh. "No, not Atlantis. We call it—" She made a sound that was impossible to understand. "In your language, it means tranquility."

"That's lovely." Jenna turned her attention to the massive structure materializing in front of them. It looked very much like an underwater castle.

"Please follow me," Dolphene said, stepping off the platform when it reached the ocean floor. The chamber of air moved with her while Jenna hesitated.

Her moment of indecision lasted several seconds, and in that time, the chamber of air moved beyond the point where she stood. Instantly, she found herself submerged in the water. The shock of the cold temperature made her gasp and she sputtered, flailing her arms. She knew she shouldn't panic, but it was impossible to stay calm when the salt was stinging her eyes and she couldn't breathe.

Then Dave was pulling her back into the safety of the air chamber. "You okay?"

She nodded, wiping the salt water from her face.

"I think we'd better keep up," he told her, urging her after Dolphene. When they reached the castle, the large front doors opened and Dolphene went inside. The chamber of air—and thus Jenna and Dave—followed.

"The boss is away at the moment," Dolphene said, "but Conrad can show you to your room."

At the mention of the man's name, alarm bells sounded in Jenna's head. She'd been lulled into thinking they were safe by Dolphene's gentle voice.

Conrad's pale form swam toward them. When he was close enough that she could make out his features, including the massive tail that now replaced his legs, Jenna gasped. "You."

He didn't look any friendlier in this form. "Follow me."

The air chamber moved after him, propelled by some magic Jenna couldn't fathom, leaving them little option but to follow. They went down a long passage, stopping when they reached the end. Conrad opened another door and stood back as the air chamber propelled them inside. Then it expanded, filling the room and giving them space to move about.

"Why have you brought us here?" Dave demanded.

Conrad remained in the water-filled hallway outside the door and merely shrugged. "All in due time."

"Who is the boss you keep talking about?" Dave asked.

Conrad gestured at someone Jenna couldn't see and the door closed, trapping them inside.

Jenna walked around the completely empty room. "At least on the ship, we had furniture to sit on."

"I don't think they're concerned with our comfort," Dave said flatly.

Agitated, she began to pace. "What do they want with us? And who the hell is the boss?"

As she passed him, Dave grabbed her arm and pulled her to a stop. "I imagine we'll find out soon enough. For the time being, we might as well save our energy." Together they sat side by side on the floor, leaning with their backs against the wall. "What I said up on deck—I want you to know I meant it. I love you."

She gazed at him, her heart in her eyes. "I love you, too."

He kissed her and Jenna found it par for her life that her happiest moment should come while she was being held in an underwater prison.

They sat for hours, wrapped in each other's arms, talking of the future as if they had one, while waiting for their fate to be decided.

At some point, Jenna fell asleep.

When she awoke much later, she was lying on the cold floor—alone.

She pushed herself to her feet and looked around. There was no sign of Dave.

She hurried to the door and pulled it open, forgetting for a moment that the ocean might rush in and drown her. It didn't. Instead, she found Dolphene hovering just on the other side, her long hair fanning out about her head like a golden halo.

"Please come with me." The mermaid's melodious voice was muted because of the water.

Jenna hesitated. "Where is Dave?" she demanded, hoping to get answers and buy time to think.

Dolphene gestured for her to follow. "Come with me." She turned and swam off a short distance before stopping.

As the air in the room contracted into a smaller chamber once more, Jenna realized that she had to follow. She walked along obediently, so worried about what might have happened to Dave that she had a hard time paying attention to where she was being led. She was surprised when the chamber finally stopped and she found herself back in the great hall.

"Stay here," the mermaid instructed before swimming off.

Jenna stared after her. "No kidding," she muttered. "Like I have a choice."

"There are always choices," a commanding male voice boomed.

Jenna twisted about to see who was speaking.

A merman appeared from a darkened corner of the room. Jenna wondered how she had missed noticing him before. He was . . . magnificent. Larger than any of the mermen she'd seen yet, he had a heavily muscled upper torso, like a body-builder's, which seemed at odds with his long, flowing white hair, mustache and beard. Despite his resemblance to a wizard, there was a spark to his eyes that had Jenna thinking this was a warrior; a leader of me—or at least, a leader of mermen.

As he drew closer, Jenna was able to make out other details, like the golden crown on his head—and the trident clutched in one of his massive hands.

"Poseidon," she breathed in amazement.

"Good. You know who I am," he said in a deep-timbered voice. He raised his trident and at his gesture, the air chamber grew larger, pushing back the water. As the wall of water retreated past him, he stepped forward, his fish tail magically replaced by legs that were as muscled and toned as the rest of him—and bare but for a cloth draped around his hips.

He strode forward, coming to stand a little too close. She had to tip her head back to look up at him, but she met his gaze steadily. The light in his eyes burned with a frightening intensity.

"Where is Dave?" she demanded, refusing to cower in fear.

"He is no longer needed."

"You killed him?" She could barely find the breath to speak.

"No, of course not. Why would you think that?"

"Maybe because you had him locked in a freezer, then thrown overboard."

Poseidon pursed his lips. "Excuse me." He waved his hand and suddenly the nearby water swirled in a violent vortex. When it stopped, Conrad was there, looking confused. "She tells me that you tried to kill her companion. Is that true?"

Conrad glared at her. "She lies."

Poseidon looked from her to Conrad, as if trying to decide who was telling him the truth. Finally, his gaze rested on her. "I find myself wondering why you would lie."

"I wouldn't," she said.

"That's exactly the conclusion I came to."

At Poseidon's first statement, Conrad had given her a triumphant smile. Now it faltered as Poseidon's meaning sank in.

"I will deal with you later," the great god said, turning on Conrad. Then he waved his hand and the merman disappeared in another swirling vortex of water.

"If Dave is alive, where is he?" she asked once Conrad was gone.

"Waiting for me. I intend to send him home because he was never the one I wanted."

She nodded, feeling a small measure of relief for Dave. "You wanted me, I get that. Why?"

"Because you killed your parents."

Though she wasn't surprised, she cringed at the harshness

of the statement. "My parents' death was an accident." She didn't know if she was trying to convince Poseidon or herself.

"You cast the spell that killed them, therefore—accident or not—you are guilty."

Now she was confused. "My parents were killed when their car was hit by a truck." Poseidon stared at her in apparent surprise. Then he placed his free hand against her forehead. Suddenly, memories of that horrible afternoon replayed in her head.

When they finished, her memories fast-forwarded to Sarah's disappearance. She remembered sitting at the dining table in the apartment she and Sarah had shared, the shock of seeing Sarah's face in the mirror and the struggle to save her sister with magic.

As the memories faded, a tear slid down Jenna's cheek. She wiped it away, unwilling to show weakness in front of her captor. Poseidon lowered his hand, a fierce scowl on his face. He was silent for several minutes and then finally said, "I'm sorry. You were sent to me as payment for a debt in the mistaken belief that you were a candidate for my ship. You did not kill your parents—nor are you responsible for the death of your sister."

"So I'm free to go?" It was too much to hope for. She would be with Dave soon. They could go home together.

"You may leave, but you will never be free."

Jenna didn't understand. "But you said—"

Poseidon raised his hand. "There is no prison I can put you in worse than the one you've put yourself in." He stepped closer to her. "What would you do to be truly free?"

"I don't understand."

He held out his hand, palm up, and a small blue globe the size of an apple appeared. Jenna studied it and saw that the globe was actually made of a clear crystal with a glowing blue light coming from inside. "What if I told you that it is within my power to offer you something you thought lost forever?"

Jenna stared into the pale blue light and was suddenly filled with a strong, familiar impression. "Sarah!" She gasped.

"This is your sister's soul."

She stared at it, mesmerized. "She's alive?"

He shrugged. "Let us say that she is not dead. When the genie took over your sister's body, he displaced her soul. I'm offering you a chance to give your sister back the life taken from her."

Jenna could barely contain her excitement. "What do I need to do?"

"You must retrieve her soul from the Well of Lost Souls."

"What about her body? The genie destroyed it."

Poseidon waved his hand, producing an egg. He held it up for her to see. Then he squeezed it and the shell broke into hundreds of little pieces. "What death magic destroyed," he said, closing his fist around the shattered pieces, "life magic can restore." He opened his hand again and the egg was whole again. "If you successfully retrieve your sister's soul from the well, I'll restore it to her body and return you both to your home."

It was too good to be true. "What's the catch?"

He smiled. "If you fail, I keep both your souls and you will spend the rest of eternity working on my ship."

CHAPTER THIRTEEN

Jenna didn't need time to think about it. "Where do I find this Well of Lost Souls?"

"Such passion and loyalty. I admire that, but why don't you think about it while I attend to another matter."

With a sweep of his hand, he was gone, leaving Jenna alone in the great hall to consider the deal. She knew that it didn't matter if he gave her five minutes or five hours to think about it, her decision was made—and when he returned a good thirty minutes later, that's what she told him.

"Very well," he said. "Let's get started." He gestured and the walls of water began to close in on them. Jenna watched with a sense of foreboding.

As the ocean passed over Poseidon, his legs reverted back to the massive fish tail. She hardly noticed his transformation. Having expected the water to stop a safe distance away, she was watching it close in on her.

Just before it reached her, Poseidon touched her with his hand.

Searing pain shot through her neck and lungs. She suddenly had trouble breathing and fought to catch her breath just as her chamber of air vanished and the ocean crashed in around her.

"Breathe." Poseidon's commanding voice filled her head. Jenna was too panicked to notice that the salt water wasn't stinging her eyes.

"Breathe," he ordered again.

As she ran out of air, her body jerked with violent spasms. Finally, it was impossible not to breathe and she opened her mouth. Water rushed in, choking her. She was dying, and a small voice urged her to stop fighting and accept her fate.

Except the most amazing thing happened. She didn't die.

Instead, air filled her lungs. It wasn't coming in through her mouth or nose, but rather through her neck. Running her fingers along her throat, she felt the slits. Poseidon had given her gills.

Realizing she wasn't about to die—yet—she relaxed and for the first time noticed that her legs felt fused together. She saw that they had been replaced by a mermaid's tale.

"The Well of Lost Souls is in the middle of the ocean," Poseidon explained, though she hadn't asked. "These changes are temporary until you have finished your task."

Jenna nodded that she understood and when he swam off, she followed. She was amazed at how easily she moved through the water. It was such a change from how she'd struggled as a child learning to swim.

Poseidon led her out of the castle and past the boundaries of his underwater city until they seemed to be in the middle of nowhere. They were swimming about fifty yards above the ocean floor, but from what she could see of it, the floor was level and comprised mostly of sand. Glancing up, she could just make out the water's surface gleaming beneath the sunlight.

"This is the Well of Lost Souls," Poseidon announced. He waved his hand and a well appeared.

Jenna swam over to its edge and looked inside. Hundreds of tiny multicolored lights sparkled up at her. "These are all lost souls?"

"Yes—and your sister is one of them."

Jenna needed no further urging. She tried to dive into the well, only to encounter an invisible barrier.

"You cannot retrieve her that way," Poseidon said. "Go to the ocean floor and the well will tip until the souls spill out. One by one, they will float downward. You must find your sister's soul before it reaches the ocean floor, for once it does, it is gone from you forever."

That didn't sound too bad, she thought.

"It's not too late to change your mind and go home," he told her.

She shook her head. "Let's do this."

"If you fail, I will come for you. If you succeed, you and your sister will find yourselves back home with no memory of anything that has occurred since she left you."

"Wait!" All her attention was on the god. "You never said anything about losing my memory." She wouldn't remember Dave? As impossible as that seemed, she knew Poseidon's magic was powerful enough to make it happen. "Why?"

"It would be too traumatic for your sister to know what she has endured—and I cannot allow you to remember the time you spent here. This is the way it must be. Have you changed your mind?"

She glared at him. He knew as well as she did that if she went back to Dave now, her love for him would always be tainted by regret and guilt for not trying to save her sister. "No."

He gestured for her to swim down to the ocean floor. A school of fish scattered when she swam too close, stirring up the water and creating hundreds of tiny bubbles. When they cleared, Poseidon had disappeared and she was alone.

From above, she caught the flash of a golden light. When she looked up, she saw a golden orb was floating down to her.

Remembering that her sister's soul had appeared pale blue, she knew before she caught the orb that it wasn't Sarah's. Repulsed by the soul's malevolent essence, she dropped the orb, letting it float to the ocean floor where it was quickly swallowed by the sand.

Jenna didn't have long to wonder where it went as another orb spilled out of the well and floated down to her. If they all came at this speed, she had a good chance of finding her sister's.

The next orb was pale blue and Jenna had to quell her excitement. She caught the soul, only to feel a rush of disappointment when it wasn't Sarah's. Releasing it, she looked up to catch the next and found that it had already fallen to within inches of her. Far above, another was just slipping over the lip of the well.

They were coming more quickly, she realized, but her confidence didn't waver. She could do this.

Soon she was catching them two at a time, then three at a time. Afraid that she'd accidentally let one slip by, she grabbed the bottom of her shirt and held it out to form a pouch.

At first, this seemed to work. She caught them in her shirt and pulled them out one at a time to examine. It seemed, however, that the faster she worked, the faster the orbs fell. How many were still in the well, she wondered? Surely it was nearly empty.

She glanced up to see the orbs beginning to fall in a steady stream. At this rate, there was no way she would be able to examine every one. There had to be a way to stop them.

Maybe if she used magic.

She called forth her power and directed it toward the stream of falling orbs, slowing the flow. So intent was she that she barely registered the dark shadow above her.

Glancing up, she saw the elongated diamond shape that had to be the underside of a ship. Not Poseidon's ship, she thought. This one was much too small—a fishing vessel, perhaps.

She was turning her attention back to the orbs in her arms when she noticed a small form swimming beneath the ship. At first, she thought it was a fish but then realized it was a small merboy.

Worried that he was getting too close to the ship, she glanced around for his parents, accidentally spilling several orbs to the ocean floor. She ramped up her magic, using it to hold back the heavy stream of orbs still falling from the well. The effort was taxing her energy and she was quickly growing tired.

She glanced back up at the boy just as a wide shadow fell

like a sheet from the ship, causing the water to ripple and the fish to scatter. A fishing net.

Jenna felt an orb roll over her hand and panicked, looking down to see that her shirt was full of orbs. She scrambled to catch the falling one before it hit the ocean floor, and she pumped more energy into her magic, trying to stem the flow. It was like trying to dam a raging river.

As she worked, she worried about the boy. Would he know enough to swim to safety?

Unable to stop herself, she glanced up again and felt her heart skip a beat. Caught in the net, the small boy struggled desperately trying to free himself. His efforts caused the net to drift dangerously close to the propellers.

"Help!" she screamed, hoping Poseidon would hear her. "There's a boy in trouble. Someone please—help."

With her attention diverted, several more orbs fell to the floor before she could stop them. Fear of failing her sister once again beat at her, as did her concern for the boy. Why was no one helping?

The boy's situation was now dire. She would fail to save Sarah if she stopped to help the boy, but the boy would die if Jenna didn't do something.

Despair filled her until she nearly choked on it while tears of frustration fell from her eyes to be swept away by the ocean. It wasn't fair. But then again, when had life ever been fair?

She abruptly pulled back her magic, letting the orbs fall freely to the floor, and began swimming as hard and fast as she could. Mother Goddess, she silently prayed, give me strength. She summoned her magic and projected it in a single powerful beam at the propellers.

There was a burst of light as the magic hit. When it faded, the propellers had stopped moving.

She reached the boy and tore at the net. When he came free, she caught his unmoving body in her arms and let their combined weight carry them down to the ocean floor, as the last glowing orb disappeared into the sand. It was over—and she had failed.

CHAPTER FOURTEEN

Jenna sat in the sand, cradling the young body in her arms, numb with shock and despair. If she'd gotten to him earlier, she could have taken solace in knowing Sarah's life had been traded for a worthy cause.

After several long minutes, she sensed Poseidon approaching. She didn't try to escape him. What was the point? With a wave of his hand, he could take away her gills and she'd drown.

"You were unable to save your sister's orb," he announced, hovering several feet above her. "Your soul now belongs to me."

"I know," she sighed, rising to her feet. "Before you take me to wherever it is you plan to take me, could you see that this child gets back to his parents?" She held him out from her body so Poseidon could see the child's face. Maybe he would recognize him.

"Tumaini," Poseidon gasped. He swam down to her and pulled the young boy from her arms, gathering him close. He held the boy with an affection Jenna hadn't expected from the great god, and it surprised her. "Tell me what happened," he demanded.

"A boat passed overhead and threw out a net. The boy was swimming too close and got caught up in it. He tried to get free but his efforts only made things worse. He was headed for the propellers." She paused. "I tried to get there in time, but I was too late. I'm so sorry."

To her surprise, Poseidon pressed a kiss to the child's

forehead. When he met her gaze, his eyes held a wealth of sadness. "He's my grandson."

She wasn't sure what to say.

"What's this?" Poseidon suddenly looked down into the child's face as the body stirred. "Tumaini?"

The boy's eyes opened and he peered up at the great god. "Grandpa?" Then he threw his arms around his grandfather's neck and buried his face against Poseidon's chest as huge sobs wracked his slight body. Poseidon simply held him, patting his back and uttering tender words of comfort.

After a long while, the boy calmed down. Poseidon shifted his weight a bit, but did not release him. He looked over at Jenna. "As I said before, you lost the challenge and by rights, your soul belongs to me now."

She nodded. "I'm ready."

"Not so fast. My grandson is more precious to me than my own life. Because you saved him, I release you from the deal we made and I will send you home." He smiled at Jenna and added, "Along with your sister."

Back at his apartment, Dave paced the length of the common area. It was killing him not to know what was happening with Jenna—just as it had killed him to leave her behind, not that Poseidon had given him much choice.

He thought back to his encounter with the god.

After falling asleep with Jenna in his arms—a sleep he now realized that had been magically induced—he'd awakened to find himself alone with Poseidon.

"Where's Jenna?" Dave had demanded before Poseidon could say a word. "What have you done with her?"

"She is safe."

"I want to see her."

"And you shall, if you still want to after we talk."

Dave had eyed the god warily, not trusting him. "What's going on? Why have you brought us here?"

"You are in my home, which does not exist in your dimension. Those who come here never come of their own free will."

"Why?"

"They are brought here to make a reckoning of their past actions, to atone for past wrongdoings."

"By serving on your ship?" Dave asked, thinking of Laura.

"Yes."

"What sins have Jenna and I committed that we've been brought here?"

"None."

Dave had been prepared to argue for his and Jenna's innocence, so Poseidon's response caught him off guard. "Then why are we here?"

"It was a mistake." The god said it nonchalantly—and without apology.

There was a time when Dave might have demanded one, but in the last couple of months, he'd had an opportunity to meet the goddess Sekhmet and knew the futility of demanding anything of the gods. "So we're free to leave?"

"Yes."

Dave didn't trust him. "But . . . ?"

This time Poseidon smiled and Dave tensed. "Jenna does not wish to go."

"What?" Dave hadn't expected that.

"Because she wishes to save her sister."

"But Sarah's dead."

"Sarah's death was by magical means. I have provided Jenna with the means of bringing her sister back. If she succeeds, I will send them both back to the lives they would have had if Sarah had never been abducted."

Meaning that Jenna's life after Sarah's disappearance—the part of her life that included him—would never have happened. "She won't remember me."

"No," Poseidon agreed. "Neither will you remember her in that altered reality."

The words sliced him like a knife. He fought past the sudden misery to ask another question. "You said 'if she succeeds.' What happens if she fails?"

"She forfeits her soul to me."

Fear for Jenna hit him. "No!" The price of failure was too great. "Let me do it. Whatever it is." He took a deep breath. "If I fail, you can have my soul."

"You love her so much you would take her place, even if it meant your own death?"

Dave didn't hesitate to answer. "Yes."

"How very noble." Only instead of sounding like a compliment, the words sounded condescending. "I wonder," Poseidon continued thoughtfully, stroking his long beard, "do you love her enough to do nothing?"

"What?" Dave wasn't sure he'd heard correctly.

"If you wish it, I will send you and Jenna back to your lives this very minute."

Dave opened his mouth but hesitated. He was missing something. "What about Sarah?"

Poseidon shook his head. "The offer is only for you and Jenna."

That was the catch. If Dave asked Poseidon to send them home, then it wouldn't be an evil genie who robbed Jenna of her sister. It would be he. He imagined her resentment and knew with absolute certainty that if he went through with it, she would grow to hate him. He took a deep breath. "You said I had a choice?"

Poseidon smiled. "I can send you back alone."

It was the devil's choice, Dave thought bitterly, his entire body itching to do battle against the god and any other foe that stood between him and Jenna.

"You must decide now."

Neither option gave him the happily ever after he wanted to have with Jenna, but there was one option that would allow Jenna a shot at having one without him. "Send me home. Just me."

Before he'd even finished the last word, he'd found himself standing in his living room where now he waited to forget the woman he loved. He'd wanted to be the hero for her. Fight for her, save her, protect her. Instead, he'd left her and loathed himself for it.

•

Driven by anger, he freed his spirit and let it soar—past the spirit realm to the dream realm. There were no barriers now to prevent his thoughts from finding Nick, and he called to his friend.

"Nick. I need your help."

He didn't have to wait long before Nick and Darius both appeared before him.

"What's wrong?" Nick asked, clearly concerned.

"It's Jenna," Dave started. "He's got her."

"Who?" Darius asked.

"Poseidon." As quickly as he could, he relayed everything that had happened. "I don't know what to do to save her," he admitted. "I don't want to lose her. I love her."

If the news surprised Nick, he didn't show it. Instead, he turned to Darius. "Poseidon's a god. Do you think your mother could help us?"

Darius shrugged. "Mother!" he shouted.

Almost at once, Sekhmet appeared before them. She smiled when she saw Dave, and he tried to smile back. He'd always liked Sekhmet and hoped she liked him enough to help him now.

Sekhmet's face grew dark and hard to read as Darius explained what had happened. "And so we thought that maybe you could talk to him, you know, goddess to god," he concluded.

"I'm sorry, Dave," she said. "I truly am, but I'm not able to interfere with Poseidon's affairs."

Dave felt his heart sink. "There's nothing you can do?"

"You love her, even though she killed her parents?" she asked.

He didn't know where she'd heard that. "Her parents were killed when a truck ran a stoplight," he clarified.

She looked surprised. "Are you sure?"

He nodded and saw Darius giving his mother a peculiar look.

"Why do I get the feeling you know more about this than you're telling us?" Darius asked.

"Don't be ridiculous," she protested a bit too quickly. Then, seeing all three men staring at her suspiciously, she sighed. "All right. Maybe I do know something."

She told them about the deal she'd made with Poseidon and why she'd offered up Jenna's name. "It wasn't anything personal against Jenna," she told them. "I would do anything to protect Zach."

Dave wanted to rant and yell at her, but one didn't do that with Sekhmet. Her temper was legendary. And in a way, he understood how she felt. "I forgive you," he told her. "But you do sort of owe me, don't you think?"

She cocked an eyebrow at him in surprise. "Is that right? Oh, all right. Tell me, does she love you as much as you love her?"

"Yes."

"Then wear this amulet and when you sleep tonight, go to your spirit mate." She held out her hand and a ruby-red amulet suspended from a gold chain dangled from her fingers. "If Jenna is your spirit mate, then when you find her in person, give this to her. If the love you feel for one another is true, this amulet will restore her memory of you. If all you felt for one another was lust, nothing will happen." She gave him the amulet. "I'm sorry. It's the best I can do."

They parted then and Dave returned to his room in the apartment. He was starting to feel as though maybe he and Jenna could have a happy ending after all when he realized Sekhmet had given him nothing to prevent him from losing his memory of Jenna.

He was about to go back to the spirit realm when the intercom buzzed, startling him. The last thing he wanted at the moment was a visitor. "Who is it?" he asked, pressing the speaker button.

"Mandi."

Dave considered asking her to go away, but changed his mind. "Come on up," he said, pressing the buzzer. Then he went to wait for the elevator to bring her up.

"Hiya, sugar," she said when the doors opened. Her smile

faded when she saw his face. "Is this a bad time?" She strained to see over his shoulder into the apartment. "I'm not here for sex," she quickly added. "Just in case you're worried about upsetting your girlfriend. I only wanted to show you this." She pulled a folded piece of computer paper from her purse and held it out.

Dave took it and saw that it was a math exam—and she'd gotten a B plus. He offered her a smile that he didn't really feel. "That's terrific, Mandi. Congratulations."

She took the paper and stuffed it back into her purse. "Well, I guess I'll go." She hesitated. "Is everything all right? I mean, you and your girlfriend didn't break up already, did you?"

"No, we didn't . . ." He stopped speaking as it occurred to him that maybe there was a way to beat this devil's choice after all. "I need you to do me a huge favor."

Five minutes later, Mandi left and Dave headed into Jenna's old room. It was still filled with her things. Dave didn't know whether to be relieved or upset. Did this mean that she was still trying to save Sarah's soul? Or had she failed?

He opened her closet and the powdery scent of her perfume, still clinging to her clothes, wafted up and greeted him. He removed several blouses from their hangers and held them up to his nose, inhaling deeply. A longing hit him so raw and deep that he tipped his head back and roared at the gods who conspired to take away the woman he loved. Nothing they did to him would ever make him stop loving Jenna. Nothing.

A second later, Dave opened his eyes to find himself standing before an empty closet. It took a second for the dizziness to pass before he could get his bearings.

When he did, he couldn't for the life of him remember why he'd been standing in one of the empty bedrooms. Shaking his head, he started for the door, only to stop when something cool ran down his face. When he touched his cheek, his fingers came away wet and he had the oddest sensation he'd been crying.

CHAPTER FIFTEEN

Unsettled, Dave went to his room, where he found a ruby amulet lying on his dresser. He couldn't remember where he'd gotten it but felt an odd attachment to it. He was so overcome by a sense of needing to keep the amulet close that he picked it up and put it on. It made no sense, but at the moment, nothing was making sense to him. Tired beyond belief, he decided he might as well go to bed.

As soon as his head hit the pillow, he felt his spirit leap out of his body. It was as though it had been waiting to be freed from its corporeal tether and now that it was, it ascended into the dream realm and began roaming. Dave was struck with the image of a bloodhound hot on the trail of a scent.

His search was interrupted by the appearance of a large merman, with flowing white hair and mustache. His tail propelled him forward until he stood before Dave.

"Being a hero doesn't always mean fighting the battle to save the woman. Sometimes it's knowing when to let the woman save herself."

The image faded, leaving Dave to mull over the words as he resumed his search, though he didn't know what he was looking for—until he found her.

She had an oval face that was daintily pointed and dark hair cascading down around her shoulders. Her blue eyes reminded him of the sky on the clearest of days and her smile filled him with such warmth, he felt like he'd just been welcomed home from a long journey.

Normally, he wouldn't see someone in such detail in his dream and though his waking mind didn't recognize her, his spirit did. She was his spirit mate. The other half of his soul, his one true love. There'd been a time, long ago, when he'd thought he'd found his spirit mate, but that experience had been false and could not begin to compare to this.

He opened his arms and she moved into them without hesitation. "I love you," he whispered.

"As I love you," she said. She caressed his cheek with her soft hand, and he kissed her with a sense of desperation, as though he might not find her ever again. Her response was nearly as intense. Easing her down, he lay on top of her, ridding them of their clothes with a single thought. He reveled in the delights of her body, knowing he'd never tire of being with her. When he nuzzled the area between the swell of her breasts, she trembled beneath him.

Her hands moved over his back, scorching the skin until he burned with barely contained need. Her legs opened to him so he could sheathe himself in her warmth. The experience was more intense than any he'd ever experienced. He wanted it never to end.

When his climax finally broke over him, he awoke. Still breathing hard, he lay there, feeling like he'd lost his best friend. The dream was disturbing on so many levels, he didn't bother trying to understand it. Instead, he got out of bed and dressed. With the morning sun just coming up, he knew it was going to be a long day.

Not wanting to sit around the house and mope, he went to the gym and was glad to see that Mandi was there working out.

"You look worse today than you did yesterday," she said by way of greeting.

Dave frowned. "When did I see you yesterday?"

Mandi stared at him. "Yesterday evening. Don't you remember?"

He rubbed his head. "No, I don't."

"Wow. You really don't, do you? You warned me this might

happen, but I thought you were kidding." She unfolded herself from the ab cruncher and wiped her face with the towel. "Wait here a second. I've got something to show you."

She walked off in the direction of the women's locker room and returned a minute later with a folded paper. "When I saw you yesterday, you told me to give this to you if you suddenly seemed to lose your memory."

He took the paper from her and opened it. "Your math exam?"

She snorted. "No, silly." She flipped the sheet over. There, written in his own handwriting, was a name: *Jenna Renfield*. Beside it, he'd written *spirit mate*.

"I don't understand."

"Yeah, I know. Yesterday you told me a story and said that when you started acting funny—like forgetting everything—I was to repeat the story back to you, so let me go get cleaned up and maybe we could go get something for breakfast? I'm starving."

Thirty minutes later, Dave sat across from Mandi, listening to a fascinating tale involving him, a woman named Jenna, a cruise on Poseidon's ghost ship and a conversation with Sekhmet. It was farfetched enough to be a joke, but he knew it wasn't. After they ate, Dave thanked Mandi and headed for his office. The advantage to working for a security company was that he had a lot of contacts and resources—all of which he was going to tap to track down one Jenna Renfield.

"You all right?"

Jenna, who'd been leaning against the kitchen counter sipping a cup of coffee, smiled down at her sister. Sarah was in her usual spot at the kitchen table, a textbook open before her. "Yeah, I'm fine. Just thinking about the dream I had last night." With effort, she pushed thoughts of her dream lover out of her head. "What do you have going on today?"

Sarah looked at the pile of textbooks. "I thought I'd do a little studying, followed by more studying. What about you?"

Jenna gave a quiet laugh. "I thought about calling in sick so we could do something fun together. Maybe go to a movie? Or do some shopping?"

Sarah's face brightened. "I'd like that. Give me a couple of hours to study and then we can play."

"Deal."

There was a knock on the door. Exchanging a curious look with Sarah, Jenna set down her coffee cup and went to look out the peephole.

A man stood there, his faced distorted by the glass but still strangely familiar. Jenna opened the door and then couldn't move. She felt as if she was caught up in a dream, a very recent, extremely erotic dream.

"Jenna." He breathed her name like it was a prayer. "Please tell me you know me."

"I . . ." She hesitated, unsure what to say. "I'm sorry, but have we met?"

He was clearly disappointed by her answer and she felt bad.

"Jenna, you need help?" Sarah called from the other room.

"No, I got it." She looked back at the man who was staring at her with a strange look in his eye. "My sister," she offered by way of explanation.

"I knew you could do it."

"I'm sorry?"

He waved it away. "Nothing. I'm sorry to bother you, but I wonder if you'd do me a huge favor," he said. "I know it sounds strange, but would you mind holding this?" He held out a beautiful ruby amulet. "Please," he pleaded when she started to refuse. "It's extremely important to me—and maybe to you as well."

Not seeing what harm it could do, she agreed and held out her hand. The amulet was heavier than she'd expected. "It's beautiful." She looked up to see him watching her closely. "Why am I holding this?"

"I'm hoping it will help you remember . . . ." His words trailed off. "Are you feeling anything?"

"No, I'm sorry."

"Never mind," he said, clearly disappointed. "I guess I was wrong. I'm sorry I bothered you."

"Wait," she said when he started to back away. "You forgot your amulet." She held it out to him but he refused to take it.

"Keep it. I got it for you."

She watched him go, then slowly closed the door.

"Who was that?" Sarah called from the other room.

"Some guy. Some cute but slightly crazy guy."

"What did he want?"

"I think he was looking for love," she whispered to herself, too quietly for Sarah to hear. Oddly, she found herself close to tears.

About to set the amulet on the foyer table, she changed her mind and put it on instead. As soon as the amulet touched her skin, a burning sensation swept through her entire body. Memories assaulted her. The cruise. Poseidon. Sarah. But most important, Dave.

"I've got to go," she shouted to Sarah as she raced out of her apartment. The elevator seemed to take forever to arrive and the ride down was interminably long. She prayed that Dave might, for whatever reason, still be downstairs.

He wasn't in the lobby, so she ran outside and searched for him. He was so far down the street that she almost didn't notice him as he climbed into the back seat of a cab.

"Dave! Wait!" she shouted, running after him.

The cab pulled away from the curb and she knew that if she didn't stop him now, it would be a lot harder to find him. Drawing on her magic, she hurled a spell at the cab to make it stop. When it did, she was already running toward it.

She reached the cab just as the back door opened and Dave stepped out. Seeing her, his eyes opened wide with surprise. "Jenna?"

She threw her arms around him and hugged him close. "You left too soon," she breathed, so overcome by emotion she could barely get the words out. "Oh, Dave. I didn't want to forget you—or have you forget me. I hated the thought of never seeing you again. Can you ever forgive me?"

"Hush, baby," he soothed, wiping the tears from her eyes. "You had a chance to save your sister. I understand that. Besides, even though Poseidon sent me home, I had no intention of losing you. Spirit mates don't forget their other half."

"Spirit mates?"

"I should have realized it months ago, when I first started dreaming of you. After my other experience, though, I wasn't sure. Not until we were both on the ship. When Poseidon sent me home, I vowed to move heaven and earth to find you and make you remember me. As it turned out, I only had to nudge a guilt-ridden goddess."

"When you first came to the door, I remembered you from my dream."

"See? I'm not so easy to forget." He kissed her just the way she remembered. "If I'm moving too fast here, tell me, but I have to ask—will you marry me?"

She smiled. "I love you, too. And yes, I'll marry you, but . . ." Her smile faded and she looked worried.

"But what?" He asked, feeling his heart tighten.

"I don't know if I can leave Sarah again after just getting her back."

"Who said you had to leave her? She can live with us."

"I'd like that."

He kissed her again. Then he paid the cab and together they started walking back to her apartment.

"I never would have made it if it hadn't been for you," Jenna told him. "Whenever I felt like I was going to fail, you were there in spirit to make me strong."

"I knew you could save Sarah," he said proudly.

She stopped and turned to face him, still holding his hand. "Actually, I failed."

"What?"

She told him about the Well of Lost Souls and trying to find the orb containing her sister's soul. She described seeing the young merboy get caught in the net and the horrible moment when she had to decide between saving him or her sister.

"I couldn't do it," she told him. "As much as I love my sister, she was already gone, but that young child had the rest of his life ahead of him. I couldn't let him die. By the time I got back to the well, it was empty and all the orbs were gone."

Dave hugged her to him, loving her more for being the kind of person to make such a sacrifice. "But if you lost, how is it you're both here?"

"The boy was Poseidon's grandson and he felt grateful."

Dave dropped another kiss on her lips. "You're incredible and I love you so much, I'd marry you tomorrow if I could. But I know women like to have plenty of time to plan these things. It's February now. How do you feel about getting married this fall? I realize it doesn't give you much time."

"I'd rather have a spring wedding."

She saw the flash of disappointment in his eyes, but he nodded. "All right. Next spring it is."

"Not next spring—this spring."

A slow smile split his face. "You realize that spring officially starts in about three weeks?"

She sighed. "I know, it seems an eternity away."

He laughed and released her so they could start walking again. "What would you like to do for our honeymoon?"

A twinkle lit her eyes. "Anything but a cruise."